Confessions of a
Serial Dater

By Michelle Cunnah

CONFESSIONS OF A SERIAL DATER
CALL WAITING
32 AA

Confessions of a Serial Dater

Michelle Cunnah

AVON
TRADE

An Imprint of HarperCollinsPublishers

HarperCollins books may be purchased for educational, business, or sales promotional use. For information please write: Special Markets Department, HarperCollins Publishers Inc., 10 East 53rd Street, New York, NY 10022.

FIRST EDITION

Interior text designed by Elizabeth M. Glover

Library of Congress Cataloging-in-Publication Data

Cunnah, Michelle.
   Confessions of a serial dater / by Michelle Cunnah.—1st ed.
      p.   cm.
   ISBN 0-06-056037-1 (acid-free paper)
   1. Dating (Social customs)—Fiction. 2. Single women—Fiction. I. Title.

PR6103.U5C66   2005
823'.92—dc22   2004025014

05 06 07 08 09 WBC/RRD 10 9 8 7 6 5 4 3 2 1

For Kevin, Rhiannon and Gareth

Acknowledgments

My heartfelt thanks to all the generous members of Deanna Carlyle's Yahoo! chick lit loop for their support and for their help with weird job descriptions.
http://groups.yahoo.com/group/ChickLit/
My heartfelt thanks also to all the generous members of the Chick Lit Writer's of the World loop for their support and for their help with weird job descriptions.
www.chicklitwriters.com
Even more heartfelt thanks to my agent, Paige Wheeler, and to my editor, Kelly Harms, for their great editorial advice.
And finally . . . much love to Lani Diane Rich and Alesia Holliday for being their wonderful wacky selves.
www.literarychicks.com
You're simply the best!

The Profiterole Problem

Rosie's Confession:

Sometimes, I wish I were a turtle.

Amongst their many other fine qualities, turtles can breathe through their asses, which would be a pretty handy fail-safe ability to possess, especially when facing death by asphyxiation . . .

On the downside, I would be hunted or accidentally killed to the point of species extinction, which is not great at all. But at least I wouldn't have to sit through dinner with Jonathan's godawful boss . . .

"This bloody country is going down the toilet," Horrible Boss booms to the dinner table at large, his jowly face flushed with indignance and too much brandy.

Normally, I am Rosie the Calm, the Organized, the Mild-tempered, the Reliable, the Logical, but after two minutes in this man's presence I am goaded beyond reason to change the habits of a lifetime.

I am sorely tempted to poke him with the heel of one of my shoes, which are too tight and are greatly adding to my general state of misery. It could be an interesting experiment to see if my pointy heel would deflate some of his pompous, self-righteous bigotry.

Trust me, I do not possess homicidal maniac tendencies, but deflation by shoe heel is a nice fantasy. . . . Can you imagine the mess Horrible Boss would make if he *did* explode? Tempting . . . but think of the cleanup job and additional work it would cause for the hotel staff. I'd *never* do that to them.

I push off my pinchy shoes under the dinner table just as my boyfriend, Jonathan, gives my free hand a friendly squeeze and smiles his charming smile at me.

My heart does a little skip, and this reminds me why I am here. To radiate the "right" company image for Jonathan. I squeeze Jonathan's hand in response. It's not as if he makes a habit of torturing me with Horrible Boss, after all, and now that my feet are liberated, I'm already feeling a million times better. My toes have blood circulating around them again, which is always a good thing.

Jonathan's smile widens in a way that says "later," because Friday night he always stays over at my place, and I shiver just a bit. Jonathan's "later" is of the very, very good variety— not exactly earthquakes good, but let's just say that the bedside table has been known to tremble. . . .

I pin a vacuous smile on my face and reach for my wineglass. In the hope of creating the "right" image, I am practically channeling "perfect company wife" vibes. And although the company at the table might be awful, at least the wood-smoked Merlot has a lot of personality. So I decide to drink a little more.

As I raise my glass to my lips, I have this really odd feeling that someone is watching me. I've been having this feeling all evening. I'm sure I'm not imagining it.

I glance furtively around the room. And freeze midsip as I nearly lock eyes with a man at the next table. As soon as he realizes I've caught him, he looks back to his companion. His exquisite, blond companion.

He's to-die-for gorgeous, and I mean that in a very dangerous, endearing kind of way. The kind of gorgeous women line up for to get their hearts broken by. And although I am not immune to a bit of male flattery, I just don't get why he's staring at me. Don't get me wrong, I'm more than okay with my body image. I know I don't resemble the back end of a bus, but I would never get mistaken for a supermodel.

Not that I'm remotely interested in him: It's just a way of passing time and phasing out Horrible Boss. . . .

Of course, Horrible Boss isn't really called Horrible Boss. He's Sidney Smythe-Lawrence, CEO of Jonathan's company. But I call him that in private, because he is one of the most obnoxious people I have ever met.

I clamp my mouth shut and fasten my attention firmly on the dessert course before I can say something rude, thereby ruining the evening for Jonathan and my fellow diners. Of course, I would never do anything like that . . .

Oh, great—profiteroles. I *love* profiteroles. All that lovely cream encapsulated in mouthwatering pastry, and dripping with chocolate. But they're just so hard to eat. I mean, one profiterole is just too big to scoop up and push into your mouth. If I were at home, I'd do exactly that, but it's not really the kind of thing you can do at a Christmas fund-raiser in a posh hotel ballroom full of posh people, is it?

"I'll *tell* you what's wrong with this country," Horrible Boss booms again.

Oh, please don't, I think but don't say. Instead, I delicately separate one profiterole from the pack and saw at it with the side of my dessert fork. This is not a top-quality profiterole, and it therefore resists my efforts. Cream squishes out of its sides, but the deflated pastry remains firmly in one piece. Inexplicably, the profiterole reminds me of Horrible Boss oozing his pompous pearls of bigotry on the world at large.

"The vast numbers of the unemployed!" Sidney tells us, wisely. "It's scandalous! To refuse work because a job offer pays less than unemployment benefits is no bloody excuse in my book," he waxes lyrical.

Resisting the strange desire to stab Sidney with my dessert fork, I stab the mutilated, deflated pastry instead and slide it into my mouth. This is the secret of my success. This is my great plan for getting through the evening—every time Sidney says something awful and solicits agreement, I simply fill up my mouth, thereby removing the need to talk.

I chew and glance surreptitiously at my fellow diners. They are all nodding sagely, hanging onto every utterance as if he were revealing the meaning of life, God and the universe. Including Jonathan.

Jonathan turns and smiles at me again. Not the charming smile, but the apologetic thanks-for-putting-up-with-this-jerk smile. Of course I can put up with it for him. After all, it is the holiday season. The season of goodwill . . . and besides, Jonathan is *such* a dear.

His lovely, angelic smile makes me feel instantly better. He's so kind and considerate—especially just recently. The least I can do is smile and nod for a couple of hours. How hard can that be? Actually, strike that . . .

I've only met Jonathan's boss twice before. The first time, shortly after Jonathan and I started dating six months ago, at the company's Summer Fête, when I "accidentally" tipped my Bucks Fizz down his cricket whites . . . Sidney and his wandering hands had cornered me by the refreshments tent, and I could barely catch my breath. He was all big jowls and yellow teeth right in my face, as he expounded on the problems of mothers in the workplace, and did I know how much money it cost the country in maternity benefits and parental time off for sick children? And wasn't I a lovely girl, he blathered on, getting even closer to me, and how lucky was Jonathan, nudge nudge, wink wink. It was either spill the Bucks Fizz or have his elbow casually brush against my chest again.

And the second time, at the Halloween Ball, when he insisted on giving me a whirl around the dance floor. I actually *did* mean to poke him in the eye with my false witchy nose. . . . Let's be reasonable, if his eye was that close to my nose in the first place, then that was too close for comfort, wasn't it? Euch. But it put a stop to his hand, which was wandering altogether too close to my bottom than was polite.

"Hit 'em where it hurts . . ."

As Sidney continues his tirade, I take a deep breath. And quickly fill my mouth with Merlot. Drinking more wine to stop myself from talking is not really a good plan—I can barely walk in my tight shoes as it is. Soused and even more unsteady on my feet will hardly help with the "right" image, will it?

But before I can stop the diligent wine waiter from refilling my glass, I get that spooky "you're being watched" sensation again.

I glance across at the neighboring table . . .

And nearly fall off my chair as the handsome, dark-haired man flashes me a sympathetic smile and raises a rather sardonic eyebrow à la Sean Connery. And *winks*.

What? What is it? Has my dress slipped down too low? Do I have food stuck to my cheek? Or is he winking at someone behind me?

Before I can turn around to check the table behind me to

test the mistaken identity theory, Jonathan gives my free hand another encouraging squeeze.

I will phase out Horrible Boss and dangerous strangers with killer eyes and sardonic eyebrows. I will think only *nice* thoughts. Like nice walks in Holland Park with Jonathan. Nice, cozy dinners with Jonathan. Movies with Jonathan. That lovely minibreak we took in Paris in September . . .

Okay, so it was a bit uncomfortable when Jonathan constantly vented at length, in public, that the French really do speak English but pretend that they don't on purpose as a kind of punishment for our beating them at Waterloo . . . and after all, he *was* trying to learn their bloody language, so they could at least give him a bit of credit. Personally, I think it was his attitude that got up their noses, rather than his beginner's French. They were all charming to *me*. . . .

But that's just an itty-bitty flaw. Everyone has them, don't they? Look at me—I have a tendency, but only a teeny one, to overplan. I like to be organized. And personally, I don't think there's anything wrong with that. I *like* predictable. I *like* knowing what I'm doing, and when I'm doing it.

I think it irritates Jonathan sometimes when I say, "No, I can't meet you on Sunday night, because I have to deal with bills, and file paperwork, and do other admin stuff," just like his flaws irritate me. But you see, we just have so much in common that we can work *through* it. We like a lot of the same things, and that's good, isn't it? Shared interests are vitally important to make a relationship work.

"Bloody begging for work . . ."

That's what Granny Elsie says. Not about cleaners bloody begging for work—I mean about relationships. A good, solid relationship is like a pair of comfy shoes.

At first, they squeeze and pinch, because your feet have to get used to them. You just have to be patient and break them in. And after all, the sex doesn't last forever, and what's left then? Affection, shared interests and a comfortable, predictable routine.

Oh, shoes . . . Now that I know that my toes are not gangrenous, better slide my shoes back on before my feet swell.

Shit. Where the hell are they? I panic as I grope for them with my toes. Thinking quickly, I accidentally drop my dessert fork on the floor. Yes, an old trick. But effective . . .

"Oops, sorry," I murmur to the table at large, but no one notices because, of course, Sidney is holding court, and they are all caught in his rapture.

I casually duck under the table. And then even further under the table. How did the bloody things get so far away from my feet? I grab for them and wrestle on the hated things.

"What are you doing?" Jonathan hisses under his breath.

Quickly. Quickly . . . In my fumbling haste, it takes an age to reunite them with my feet.

"Rosie," Jonathan hisses again, and I notice that the table has gone quiet.

"I say," Horrible Boss booms. "What on earth are you doing under there, Rosie?"

"Um—" I grab the dessert fork.

"I've heard all about what young ladies get up to when they duck under tables at dinner," Sidney says suggestively, and the table laughs along with him.

"Got it." I hold up the dessert fork. All eyes are on me, and I know that my face is burning with embarrassment.

"That's what they all say." Horrible Boss laughs his horrible laugh, and I flush even more as the waiter takes the dirty fork from me and hands me another.

I wish for the ground to open up and swallow me, but fortunately Sidney, aided by the brandy he has consumed, moves on to another diatribe.

Oh, why did I lie when Jonathan casually asked me my

shoe size? There was just no way I was going to admit that I took the same size as him. So I told him two sizes smaller.

I didn't think there was any harm in that—no woman wants to admit to having big clodhoppers (as Granny Elsie so charmingly refers to my feet), does she? Especially as I am only five feet two inches tall. . . .

It never occurred to me that Jonathan would bring me back these lovely Jimmy Choo black satin slingbacks from his business trip to Manhattan, size nine. I mean, they're gorgeous and divine, but it was a surprise, because things were cooling off between us. I was even thinking of breaking up with him. . . .

But I couldn't break up with him after that, could I? As best friend Jess says, you really have to give someone a chance. You can't just ditch them after a few dates because you haven't given the relationship time to fully develop. Especially after such a lovely gesture. And I'm glad I didn't. Jonathan and I really have become a lot closer since then.

The shoes were a bit of a problem, though. I couldn't return them, because I would have had to ask Jonathan for the receipt. But, thanks to the marvel that is the World Wide Web, I ordered the exact same pair online in my real size. They're still a bit too narrow, because they didn't come in a wide fitting, but at least I can wear them without fear of crippling myself for life.

Unfortunately, the shoes that nearly fit are currently with the cobbler because the underneath part of the heels needed to be replaced and, amidst the utter chaos that has been my day, I ran out of time to collect them. And Jonathan asked me to wear them tonight, especially . . .

"*Ça va bien, chérie?*" Jonathan mutters for my ears only. He's such a sweetie.

As I glance around at Jonathan, I can't help but catch sight of the handsome stranger again. He really is, well, handsome.

In a dangerous, Hugh-Jackman-being-James-Bond kind of way. He looks like the kind of man who dates gorgeous, exciting women, rather than unexciting, okay-looking women like me. As he lowers his head to listen to his partner, he laughs, and something in my stomach contracts. His date really is breathtaking—slim, blond, straight out of James Bond. . . .

"*Chérie?*" Jonathan nudges me, and I try to forget the handsome stranger and focus on my own very handsome boyfriend. Jonathan is handsome in a kind, trustworthy kind of way, and I'm very lucky to have him.

"I'm fine. I mean, *je vais bien,*" I lie, crossing my fingers.

It's sweet that he talks to me in French, it really is. And if it weren't for a shared interest in French, we'd never have met. We fell for each other over conversational phrases at night school, which is romantic, isn't it?

I was there because it seemed like a good plan to, you know, expand my boundaries. Also, because I quite fancied going to France on vacation, and it's nice to be able to at least say the basics in the language of the country you're visiting. It's good to make a bit of an effort, isn't it?

Jonathan took the class because his company deals with Europe, and he wants to be able to talk to "those arrogant bloody Frenchmen," as he rather annoyingly refers to them, in their own language.

"If they're claiming benefit from the State, then they should be put to work digging holes for the State. And filling them up again. That would teach the lazy sods," Sidney booms, looking around the table for agreement.

Heads nod in affirmation. All, of course, except mine.

"Absolutely." Graham Hurst, Jonathan's main competition, and his wife, Cynthia, nod their heads in perfect time. They remind me of those little "nodding head" puppies and kittens you can buy to put in the back of your car.

"What say you, Jonathan?" Horrible Boss asks.

"That's certainly an interesting concept to tackle the un-employment problem," Jonathan says smoothly, also nodding his head, and I squirm in my seat.

Jonathan squeezes my free hand under the table again, and I bite my tongue. And when Sidney's beady eyes shift to me, I panic, because I know that I won't be able to say any-thing remotely agreeable.

What can I do? I don't want to cause any unnecessary fuss, but neither am I about to concur with such pomposity. Quickly, I stab a whole, unmutilated profiterole and stuff it into my mouth.

"And you, Rosie. You must see it all the time at your, er, little employment agency." Guffaws follow. Graham and Cynthia's are the loudest, I note. Sidney finds it highly entertaining that I match people to the right jobs. I find it highly irritating that he callously dismisses my—I have to say—rather suc-cessful "little" agency.

"Hmmff," I say, pointing to my mouth. Actually, I think that attempting the whole profiterole might have been a mistake. . . .

"I bet you find it difficult to fill the lower-paid jobs, don't you? All those lazy bastards shying away from honest toil?"

"Hmmff," I say again, as the huge amount of pastry and cream in my mouth threatens to choke me.

"Rosie's agency is doing very well," Jonathan says very loy-ally as my face burns, and I gag as I try, ineffectually, to swal-low some of the profiterole.

I think I'm going to be sick. I really think I *am* going to be sick . . . either that, or I will be in need of the Heimlich ma-neuver.

The handsome stranger raises a questioning do-you-need-help? sardonic eyebrow at me and looks poised to stand and come over. He looks a bit worried. But I am getting worried, too—especially as no one at my table has realized that I might be in danger of expiring on the spot. James Bond to the rescue, I think, as he gets to his feet and as my eyes start to bulge.

"Yes, but it's only a second income," Sidney sneers. "But you'll be giving it up when the little ones come along. I've always said that working mothers are a drain on society—"

And it's then, at that moment, that the too-big mouthful of profiterole *completely* overwhelms me, and I crazily think of turtles. As I start to gag even more, I grab desperately for my napkin and hold it to my face. Just in time to cough and splutter out the whole, sodden, chocolatey mass.

The sudden silence that envelops our table is painful, despite the noise of the thirty or so other tables in the ballroom. Our fellow diners are flashing Jonathan faux sympathetic smiles whilst mentally congratulating themselves on having such a well-behaved partner or spouse.

I am mortified. And relieved to be alive.

I cannot believe I have just coughed up the contents of my mouth in front of these people.

"Er, sorry everyone." Jonathan jumps to his feet. "I think Rosie needs some fresh air." Jonathan tugs at my elbow. "I'm always telling her not to bite off more than she can chew, ha, ha, ha," Jonathan continues, and I flush with humiliation. And a little bit of annoyance.

As Jonathan hustles me away from the table, and I hobble along in my too-tight shoes, I am wretched and wishing I were anywhere but here.

And as we pass the neighboring table, the handsome stranger is smiling sympathetically at me again. This time, instead of winking, he gives me a discreet thumbs-up.

Kindly meant, but my embarrassment is now complete . . .

* * *

"But what were you thinking, stuffing the whole thing in your mouth?" is Jonathan's opening sentence as we reach the hotel foyer. Not the right choice of words.

I bristle a bit more, because I am the injured party and am in sore need of some sympathy and understanding. And my feet hurt.

"It was the only thing I could think of to stop myself from telling your boss what an obnoxious prick he is," I say without thinking.

"*Rosie.*" Jonathan's eyes widen in shock, because I'm not usually so blunt. At least, not with him. "That's a . . . a bit strong."

"Well, Horrible Boss has that kind of effect on me," I say, sinking into one of the lush, overstuffed sofas.

"You must remember not to call him that in public," Jonathan hisses as he quickly checks out the surrounding area for eavesdroppers.

"Don't worry," I tell him, leaning my head into the sofa's comfort. "Everyone's too busy fawning over him to bother spying on us. And believe me," I say, as I try to flex my toes a bit, "I could think of a lot worse things to call him. Doesn't he ever get to you?" Thank God I can take the weight off my feet!

"Look, I know he can be a bit difficult," Jonathan says as he sits down next to me and takes my hand, "but he really doesn't mean half of what he says. He just blusters a bit."

I am not that easily mollified.

"And what were *you* thinking, apologizing for me like that? Bit off more than I could chew? You made me sound like a complete idiot." Tired and depressed by my long, disastrous day, my voice wobbles and I am unexpectedly close to tears.

"I'm sorry, darling." Jonathan's arm is around me in an instant, and I lean into his reassuring warmth, inhaling the familiar scent of his skin and cologne. "I didn't mean to hurt your feelings. It's just—you know how *très* important this promotion is to me."

I worry, sometimes, that his promotion is more important to him than I am.

"Not more than you, *naturellement*," Jonathan adds, dropping a swift kiss on the top of my head. "But it's only for *ce soir*, after all. It's not like you have to even socialize with Sidney that *souvent* . . . "

He does have a point. I lift my head from his chest and look into his sweet, worried face.

"Did you see the look on Graham Hurst's face? You know how hard I've worked for this promotion, and how desperate he is to steal it from me," Jonathan says, his forehead creasing.

Poor Jonathan. I *do* understand the importance of getting on in one's chosen career. I'm pretty much like that with my employment agency. In the beginning, I had to work even longer hours than I do now to get it up and running. I also understand how important it is to have a sympathetic partner. Ivan, my two-years-ago ex, very quickly ran out of patience with me.

"I'm sorry, too," I tell him, reaching up a hand to his face, and he turns his cheek and kisses me right on the palm. "It was just after the Mum episode, and the burning toaster incident and everything, I got a bit short-tempered."

"Poor baby, you've had a *jour terrible*. You're such an angel," Jonathan tells me, pressing another kiss to my palm. "Whatever did I do to deserve you?"

How lovely is that? You see, sometimes I worry that we're not exactly right for each other. But is that just on account of my commitment phobia coming out? Not that *I* think I have a phobia about commitment. . . .

"Tell you what we'll do," Jonathan tells me. "You stay here. I'm going to get you a nice medicinal brandy, and you'll feel so much better."

"Okay," I say, happy to take refuge in the foyer for a while. See, Jonathan knows how I feel and is adapting to my needs.

Before Jonathan, I hadn't had a boyfriend for two years. Since Ivan, in fact. My friends said that I spent too much time at work to actively avoid looking for Mr. Right. And to avoid missing Ivan. In fact, they also think I actively pushed Ivan away because he was getting too serious. But that's not true at all. At least, I don't think it was.

"*Voilà.*" Jonathan arrives back, and I smile. I knew I could rely on him. "Now, you take your time to—you know—pull yourself together," he says as he places my brandy on the coffee table. And then I notice that there *is* only one brandy glass.

"Aren't you having one?"

"Er, not right now. You don't mind if I go and do a bit of networking, do you? You'll be okay here for a few minutes by yourself, won't you?"

I'm tempted to make my medicinal brandy last as long as possible to avoid going back to the fund-raiser, but I feel strangely abandoned sitting here by myself.

Of course, I do understand how important it is to network at these functions—you just never know who you're going to meet, and let's face it, the tickets were *very* expensive. But raising money for children's charities is such a good cause. Sidney's sister is some kind of fund-raising guru, and she arranged the whole thing. Bossiness must run in the family . . .

Briefly, I consider checking my cell phone for messages. I switched it off when we arrived because my mother has the habit of calling me at all hours of the day, even when I tell her well in advance that I will be incommunicado.

But I just can't face any more Mayford family disasters at the moment, of the real or imagined variety. They'll just have to manage without me for one night. I will check it when I get home. Or tomorrow . . .

I could use a lifeline and call a friend, therefore creating the impression that I am not a sad, lonely person on her own but someone who has just escaped the party to make important business calls.

But Carmen and Paul will be engaged in their usual Friday-night fight and will not appreciate the interruption as they smash plates and generally scream at each other. I don't know why they do this, but Carmen says it's just a form of self-expression. And the sex afterwards is phenomenal. But expensive in terms of crockery.

Jess will be at Friday-night knitting class. She says it's all the rage now, and not like some old women sitting together in a circle at all. Apparently, it's all dragon patterns and skulls and crossbones—the "new" rave party.

The brandy has helped, it really has. I get to my feet and smooth down my dress. And despite my aching feet, I now feel able to face the rest of the evening, whatever it might bring.

This thought holds me until I reach our table. It is practically deserted, and I cannot see Jonathan anywhere. Instead, only Cynthia is on hand, so at least it means I will not be sitting alone. This would normally be fine—even if she *did* want to wax lyrical about her and Graham's au pair, or new super-deluxe vacation home.

On this occasion, however, it is a disaster. The music has begun, and people are slow dancing to "Have Yourself a Merry Little Christmas," and Sidney is heading back toward the table from the direction of the men's room. I know he has spotted me and is thinking that slow dancing with me is next on his agenda, because his squinty eyes are fixed on me. He is a man on a mission.

It will be hard to refuse him, especially as it will seem churlish of me not to have a Christmas dance with him. But I just can't face it. Apart from not wanting his hands anywhere near me, I don't want to ruin things for Jonathan by saying something stupid. I need my own mission to avoid him.

Before I can consider the consequences of my actions, I grab the arm of the man who is passing me. Anything—anything at all to avoid Horrible Boss.

"Excuse me," I say, just a bit hysterically as Sidney gets closer. "I know we've never met, and will probably never meet ever again, and I know this is the kind of thing that people do in movies, and not in real life, but would you consider saving a complete stranger from certain disaster and evil wandering hands? It should only take a couple of minutes. I will give you my firstborn."

"That's a rather dramatic offer, but drastic times call for drastic measures," a pleasant, amused baritone voice replies. "As it happens, you're in luck. Saving damsels in distress is one of my specialties."

And as I look up into my ad hoc rescuer's face, he raises a sardonic eyebrow at me.

Oh.

It's him.

Dancing Queen

Rosie's Confession:

Did you know that being fluent in at least two languages could, apparently, help to protect against mental decline in old age?

I wish I hadn't given Jonathan that article, though, because the study meant people who speak <u>both</u> languages fluently, rather than one fluently and only a smattering of the other. I wish Jonathan wouldn't speak French to me in public. I know he doesn't <u>mean</u> to sound pretentious, but it does make me cringe a bit . . .

Escaping Sidney is now the least of my problems, I think, as warning sirens blare in my brain, and I wonder how one man can be so lethally attractive. It's just so unfair to womankind. . . .

My traitorous ovaries rejoice as they leap to immediate attention, closely followed by all other traitorous organs. And, in fact, all other traitorous body parts. Even my toes find room to curl.

And I know that I am standing here with my mouth hanging open in an unattractive manner. Drooling is so—so undignified. I must remember how to speak. Breathing might be good, too. This is only a man. A fellow human being . . .

I clear my throat to test my failing vocal cords. Now, there are many witty, amusing things I could say at this point to charm him with my sparkling personality.

"Oh, it's you," which is what actually comes out of my mouth, is not one of them. Not that I *want* to charm him, of course. Why should I care what he thinks of me? *Of course* I don't care . . .

"Yes, I think we can be sure that it is, in fact, me," he says, smiling down at me from at least six feet up.

His dark, wavy hair flops over his forehead, and I want to reach up and touch it. His teeth are ever so slightly crooked, which is endearing. His eyes crinkle so nicely, and twinkle so . . . dangerously.

"I'd love to stop and chat, and get to know you a bit better before I take such a liberty as placing *my* hands on your person, but I think the root of your distress is about to descend on us," he says, nodding his head just a little in the direction of Sidney the unstoppable Sherman tank. "We should make your escape now. Do you think you could bear to dance in those shoes? It's a slow number, and it will involve little actual movement of feet."

"Dancing. Yes. Good plan," I say, babbling like a complete idiot.

"I apologize for having to put my arm around you in such a familiar way, but I promise not to let my hands wander too far," he says, and I almost forget to breathe again as he takes one of my hands in his and slides his other around my waist. "Oh, good. Bing Crosby—always a wise choice for any Christmas party, don't you think?"

"I, um—" I stutter, groping desperately for a thought. Any

thought at all . . . oh, but he smells lovely. No! Forget that. *Not* a good thought.

"You know, you could put your arm around my waist too. I've always thought that free-form arms during close dancing are a bit noncommittal."

"How can you tell?" I blurt as I tentatively place my arm around him. God, it feels good. Too good. Another bad thought. "About the shoes," I say, as we start to sway in time to "I'm Dreaming of a White Christmas."

"Ah, that would be because of my medical training." He smiles even wider. "We doctors have our secret methods of discerning tight-fitting shoes."

Oh, this is even worse than I thought. Not only is he adorable, and dangerous, and smells lovely, but he also *saves lives!*

"Or it could just be the way that I hobbled out of the room after the near-death experience," I say, just a bit cynically.

"Well, that shatters my secret methodology," he laughs down at me, and my heart misses a beat. "The hobbling was a large hint. Why *are* you wearing shoes that are too small? It's something that's been fascinating me all evening."

"Trust me, the shoe story is not interesting," I tell him, because, well, he makes me feel petite. I don't want to shatter the petite image with my big feet issue. "Do you make a habit of looking closely at women's shoes? Is this something that the Royal College of Physicians needs to be warned about?"

"No," he laughs, and I have to bite my lip so that I don't sigh at just how good his laugh makes me feel. "As concerned as I might be, in a totally professional capacity, about the state of the health of your toes, they were not my primary concern. Would it be cheesy of me to say that I couldn't stop myself from watching you because you are by far the most interesting, beautiful woman in the room, and I was wondering how I might escape the boredom of the evening and sweep you away?"

His words shower me with just the right dose of hypothetical cold water that I need. I am medium sized. My hair is straight, and almost black, and falls to just below my ears. I have a good complexion, and nice blue eyes. I am attractive in a normal kind of way.

"Cheesy doesn't begin to describe it," I say, coming back to earth with a bump. A lump is building in my throat. This guy, whom I immediately christen Dr. Love, has a great line and a charming bedside manner, I'll bet. But no way, no how, could he think I'm beautiful. *Especially when comparing me to his own dinner companion.*

"Well, that's what I thought. I shall remember to avoid cheesy compliments at all times. You have a very expressive, tactile face," Dr. Love tells me, and I cringe at my own disappointment. I don't want him to flirt with me, I definitely don't, but "expressive, tactile face" just doesn't hold the same allure as "most interesting, beautiful woman in the room."

"What's that thing with the James Bond sardonic eyebrow?" I ask, just a bit crankily. "I bet it took years in front of a mirror to perfect."

"What can I say? Just the right amount of sardonic is so hard to achieve." He raises his eyebrow and laughs. "I can see you're not impressed."

"Sorry. But charming, sardonic eyebrows have no effect on me. Give me a man who can waggle his ears, every time," I lie, and he throws back his head and laughs even more.

God, but a man who can laugh at himself is so . . . endearing. I stop that thought in its tracks. I don't want him to be charming, or endearing. I want him to be self-obsessed, with an ego the size of London. At least that way I could dislike him.

"The ear thing I can't do, but the eyebrow thing is a God-given talent. It drives my mother mad—she says I use it when I'm agreeing with her, but really disagreeing with her."

"And do you?"

"All the time. I'm all for family harmony—not that there's a great deal of it when we all get together."

"Sounds like mine," I tell him. I want to know more about his family and its harmony. I wonder if he's married . . . Before I can stop them, my eyes home in on our entwined hands. I can't feel a ring, but then it's the wrong hand for a wedding ring.

What am I doing? I've known this man for five minutes. I don't *care* if he's married. After all, I'm practically engaged myself.

Oh. In my bedazzled-by-Dr.-Love state, I forgot all about Jonathan. How could I do such a thing? I look over to our table as we sway around again. Jonathan is there, and is scowling across the room at me. I think I should get back to him. At least there's no sign of Sidney.

"The wanderer returns," Dr. Love comments, following my line of vision. "I take it that's your boyfriend?"

"Yes."

"Ah, thought so," he nods, not smiling anymore. And I don't know if it's my imagination or not, but he sounds just a bit disappointed. Which is ridiculous.

"I really should be getting back," I tell him, as Bing Crosby fades out.

"Which is a shame, because 'Rudolph the Red-Nosed Reindeer' is one of my favorite pieces," he says, his mouth crinkling in a half smile. "At least you will be safe from Sidney of the wandering hands."

"You know him?" Oh. That's not one I was expecting.

"Unfortunately," he tells me, removing his arm from around me. I shiver slightly and try to convince myself that no arms around me is a good thing. "We're related."

"Oh, God. I didn't mean to be rude about—"

"No worries," he says, holding up a hand. "We can't choose our relatives. Sidney is an obnoxious fellow, which is exactly why I take the approach that you did over dinner," he tells me, and I nearly stumble as he leads me back across the room. But not because of my shoes.

"What?"

"Whenever I'm in his company, I just keep filling my mouth with whatever is handy so that I don't have to actually talk to him."

"Well, it seemed like the best thing to do."

"I know—great minds think alike. In another reality we're probably soul mates," he says, winking.

"You really need to work on the cheese angle of your conversations," I laugh, taking it as a joke, because it must be a joke, mustn't it?

We are now at the edge of the dance floor. For some strange reason, I don't want to introduce him to Jonathan. And I don't want to think about soul mates, either. Better to break things off now. Not that there's anything to break off, of course.

"Well, thank you for rescuing me," I say, looking down at my too-tight shoes, and my feet begin to throb again. Oddly, I'd forgotten about them hurting just for a few minutes. "I think it would be better if . . . ," I break off, indicating Jonathan with my head.

"I understand," he says, with a half smile. "I don't want to be the cause of any unintentional disharmony. It was my pleasure. And thank you for not choking to death on the profiterole. It was the highlight of my evening, apart from dancing to Bing."

I don't want this conversation to end, which is also ridiculous.

"Well, good-bye then," I say, holding out my hand. "And thank you."

"My pleasure. Try not to expire over the cheese course," he says, briefly taking my hand. "Chew well."

"Who was that?" Jonathan asks by way of greeting as I slide into my seat.

"Oh, just some bloke," I say, hoping that my face is not as flushed as it feels.

"Only I was looking all over the place for you. I thought you were still in the foyer. I missed you."

How could he have missed me? He was too busy networking to even sit with me in the foyer. I squash this thought. Because it's actually quite nice that he's jealous. It shows he cares.

"I don't even know his name," I say evenly, because I've had enough disharmony today to last for a year. "He's just someone who happened to be passing when I needed to be saved from dancing with Sidney."

"Well, I don't like the look of him," Jonathan says, still looking a bit petulant. "And would it hurt you to have one dance with my boss? It *is* Christmas, after all. Cynthia danced with him."

Lucky Cynthia.

"Don't you remember the Halloween Ball and the false nose incident?" I ask. I'm a little hurt, because Jonathan could be a bit more understanding. I know he needs to focus on this promotion, but how can he bear the thought of his boss's hands wandering all over his girlfriend?

"Yes, yes," he says, taking my hand and smiling. "That was *très* quick thinking of you," he adds. Whew. For a moment there I thought he was really going to take Sidney's side. "It has to be said, you can be *un peu* clumsy on your feet—you nearly took out Sidney's eye with that false nose, and we don't want any more accidents."

That wasn't quite the response I hoped for. But before I can say something, Graham and Cynthia return from the dance floor to take their places at the table, and Jonathan, Graham and the company's accountant commence their usual one-upmanship chat about how their respective departments are doing really well. An "I'm the man" exercise to prove their superiority over each other.

And when Cynthia strikes up a conversation with the company accountant's wife about their new yacht, or château, or something equally fascinating, I am still smarting from Jonathan's remarks and excuse myself in favor of the ladies' room.

As I get to my feet I do not glance over to Dr. Love's table to see if he is there. Or, indeed, to see if he is watching me. I wonder how much longer we have to stay for decency's sake before we can leave. . . .

"There she is," a familiar voice behind me bellows, just as I am turning around to leave the table, and I cringe. "Haven't had a chance to talk to you tonight, Rosie," Sidney tells me, swaying.

That's because I have been avoiding you, I think but don't say. In fact, I don't say anything at all. Because the sight of a tipsy Sidney, brandishing a sprig of mistletoe, is too awful for words.

"Come and give your Uncle Sidney a little Christmas kiss," he says, lurching toward me, lips puckered as he reaches for me. He's aiming right for *my* lips. And as his face reaches mine, and as his hand slides around my shoulder like a vice, ruining Jonathan's chance for promotion is the last thing on my mind.

I am trapped.

The music has switched from slow to upbeat, and Slade's

"Well Here It Is, Merry Christmas" is now booming in the background. It's a bit ironic, really, because I'm not feeling much Christmas cheer right at this moment.

Just as I get a wave of brandy breath blown in my face, just before Sidney's lips reach me, I know that I have to do something to escape. I turn my head and tilt it away from him. And accidentally stomp on Sidney's foot.

"Aaargh," Sidney cries, dropping his mistletoe as he tumbles backward and narrowly misses falling on a woman at the next table when he hits the floor.

"Oops. Sorry," I say, mortified. I didn't mean to send him flying. I just meant to stop him from kissing me, that's all. "Um, accidents will happen."

"Sidney, you poor, poor man," Cynthia twitters, out of her seat and kneeling by his side before I can blink. She looks up at me and shakes her head.

"Let me give you a help up." Graham, also one not to miss a beat, is reaching down a hand to him.

"Ouch," Sidney bellows as he's levered into a sitting position. "I think my toe's broken."

"What did you do?" Jonathan jumps to his feet. "How did this happen?"

"He tried to kiss me—I mean really kiss me—and I stood on his toe," I tell him, leaning in so that only Jonathan can hear me. Not that it's a worry, because the music is practically deafening. "But I didn't mean to cause Sidney any actual bodily harm."

Sidney, now on his feet, is being helped to his chair by the overly concerned Graham and Cynthia. He is still bellowing, but fortunately, I can't hear him. As Noddy Holder belts out, "Everybody's having fun," I sigh, briefly, because I am definitely not having fun. I hope I didn't break his toe . . .

"God. This is terrible," Jonathan says, pushing a hand through his hair as Noddy sings about looking to the future, and I feel bad for Jonathan, because he's obviously worrying about *his* future within the company. It's a tricky position to be in.

"Come on, we can rescue the situation," he says, reaching for my arm. "Let's get in there before Cynthia and Graham end up with all the credit. I don't know—er, you slide off his shoe and check out his toe or something. Look, there's the mistletoe—you could, you know, kiss it better."

"What? No way am I kissing his toe, or any other part of him." I mean, really!

"But that would show that it was just a clumsy accident— I'm sure he won't hold a grudge against you."

"What about *me* holding a grudge against *him*?" I squeak. Jonathan *must* understand. "Can't we just, you know, leave quietly and let the fuss die down?"

"Are you mad? Of course I can't leave. Graham will poison him against me if we do that. What grudge?"

"He tried to kiss me. And not a peck-on-the-cheek, innocent kind of kiss. And I'm not mad—I'm furious."

"Don't you think you're overreacting just a little bit?"

"Don't you think you're *underreacting* just a little bit?"

"What are you talking about?"

"On several occasions he has attempted to manhandle me, and I have overlooked them for your sake," I tell him, my temper flaring. "But this is just too much." How can Jonathan be more worried about his boss than me?

"Now, Rosie, I think you should just calm down a little—"

"Calm down?" I raise my voice, really seeing red. "I should be uncalming up, not calming down. And you should be supporting me."

"But I do support you," Jonathan says reasonably. "Maybe you shouldn't have worn such a—a tight-fitting dress," he adds, and I want to scream. It is the last straw.

"My dress," I clearly enunciate each word, "is not an issue.

Your boss is the issue. He is a lecherous, overbearing ass, and quite frankly, I can't understand why he's never been sued for sexual harassment."

As I deliver that last sentence, I realize that the music has stopped for the master of ceremonies to take center stage, and everyone in the immediate vicinity heard my last remark. And are all looking at me. Including Sidney, Graham and Cynthia.

Graham and Cynthia are wearing cat-who-got-the-cream expressions, whereas Sidney resembles a storm cloud.

"Er, yes, I think you're right, Rosie. I think you definitely *should* tell your cousin to sue," Jonathan, ever quick on the recovery front, ad-libs for our audience at large. "Don't worry," Jonathan says as an aside to me as the MC announces the winner of the raffle. "I can fix this. I think you'd better slip out and go home before you can do any more damage. I'll sort this out. I'll follow you as soon as I can."

"Don't bother," I say, because at this moment I don't care if he can fix it or not. In fact, I don't care about Jonathan coming home with me, either. And as I hobble forlornly across the room, I stop and take off my pinchy shoes.

Time for Cinderella to leave the ball without the prince . . .

"Marvelous exit," Dr. Love says in my ear as he takes my coat from the cloakroom attendant, which is a surprise, because I was expecting her to put the coat in *my* outstretched hand. Plus, I wasn't expecting Dr. Love to follow me, either.

"Here, let me help you with this," he says, giving me a lopsided smile.

I know I shouldn't be glad to see him. But I can't help it. As soon as I hear his voice I feel just a bit better. It's just because he's being friendly, that's all—and right now, friendliness is something I'm sorely in need of.

"Well, I thought I'd make it something memorable," I tell him, trying not to cry as he holds my coat and I slide in one arm. "Something to really crown my miserable day. Why are you here? Shouldn't you be ministering to Sidney's broken toe?"

"The toe is fine. Sidney will have forgotten all about it by tomorrow. Here," he says, pausing to reach into his pocket for a tissue.

"Thank you," I say, dabbing my eyes. "I'm fine now. You should go back to your date."

"Trust me when I say that I won't be sorely missed," he tells me, which is very interesting, because I cannot imagine anyone not sorely missing him. "You look like you could do with some coffee. Let me take you for coffee, and you can laugh at my sardonic eyebrow and tell me about your miserable day."

Coffee with a dangerously attractive, friendly stranger as opposed to slinking home to my own miserable company, where I will no doubt replay the whole disastrous evening again and again, is definitely appealing, but I cannot think for the life of me why Dr. Love is bothering.

"Why are you doing this? You don't even know me," I say as I swap my shoes over to my other hand, and he eases my other sleeve onto my arm.

"After our dance and our shared love of Bing? You wound me to the quick," he says, dramatically placing a hand on his heart, and I can't help but laugh with him. "Plus, you promised me your firstborn if I rescued you, and I'm calling in your debt."

"You might have to wait a long time for that," I say morosely, thinking of Jonathan. "The way things are at the moment, I'm not even sure I have a boyfriend anymore."

"So therefore far better to have coffee with me than go

home and think suicidal thoughts." He buttons my coat with nimble, elegant fingers. I shiver, imagining those fingers and what else they are capable of doing. I also notice that they are ringless. "I'd never forgive myself if you slit your wrists or something," he adds.

"I'm much too sensible," I say, just a little bitterly. And far too sensible to have coffee with handsome strangers, too . . .

"Well, then, break the mold of sensibility. I think McDonald's in Piccadilly Circus is our best option at this time of night. Not exactly high on the scale of sophistication, but it's close, convenient, and packed with people in case you're worried that I have nefarious motives."

His choice of venue is surprising, but at least it proves he's not a snob. I really shouldn't do this . . .

"I don't think—" *it's a good idea,* I nearly say.

"Don't think," he says, his handsome face earnest as he holds up a hand. "Just come. Besides, you'll be saving me from self-imploding through boredom. A necessary evil to raise money for worthy causes, but I hate these shindigs," he adds, with a grin, as he shrugs on his own coat.

What if I did? Do I really want to go home and sit by the telephone and wait for Jonathan to call?

To hell with sensible, I think as I smile back into his face. For once, common sense and practicality be damned.

"So your miserable day began—"

"This morning before I woke up," I tell him as he tucks my hand in his arm and we walk to the door.

"Miserable days often start that way—mine usually involves a loud beeper in the wee hours of the morning to request my presence at the hospital."

"I can't beat that." I shake my head. "My mysteriously nonfunctioning radio alarm fades into insignificance compared to, oh, saving lives."

"Not at all," he says, smiling ruefully. "I'm completely fascinated by mysterious radios. So, I take it this caused you to oversleep?" he prompts me.

"By an hour, but then the radiator in the living room decided to muscle in on the action."

"A-ha. I'm guessing that until this point in time it was a very well-behaved radiator?"

"The height of radiator perfection," I laugh. "It developed a sudden and violent leak," I tell him, falling in easily with his rhythm of speech. This is actually quite fun . . . not that I should be having fun at a time like this.

As the doorman holds open the door for us, Dr. Love removes my hand from his arm.

"Hold on tight," he says, and before I can ask him why, he scoops me up into his arms.

Cinderella Syndrome

Rosie's Confession:

Venus, apart from being the Roman goddess of love and beauty, is the only planet in our solar system that rotates in a clockwise direction.

I mention this trivial fact (although obviously not so trivial to Venus) because at the precise moment Dr. Love picked me up, I got this dizzy, falling sensation, as if all the planets in my metaphorical internal solar system had ground to a halt and then begun spinning in the opposite direction, <u>and nothing would ever be the same again.</u>

Which is ridiculous, because I don't believe in love at first sight.

Never before in my life has a man lifted me into his arms and carried me—except for my dad, when I was little. But a hundred and twenty-five pounds of woman is a lot of weight to haul around compared to, say, thirty pounds of toddler.

What if he drops me? What if I'm too heavy?

"Relax, I'm not going to let you fall," he says.

Actually, it does feel safe, and secure and . . . rather nice. Too nice. He's just being *nice* to me. This is not an invitation to cuddle closer and run my fingers through his endearingly floppy, yet well-cut, hair.

"You're doing the free-form arm thing again," he says in my ear, and I have to force myself not to shiver at the warmth of his breath. "You might want to put one around my neck for balance."

"But—" That would mean even more intimate contact with his person. *Yes*, every nerve ending in my body sings. *No—think clearly, logically*, I tell myself.

"Your poor feet have had enough torture—the last thing they need is to walk the streets of London clad only in panty hose. And besides, it's starting to rain a bit."

"But—" I tentatively slide my arm around his neck. Hmmm. He really does smell good . . .

"No buts," he says, his face so close to mine that I could kiss him. . . .

I squash that thought immediately. This is about *coffee*, I remind myself. Think about coffee. Think about Jonathan. How can I even consider kissing another man?

"So, where were we?" he asks as we reach the line of cabs outside the hotel, and I can't remember, because his arms are so lovely and strong and warm. "Ah, yes—the badly behaved radiator. I'm thinking this involved a long wait for the plumber—"

I can't stop myself from grinning back. He's just so charming. He places me into the cab, and as he climbs in the other side, I'm wishing he'd carried me for longer. Which is totally ridiculous . . .

"Piccadilly Circus, please," he tells the cab driver. "And?" he prompts me. *Where was I?* "Waiting for the plumber," he prompts me again.

"And moving vast quantities of furniture and books, so that I could save the carpet from certain ruin," I tell him.

"Always a good plan."

"Yes, but while saving the carpet from certain ruin, my toast caught fire on the grill."

"They don't make grills the way they used to. The new ones are just too sophisticated and efficient—damn shame, the way they burn the toast," he says, shaking his head as if burning toast was the most normal thing in the world to do.

"At least I know that my fire alarms are in good working order," I say, as we reach McDonald's and he scoops me out of the cab. I nearly forget to breathe as I try to focus on the conversation. "The firemen were very understanding about being called out on a false alarm," I tell him as we reach the doors and he places me back on my feet.

"Better a false alarm than a real emergency. Two large, normal coffees, please," he says to the assistant. And then to me, "Is that okay? I can't get to grips with all these newfangled coffee options—it's all latte whatsits, skinny this, and mocha that—very confusing."

"Normal coffee is great," I say. And then, as we sit down at a table in the corner, "This must be so trivial compared to your days." I must sound like a complete idiot, chattering on and on.

"Not at all trivial." He shakes his head. "We've barely scratched the surface. Lunchtime."

"Okay. So at lunchtime—"

"Which you planned to work through in order to catch up on the work you missed this morning—"

I think he's psychic.

"My mother called. This involved a detailed description of her latest crisis—the gas supply was disconnected—"

"And I'm guessing here that your mother is like mine,

therefore this also involved you fixing it," he says, stirring sugar into his coffee.

Definitely psychic! And he's good to his mother.

"A lengthy trip to the energy company to pay the late bill, and threaten, cajole and plead until they agreed to reconnect this afternoon."

"My God, you're good." He raises that sardonic eyebrow again. "It usually takes them at least a week. Sorry—old habits die hard," he adds, smoothing his eyebrow.

"Granny Elsie was my ace card," I tell him dryly. Actually, the eyebrow thing is very cute. "She lives with Mum, and I simply pointed out that it would not be good publicity to allow an eighty-six-year-old grandmother to spend the weekend in a freezing house."

"Clever move."

"Well, I thought so. I didn't mention the alternative plan to the company representative—Mum's covert threat that she and Granny Elsie would move in with me until it was fixed."

"And although you love them, this was not a tempting alternative?"

"You don't know my mother."

"I'm with you, trust me," he nods. "My mother, much as I adore her and am grateful to her for carrying me for nine months, and generally making sure I grew up without killing myself on motorbikes and such, would drive me mad within the hour—far too tidy."

Another reason why Dr. Love and I would never be compatible. Not that I'm making a list here, of course . . .

"My mother's the opposite," I sigh and don't add that I am a neat freak. I'd drive him crazy.

"Mine would be ironing my socks and scrubbing between the tiles in the bathroom with a toothbrush before I could blink. Or rather, she'd hire a maid to do it."

I flush. *I* iron socks and clean between the bathroom tiles with an old toothbrush.

"Um—" His folks have *maids?* Mine can barely afford the gas bill, and his have *staff.*

"Oh, God—I didn't mean to insult you," he says, his eyes crinkling as his hair flops onto his forehead. "Nothing wrong with being clean and tidy—in fact, they do say that cleanliness is next to godliness. Now back to your day," he says, pushing his hair back.

"Well, because I was running so late, *of course* I missed the cleaners by five minutes, which means that I couldn't retrieve my discreet black velvet evening dress. This also means that instead, I am wearing a much more revealing evening dress."

"I, for one, am rejoicing. That's a very attractive dress you're wearing."

"Thank you," I tell him evenly, but my pulse is humming, and my heart is pounding just a bit harder at the way he's looking at me. Even though he can't see the dress, because my coat is covering it. "But this was not my choice of dress for tonight. I didn't want to encourage Sidney's wandering hands."

"Sidney should be in complete control of his hands at all times. Trust me—the dress is not an issue."

Why couldn't Jonathan have said something like that? Thinking of Jonathan depresses my mood. I wonder what he's doing and what he's thinking . . .

"It is when your boyfriend is really hoping for a promotion and you don't want to piss off his boss," I say, looking into my coffee cup. I don't need to point out that my boyfriend chose to stay with his boss, rather than leave with me. How pathetic must I seem?

But I still can't believe that my boyfriend, whom I love—at least I'm nearly sure I love him—could not see the situation for what it was.

"That's a sticky one. Yet your boyfriend, I'm sure, will come to his senses, and by tomorrow this will all be a storm in a teacup. They say that everything seems a lot better in the morning."

"But not—"

"—the mornings when your alarm clock fails to work," he finishes my sentence for me again.

Dr. Love is a complete stranger, yet I feel like I know him. How odd is that? But maybe he understands because he's removed from the situation. It's sometimes hard to see something if you're too close, isn't it?

"So, after your surreal, stress-filled day—"

"I had only fifteen minutes to get ready for this surreal, stress-filled evening."

"I'd never have guessed," he says. "You look lovely, and if I were your boyfriend I'd be completely proud to have such an amazing girlfriend who worries about my promotion prospects."

I break eye contact and refocus on my coffee.

"It's late," I say eventually, my cheeks still on fire at his last comment. He's just being nice, and I am far too sensible to read more into his words. I should go home. For all I know, Jonathan might be trying to call me right now to explain and apologize.

"Yes. Of course. I'm sure your boyfriend will be worried about you. I'd be worried about you. Oh, excuse me one moment," he says as his beeper rings. "I suspect that Baby Woodbridge has decided to make an appearance, which will be a relief for poor Mrs. Woodbridge, because she's a week past her due date."

And as he calls the hospital on his cell phone, I can't help but think back to his comment earlier this evening when I first grabbed his arm at the fund-raiser. He really *does* make a habit of saving damsels in distress . . .

"Sadly, I have to go, too." And his smile really is sad, as if he's really going to miss me. I must get a grip on reality.

"Which is not sad for Mrs. Woodbridge, though," I say, getting to my feet and picking up my shoes.

"It looks like she's in for a long night." He takes our cups and places them in the trash. "Ten hours of contractions and she's still only dilated by two centimeters."

"I'm sure she's in the best hands." I pause as we reach the door. "Well, thank you so much for coffee and the shoulder to cry on."

"Not so fast," he tells me, and my heart leaps into my mouth. Maybe he's going to ask me for my number. "Hold on tight," he tells me, scooping me up into his arms again. I could get used to this—used to him, I think, as the blood in my brain pounds in my ears. "Let's get you safely into a taxi."

"Really, there's no need—I can walk," I protest just a bit but am secretly delighted at the close contact. My body is even more delighted, and hums, aching to get closer. Even if only for a few seconds. Even if guys like him never ask for telephone numbers from girls like me.

"Well, here we are," he says, turning his head to look into my eyes just as a black cab pulls over. And what I see there freezes me.

"Yes," I breathe, my heart racing, because he's looking at me as if he is starving and I am a delicious meal.

"I'd better put you down," he says, as if he never wants to put me down.

"Yes," I breathe again, swallowing as he begins to bend to place me in the cab, and all I can hear is the pounding of my heart and the whisper of suggestion in my ears.

And in that moment, I want to be rash. I forget that I am Miss Sensible and *know* that I am about to do something exciting. Impulsive. Irrational. Instinctively, my arm tightens around his neck, and his face moves closer to mine. And I, Rosie Mayford, take the final step and kiss him.

It is soft, and sweet, and gentle, and tastes of coffee. And my God, I want more.

And when he pulls back, probably shocked to his core that a complete stranger has kissed him, and he was only being kind to the poor girl, after all, I hardly dare open my eyes. But when I finally do, his are hot and blazing.

This time, the kiss isn't soft at all.

It's hot, and wet, and explosive, and exhilarating. Every nerve ending in my body is screaming with joy.

I don't notice when I drop my shoes and wind my other arm around him, pulling him closer, sliding around in his arms to press more closely to him.

I don't notice the damp as my feet touch the wet ground.

I don't notice the chill in the air, or the noise of the traffic, or the bright neon lights of Piccadilly Circus, because of the fireworks exploding in my head.

But the impatient honking of the taxi is a reality check. What the hell am I doing, playing with fire like this?

"Come on, love, is he getting in the cab with you or not?" the cab driver yells through the window, and I pull away and gasp.

Dr. Love looks as stunned as me. But probably not for the same reasons.

How can I kiss another man so passionately, when only an hour or two previously I was thinking of Friday-night sex with my boyfriend of six months? What kind of woman does this make me?

"Um. I'd better go. You'd better go," I babble, jumping into the cab.

Dr. Love, for once, doesn't have much to say. He is still standing there with that dazed expression on his face, but lunatic women who kiss you passionately in the middle of a busy London street can have that effect on you.

I pull the door closed, and as the taxi pulls away, I cannot resist turning around to get one last glimpse of him. What must he think of me?

"I said, where to, love?" the cab driver asks me.

"Notting Hill. Princedale Road," I tell him, realizing the irony of my street address as I watch Dr. Love pick up my forgotten shoes from the sidewalk.

But he's not my prince, I remind myself. And the shoes don't even fit.

And then I realize something else.

He kissed me right back.

Sense and Sensibility

Rosie's Confession:

I think I might be a slut.

I have a boyfriend, who, despite his little flaws, I think I love. So how could I have been so tempted by Dr. Love at the first sign of trouble? I must be a slut.

Apparently, scientists have developed a method of inserting a single monogamous male prairie vole cell into the brain of promiscuous male meadow voles, which makes them faithful.

Wonder if it works on human females?

Yes, I am a coward.

Instead of staying home this morning to answer my phone messages from Mum, and possibly from Jonathan, I am hiding in a coffee bar on Portobello Road with best friend Carmen. Actually, I'm not technically hiding at all, because I always meet Carmen and Jess (who is always late) for coffee on Portobello Road on Saturdays. The fact that I've also left my cell phone at home was just—absentminded of me, that's all . . .

Okay, so I left it at home on purpose. I just need to clear my head a bit. You know, to regain some sense of normality. But I'm beginning to wish that I hadn't told Carmen about last night.

"You did *what?*" Carmen asks me, her lovely gypsy eyes widening to saucers as she leans back in her chair.

She is peering at me as if I have just announced that I have developed a sudden, passionate interest in poisonous arachnids, am leaving behind all that is near and dear to me, and am emigrating to Australia to better study my subject matter.

This shock, I suspect, is because we usually spend Saturday mornings rehashing her current drama with Paul from the night before, and what should she do, and I give her advice that she usually ignores, and then I tell her about my mother's latest drama, and she gives me advice that I try to take but don't quite manage. But the drama doesn't usually revolve around me, personally.

"That's just so—so *nonsensible* of you," she says.

I pick up a teaspoon and carefully focus on stirring my coffee—unnecessary, since I don't take sugar, but my face is flaming, and I'd rather not share my embarrassment with the whole coffee shop.

"I know," I say to the tabletop. "I don't know what came over me. I *hate* nonsensible."

Carmen, not the kind to be shy about voicing her opinion, is unusually silent. But then, despite the fact that she has complained about Paul nonstop since the moment they met eighteen months ago, she's totally besotted and would never cheat on him by kissing a complete stranger.

"Sooooo," I say too brightly, in my bid to change the subject. "You and Paul smash any good plates last night?"

"Darling, just because Paul and I like to voice our opinions and discuss our personal issues in an adult, open forum, doesn't mean that we fight *all* of the time, you know," she says, frowning as she twirls a handful of her long, red curls. "As a matter of fact, we had a nice, quiet evening with take-out Indian and a bottle of wine."

"That sounds very, um, romantic," I say but am instantly suspicious. As Carmen twirls her hair even more furiously, I wonder if everything is okay between them. You see, the hair-twirling thing means either (a) that she is worried about something, or (b) thinking deeply and meaningfully about something.

"Paul did a fourteen-hour shoot for *Free Your Food* magazine yesterday. He was just tired, okay? So don't go reading anything into it, Miss Rational," she says, abandoning her hair twirling.

"I wasn't," I tell her, a bit surprised by the vehemence of her tone.

"And don't change the subject. No wonder you look like shit." She shakes her head in wonder. This is not quite the response I was hoping for.

It's a good job we've been friends since school, and therefore I know that when she says things like "You look like shit," she is not being a bitch—she's trying for empathic.

But after the night I spent tossing and not sleeping, I think I look relatively good. And at least I finally got around to alphabetizing my CD and DVD collection.

"Thanks for the brutal honesty," I say, sipping my coffee. "You should have seen me this morning pre-emergency Clarins and eyedrop treatment. God, do I need this caffeine."

"Darling, I really didn't think you had it in you," she says. And then utterly confuses me by grinning like a Cheshire cat. "This is *great*. This is *fabulous*. Totally un-fucking-believably *fantastic*. Although I may need years of therapy to recover from the shock."

I don't see what's so fabulous about it and am about to say so when Jess comes dashing over to our table.

"Hello, hello, sorry I'm late," Jess chirps to us, and Carmen and I pick up our cups before she places hers on the table. The table rocks, and her herbal tea sloshes into the saucer.

"Darling, we were beginning to think you'd been abducted by aliens again," Carmen says, her eyes still on me.

Jess really does believe she was abducted by aliens once, briefly, in college. But Carmen and I are convinced it was a hallucination due to her roommates' fondness for "herbal" cigarettes.

"My God, it is *madness* out there." Jess rummages in one of her bags. "*Madness*, I tell you. Portobello Road on Saturday in December! What else can I expect? I know, I know, but look at these," she says, her cheeks pink and flushed from the cold and excitement as she brandishes a pair of fuzzy, bright orange earmuffs.

"Bright orange earmuffs contrasted with bright pink hair and a bright purple sweatshirt. Interesting fashion statement," Carmen says. "Today is just *full* of madness and surprises," she adds, glancing slyly across at me. "Take our Rosie, here—she had a *very* surprisingly mad evening."

"Oh, they're not for me—they're for Mummy." Jess, who still hasn't quite caught up with the conversation, shakes her head, and a curtain of pink hair falls around her sweet face. "To go with the orange sweater I made her for Christmas. I think they're perfect."

It's hard to imagine Jess's mother, Lady Etherington, wearing anything except Burberry, but I don't tell Jess this because she is one of the most well-meaning people I know.

"The pink hair is adorable," I tell her, because it is. Not many people can carry that off with aplomb.

"Stop changing the subject, again," Carmen tells me.

"What? What? Did I miss something?" Jess pulls her chair up to the table, and Carmen and I grab for our coffees again, just in time to save them from getting sloshed. "Sorry, sorry."

Jess holds up her hands as more of her herbal tea leaps over the rim of her cup. "Aster's always telling me I'm a clumsy clogs."

"You're not clumsy," Carmen says loyally, her lips pursing.

"No, not clumsy. Just always in a hurry," I say, remembering that Jonathan called *me* clumsy, too.

Carmen doesn't like Jess's boyfriend, Aster, very much. I'm not terribly keen on him, either. His real name is Glen, but Aster, short for Asterisk, meaning *star*, apparently has more kudos when you're a budding pop star on the verge of fame.

"I'm making him a black sweater with a white star on the front for Christmas. Do you think he'll like it?" Jess asks, chewing on her lip.

"I'm, um, sure he will," I lie. Not because the sweater won't be great, but because Aster, although a poor, struggling artist on welfare, has developed fine tastes in designer grunge clothes. All purchased with Jess's trust fund.

"He'll love it," Carmen says in a way that implies "I will strangle him with it if he doesn't."

"But anyway, anyway, what did you mean about Rosie's evening? Not trouble with Horrible Boss again? Horrible, horrible man," Jess says sorrowfully. "How did it go?" She leans across the table to give my arm a sympathetic pat.

"Well," I take a deep breath.

"No, let me," Carmen says, grinning. "Please—it would make my year. What would you say," she leans into Jess, "if I told you that Rosie threw Sidney violently to the floor when he tried to snog her, broke his toe, made a grand exit minus Jonathan, got picked up by a handsome doctor, and passionately shared tongues with him in Piccadilly Circus? And then forgot to ask him for his name." Carmen falls back in her chair laughing.

"No, no. You didn't!" Jess puts a hand to her mouth.

"Well, it wasn't quite like that," I say, squirming in my seat. "I didn't actually push Sidney . . ."

"But what about poor Jonathan?" Jess is highly invested in my relationship with Jonathan. She likes him and thinks he's perfect for me. Also, there's nothing she likes more than a good wedding. She spends a great deal of time fantasizing about them—especially her own.

"I know," I sigh. "I'm seeing him tonight. What am I going to say?"

"It was only a kiss," Carmen says. "Why say anything at all?"

"With tongues," I point out. "We exchanged body fluids."

"Darling, don't get carried away by a bit of saliva." Carmen starts the hair twirling again, and I think she's about to get serious and meaningful.

"You know, Aster has to kiss a lot of girls in his business." Jess frowns.

"*Does* he?" Carmen says, rather dangerously.

"I mean, the girls kiss him. They just get so overcome by him on stage, they can't help themselves."

"That's . . . remarkable." I just can't see Aster's appeal, myself. Despite his penchant for designer clothes, he is thin to the point of emaciation. But he does have an Iggy Pop thing going on.

"I think that your brief encounter with Dr. Love happened at a crisis point in your relationship with Jonathan," Carmen says slowly.

"Well, I'd call Jonathan loving his boss more than me fairly crucial."

"No, that's not the point. You're at that stage where you have to think about the future, and you're getting ready to move to the next phase. Quite possibly," Carmen tells me, thoughtfully, "you were looking for a way out of your relationship with Jonathan before things get too serious."

"Exactly," Jess jumps on the bandwagon. "You let a man get close to you, but once they start wanting more commitment, like living together or something, you find a reason to finish it."

"But on the other hand," Carmen adds, "Jonathan does have a blind spot with his boss's attitude to you, which pisses me off greatly on your behalf. And while Jonathan is a great all-round kind of bloke, I suspect that he could do with more backbone. I think that you need some risk in your life."

"But I hate risk."

"The sexual excitement doesn't last forever, you know," Jess adds. "Although six months isn't very long for things to get boring."

"Jonathan's not boring."

"I mean, Aster and I have been together for seven months now, and our sex life is really hot. Maybe you just need to be—you know—more adventurous in bed."

"Our sex life is exciting enough, thank you very much." I blush a bit, but it's true. Jonathan's no slouch in that department.

"But you plan it. You even know what nights of the week you're going to have sex. Maybe a bit more spontaneity would help things along."

"What's wrong with sex in bed?" I've just never seen the appeal of sex on the kitchen table. I mean, it's just too uncomfortable.

"Let me finish." Carmen holds up a hand as she takes a sip of coffee. "This isn't about sex at all. It's about emotional commitment. And you don't hate risk, you're just conditioned to take the safe option every time. So what you do is opt for Mr. Nice Guy, because he's Mr. Safe Guy."

"But that's not—" *true*. Is it?

"I think you should, you know, talk it through with Jonathan," Jess says patiently. "I mean, if all that's wrong with him is his need to please his boss overly much, then it's hardly the end of the world. It's not as if he's, you know, secretly checking out pictures of naked grannies on the Internet."

Jess does have a point . . . and I *am* very fond of Jonathan—most of the time, when all's said and done.

"So—you're saying I *should* stick it out with him?" I think I want to. And she's right—I should give it more time. And it would be a bit of a relief to attend Christmas parties as a couple, rather than as a single . . . Besides, we've had a lot of good times together, and the Sidney thing is a minuscule part of our relationship.

"Just for a bit longer," Jess smiles with relief. "Talk to him. You owe it to yourself to see where it's going. Take that risk. Take your relationship to the next phase."

I can see from her dreamy expression that she's daydreaming about me in a puffy white dress, exchanging vows with Jonathan. I envy Jess a bit, truth be told.

You see, I don't daydream. Not really. Not unless you can count daydreaming about winning the lottery—not a huge amount, just enough to ensure financial security. Or of a peaceful weekend where Mum doesn't get panicked about something or other. Or I dream of finding the perfect person for the perfect job. Not the most exciting of things, but then *I'm* not that exciting, and besides, that's what I do at work. But it's not exactly boring, either . . .

Picture this: It's a cold, rainy December day at work. The phone rings, and it's, oh, some gorgeous, handsome actor. And he needs *me* to find him the perfect live-in assistant. He's trusting me to find just the right person who, amongst other things, will . . . chop his broccoli for a late night snack after a busy evening treading the actorly boards of the West End . . . if he actually eats broccoli. Okay, so maybe my daydreams *are* a bit boring . . .

"Hell, I wasn't talking about Jonathan," Carmen grins, and

I don't like her tone of voice. "I think Dr. Love is the most risky, exciting thing that's happened to you in years," she tells me. "I think you should track him down and sleep with him."

I think I need to go home and lie down. My brain hurts . . .

Have you ever wondered at some of the squirrelly label warnings that manufacturers deem it necessary to include with consumer goods for the benefit of us poor, hapless customers?

I mean, we don't really need to be alerted to the fact that our food products "will be hot after heating," or that we really shouldn't attempt to iron our clothes when they're actually on our bodies, do we?

I kid you not, that's exactly what the information pack that came with my iron warned me not to do. And let's face it, if the company feels beholden to warn us of such antics, then at least one poor (although incredibly stupid) person must have tried it . . . the mind boggles.

It's the Swedes I feel sorry for. Poor, uninformed sods. Who knew that they were so sorely in need of being admonished not to attempt to stop their chainsaw blades with their hands. Or with their genitals . . . euck.

But I do firmly believe that dishwashers should come with the warning "Do not under any circumstances whatsoever attempt to wash horticultural features in me," just to make it abundantly clear to people like my mother, whom I love dearly, but whom I also suspect inhabits a parallel universe, that garden gnomes should be consigned to the garden.

After Carmen's rather shocking advice (which, no, I am definitely not going to take) and Jess's more sensible advice (which I think I *am* going to take), and after elbowing my way through the Saturday morning chaos of Portobello Road market (otherwise known as Shopping with the World and His Wife), and chewing the fat about my forthcoming dinner with Jonathan tonight, because we always go somewhere nice for dinner on Saturday nights, and what the hell am I going to say to him, and what the hell is he going to say to me, I finally reach the sanctity of my house. And finally check my telephone messages.

All ten of them are from my mother.

Not a single one of them is from Jonathan.

But before I can worry about Jonathan's silence, or wonder what new tizz my mother has got herself into, the telephone rings, and it's my mother.

"Darling, thank God you're not dead," is her opening remark. I'm pretty ecstatic not to be dead, too, but I don't say this, because my mother doesn't give me the chance.

"Where were you? We've been so worried. You've been incommunicado since yesterday, and I've been calling and calling on your home phone and your cell phone," she panics down the line at me.

"Sorry, Mum," I sigh. Because I *am* sorry. I truly don't mean to worry her, but it doesn't take much to get her going. She's turned it into an art form. "I told you yesterday that I had to go to—"

"Yes, but you should have called me when you got home. You could have been mugged by a drug trafficker on Ladbroke Grove, or dragged into Kensington Gardens by a serial rapist," she says, building up to a crescendo of horrification.

This picture of doom and desperation is in direct relation to her belief that the only safe place in London to live is Hampstead, where she lives, and her desire for me to sell my nice little house and move back in with her and Granny Elsie.

Yet again, I thank God for the housing trust that got me onto the first rung of the ladder of home ownership. Six years ago, after a year of residence in the Royal Borough of Kensington and Chelsea, as it is so grandly called, I was able to take part in a shared ownership scheme for young (and therefore unrich) singles. It was only one room, plus a small bathroom and kitchen area, but it was mine. And came with a huge reduction, thanks to the housing trust.

I also thank God for the bequest that Granddad Mayford left to me, which enabled me to sell the studio apartment two years ago (at an astonishing profit) and plough all my money into my partnership in Odd Jobs and a huge mortgage for my sweet little terraced cottage. My haven of calm and serenity.

"Please calm—" *down*, I don't say, because Mum is barely pausing for breath.

"I nearly called the police to report you missing, but Granny Elsie said that you can't report a missing person until they've been missing for at least twenty-four hours. She heard it on *Crime Watch*."

Thank heaven for Granny Elsie, I think, rubbing my temple as it begins to throb in a familiar way.

"But darling, you have to come over *right now*," Mum tells me, her voice hitting a peak of panic. "Granny Elsie stuck Percy's head to her hand with the superglue, and we can't get him off."

Or maybe not . . .

Percy, I should tell you, is one of Granny Elsie's vast collection of garden gnomes. And Granny Elsie, although inexplicably potty about her garden gnomes (much to the horror of half of the posh residents of Mum's Hampstead address), does not have the steadiest of hands when it comes to fixing things with superglue. She does not have the greatest eyesight, either.

"How did it happen?" I sigh, because there is always a tale to tell.

"The *why* doesn't matter now," Mum says very quickly, and

I know that she is somehow responsible for Percy's current predicament.

"It was putting him in the hot cycle in the dishwasher as did it," Granny Elsie pipes up in the background, and my temple throbs even more. "I told you, Sandra. Didn't I tell you it should have been the cold cycle?"

"Shush, Mother," my mother tells her. And then to me, "The *how* we get Granny unstuck is the only thing that's important."

"You put Percy in the dishwasher?"

"Well, he was dirty, and I didn't want him in the kitchen sink, did I? Everyone knows the dishwasher is more hygienic."

I don't bother pointing out that she's not exactly planning on eating off Percy and that a quick sluice down with the garden hose would have been just as effective. This will only add to her arsenal of weapons in the Why I Should Move Home war.

"Have you tried soapy water? Or nail varnish remover?" I ask, remembering Jennifer Lopez's nifty little trick in *The Wedding Planner*, where she removes a statue's testicles from Matthew McConaughey's hand. See, you learn so many things from movies. Thinking of Matthew McConaughey makes me think of doctors, which leads me inexorably back to Dr. Love . . .

"She needs hospital treatment," my mother insists, building up to another panic. And before I can tell her not to get carried away by a flight of fancy, I get carried away by one of my own.

It ambushes my brain, and before common sense can overcome its surprise at being hijacked in such a way, and ruthlessly squash my flight of fancy, I'm off and running. In fantasy land.

I'm in the hospital with Granny Elsie for emergency Percy removal. Of course, I'm wearing the gorgeous, unsensible, red crushed-velvet top I saw in Carmen's vintage clothing store last week, which, although I craved, I dismissed as too revealing. I'm also wearing tight, sexy, distressed jeans, which I also saw in her store and didn't buy, but which turn me into a sex goddess. My hair is glossy and immaculate, and in between the dash from Mum's house to the hospital, I've found time to apply full makeup.

I've just settled Granny Elsie in her cubicle and am making reassuring noises of comfort to her when the privacy curtains part. And there he is. Dr. Love.

The harsh hospital lighting dims to a romantic glow. "Sweet Mystery of Life, at Last I've Found You," plays in the background with full orchestra, because, of course, my astonishing daydream comes complete with sound effects.

Dr. Love is instantly smitten by my sexy, glowing persona, combined with caring, granddaughterly concern. He's a bit haggard, but in a sexy, rumpled kind of way because, apart from delivering Baby Woodbridge, he spent the night fraught with regret that he didn't obtain my name or my telephone number, thinking he'd never see me again and had lost his chance of One True Love.

"Darling, you're so much better at this kind of thing than me," my mother's pathos-laden voice interrupts my daydream, just as Dr. Love has taken me into his arms and is about to *kiss* me.

I kill the daydream.

I would never use Granny Elsie in such a way. And besides, there are so many hospitals in London that the chance of me ending up in Dr. Love's is, well, just not going to happen. Not that I want anything to happen, of course I don't.

"I don't know how we manage without you," Mum says,

and I can hear the tears building in her voice. "It would be so lovely to *see* you," she says plaintively.

She saw me yesterday, but pointing this out will only lead to a further diatribe about being old and alone in this world, and what a comfort children should be to their poor, widowed mothers, even though she is only fifty-four and has Granny Elsie for company.

I concede this round and fortify myself to do battle with the chaos that is the Northern Line.

Better just call Jonathan first . . . I take a deep breath and dial his number.

Ties That Bind

Rosie's Confession:

Banging your head against a wall apparently burns one hundred and fifty calories per hour.

This is interesting, but I cannot help but wonder (a) why someone thought this would be a good measurement to test (I mean, how many people do you know who consistently bang their heads against walls in the first place?), (b) how they actually persuaded anyone to volunteer for this, and (c) if anyone has thought of measuring how many calories per hour it burns when dealing with a mother not quite in this reality...

"You're such a comfort to your poor, widowed mother," Mum tells me two hours later, after I have successfully removed Percy's head from Granny Elsie's hand, glued his head back on his body, placed him in his familiar spot in the garden with all the other gnomes, and rinsed down all the other gnomes with the garden hose to avoid further disasters.

And discovered the unpaid phone bill.

Inexplicably, the thought of hitting my head repeatedly against a brick wall is very tempting. . . .

"Mum, you have to stay on top of things," I say, checking through the heaps of papers on the kitchen table. "This is a final warning."

"I know, I know, dear. I, er, just forgot. How about a nice mince pie?" She deftly changes the subject, whisking the pack out of the cupboard and placing it on the cluttered table.

Odd that she worries so about the cleanliness of the garden gnomes. She doesn't have the same feelings about the tidiness of the kitchen, that's for sure.

"They're from Marks & Spencer—your favorites."

"But I set it up as a direct debit from your bank account so you wouldn't have to worry about stuff like this." Such as the gas bill, too, it suddenly occurs to me.

After Dad died just over a year ago, I went through all the financial details with her. Apart from the Hampstead house, there is also a monthly pension and a government widow's pension. It's not a huge amount, but enough to cover bills and property taxes and leave her with enough money to spend on herself. And Granny Elsie contributes to the bills.

"December is such a busy month, all that shopping to do—I'm just a bit overextended at the bank until next month," Mum tells me, a bit flustered as she pours boiling water into the teapot. "I just—canceled it for this month, you know, to give me a bit of extra cash for Christmas."

"It doesn't work like that." I close my eyes. Mum and financial affairs are not a match made in heaven. "You can't just not pay a bill for one month, then catch up the next. I'm guessing here—call it a wild stab in the dark if you like—but maybe that's why the energy company got so upset yesterday."

I don't suggest that she sell the house and move somewhere cheaper and smaller, thereby setting herself up with a nice lump sum to live off. We've gone that route before, and she just can't bear to leave the house she's lived in all her married life. I do understand, but am concerned that she's getting even flakier.

"I just wanted to buy you a nice Christmas present," she says, spilling milk on the side as she pours it into the cups. I know she means well, but this is another ploy to enforce mother guilt on me.

"Why don't I see what part-time jobs I've got on the agency books?" I ask her for the millionth time. "I'm sure I've got something that would suit you. It would, you know—get you out and about and meeting people, and give you a bit of extra cash."

"Your father never held with working wives," she tells *me* for the millionth time as she purses her lips. Dad was a bit old-fashioned, but I think he meant working wives with small children, rather than working wives in general.

"But I'm sure Dad would—" I grope for the right words. It's hard, because she still misses him so much. So do I.

"It's a full-time job just keeping this house going and looking after Granny Elsie," she says, her voice quavering as she gesticulates at the clutter. And then she makes a quick recovery and says cheerily, "You know, the basement's so lovely and light and spacious. Plenty of room for one—or even two—people. With a bit of work, it could be transformed into a completely separate apartment, with its own front door and everything."

This is not a new idea. This is the same idea she comes up with oh, say, once a month. I suddenly yearn for Jonathan's understanding smile and easygoing, uncomplicated company.

"Ooh, you didn't tell me you'd got Marks and Sparks pies." Granny Elsie, a small, rotund, perfumed vision in lilac polyester, wanders into the kitchen and grabs one from the pack.

Saved by the octogenarian with the pink rinse, I think, because Mum's next line would be that the basement would be perfect for me. And for me and *Jonathan* after the wedding, which my mother assumes will be the next logical step.

I do try to understand her, I really do. She really loved my dad. He was her whole life. He took care of her, and they did *everything* together. And although I don't want to spend my life alone, I don't want to end up like my mother, either. I just couldn't stand such a claustrophobic arrangement.

In that moment, I am certain about what I am going to do. I'm going to forget all about handsome, tempting doctors and concentrate on my unclaustrophobic relationship with dear Jonathan.

Jonathan certainly isn't the claustrophobic type, that's for sure. He wasn't home when I called earlier. I left a message, but he hasn't called me back. At least, not on my cell phone. Or my mother's phone, and I know he has the number, because I told him in the message—just in case.

"Mother, are you wearing the old girdle?" my mother asks. Granny Elsie, it has to be said, has dangling body parts. But at least it's distracted Mum from her basement crusade. "Your bits are hanging out everywhere. And down."

"I can't wear the new one you got me, Sandra. It squashes my intestines, and I need plenty of room down there so's I can eat plenty at dinner," Granny Elsie says, shoveling the rest of the mince pie into her mouth and taking another.

"That old thing's a disgrace—it's full of holes." Mum is indignant. And she's also right. Granny Elsie's old girdle is not something you want to see dangling from the clothesline amidst the clusters of gnomes.

"All the more easy for, you know"—Granny Elsie crinkles her already crinkled face into a lascivious grin—"accessibility."

I'm so glad she shared that with me. My grandmother's sex

life is just the picture I need in my head. Thinking of sex lives reminds me that I'd better go home and get ready for tonight.

I'm really going to talk things through with Jonathan. But I don't think he needs to know about the kiss. After all, we're not married yet, and it was only a kiss. But what a kiss . . .

"Mother!" my mother shakes her head. "Please."

"I'm having dinner with my new gentleman friend." Granny Elsie digs me in the ribs with her elbow. "He's a bit crinkly, is Alf, but at my age beggars can't be choosers. Speaking of sex," she cackles, and her false teeth slip a bit. "Did your mother tell you about the Immaculate Conception and How We Should All Come Together As a Family to Celebrate the Wondrous News?"

"Why are you speaking in capital letters?" I ask Granny Elsie, because it sounds like she's implying that Mum has joined a religious cult.

"Your cousin Elaine's pregnant," my mother sniffs, and I nearly faint on the spot. "She's going to be one of them single parents."

"You're kidding me," I say, sitting down on a kitchen chair. On top of the mound of clean, folded washing also inhabiting the chair, but I barely notice, such is my surprise.

Elaine is not one of my favorite people, and to be honest, if she weren't family then I would strike her forever from my Christmas card list. Or re-gift her with something horrible and used that I don't want, because that's exactly what she does to me.

Except for last Christmas, of course, but that was by accident. She gave me the Body Shop gift basket I'd bought her the year previously, but it backfired on her, because I happen to love Body Shop stuff, and I enthused about it all evening at length, because it really pissed her off. And although I don't make a habit of pissing people off, I make an exception for Elaine.

But pregnant? This will probably mean that I have to be nice to her. I can't imagine how Auntie Pat's taking this, though—think of her social standing at the Women's Institute!

"What did Auntie Pat say?"

"Apparently, yer Auntie Pat and Uncle Bill are as pleased as punch—they're even throwing this year's Christmas Party in her honor," Granny Elsie says, hitching up her panty hose. "It's not just family this time around—they're invitin' everyone they know."

I'm shocked that Aunt Patricia (or "Auntie Pat" as we call her, to annoy her) is taking this so well. She comes from a very grand old family with failing fortunes (although she lowered herself to marry Uncle Bill because, we suspect, of his self-made fortune). She's always had very grandiose ideas about people's situations in the grand scheme. Particularly her own.

"Yer cousin Elaine called and invited me personally," Granny Elsie adds, slurping her tea to wash down the mince pie.

Elaine called Granny Elsie personally? I'm trying to imagine Granny Elsie in Auntie Pat and Uncle Bill's house on Hampstead Heath. It is immaculate and full of expensive things that make you scared to touch anything. I'm also trying to imagine Elaine being nice, but it's just not gelling.

Uncle Bill's my dad's brother, so Granny Elsie isn't, strictly speaking, related to that side of the family. And Auntie Pat usually ignores her existence.

"I know yer Auntie Pat don't like me. I know she thinks I lower the tone," Granny Elsie adds.

"I don't know where you got that idea," Mum says rather

dryly. "Of course, it could be the old corset. Mother, I do wish you'd wear the new one. And your new teeth." But before she can launch into one of her diatribes, something odd happens. Mum's whole face shifts gear into a huge smile.

"Oh, but I haven't got a thing to wear to the party. I shall have to get something new," she says, her eyes lighting up. "You'll have to have something new, too, Mother."

"I'm all fixed up." Granny Elsie heads for the door. "I'm wearin' me red-and-green stripy number with the black flowers, because it's festive."

I grin, because Granny Elsie in that dress is a sight to behold. Auntie Pat's going to hate it.

"Plus," Granny Elsie winks at me from the kitchen door, "it'll really irritate your Auntie Pat. Now I've got to go and touch up me makeup. I'm due at Café Rouge in ten."

"I bet you could do with a nice new dress, Rosie. Call it a little extra Christmas present especially from me. Let's plan a girly shopping trip."

"But—"

I am about to remind her about money, and how she's overspending, but I stop when I see her overdue MasterCard statement on the floor under the table. The total is only twenty-five pounds, but it does have to be paid.

"Mum, what's this?" I ask rhetorically, waving it at her.

"Oh, that?" She snatches it from my hand. "It's just—a little something extra I bought for you, dear," she squints at it. "It was from one of those shopping channels, and I had to use a credit card because it's just easier with a credit card on the phone, isn't it?"

"Mum," I say, just a bit wearily. "We need to have a chat about all these unpaid bills."

"Don't be such a killjoy, darling, I just want you to have a lovely time," she tells me, sniffing indignantly. "You know—

just like it used to be when Daddy . . . oh, darling, remember all those lovely times when we were all together." She pulls a tissue from her pocket and dabs at her eyes.

"Mum," I say gently, touching her arm.

"Now then, dear," Mum says, straightening briskly. "Can you stay for dinner? How about I rustle you up something nice to eat?"

I manage to drag myself away because my mother has grand ideas for Jonathan and me and approves of the fact that I am having dinner with him. At least I think I am. He still hasn't returned my call . . .

But I only escaped after promising my mother to come for lunch the next day as a thank-you for my insistence on paying the telephone and MasterCard bill (despite the fact that I nearly always go for lunch on Sundays), writing checks for both bills and mailing them on my way back to the Northern line.

As the tube roars through the bowels of London, I worry about Mum. I mean, she's always lived in her own little world, even before Dad died, but I think she's getting worse.

Also, I'm still completely stunned about Elaine. I can't believe that holier-than-thou, cannot-put-a-step-wrong-in-everyone's-eyes, Goody Two-shoes Elaine is pregnant. I climb off the Northern line tube and head through the deep passageways toward the Central line.

And what's more, she won't say who the father is. Probably because she can't remember, I think evilly.

Elaine is tiny, petite, has small, narrow feet (of course) and looks like a China doll in a beautiful, fragile, butter-wouldn't-melt-in-her-mouth kind of way. Unfortunately, she has the heart of Chucky and always wants what other people (i.e., me) have.

When I was ten, I really, really wanted a pony for Christmas. I yearned for one with all my Barbie-and-My-Little-Pony-adoring soul. Yes, I know now that ponies are expensive and require (a) a stable, because they cannot live in the basement apartment of a Hampstead house, which was what I planned, and (b) plenty of space to run around in—not a small garden like ours. Although I promised to take Candy (yes, I'd already chosen a name for my perfect pony) for extensive walks on Hampstead Heath every day. As I said, I was ten, and the world was a wonderful, hopeful place.

Elaine knew all about my pony longing, because she threatened to bite the head off my Princess Aurora Barbie if I didn't show her my letter to Santa.

Needless to say, she got her very own pony that same Christmas. And I tried to be happy for her, I truly did. And I was more than happy with the toy horse I got for Princess Barbie to ride. I was even happy to clean out Candy's stall (yes, Elaine even stole the name) for months, because Elaine let me have a weekly ride on her. It was almost like having my very own Candy . . .

Until I turned up one day to clean out Candy's stall and she'd gone. Elaine took great delight in telling me that Candy had been sold because Candy loved me more than Elaine, and no one was allowed to love me more than Elaine.

I should have kept my mouth shut and let the bitch bite off Princess Aurora's head.

Yes, I know it's childish to hold a grudge for eighteen years, I think, as I exit the station at Holland Park and head toward home, but Candy wasn't the last love Elaine stole from me.

I'll never forget the humiliating scene at my twenty-first birthday party. The scene where I go to my parents' bedroom to find Auntie Lizzie's coat and instead I find dear

Elaine showing Harry, my then boyfriend, her blow-job skills . . .

At least Jonathan would never do anything like that.

And as I push open my front door, the telephone is ringing, so I dash for it and pick up, because it's probably Jonathan.

Thank God for safe, dependable Jonathan.

"Hello?"

"Darling," Elaine purrs down the telephone, and I'm confused, because she never calls me.

"Elaine," I say, a bit breathlessly on account of being breathless from dashing for the phone. "Lovely to hear from you," I lie. "Lovely news about the, um, baby."

"I'm just so excited," she squeaks in her little-girl voice. "Just imagine, I'm the first of us four cousins to bring a new life into this world."

"Isn't it amazing," I say, conjuring up a very unflattering image of Elaine, all fat and bloated and whalelike at nine months pregnant. And then, because I can't help it, "I hope the, um, lucky dad is excited, too."

"Oh, but darling, things are a little tricky for him right now and I'm sworn to secrecy."

I'm intrigued. Obviously a married man, then.

"Married, is he?" I say before I can stop myself, because although I would never knowingly sleep with a married man, Elaine is not so scrupulous.

"Naughty Rosie," Elaine purrs down the phone at me. "Let's just say that we have his public image to think about, but trust me, as soon as the time is right, I'll tell you all about it."

Is it just my imagination, or does that sound like a threat?

"You simply *must* come to the party at Mummy and Daddy's next Thursday," she stresses. Which is odd, because I always go to the family Christmas party. Under sufferance, but I do have an arsenal of family I actually like who will also be in attendance. And Jonathan, of course.

"I can hardly wait," I say carefully as I wait for the real reason for her call.

"It seems like so long since we last had a chance to chat," she says, hiking up the charm. "And you must bring your wonderful boyfriend with you," she adds, and my suspicious nature immediately jumps to the conclusion that she means to try to steal him from me. Why else would she bother?

"I'll certainly try," I say, as Elaine, Harry and the Blow-Job Episode spring immediately back to mind. I wonder if there's a way I can uninvite Jonathan, because he's already got it booked in his diary. Maybe I can pretend the party's been called off due to—

What am I doing? The one and only time she met Jonathan at Uncle Bill's sixtieth birthday party back in August, Elaine barely looked at him, because she was dating some rich, handsome investment banker. And besides, Jonathan is a complete sweetie and would never do that to me. It's one of the reasons I'm so fond of him.

But I wouldn't trust Elaine with the Pope . . . even if she *is* pregnant.

"And you must tell Granny Elsie it wouldn't be the same without her," Elaine trills, which is plain weird. Elaine can't stand Granny Elsie.

"Er, yes, she's very excited about it," I say, because she is. More about the lavish spread Auntie Pat always puts on, I think.

"And your lovely friends Carmen and Jess—and Charlie, of course." This is getting weirder by the second, because I know for a fact that Elaine can't stand my friends, either. "I'm just so happy," Elaine squeaks again. "I want to put my arms around the whole world and hug it."

I wonder, as I try to wind down the conversation and get rid of her, if pregnancy has wreaked this miraculous personality change on Elaine?

It is the season of goodwill, after all.

"For indoor or outdoor use only," the packaging on the Christmas lights wisely instructs me, as I open the box and unravel the long string. As opposed to say, what, exactly? Underwater or in space?

My gorgeous Douglas fir's been in the back garden all week, just waiting for me to bring it indoors and decorate it, so I thought I might as well get it out of the way. It's just not the same at Christmas without the smell of pine, is it?

As I place the final bauble on a branch, I take a step back and admire my handiwork. This year, I've decided that red and silver will be my tree theme, because they go so well with green, and are very Christmassy, too. I need all the Christmas cheer I can muster.

And now I'm going to watch a movie—something with blood and guts in it—something that doesn't include cute doctors or beautiful heroines who always get their man.

Jonathan broke up with me earlier.

After hanging up on Elaine, I checked my home phone messages, because time was getting on and I thought it was odd that I hadn't heard from Jonathan, so imagine my relief when I heard his dulcet tones speaking to me via voice mail. This is what he actually said.

"Er, hi, Rosie. It's me. Jonathan. Er, it seems Sidney's toe wasn't broken after all, hahaha, just a bit, you know, bruised. Just thought you'd like to know."

That's sweet, I think momentarily, barely noticing that his sentence does not include a word of French. And then he drops his bomb.

"Er, I know this is a bit sudden, and I don't know the best

way to tell you this, but it's been on my mind for a while. Rosie, you know I wouldn't willingly do anything to hurt you, especially at this time of year and all. But I think we should take a bit of a break from each other," he says, and I'm floored. I mean, I know I was thinking we needed to take a break, but I've worked through it.

Oh, I just bet he's met someone else.

"Er, it's not that I've met someone else. Just thought you might want to know that. I'm extremely fond of you, but I think we need to cool things down. Just for a while. Just for a few weeks. Well, take care. Speak to you soon. If you feel you need to, er, talk about it, well, er, I'm here."

That's it? That's my *breakup*?

Due to the suddenly boneless quality of my legs, I slump onto the sofa and look up at my Christmas tree, all twinkly and glittery, and I feel so alone. Everyone deserves to have someone to share Christmas with, don't they?

I just can't take it in. I bet Jonathan will call tomorrow, and it will all be a mistake, and am definitely *not* going to think about it right now.

Instead, I load *Terminator III* into my DVD machine and settle back for some world destruction. And as I watch people getting terminated, *I* terminate my way through a large pack of tissues and peanuts. Unsurprisingly, the peanut packaging contains the following consumer advice: "Warning: contains nuts."

I may have to write a thank-you letter to the consumer affairs manager for that one . . . just as soon as I've scraped my heart up off the floor.

Mistaken Identity?

Rosie's Confession:

Sometimes, when things are messy, I wonder what it would be like to be a snail...

Not because I think that slithering gastropods with coiled shells are particularly attractive creatures but because they can sleep for three years. Can you imagine that? Something horrible happens to you, and all you have to do is take a nice, long nap, and by the time you wake up, you're well over it!

Of course, being a French snail is not so attractive, on account of the possibility of being eaten...

"Jonathan casually broke my heart and dumped me via voice mail yesterday," I announce, just a bit dramatically, to my friends the following afternoon.

Oh. I really didn't mean to sound so melodramatic. It's just that I've been holding this information tightly squeezed up inside my lungs since last night, and it's grown, expanded, and I have to say something to someone or I'll burst with it. But I just couldn't face calling anyone last night.

Dumped. With only five days until Christmas. I mean, it just sounds so pathetic, doesn't it? I am so unlovable that my boyfriend can't even wait until the New Year to get rid of me.

Jess, who unfortunately has chosen this exact same point in time to arrive at our table with huge Aster stars in her eyes, shrieks, "Well? Well? What do you think? Isn't he fabulous? Totally fabulous?"

Poor Jess. Her enthusiasm is totally lost on everyone as they fall into stunned silence.

We are all sitting in the Duck & Drake, a small, smoky, dingy, off-the-beaten-track pub in Camden. It is so far off the beaten track that I spent half an hour hunting it down, which is fortunate in a way, because I arrived so late that I was just in time to hear Aster and his band brutally murder their second set.

I briefly considered canceling and going home after lunch at Mum's, to brood and regain my equilibrium a bit before I told my friends about Jonathan, but I promised everyone I'd be here for Aster's debut London appearance with Asteroid Attack. Especially Jess.

When I say everyone, I mean Carmen, Jess, my *nice* cousins Flora and Philip, and Charlie, with whom I co-own Odd Jobs.

Philip is the first to absorb my news and recover his tongue.

"Oh, no. I'm so sorry, Rosie," he tells me sympathetically. "I thought he was rather a nice chap."

"Nice chaps don't dump their girlfriends a week before Christmas. What a complete fucking bastard." Carmen bangs her empty pint glass down on the table.

"I thought you rather liked him," Flora, sister of Philip,

says to her. "Poor darling," she adds to me. "I know the future seems bleak and empty, but you will get over—"

"He could at least have had the decency to wait until the New Year, like any normal person," Carmen jumps back in before Flora can finish. And then, "Sorry for the 'fucking bastard' part, Phil," she tells Philip, who, when not inhabiting pubs dressed in jeans and a sweater, inhabits a Church of England church, dressed in a robe and a dog collar, because he's a vicar.

"No worries," he smiles good-naturedly. Philip is always good-natured and tries to see the best in people, but I expect that's part of his job description. "I don't suppose it would be of any help to say that it's the will of God, and that He works in mysterious ways?" he asks me. Then, when I shake my head, "Thought so. Bad luck, though, dear girl."

"Do you want me to hunt him down and break his legs for you?" Carmen jumps in again, her eyes narrowing to slits as she picks up her next pint and takes a swig. "Sorry, Phil—just pretend you didn't hear that."

"But only yesterday you were telling *me* to dump *him*," I say. She's already downed two pints of Theakston's Old Peculier ale since I arrived, and I suspect that her vehemence is directed at her boyfriend, Paul, rather than at Jonathan, since Paul is mysteriously absent.

"That's not the point," she says, and I'm thoroughly confused. "You were convenient for the sex, of course. And handy to take along to his Christmas bash. But once you served your usefulness, he dumped you. Therefore he doesn't have to buy you a Christmas gift."

"Well, thanks," I tell her, even more miserable now. "That really makes me feel better about the whole situation. Dumped because he's trying to save cash."

"He's not the only one. Honestly, since Paul turned thirty,

he's become a real old man about some things. I've come to the conclusion that all men are selfish, egotistical bastards who don't deserve the time of day. Present company excepted," she adds rather tipsily, looking around at Philip and Charlie. "And, of course, it's always better to be the dumper than the dumpee."

"But I thought you were so happy together." Flora always says this when one of us breaks up with someone. "You seemed so well suited," she sighs. Flora always says this, too.

Flora, at five feet ten inches, and one hundred and eighty pounds, is very blond and attractive in a Valkyrie-esque, Wagnerian kind of way. She is exuberant and interesting and one of the nicest people ever, but men tend to see her as sister or nanny material rather than wifely material.

"You've just got to push out that stiff upper lip, darling," she advises me. "You've got to just climb back in the saddle—jump back into the dating pond as quick as poss."

Or they are put off by her plummy, modulated, well-meaning bossiness. Her last boyfriends, both of whom were recently separated at the time they met Flora, dumped her and went back to their wives. Apparently, all those long chats and reasoning it through with Flora really helped them sort out their feelings and stiffen their backbones.

Poor Flora. All she really wants is to find someone nice and friendly with whom she gets along.

"Right before Christmas. That's so—" Charlie, who hasn't said a word until now, shakes his head and pulls a tissue out of his leather jacket. And dabs at his eyes. "I know what you're going through, darling—" He breaks off. Charlie got dumped by his One True Love just before Christmas last year.

"I didn't mean to bring back sad memories," I say quickly. Until this moment I'd forgotten. . . .

"You *will* get over him and move on," he tells me, patting my arm. He's never quite gotten over it, though, and has apparently given up on love forever. There have been a couple of guys since One True Love, but they fizzled out before they got going.

"You hated him, didn't you?" Jess, who, as usual, is still not quite up to speed with the conversation, slumps down on her stool, and we all lunge for our glasses as the table rocks. "I know Aster can be a bit . . . difficult at times, but he's got a heart of gold. Truly."

"We weren't talking about Hot Stuff over there," Carmen says, glancing across to the bar, where Aster is chatting up two very attractive women. "Jonathan dumped Rosie yesterday. Via voice mail."

"Oh. Sorry, sorry, that's terrible," Jess says, also sniffling in sympathy. "I don't know what I'd do if Aster broke up with me. I'd be heartbroken. Heartbroken," she adds as Charlie hands her a tissue.

"I wouldn't," Carmen mutters under her breath just for my ears, because Aster is getting very friendly with those two girls at the bar. He's practically ignoring poor Jess.

"You poor, heartbroken *soul.*" Jess shakes her head.

"Look on the bright side," Flora adds in her stalwart voice. "There are more fish in the sea than ever were caught."

But I want the one that slipped off my hook.

I know that Jonathan can be an idiot at times. And I know that I considered taking a break from him, but that was only my reaction to the Sidney thing and the Dr. Love thing . . . before I had time to put things in proper perspective.

Since last night, I have run the gamut of all emotions as I flounder alternately from loving Jonathan, to hating him, and then remembering all those kind little things he did for me, like buying me shoes, and helping me with my French, and I get all gooey inside and close to tears.

I didn't mention the breakup to Mum and Granny Elsie over lunch. Mum spent the whole time rattling on about

Mrs. Henderson at number sixty-three, and how her daughter moved back with her after splitting with her live-in boyfriend, and how nice it was for Mrs. Henderson to have Her Shirley back home. So after that, I just couldn't face Mum cross-examining me about what I did wrong this time.

I don't deliberately set out to sabotage my relationships . . . maybe I'm just not coupledom material, after all.

"Well." Charlie shakes his head, and we all sigh into our drinks and shake our heads as we fall into a morose silence. I certainly know how to kill ambience.

"Did we all rock or wot?" Aster asks, swaggering over to our table. "Man, did we bring the house down, dontcha fink?" he says. "How about you, Vicar—wouldnta fought this was your cup of tea," he says, sniggering as if he's just told a really funny joke. "I would've fought that choirs singing hallelujah was more your cup of tea," he sniggers even more.

"Well, I'm a vicar of very eclectic musical taste," Philip tells him solemnly. Aster, who has a small vocabulary that obviously doesn't include the word *eclectic*, stares at him blankly for long moments before answering.

"Sorry, Vicar, just can't see you wiv an electric guitar."

And I wonder for the umpteenth time why Jess, who is intelligent, and kind, and rich, and pretty in an odd kind of way, has hooked up with Aster, who is ignorant, and not pretty, and squeezes her for money. At least I think he does.

See, although I am devastated by Jonathan's callous behavior, I am not quite so devastated that I can't see my friends' problems. But who knows what hidden depths Aster has? I suppose it's all in the eyes of the beholder.

"Er, quite," Philip says, puzzled. "Very enthusiastic performance." His eyes soften as he glances from Aster to Jess.

"You were, um, unique," I say, because they were loud and unmelodic, and Aster cannot carry a tune, but it's so important to Jess that we try to like him. Actually, I've always thought that Philip had a soft spot for Jess . . .

"You were loud. And unimaginably unmel—" Carmen begins, and I swiftly kick her leg under the table before she hurts Jess's feelings, because she's had a bit too much to drink and would not forgive me if I didn't stop her. "Unmissable," she says, glaring at me.

"Remarkable," is Charlie's response.

"Interesting, um, arrangements." Flora pins a diplomatic smile to her face.

"See? I told you how amazing they are, didn't I?" Jess leaps up like a boisterous kitten and throws her arms around Aster's scrawny neck, and we all grab our drinks again as the table rocks.

"Watch out, babe," Aster tells her, removing her arms as he glances back to his fan club at the bar. "I got a persona to maintain. I can't be having me girlfriend attached to me like a leech the whole bleedin' time. And you nearly sent them drinks flyin'."

"Oh, sorry, sorry," Jess says, her smile faltering just a bit. And I want to smack Aster for being so awful to her. I nervously look around at my friends and know that they want to hit Aster, too. The uncomfortable hostility is so thick you could cut it with a knife.

"She's not clumsy," Carmen, unsurprisingly, pipes up, and I give her a warning frown, but she blanks me. But she does smile, and sweetly adds, "Neither is she an avaricious, irascible corsair."

I hold my breath as Aster absorbs Carmen's words. Everyone else around the table is holding their breath, too, except for Jess, who instead resembles a small, hurt animal.

"Right you are." Aster gives Carmen a puzzled smile. I don't think Aster understood that Carmen just called him a greedy, bad-tempered fortune hunter. "Er, can I have a quick word," Aster says to Jess, tilting his head toward the bar. "In private, like."

"Um, yes. Yes. Excuse me a minute," Jess says a bit too brightly, her face flushing as she reaches under the table for her bag and follows Aster across the room.

"Carmen, darling, I know you mean well, but *really*. Did you see poor Jess's face?" Flora says as soon as Jess is out of earshot.

"She is *right*, though," Charlie tells the table at large. "How else could he afford to buy that new guitar?"

"A bit quieter, old chap," Philip says to him. "You don't want Jess to hear you. She'd be very upset if she knew we thought her boyfriend was using her for money."

"He *is* using her for money," Carmen says, taking another swig of her beer. "Just watch. He's an obnoxious prick with no personality. Sorry, Phil."

"No worries about the language," Philip tells her. "I've heard it all before, you know."

And sure enough, Jess is reaching into her bag for her wallet. She pulls out some notes and hands them to him.

"But what are we going to do about it? He can't fucking well keep getting away with it." Carmen's face is getting redder by the moment as she gets into her stride. "Anyone with a brain cell can see he's using her."

"Maybe we've got the wrong end of the stick," Flora reasons with her, but her heart's not in it. "It's entirely possible that Aster intends to pay her back." She doesn't really believe that, but she always tries to be so evenhanded in her judgement. "It's obvious that she completely dotes on him. I don't think she'd thank us for mentioning the money thing."

"Yes, she does rather seem fixed on him," Philip smiles, but his eyes are unhappy. "We need to be here for her, but we shouldn't, you know, alienate her by maligning her boyfriend.

She might not feel comfortable coming to us for sympathy later if she sees it for herself and breaks up with him."

Philip does have a good point.

"He does have a point," Charlie says. "I mean, Carmen, darling, if we all told you that Paul was a loser, which of course he's not because he's completely adorable, and that you could do a million times better, how would that make you feel about us?"

"The way things are at the moment, I'd probably buy champagne and offer to bear your children." Carmen takes another swig of her beer, and I worry more.

"Ha, ha, good one," Charlie says. "Come on, you know you don't mean it."

"Of course she doesn't mean it," Flora adds. "You and Paul are just so well suited."

"Um, is everything okay between you and Paul?" I ask, because I'm not so sure that this is just a normal fight.

Carmen looks around at us for long seconds before replying. "Sorry everyone, take no notice of me. I'm just being my usual pissy, difficult self," she says, a bit bitterly. "Really. It's nothing. Paul got a call from one of his photographer friends. The guy was sick and asked if Paul could cover a wedding, and instead of being a reasonable, understanding kind of girlfriend, I overreacted. But he hasn't exactly missed the musical event of the century, has he? And as Paul says, we have to start thinking about our old age, and pensions, so we can do with the extra money. Oh, enough about me. Let's rip Aster apart some more, that'll be sure to cheer me up."

Before I can focus on what Carmen has just said, Jess arrives back at our table, a flurry of red-faced embarrassment. Within seconds, Aster has bought drinks for himself, his three band members, and the two women. But not for Jess.

"Um, um, I think it's my round," Jess says brightly, but her eyes are suspiciously shiny. "I did ask Aster to get the drinks in for me, but I think he's forgotten," she says in a rush. "Same again, everyone?"

"Absolutely not." Philip, ever the gentleman, jumps to his feet and pats her on the shoulder. "Sit yourself down. My turn, dear girl."

"Bring that medicinal brandy for Rosie," Flora commands him. "Darling, we're neglecting you," she turns to me. "Tell us about your breakup with Jonathan. But only if you want to. It might help, you know, to get it off your chest."

Actually, in the midst of the dramas at the table, I had forgotten all about Jonathan . . . I am instantly flooded with misery and guilt as I remember the disastrous events of Friday night. I mean, how humiliating is it to be ditched because your boyfriend is more committed to his career than to you?

And so I spend the next ten minutes telling them about the horrible fund-raiser, and about the near kiss with Sidney and the near broken toe event. I don't get the chance to tell them about my encounter with Dr. Love, because, of course, Carmen enthusiastically hijacks the conversation at this point and wildly embellishes the details.

"You're a dark horse." Charlie is impressed. "I didn't think you had it in you."

"But how could I do something like that?" I wail. "I mean, does it make me a callous, unfeeling person? Does it make me a slut?"

"No, no, not a slut." Jess shakes her head.

"Of course not, dear girl." Philip hands me a glass of brandy. "People *do* tend to react to traumatic emotional situations in odd ways. I see it all the time in my parish."

"Gosh, I think it's rather romantic." Flora's eyes mist with emotion. Which shocks me, because she's usually so sensible.

"I still think you should have taken him home and shagged

him." Carmen has now switched from pints of beer to whisky, and is slurring.

"Although I do think that Philip is right," Flora continues. "You felt neglected and misunderstood by Jonathan, therefore your resistance levels were low. Dr. Love was conveniently on hand, and you transferred your feelings for Jonathan onto him."

"You know, that makes sense." It really does. This cheers me enormously. At last, a logical explanation for my odd behavior.

"I have to say, though, I always did like a nice doctor," Charlie sighs, and I think of Dr. Love and his sardonic eyebrow and sigh too. "It's the white jacket and stethoscope thing they have going on. Flora, you're so lucky to work in a hospital."

"I know." Flora's face lights up in a huge smile, and then she flushes. Which is strange, because Flora frequently complains that it's difficult to meet men at St. Charles' Hospital, where she is a high-up administrator, because they are either (a) her subordinates, which is a no-no, or (b) married or gay.

"You know, you've got to admire Rosie's doctor," Philip says. "I'd never have the nerve to pick up a stranger like that. I think I need to get out more."

I hadn't really thought about Philip and girls. I mean, he's nice and attractive, in a big-bear kind of way. And he has had girlfriends in the past, but thinking about it, not for a long time. It must get lonely, ministering to the flock and not having anyone to minister to you.

"I just don't get the opportunity to meet girls," Philip adds. "I think the dog collar puts them off. You know, not exactly sexy, is it?"

"Well, I wouldn't be put off by a dog collar if I liked a man," Jess tells him.

"Wouldn't you? Oh, I say, that's very nice of you, dear girl," Philip beams at her.

"It's the worst time of year to be on your own, though," Charlie says, and I worry that he's going to get all introspective and depressed like he did last Christmas.

"You're not on your own," I say. "You have all of us. Well, Philip, Flora and me, at any rate. Carmen and Jess have significant others, but that's only two out of six. Only thirty-three percent, when you think about it logically."

"Actually, make that fifty percent," Flora says, blushing.

"You've met someone? When? Who is he?" Although I'm delighted for Flora, who obviously *has* met someone, I can't help but feel a little pang.

"Well," she says, pausing and glancing around at us before leaping in. "He's a doctor. I met him at a conference in September." And although she's grinning like an idiot, I feel another little pang of jealousy.

"And you've kept it to yourself since then? Come on. Spill," Carmen commands her. "Just please don't tell us he's separated."

"Actually, he's divorced. I know, I know." Flora holds up her hand before we can say anything. "But this time it's different. I think he might be The One."

"But why didn't you tell us?" This is amazing.

"I didn't want to tempt fate. You know—after my disasters with James, and then Lucian. And I wasn't sure if I should say anything today, especially after your news—"

"I'm delighted for you," I tell her, because I am. How horrible is it of me to be jealous of my own cousin?

"Details, please," Charlie says, edging closer in his eagerness. "And don't leave out a thing. Taking special note to tell us all about his bedside manner."

"Well." Flora pauses again, looks around at us again, then plunges in. "I'm bringing him to Auntie Pat's party on Christmas Eve, so I've got to tell you sometime soon. You are all coming to that, aren't you?"

"What *is* that all about?" Carmen frowns. "I'd almost forgotten, Rosie—blame it on my alcohol-saturated brain if you like, but I had the most weird telephone conversation with Elaine."

"Me, too," Jess nods. "She's invited us to the family party. Me and Aster, I mean, which is nice because she's never even met Aster."

"Which is completely fucking odd, don't you mean, because Elaine never does anything nice," Carmen interrupts her. "Tell me, you three know her better than anyone." Carmen looks at me, Flora and Philip. "Why has she invited us? And don't say it's to celebrate her forthcoming bundle of joy, because I'm not buying that."

"Er—the season of goodwill?" Philip says.

"Or to make mischief. I still haven't forgotten Rosie's twenty-first." *Thanks, Carmen, for reminding me of that*, I think. "Sorry, Rosie—I didn't mean to remind you about that fucking—"

"So, about Flora's new chap." Philip is so sensitive to people's feelings. I flash him a grateful smile. "I can't wait to meet him."

"It's lovely news, lovely news," Jess clasps her hands together. "We're definitely coming to the party now, because we're all dying to meet him, aren't we?"

"Absolutely. And if Elaine causes any fucking problems, like trying to sneak off with your bloke so she can give him a blow—"

"So what is he like?" I ask brightly, partly to stop Carmen from putting her foot in it any more than she has, and partly because I am working hard on my enthusiasm and trying not to think of my tall, dark, handsome obstetrician. Or Jonathan, of course . . .

"Well. His name is Edward, but everyone calls him Ned. He's thirty-two—"

Right around the same age as Dr. Love, I think.

"And I know it's a cliché," Flora laughs, "but he's tall, dark and handsome—"

Dr. Love, Dr. Love, Dr. Love . . .

"He's charming and funny—"

Check. Check.

"And he's an obstetrician. At St. Mary's Hospital."

My God.

The Season of Goodwill

Rosie's Confession:

I hate Christmas. Well, this one, anyway . . .
    Bah, humbug!

Christmas Eve. Four days since Jonathan's breakup voice
mail message, and I still keep expecting him to call. . . .

I mean, you would call someone if you broke up with
them via voice mail, wouldn't you? Just in case they didn't
get your message, because we all know that voice mail isn't
one hundred percent reliable, and if the person didn't get
your message in the first place, then they wouldn't even
know you'd broken up with them. Oh, telephone . . .

"Let me put a hypothetical scenario to you," Carmen says,
and I can just tell from the succinct punch of her voice that
she is twirling her hair. Which, as we know, means she's either pissed off about something or thinking deeply about
something.

"Just suppose. *Just suppose* that you spent *months* hinting
frequently and at *length* to your boyfriend that what you *re-*

ally would absolutely love, what you really, absolutely would adore as a secret, surprise gift for Christmas was a *romantic weekend* in Paris. *Or similar.* I mean it doesn't have to be Paris, think a minibreak anywhere romantic, *anywhere at all*, because spending quality time together would be lovely, and said boyfriend seems to spend all his time working these days—" She finally pauses for air. "Are you still there?"

"Absolutely." Pissed off, then, I think, wishing that I actually still had a, you know, actual boyfriend.

"And just suppose. Just suppose he totally, utterly misses the whole bloody point and buys you *tropical fish* instead. I mean, what the fuck was he *thinking?*"

Interesting choice of gift. And then something else occurs to me.

"Someone's obviously been sneaking around looking for their secret Christmas gifts. Carmen," I say, exasperated. "The whole point of secret gifts is the actual secret part. I thought you wanted a surprise."

"I do, but not this kind of surprise. And I didn't go looking, I just—accidentally overheard Paul on the phone to the pet store when he sneaked off downstairs to make a secret call. Besides," she sniffs, "I suspected he'd fuck up, somehow, and I wanted to be prepared. You know, take out my disappointment on someone else so I can practice being excited when Paul actually gives the bloody fish to me. I mean, I did want some spontaneity in my life, and here I am bloody complaining because he's spontaneously bought me tropical fish. And I don't want to hurt his feelings . . ."

This is one of the things I love about Carmen. She might be all mouth, but she does care about her friends and hurting their feelings. But it's nice to get any kind of gift, and I've always thought that tropical fish were very, you know, calming and pretty.

"Well, tropical fish are very calming and pretty," I soothe her. "And I—"

"Yes, yes, but don't you see? It's the first step on the slippery slope to—to—*staid coupledom*," Carmen leaps right back in. "I mean, it's a *commitment*."

"Carmen, it's only fish." I think she's overreacting just a bit.

"Yes, but you know what it means, don't you?"

And I'm trying—I'm really trying . . .

"Um—don't forget the fish food with the weekly shopping?"

"It means we're tied to the house. How can we go on a bloody minibreak, or vacation, when we have—*dependents*."

"This is why you have friends," I tell her, keeping my tone smooth and soothing. I know she likes to think of herself as a bit of a free spirit, but taking care of fish isn't exactly rocket science, is it? "It's simple," I add. "You book a minibreak, then you ask me to drop by your house and feed your fish while you're away. Problem solved."

There is a long silence as she absorbs my words.

"God, I'm sorry, Rosie," she sighs. "I know I can be a selfish bitch sometimes. You're right. Thanks for the reality check. How are *you*?"

"Oh, you know, fine," I lie, my voice trembling just a bit.

"Well, don't think about Jonathan," Carmen commands me. "Think about hot doctors instead. Oh, gotta go, a customer just came in."

And that, my friends, is the crux of the matter. See, in between thinking about Jonathan, my mind keeps wandering back to Piccadilly Circus . . .

I blame Christmas.

See, it's a traditionally quiet time in the employment agency field, even for an agency like Charlie's and mine, which supplies staff for some of the oddest jobs you can think of. Normal people are just too busy going to parties, or shopping, or generally having too much festive fun to think about changing jobs.

With one or two exceptions to the rule . . .

I mean, we did have a flurry of last-minute requests last week from department stores and various other organizations for Santas, elves and fairies, but we'd already anticipated seasonal demand and had several of our regulars lined up, just in case.

Also, Charlie's been up to his neck in the final preparations for various drag acts he's arranged for Christmas extravaganzas, and is currently in a Hammersmith gay bar soothing ruffled Karmic Kitty egos.

Apparently, Kitty Princess Cherrie of the group Queen KiKi and the Karmic Kitty Princesses (otherwise known as Nigel from Clapham) is convinced that his version of "I Will Survive" is far superior to that of Kitty Princess Jancie's and wants to switch.

Kitty Princess Jancie (John from Leeds) is not happy about a last-minute rearrangement, nor does he want to perform Kitty Princess Cherrie's "I Am Who I Am," because he hasn't got the right costume for that particular number, and everyone knows you shouldn't mess with costume karma.

This is further complicated by the fact that Queen KiKi (Lionel from Brighton) has decided that as he is the main star of the act he should have special privileges and has demanded a separate dressing room in the tiny backstage area of the Hammersmith pub, plus free drinks from the bar.

And if he doesn't get his dressing room and free drinks, his headache will turn into a migraine, and possibly a brain tumor, and he will therefore be unable to perform.

That's Charlie's field, thank God. He arranges drag acts or other performance-related acts for companies, conferences and private functions.

My personal favorite has got to be the increasingly popular Japanese-style boot camps. We provide professional shouters. People with loud voices to insult their senior managers or students to encourage better performance—can you imagine being paid to yell at people? I may volunteer my own services next time . . .

But back to the point. See, because it's Christmas, things are just too quiet, and it gives me too much time to brood.

Oh, telephone again. I grab for it, because it might be Jonathan, and . . .

"Miss Mayford, she just won't do," Mrs. Granville-Seymour booms down the telephone line at me.

Another exception to current quietness is the job, or should I say *honor*, of babysitting Maximillion d'Or, a colorpoint red point Persian cat, belonging to Mrs. Hermione Granville-Seymour of Kensington Place.

"But—" *I thought it was all arranged*, I don't quite manage to say.

Mrs. Granville-Seymour and her lady companion are flying off to Aspen, or similar, for her annual New Year gettogether with old school chums, and her current agency just couldn't provide satisfaction.

This could be our entrée into the world of rich people's pets! You wouldn't believe just how extensive is the need for pet minders, or poop scoopers, or dog walkers in the hallowed halls of the rich within the Royal Borough of Kensington and Chelsea. And if we can give satisfaction to "dear Maxie's" owner, Mrs. Granville-Seymour will talk about us to her rich friends, who will also consider switching to Odd Jobs for their pet-caring needs.

"I just don't feel quite right about her now. I just don't think she's fully committed to dear Maxie," Mrs. G-S booms again.

I'm more than a bit cross about this, because I lined up a

selection of perfectly good people with cat experience from whom Mrs. Granville-Seymour could select "dear Maxie's" perfect carer.

Each candidate was required to spend a morning or afternoon getting to know dear Maxie and to learn about his needs. (Talking to him, playing with him, watching TV with him, listening to music with him—the list goes on.)

Unfortunately, I thought Mrs. G-S had settled on Claire, who is a very nice med student in need of some extra cash over the holidays, and Mrs. G-S is paying very, very well. Unfortunate, because Claire, it seems, wants her fiancé to spend New Year at Mrs. G-S's with her and dear Maxie (I mean, the cheek of the girl, wanting to see in the New Year with more than just a cat for company), and Mrs. G-S doesn't want a stranger in her home getting up to, well, whatever she thinks Claire's fiancé, also a med student, will get up to. Playing doctors, possibly? Oh, I didn't mean to think about doctors. . . .

And despite reassurances from Claire that she's prepared to continue with the arrangement sans her fiancé, Mrs. G-S does not, now, trust her to keep her fiancé at bay.

And so, on Christmas Eve, Mrs. G-S has decided to change her mind, as is her prerogative, of course, because the client is always right.

"Dear Maxie just didn't take to any of the rest of the candidates, and time is running out, Miss Mayford."

"I appreciate that, Mrs. Granville-Seymour, I really do," I soothe her, completely hiding my crossness as I wrack my brain for another possibility.

But I've sent all of my best people to her already. Mrs. G-S is leaving on December thirtieth, which means that I have six days, excluding tomorrow, which is Christmas Day, also excluding the following three days because they incorporate Boxing Day and the weekend, to find a replacement.

Which means, in effect, that I have this afternoon and next Monday, only, to get someone in place.

"Let me run through our books, make a few phone calls and get back to you," I tell her with a sense of impending lost-rich-pet doom.

"I personally feel that someone of an educationally higher level would be more appropriate," Mrs. G-S booms, and I'm thinking, *Why?* Because looking after a cat isn't exactly brain surgery, is it?

Oh, I didn't mean to think about brain surgery, because that, inevitably, reminds me of doctors again . . .

"Dear Maxie is such an intelligent darling," Mrs. G-S continues. "He needs *intelligent* conversation."

But Maxie doesn't speak English. I mean, how ridiculous is it? Surely the woman isn't crackers enough to be suggesting that only a degree-level person could possibly handle caring for dear Maxie?

"I was thinking along the lines of someone with a degree," Mrs. G-S immediately adds. "Preferably one with a degree in literature. Or a language."

I give up! Really, at this point in the conversation I'm waving a mental white flag of defeat.

"I'll see what I can do," I tell her, thinking that there isn't a cat in hell's chance of fixing this one. Which would be tragic, because it would blemish our, well, unblemished reputation.

See, when Charlie and I quit our respective jobs two years ago and formed Odd Jobs, we adopted our company ethos: to find exactly the right jobs for the right people. Or the right people for the oddest of jobs. Our guarantee: successful placement for all.

I don't think we've ever turned anyone away before . . . except for the company searching for chicken sexers, because it was just too, too horrible to think about. And immoral.

The reason we turned it down: In order for the large company to capitalize as much as possible on its profits, it wanted to feed and raise only female chicks. Therefore it needed to determine the sex of the chicks as soon as they emerged from their eggs.

The chicks would be placed on a conveyer belt, and the sexers on either side would check the chicks for tiny testicles. The male chicks' fate was to be thrown into barrels with hundreds of other male chicks. Result: Chicks would either be squashed by the weight of their brothers or generally be left to die, or be horribly disposed of.

Euck. I mean, how inhumane is that?

Anyway, it didn't even sound legal, so I complained to the Royal Society for the Prevention of Cruelty to Animals. Plus I also wrote a strong letter to the Ministry of Agriculture.

But since we started out, just Charlie and I, we've had a good deal of success. So much, that we now have books full of people we can call on for different odd jobs, and we also have three employees to cope with the workload. At least we usually have three employees, but as I said, things are unusually quiet because of the holidays.

Today it's just myself, Charlie (when he's finally settled the Kitty Princesses) and Colin, who is manning the front office and the phones.

I have to find a carer for Maxie on my own, it seems . . .

I lay my head on my desk in the hope of some kind of inspiration, until there is a knock on my office door.

"I've got a failed sex kitten in the front office," Colin tells me in his monotone voice.

Due to the special nature of our agency I'm not exactly surprised. However, I'm also wondering if Colin has finally cracked.

"Says she wants a new job with low responsibilities and no sex."

Colin's monotone delivery is not deliberate. He says it's a

reflection of his monotone personality, which is why he kept getting "released" from jobs before he came to us.

Poor Colin. He suffers so from lack of self-esteem. I mean, he's very interesting when you get to know him. And he has a real knack for fitting the right people to the right job.

But sometimes, entirely due to his monotone voice and beige clothes, Colin does tend to fade into the background a bit. We all tend to forget he's there. I feel guilty about this because I don't mean to hurt his feelings.

On infrequent occasions, to compensate for his lack of intonation (and to shake us up a bit), he sprinkles his sentences with unignorable words.

"Says she's had enough of porn flicks and having to arouse all those penises."

Because "porn flicks" and "penises" are extremely unignorable words, aren't they? This is obviously a cry for help.

"Come in and sit down, Colin," I say, because it's not Colin's fault that he's so lonely and has to say strange things in order to get people to actually hear him. I mean, if I was forty-six and lived with an aging, deaf, demanding mother, I might get lonely and depressed from time to time.

"Would you like some coffee?" I ask, because I don't want Colin to think I am only going to spare him five minutes before carelessly giving him the brush-off. "Tell me all about it," I tell him in my best I'm-here-for-you voice.

"This is not a cry for help," Colin deadpans at me. "I'm not due for another depression until next month. I really do have a failed sex kitten in the front office. She's a fluffer. I've never heard of a fluffer before, but she says it's her job to, you know, warm up the male actors before the performance."

God, why me? Why today? I think as I also wonder if she likes cats.

"She's got a degree in French and German, if that's of any help," Colin adds.

* * *

An hour later, as I send Grace (who seems lovely and normal) off to visit with dear Maxie and Mrs. G-S, I am mentally congratulating myself for such a brilliant stroke of genius!

All Grace needs to do is charm Mrs. G-S, make a fuss of Maxie, and remember not to mention her involvement with the porn industry, and all will be well.

Of course, we'll have to wait for the final decision until after the background checks come back in on Grace, but I'm confident that this will work out. I have a feeling . . .

Strangely, I'm already missing having a Mrs. Granville-Seymour problem to work on, because it's quiet again, just like it has been all week.

So, of course, this means that I have a lot of time to (a) miss Jonathan, (b) daydream about Dr. Love, because I can't stop daydreaming now that I've discovered how to—it's a complete nightmare and I wish it would cease—and (c) obsess that Flora's doctor and my Dr. Love are one and the same.

At least Mum hasn't been panicking about anything much this week. Or so I thought until about two minutes ago, when the phone rang, and it was Mum.

Today's crisis, it would seem, is grand theft.

"Honestly, what is the state of the nation coming to when the constabulary is no longer interested in a domestic burglary?" is Mum's opening line.

I'm actually glad to hear from her, because she's just interrupted a rather annoying daydream in which Dr. Love saves me from certain death. Yes, I know, a cliché. But I can't seem to avoid them.

Picture this: I am walking along the canal at Camden. A hit-and-snatch thief has just grabbed my handbag, and in the process of the struggle (I'm not about to let a thief get away with that, daydream or no daydream), I successfully kick the thief where it hurts and yank my bag back from him.

Unfortunately, the momentum of him letting go of the bag propels me backward into the canal, and I hit my head on the way down, and am therefore rendered unconscious.

Dr. Love, who just happens to be passing, has seen the whole thing (and is now in love with me, because I am such a kick-ass, feisty, and also beautiful gal), and he dives in and heroically rescues me from the murky waters.

He has just given me the kiss of life.

I open my eyes, and our gazes lock.

"Sweet Mystery of Life, at Last I've Found You," is once again playing in the background (I definitely need to imagine a better soundtrack).

And although I am wet and murky, it's in a beautiful, disheveled kind of way. And as I am transported to the hospital to be checked out for canal germs, Dr. Love holds my hand in the ambulance.

I'm kept in overnight for observation, and Dr. Love pops in to see me in between Mrs. Woodbridge's contractions.

True love springs eternal between us, and when I am released the next day, Dr. Love is awaiting me with his car, a huge bouquet of flowers, and a magnum of champagne . . .

And as we drive off into the sunset to live happily ever after (because my daydreams tend toward the romantic rather than the erotic, which is a bit disappointing), Mum says, "Granny Elsie will be devastated if she notices. What are we going to do?"

"Sorry, Mum? Rewind that. What, exactly, happened? Are you telling me the house has been burgled? Did you call the police?"

"No, no. The house is fine. Didn't you hear a word I just said?"

"Sorry—the line was fuzzy," I lie. Really, this daydreaming nonsense will have to stop.

"I said that Gertrude is missing. She's been stolen from the front garden, and the police aren't interested."

Gertrude is another of Granny Elsie's garden gnomes.

"Mum, I'm sure they want to help, but you know, limited resources and everything."

"But Granny Elsie's had Gertrude for ten years. This is a serious matter."

"Well, on a sentimental level . . ." I mean, the theft of a garden gnome is hardly as important as, say, some thief breaking in and stealing all of little Jimmy and Suzie's presents from under the Christmas tree, is it?

"She's practically an antique," Mum wails, building up for a good, rollicking panic. "What are we going to do?" she asks again, but what she really means is, what am *I* going to do?

"Okay, calm do—"

"Granny will be heartbroken. Heartbroken. Granddad Smith bought it for her for their fiftieth wedding anniversary."

"It's okay," I tell her. "Just remind me exactly what she looks like."

"Don't be silly, darling, she's your grandmother—you've been seeing her several times a week for your entire life."

"I meant Gertrude, Mum." It's only eleven-fifteen, and I already feel a headache coming on.

Mum gives me a refresher on Gertrude, detail by excruciating detail, and I wonder why she's so completely familiar with a garden gnome. But at least it will give me something to do for the rest of the day, which I plan to spend checking out garden gnomes on the Internet.

Unfortunately, by eleven-thirty I have located a Gertrude clone, complete with fishing rod and red skirt, and have ordered and paid for her by express courier delivery.

And after I call Mum to give her the good news, and after she reminds me that I have to be at her house at seven sharp because she and Granny Elsie are expecting me to take a taxi with them to the party (because they can't manage in the taxi without me), I now have nothing else to do.

So, of course, I begin to obsess about tonight's party again and slide into another daydream about Flora's doctor . . .

I am wearing my formfitting, "fuck me" black dress. My makeup, as usual in my daydreams, is immaculate. My elegant, *small* feet are encased in the sexiest "fuck me" shoes you have ever seen. My hair swings like a bell around my face.

I enter Auntie Pat's drawing room, unaware that my heart is about to be shattered in two.

Flora and Ned have their backs to me, but something about Ned is totally familiar.

"Rosie," Flora booms as she spots me. "Come and meet Ned, my fiancé." Fiancé? That was quick work. And as he turns, my stomach clenches, my heart thuds, and I break out in a nervous sweat. Even my fingertips break out in a nervous sweat.

It's my mysterious doctor.

"Sweet Mystery of Life, at Last I've Found You," annoyingly cranks up in the background again, only to come to a screeching halt as I realize that telling Flora that her doctor is also *my* mystery doctor will ruin her life while presenting me with yet another unpalatable dilemma.

Dr. Ned kissed me passionately while engaged to Flora. Do I tell her, or should I let it go? Will he cheat on her, or was last Friday night a one-time slipup?

"Stop obsessing," Charlie tells me, poking his head around the corner of my office door.

"Who, me?" I ask, my face flushing with embarrassment. "How are the Kitty Princesses?" I ask, to cunningly change the subject from my red-faced, obsessive self.

"Karmic, once again, thank fuck. This just arrived for you," he says, coming into my office and placing a box on my desk. "And I'm completely jealous, because this is obviously a Christmas gift, and no one's sent any to me."

"Don't get excited," I tell him, getting excited myself as I slit the tape with my scissors, because the return address on the packaging is from Selfridges on Oxford Street. It's probably something for Odd Jobs as a thank-you from a grateful client.

And as I finally wrestle open the box, I gasp.

It's a pair of shoes. Pretty, black, kitten-heeled shoes.

The note inside says, "Kitten-heeled shoes for my own special kitten, love Jonathan XXX."

He obviously ordered them before we split up, because the order date is for last Thursday.

I burst into tears. Last Thursday, my life was so ordered and neat, and now I'm suffering from lust transference and daydreaming about cheating, ratbag doctors.

"Hey, come here, sweetie," Charlie says, pulling me into his arms. "Shush, now." He pushes a tissue into my hand.

"Sorry," I sniffle. "It's silly, but I just didn't expect to receive anything from him after our breakup."

"I know. It's like getting a gift from someone after they died a few days previously. Spooky."

Well, I wouldn't put it as drastically as that . . .

"And looking on the bright side, at least you get a gorgeous pair of shoes as a parting gift." Charlie lifts one out of the box. "But you'll have to see if you can exchange them. They're the wrong size."

They are, of course, two sizes too small.

The Ghost of Boyfriend Past

Rosie's Confession:

The tongue is the strongest muscle in the human body.
  Strongly suspect that cousin Elaine spends hours each day exercising hers, because in her case it is a lethal weapon . . .

By the time Mum, Granny Elsie and I arrive at Auntie Pat's party later that night it is in full swing because, of course, we're late.

Late because—apart from my cab arriving a half hour late—when I finally arrived at Mum's to collect her and Granny Elsie, complete with Christmas gifts and an overnight bag, because it is written in stone that All Single People Must Spend Christmas at Their Parents' Homes, instead of being ready to leave the house instantly, Mum was peeling enough vegetables to feed Hampstead.

This is what happened.

"It's tradition, darling," she tells me, adding a millionth potato to a pan of water and wiping her hands on the floral pinafore she's put on to protect her new dress. "It will only take five minutes."

"But the taxi driver's waiting for us." Honestly, am I the only one in this family who thinks that punctuality is important? I called her as I was leaving just to make sure she and Granny Elsie were ready. The "coats on" variety of ready. Granny Elsie, naturally, is nowhere to be seen . . .

"I'm sure he can wait a few extra minutes," Mum says as she serenely takes a bag of carrots out of the refrigerator and starts peeling one.

"But—"

"Besides, we can always ring for another cab."

"Not on Christmas Eve we can't, because—" the entire population of the city of London is out partying and also requires cabs. And because I knew this, I took care to book the cab in advance. I don't say any of this, because Mum plays her ace card.

"But I always prepare the Christmas Day meal on Christmas Eve," she says, building up for a panic. "You know how I always like to spend Christmas Day with my family, without having to fuss too much in the kitchen. Your father always loved my turkey and special stuffing . . . oh, it just won't be the same without him . . ." she trails off plaintively.

"Okay," I sigh. I know I should try to be more patient with her. It is only our second Christmas without him, after all.

I am an island of peace and serenity, I tell myself.

"Now if you could just measure a pint of milk for me, we'll get the custard under way."

I clench my teeth. "Right. I'll just go and beg the cab driver to wait, first, shall I?"

When I say "beg the cabdriver to wait," I also mean "bribe him," due to the laws of low supply (him) and high demand (did I know how many other jobs he was missing out on?).

But after I promise him a breathtaking amount of cash, he agrees to wait for ten minutes.

And when I get back to the kitchen, Mum has finished the carrots and has her hand up inside the turkey.

"Mum—" I break off, because I think that I am wasting my breath.

"It won't take more than a few minutes, dear," she says again, as if keeping the cab waiting to stuff the turkey is something people do every day of the week. "It always tastes better when the turkey has time to absorb the flavor from the stuffing."

I roll my eyes, but nothing is coming between my mother and her mission.

"Have a nice little sherry, dear." Granny Elsie wafts into the kitchen on a cloud of Youth Dew. "It'll steady your nerves."

Honestly, I give up. I really do!

Peace and serenity, I remind myself again.

"Thanks, Gran." I grab the sherry and drink it down in one gulp. "How about another little sherry?" I say, holding out my glass. "Perhaps Mum should have one, too."

"Alf took me for a turkey dinner today," Gran tells me, topping up my glass from the bottle she's wielding. "I think he's tryin' to sweeten me up," she winks, "you know, for sexual favors and such."

This, I truly needed to know.

"Mother," Mum sniffs as the taxi driver honks his impatience. "Really."

"Mum, we *have* to go," I say, draining my second glass. The turkey is now safely stuffed.

"He wanted to come to the party tonight," Granny Elsie adds. "Alf, I mean. But I thought that was a bit much. We've had three dates this week already and I want to keep 'im keen. And you know that old saying, Treat 'em mean, keep 'em keen," she cackles.

So that's where I went wrong with Jonathan, I think sourly. *Obviously I wasn't mean enough.*

"Besides," Gran adds, "you never know, I might get a better offer at the party."

I wonder sometimes how I turned out to be so normal, I think, not wanting to contemplate Gran and her better offers.

The honking of the taxi horn spurs me to action.

"Right," I smile brightly and take the initiative. I cover the turkey with aluminum foil and push it into the refrigerator. I also take the carrots from Mum, cover the pan and place it in the refrigerator, too. "Coats on, everyone."

"I think I'd better just pop to the lav before we leave." Granny Elsie promptly heads toward the stairs. "I don't want to be caught short."

"But can't you wait? Auntie Pat—" *has six bathrooms*, I nearly finish saying to the back of her head. I am wasting my breath.

"Really, cab drivers these days have no manners," Mum sniffs, drying her hands and taking off her pinafore. "Well, he can jolly well wait while I freshen up my makeup."

"Mum, you look fine." The taxi driver honks his horn again. "Gorgeous, in fact," I add, because she does. The new, pale green dress really brings out the green in her eyes. Plus, it is silk and looks expensive. But before I can think straight, the taxi honks yet again.

"I'll only be a minute, dear." Mum follows Granny Elsie up the stairs.

I go outside and prostrate myself in front of the cab, promising even more cash to the now irate driver.

I should have known that it was going to be one of those evenings . . .

And so, because we're so late, by the time we get to the

party, I don't have time to absorb the first unpleasant shock of the evening without a full audience in attendance.

We have just been let into the front hall and relieved of our coats by one of the small army of staff that Auntie Pat has hired for the evening.

"Good evening, Rosemary. Sandra. Elsie," is Auntie Pat's dry, disapproving greeting as she, well, greets us at the drawing-room door. "I'm so happy you decided to join us," she says, making it sound more of an accusation.

It really irritates Pat that Dad married my mother, who hails from Bethnal Green, an area of London that Aunt Pat considers dreadfully common and depraved.

"Oh, sorry—we . . . we had to . . ." my mother flusters, because in the presence of Pat's condescension she always gets flustered and confused. It annoys me that Pat feels the need to put her so ill at ease. It used to bug Dad, too.

"Hi, Auntie Patsy," I say with false cheer, deliberately not calling her Aunt Patricia, which we all know she muchly prefers. "It's lovely to see you, too."

"Elsie, what an *interesting* dress," Pat adds, looking down her patronizing nose at Granny Elsie, because Granny Elsie is also from Bethnal Green.

"I chose it specially," Gran says, cackling. "Right, best wishes of the season to you, Patsy—thanks for the invite. Now I'm going to mingle for a bit and check out the lovely grub." Gran the Imperturbable cuts an unmissable red, green and black swathe across the room in the direction of the buffet.

"Sandra, is that a new hairdo?" Pat asks my mother. "Remind me to give you the number of my personal stylist—Roman is such a whiz with fly-away hair."

"How is the mother-to-be?" I jump in, because I don't like the supercilious way Pat insults people by making it sound like false praise, and I want to rattle her a bit. *Any clues as to the identity of the father yet?* I don't ask, because I am trying for peace and serenity, but I am sorely tempted. I know it's a bit horrible of me, and I have no issue at all with unmarried mothers. Really. I think it's all about personal choice.

But until now Pat has had An Opinion about babies out of holy matrimony. An unfavorable one. And she hasn't been afraid of voicing it to anyone who would listen, either.

"Dear Elaine," Pat says, making a one-hundred-and-eighty-degree turn on previous policy. "Such a brave girl to do this by herself. I've always said that too many opt for terminations because they just cannot be bothered to shoulder their responsibilities. But my Elaine is soldiering on alone."

I hardly think that Elaine will be alone, friendless and living in squalor, desperately trying to make ends meet.

"Sandra, Rosie, how lovely to see you both." Auntie Lizzy, mother of Flora and Philip, saves the moment. "Sandra, what a lovely dress. Now I'm sure our hostess has a lot to do," she says, flashing Auntie Pat a false smile as she takes Mum's arm and leads her into the heaving drawing room. "Let's get you fixed up with a drink."

It also fires up Pat's blue blood that Uncle Gregory, Dad's other brother, married Auntie Lizzy, and therefore far above himself. Auntie Lizzy's father was a Lord of the Realm. This means that Auntie Lizzy, who also has a very aristocratic nose, but a very nice one, is above Aunt Patricia in the social pecking order.

This is a fact that delights us all enormously, because when Auntie Pat is unbearable (which is a frequent occurrence), Auntie Lizzy puts her in her place.

"Elaine's just about to make her Christmas speech, and it would have been a *shame* for you to miss it," Pat tells me, and I wonder *why* Elaine needs to make a speech.

I have a bad feeling about this, I really do. But instead of rising to the bait, I rise above petty sarcasm.

"Lovely," I say, brightly.

"Go ahead," Pat smiles evilly. "I'm sure you know everyone in the room."

And as I walk into the noisy, heaving drawing room, I scan the room for my friends, because after the day I've had with the rich cat and the shoe gift, I need a reality check. They are not hard to spot on account of Jess's pink hair.

And as Carmen waves at me from the far corner, and as I begin to weave my way through the masses, I realize that I have forgotten all about Flora's mysterious Ned. And then someone taps me on the shoulder.

I am so glad that I wore my "fuck me" little black dress, plus the uncomfortable, yet also "fuck me," stiletto heels. I am also glad that I took extra care with my makeup and hair.

Glad, because it's always a good plan to look one's best when confronted by a cheating ex-boyfriend, don't you think?

"Hello, Rosie," the tall, handsome man says in my ear, and I wish I had a stiff drink in my hand, because I could do with one. Or possibly more . . .

It is Harry Winterton.

Odd, how I was thinking about him only the other day . . .

Thinking of stiff drinks inevitably reminds me of the last time I saw Harry, because it was upstairs in my mother's bedroom.

Harry of the Elaine blow job.

"God, it's lovely to see you. You're looking as gorgeous as ever," he tells me, his white teeth gleaming as he smiles his naughty-boy smile. "If not, in fact, more gorgeous."

So is he. The preceding seven years have been very good to him, and at twenty-eight, he is as charming and blond as ever, with that same naughty-boy glint in his eye, as ever. Actually, his hair is *blonder*.

"You're looking blonder than ever," is not the most friendly riposte in the world, but that is precisely what comes out of my mouth. "Great highlights. Expensive highlights."

"Well, I had it done especially because I knew I'd see you tonight," he flirts at me, ignoring my sarcasm. "Was it worth it, do you think?"

"Oh, I make it a policy never to trust a man who spends more on his hair than I do. Still as vain as ever, then."

What the hell is he doing here?

As soon as the question pops into my brain, I know the answer. Elaine asked him, of course. Although *why* is a mystery. . . . Could Harry be the mysterious father?

"Still as unforgiving as ever?" His words are gentle, pleading, little-boy cute, and for a moment, just for a moment, I remember the good times, and my pulse picks up speed.

And then I see Carmen and Jess weaving their way through the crowd to rescue me. Lovely of them, but there's no need because this man broke my twenty-one-year-old heart, and no way will he get the chance to do it again. And do it again he surely would.

Harry the Heartbreaker was his name at university. The same age as me, but years ahead in terms of sophistication and charm, I didn't stand a chance when he set his sights on me and wooed me into his bed. I should have realized that handsome bad boys such as Harry never settle for less-than-gorgeous girlfriends like me. They settle for people like Elaine.

I can rescue myself.

"It's kind of a hard image to get out of my mind. You know, you, on the bed, with your pants down, and your di—"

"I'm sorry," he interrupts, holding up a hand. More little-boy cuteness. "I never meant to hurt—"

"Did you fuck her?" Oh. I'm not usually so crude. But then, I don't usually find myself chatting to Harry. In fact, I haven't spoken to him since that fateful night.

I never asked Elaine if she'd actually slept with him, because she would have lied to me either way and said yes, just to dig the knife in a bit deeper.

"It wasn't like that—"

He's about to tell me that it was just a bit of fun gone too far, and that it was me he cared about, really, but I don't give him the chance.

"Harry, what *are* you doing here, anyway?"

"Darling, Rosie, so lovely to see you," Elaine squeaks. And then, "Oh, I hope it doesn't bring back too many bad memories, you know, seeing Harry again after all this time."

"I'd practically forgotten," I lie, but my face is red.

"It's just that my pregnancy has made me want to reconcile the whole world," she tinkles. "And when Harry and I bumped into each other in Fortnum & Mason's, it seemed like fate."

Spite, more like, I think as Elaine smiles spitefully. And I wonder, as I have done over the years, why she makes such an effort to hate me and belittle me. Well, not only me, because she does it to Flora and Philip, too. I mean, it must be so tiring.

"And when she asked me to the Christmas party, I couldn't resist seeing you again," Harry flirts at me again, which brings a frown to Elaine's brow. "We parted under such a black cloud, I never forgave myself for—"

"Well, that's all water under the bridge now, isn't it?" Elaine says brightly as she places a hand on his arm. At that moment I could almost kiss Harry for flirting with me, rather than with Elaine. Almost.

"Look, here's my phone number," Harry says, reaching into his jacket pocket and handing me his card. Which under the circumstances is rather presumptive of him. "If you ever feel like going out for a drink, or for dinner—"

"Oh, but didn't I tell you?" Elaine jumps right back in.

"Silly me, I must have forgotten, but Rosie's practically en-gaged, aren't you, darling?" Elaine smiles her little cat smile of satisfaction. "Speaking of which, where *is* your lovely man?"

"Oh, things were getting far too serious," I tell her, all non-chalant. Because I'm suspecting that the whole point of this encounter is to embarrass me in front of my family, friends and Jonathan. "I decided to cool it a bit. You know, take a break from each other, see how I felt come the New Year."

"But you seemed so happy together." Elaine is nonplussed. "I mean, he's such a lovely man."

"Well, if you're that interested, I'd be happy to pass him on to you. Just let me know if you'd like his number." No, I have no intention of doing so, but it is worth a shot just to see the expression on her face. *Take that, Elaine,* I think.

"Well, I, for one, am rejoicing," Harry says, and Elaine scowls even more.

"Don't get too rejoyceful," I warn him. "It doesn't mean that I'm even vaguely interested in picking up where we left off."

"No, she certainly isn't," is Carmen's opening line as she and Jess finally reach me on their rescue mission.

"The cavalry to the rescue." Harry inclines his head. "Hello, ladies. How are you both?"

"Dandy and fine," Carmen tells him airily. "And don't bother with the charm, we're immune."

"Yes, I remember that aspect of your personality," Harry says. "Still manless, Carmen?"

"Oh, didn't Rosie tell you?" Carmen's voice is deceptively sweet. "We decided to ditch our men and form a lesbian mé-nage à trois," she adds.

"No," Elaine squeaks, then laughs her tinkly little laugh. "You are too funny."

"You think I'm joking? Come, oh, Sapphic sisterhood,"

Carmen says, sliding an arm around me and Jess. "Have fun, you two," she says, winking at Harry and Elaine. And then, "Oh, I forgot, you already did that."

"Naughty," I say, breathless with laughter.

"Yeah, but it was worth it just to see their faces."

"Are you alright?" Jess asks me. "It was awful, awful of her to do that to you."

"We didn't notice him until a couple of minutes ago," Carmen says.

"I'm fine, truly," I say. Although my stomach is still wobbling a bit. "It was just a bit of a shock, seeing him after all these years."

And as we reach the corner, where Philip is deep in conversation with Flora and a tall, handsome man, my stomach starts to wobble some more. At least, I think he's handsome, because I can only see the back of his head.

"Here she is," Flora booms. "Dreadful business," she adds just to me, under her breath. "I wonder, sometimes, how we can be related to Elaine. But anyway, you're here now. Darling," she touches her tall, dark doctor on the arm. "There's someone I'd like you to meet."

I hold my breath as he turns around.

"You must be Rosie," he booms, his eyes crinkling nicely in his pleasant face. "Flora's told me all about you. I'm so pleased to meet you."

Not a sardonic eyebrow in sight. Whew.

And as he looks back adoringly to Flora, the way he really *looks* at her as if she is the only woman on the face of the planet, I can't help it. I suddenly imagine "Sweet Mystery of Life, at Last I've Found You," playing in the background.

"I really like Ned," I say two hours later, as Jess, Carmen, Philip and I watch him charming Auntie Lizzy and Uncle

Gregory. He's completely perfect for Flora. In fact, he's like a male version of her. I think this time she really has got it right.

"He's perfect for her, perfect," Jess says, smiling. "Especially the way he looks at her. You can just tell he loves her," she adds a bit wistfully.

Aster couldn't make it because Asteroid Attack was, it seems, booked for a private rave in Chelmsford at the last minute. Jess was a lot disappointed, because she won't see Aster until New Year's Eve. He's heading to his parents' house for Christmas, followed by a brief, yet unexpected, sojourn to Amsterdam with his friends. But without Jess.

Personally, I want to break both of his legs for letting her down, but it's the band's first paid gig, so also want to actively encourage him. Plus, if I were rich, I would bribe him to stay in Amsterdam and away from Jess forever.

"Yes," I say, watching the way Ned's hand is never far away from Flora's arm. He can't seem to stop touching her. "The highlight was the point where Elaine tried to lure him away for the grand tour of the house, and he insisted that Flora go, too. Did you see her face?"

It was actually quite funny. Elaine really worked the charm, but Ned, it would seem, is immune. She's not having much luck with men tonight; Harry took off shortly after our brief encounter, and he made a point of reminding me to call him. Elaine was not pleased when I flirted back at him and said I might just do that. Not that I'm going to, because I have more sense, but it was worth it to see the look on Elaine's face.

"I foresee wedding bells in the not-too-distant future," Carmen says a bit bitterly. "Which is lovely for them," she adds, trying for upbeat, "but not for everyone."

She's worrying too much about the implication of the tropical fish and Paul's desire for stability.

"What could be more stable than living together?" Carmen asks us again, rhetorically. "What does he mean, he wants more commitment? They don't come any more committed than me. My God, I mean, I'm raising his fish, aren't I?"

Paul couldn't make it to the party because he had another emergency photo shoot. Yes, on Christmas Eve. Apparently, his photographer friend is still sick, couldn't make a swanky, executive party, and asked Paul if he'd do it in his stead.

Carmen says it's a lot of money, but she's not very pleased at being boyfriendless on Christmas Eve.

I'm pretty unhappy to be generally boyfriendless.

"It will all sort itself out, you'll see," Philip tells her. And then, "Well, I must go and ready myself for the midnight service. I don't expect there will be many there, but one can only live in hope. Don't suppose you three want to come and, you know, be my congregation?"

"That sounds lovely," I tell him, because it does. A bit of quiet, serene peace and Christmas carols would be very welcome after the week I've had. "But I can't. I have to get Mum and Gran home. Especially Gran," I add, because Gran has had a very good time with Auntie Pat's buffet and hot punch, and is weebling just a bit.

If we stay much longer she will take control of Auntie Pat's baby grand piano and treat us all to some Old Time Music Hall songs. She's quite a nifty piano player, and she sings very enthusiastically, but her songs tend toward the bawdy.

"Count me in," Carmen says, which is a surprise, because she's not a church kind of person. "This has got to be one of my worst Christmases so far, and I could do with a bit of spiritual nurturing."

"Me, too," Flora tells him, and Philip beams.

"Really?"

"Go on, then," I tell them glumly. "Desert the sinking ship."

"Poor darling," Carmen hugs me. "You've had a shit time just recently." And then, "Let's do something special for New Year. Just the gang—I want to spend it with only the people I really love. And Charlie, if he's not working a gig. You, too, Phil—you don't have to work, do you?"

"Er, no. That would be wonderful," he says.

"I'd love that," Jess says, and Philip beams at her again. "But that does include boyfriends, doesn't it?"

Before Carmen can say something nasty about Aster, and before Jess can see Philip's smile slip, Auntie Pat calls for a hush for Elaine's Christmas message. I thought they'd forgotten, but it seems that we must be tortured.

"Dearly beloved friends and family," Elaine says serenely as her blond head shines like a halo in the lamplight. "Thank you for taking the time to spend this evening with us to celebrate the coming of the Lord, and, of course, my own special news."

"God, she sounds like the bloody Madonna," Carmen whispers in my ear.

I hope this isn't going to take long.

"I'm not going to make a long speech," she says.

Thank God.

"I just wanted to wish you all a very Merry Christmas."

That's it? I can't believe Auntie Pat made such a performance about Elaine's speech and that's it.

"Christmas is a time of joy, and birth, and giving thanks, but we should also spare a thought for those less fortunate than ourselves—"

"Watch out, Phil," Carmen says under her breath. "I think she's after your job."

"Such as the starving, sick and lonely," Elaine goes on. "I know how it feels to be alone," she continues, almost tragically. "And I just wanted to add to my cousin Rosie, whose boyfriend tragically broke up with her just before the festive season, that life does go on, and I'm sure she'll find inner peace if only she places her trust in God."

"Jesus fucking Christ," Carmen says under her breath as all eyes fall on me. "Sorry, Phil—but I think I may have to kill your cousin."

Not if I get to her first, I think as I see Mum's face. I hadn't actually gotten around to telling her about Jonathan yet.

"Thank you, Elaine," I say, rising to the occasion as I also raise my glass of punch. I've had quite a lot of this very alcoholic punch and am feeling quite brave, as well as enormously pissed off. "It's very sweet of you to worry about me. So I ask you all to raise your glasses and wish Elaine peace, happiness, and a reconciliation with the father of her child—whoever he might be."

There is a sudden, embarrassed silence as people absorb the words that they have all been thinking yet have not dared to utter.

"Friends," Ned steps into the breach. "At least I feel that you're my friends after the warm welcome you've all given to me this evening, so I hope you won't feel I'm being too presumptuous by asking you to share in my joy. Flora has just made me the happiest man in the world by agreeing to marry me."

It is New Year's Eve.

I have a bottle of champagne, luxury Belgian chocolates, luxury caviar, strawberries and a selection of books written by such wonderful authors as J.K. Rowling and Stephen King.

I also have a selection of completely unliterary movies such as *The Little Mermaid* and *The Lion King* at my complete disposal via the touch of the remote control.

I also have a date, but it has to be said, not quite the date I was hoping for . . .

Instead of my lovely friends, who are all carousing somewhere in Trafalgar Square, for company, I have Maximillion d'Or, beloved, adored, prizewinning colorpoint red point Persian cat.

I'm giving him a taste of popular, rather than classical, culture as a New Year's treat, but somehow I don't think he'll tell on me to Mrs. G-S.

Ex-fluffer Grace has a very slight cold, and although she felt fit enough to cope with the highly untaxing job of caring for dear Maxie, Mrs. Granville-Seymour just couldn't bear risking his health. Although I didn't think that cats could catch colds from humans . . .

I take a long swallow of my third glass of excellent champagne. And, in my tipsy haze, as Big Ben approaches two minutes to midnight, I have A Brilliant Idea. Dear Jonathan. I miss him so much. I bet he's missing me, too . . . I bet he's too embarrassed to call me and is also miserable and lonely . . .

I reach for the telephone and punch in Jonathan's number. And hang up the moment I get switched to voice mail.

He obviously isn't home brooding about our failed relationship, then. He's probably out with a hot new woman with small feet.

"Happy New Year, Rosie," I toast myself sadly as I watch the seething mass of people in Trafalgar Square laughing and cheering and kissing as Big Ben strikes midnight.

Maxie opens an eye, then flops back to sleep.

The label on the champagne bottle warns me not to operate heavy machinery or drive a vehicle while under the influence, which is a shame, because I was just sitting here thinking that I might trim Mrs. Granville-Seymour's bushes with one of those Swedish chain saws, whilst also driving her BMW.

Oh, well.

I'll just have another little glass, then . . .

St. Valentine's Day Disaster

Rosie's Confession:

It is medically proven that a good sex life really helps seniors to stay healthy. It relieves stress, boosts self-esteem and makes them feel younger.

It's no wonder, then, that Granny Elsie has a better sex life than I do . . .

"That's got to be the most pathetic excuse for a list of New Year's resolutions I've ever seen," Carmen tells me just over six weeks later, on Valentine's Day afternoon, as we sip coffee in the back room of her vintage clothes store in Pembridge Road.

I snatch it back from her because I think it's pretty good.

1. ~~Spring clean entire house.~~ Check.
2. ~~Take up horse riding to annoy Elaine.~~ Check.
3. ~~Join Jess's Friday night knitting group.~~ Check.
4. ~~Get Mum's finances back on track.~~ Check.

5. ~~Get Mum back on track.~~ Check. Well, nearly . . .
6. ~~Threaten plumber with legal action for botch job on bath-room and resultant leak through kitchen ceiling.~~ Check. Although no response from him has actually been forthcoming . . .

I don't tell Carmen about the seventh resolution, which I resolutely left off the list. *Stop daydreaming about Dr. Love* is hardly something I want her to know about. I don't want *anyone* to know about it, because it's, well, fucking pathetic, and after nearly two months I should have gotten over such a childish crush.

The latest daydream, this morning, involved chocolate, and red roses, and romantic dinners. And garden gnomes arranged in the shape of a heart. What kind of daydream is that, I ask you? There was no *sex*. Plus, the background music still needs some work . . .

"Well, it was *your* idea." I'm beginning to wish I hadn't bothered with the list. Actually, I *didn't* bother on actual New Year itself, but Carmen says I have to have goals. It's lovely of her to worry about me, but she needn't. I'm perfectly happy the way I am.

"Yes, but giving the plumber short shrift wasn't what I had in mind—"

"And if I'm going to have a list at all, it might as well be a list of fairly *achievable* goals." Or, in fact, ones that I've already achieved.

"But the whole point, *my* whole point, is that you need to get out and have fun, meet people. Men, specifically."

"Plumbers are generally men," I point out. Although Greta, at Knit One Purl Jam, is a plumber, and she's definitely not a man. I'm thinking of asking her advice about *my* plumber situation. "A lot of men ride horses, too," I say.

What I don't add is that the group I'm currently trotting with is all female. I definitely don't want to meet any more men. But I have to say I am enjoying my twice-weekly trots around the training circuit. We'll be ready to actually trot around Hyde Park soon.

Elaine bought me a course of ten horse-riding lessons for Christmas. Actually, she didn't buy it for me at all. I remember that it was a gift she received for her birthday, last November, because I was at the party, and I was standing next to her when she opened the gift certificate.

Although it was an expensive gift (three hundred and forty quid, because I checked), I suspect this was to enhance my grief about Candy, the lost pony, and if I were paranoid, which I'm not, I might also suspect that it was a veiled threat. That the reminder about Candy was also to remind me of what she said to me that day. That no one could love *me* more than *her.*

But that would also be completely fucking psychotic of me. And also pathetic.

On the other hand, it could just be that she couldn't take the riding course on account of being pregnant. I worry too much, sometimes . . .

Whatever the reason, it has backfired on her, because I'm having fun on Tuesdays and Thursdays with the gals and a gentle mare called Tansy. I'm seriously thinking of keeping up the lessons after the course finishes.

You know, during the last few weeks I have settled into a very nice manless routine, and I'm a bit ashamed to admit that instead of feeling more shattered by my disaster with Jonathan (from whom I have not heard a peep), instead I am just a bit relieved.

It's such a release to be able to be myself without having to be on my best behavior for someone. And I'm not lonely, not really, because who could be lonely with such a lot of things to do? In fact, I'm so busy these days that I haven't got time for a man—where would he fit in my schedule?

On Saturday mornings, I have coffee with Carmen and Jess. Afternoons I catch up on shopping and cleaning. Evenings I have dinner with my friends. It's a new tradition that Flora and Ned started—they invited us all for dinner at Ned's house (Flora moved in just after Christmas), and we had such a great time that it then became The Thing To Do on Saturdays.

On Sundays I have lunch with Mum and Gran, spend the afternoon with Mum, because Gran disappears on a date, then I spend the evening catching up on admin and stuff, and maybe watch a movie.

On Mondays I go to cooking class. I mean, it's pathetic that a woman of twenty-eight can't cook, isn't it? Plus, I want to reciprocate and surprise all my friends by cooking them a meal at my place soon. We're doing spaghetti sauce next week. Once we get as far as the chocolate mousse, I'm going to have a practice run before I actually invite everyone, because it's good to have a practice run or two to get it right, isn't it?

On Tuesdays, after tea at Mum's I go riding, and then I'm too tired to do anything except shower and veg in front of the TV.

On Wednesdays, I have French conversation. I was a bit worried at first that Jonathan would show up for the new term, but then I thought, that's his problem. I mean, why should I disrupt my French classes just because he dumped me? I mean, if I'm going to be bilingual and delay the onset of dementia, I need to keep it up. At least he had the decency not to. Show up, I mean.

Thursdays are a repeat of Tuesdays, except I go to the pub for a couple of drinks with my new riding buddies afterwards.

Fridays is Knit One Purl Jam with Jess and my new knitting buddies.

So, the myth that all single women must be in need of a man to make them complete is, in my opinion, exactly that. A complete fucking myth. Of course, I do miss the sex . . . but that's why God, in Her wisdom, invented vibrators. Ahem. Enough about that.

"And this—this knitting thing. Really, Rosie, it's so 'grandmother.' You need a life."

Actually, my grandmother's life is pretty interesting at the moment. It involves a love triangle, and garden gnomes, and cowboys. But even thinking about it is too tiring and makes my head ache, so I don't mention it to Carmen.

"Don't you like my sweater?" I ask instead, the picture of innocence. "Just look at this sweater and tell me that knitting is boring." I am wearing my knitted-by-Jess sweater. She made us all one for Christmas, and I have to say they're positively fabulous. Definitely not boring or grandmotherly. Who knew Jess was so talented?

Mine is bloodred angora, with three-quarter sleeves, semi-fitted and cropped. It's very French, which is exactly what Jess was aiming at, because she says I look French. Very Audrey Tautou in the movie *Amélie*. Actually, I quite like the idea of adopting an Amélie look. I quite like the idea of adopting the Amélie approach to life, too.

You see, I really think that the way to happiness is to improve the lives of those around me, just like Amélie. That's the secret of my happiness, apart from such a busy agenda.

Carmen's sweater is a lovely mottled turquoise/blue/green roll neck and is completely sexy, in a mediaeval kind of way, and molds her lush curves. Jess really captured our personalities. It's incredible.

I don't have Jess's skill, but it's fun to sit around and gossip at Knit One Purl Jam over coffee, with Pearl Jam playing in the background. Kitty, the founder of the group, loves Pearl Jam with a passion.

"Of course I love the sweaters. I just don't see what kind of lure there is to spend Friday evenings gossiping over knitting needles and coffee, instead of getting out there and, most importantly, getting laid."

"It's not like that at all," I say, although truth be told, I do miss sex with an actual, you know, man, rather than a vibrator. "It's really hip." Which surprised me at first. "It's all young, trendy women. It's fashioned after a knitting group formed by a Manhattan feminist," I tell her, because even Carmen should approve of that. "We all talk about sex." Well, the others talk about sex.

"And you, on account of not having any, live vicariously." Carmen shakes her head. "It must be seven weeks since you last did it. This is not a healthy situation."

"So what did Paul get you for Valentine's Day?" I ask, moving swiftly away from my non-sex life.

"Don't change the subject."

"I got a card. An anonymous one." Secretly, I was thrilled and surprised to get one at all. It's pathetic of me, but I was so happy when that red envelope slipped through my letter box onto the hall floor. I suspect it was from Harry, which doesn't count, but I don't want to share that with Carmen.

"That's a good start," Carmen says approvingly. And then, "Paul got me red roses, chocolates and a date with a lawyer."

"Oh. Um, the date with the lawyer is—unique."

"He wants us both to make a will. Says it's only sensible, seeing as we're approaching old age," Carmen adds, eyeing the fish tank in the corner.

Paul, who is lovely and perfect for Carmen, wants more stability. What he actually means by that, as well as a cut down in the plate throwing, is less sex in odd places. The sex in odd places thing is one of Carmen's New Year's resolutions—a quest to remain young, unfettered and spontaneous. But Paul, apparently, likes comfort, now that he's in his dotage.

I have to admit, I'm right with him on that front. Carmen's idea of sex in odd places can be a bit, well, daunting sometimes. The minibreak hasn't worked out yet, on account of Paul working such long hours and saving extra money for their pension plan. As a compromising alternative, Carmen has plans to get him onto the fire exit stairs at the posh hotel tonight.

"But at least it beats more tropical fish." Carmen shakes her head. "He was very disappointed about the fish."

It has to be said that the fish experiment didn't turn out too well, on account of one of them, whom we've christened Malevolence, having cannibalistic tendencies and eating all of the others.

I glance across at the aquarium in the corner. Carmen moved it from the store because, she said, Malevolence was giving customers the evil eye. Actually, I think she's right . . . it is a very demonic-looking fish . . .

"Well, getting any kind of Valentine's Day gift is nice," I tell her, because it is.

"I know, I know," she says, shaking her head, then she laughs. "God, I'm beginning to sound like Jess."

"Anyway, what's the big mystery?" I ask her quickly, because talking about Jess will inevitably lead to a diatribe about Aster again. Plenty of time for that tonight. "Why, apart from the additional pleasure of my company, since we already had coffee this morning, was it so vital that I immediately drop everything and hightail it to your wondrous store?"

"Something came in," she tells me, riffling through the garment rack. "It just screamed 'Rosie' at me, and I think you should wear it tonight."

It is a piece of wine-red velvet and wine-red silk. It doesn't look like much . . . actually, it looks very Amélie . . .

"But I'm sorted," I resist. But I'm weakening.

Tonight is Flora and Ned's engagement party. It's going to be a huge, swanky affair with approximately three hundred people. I had intended to wear my safe black velvet number, on account of not wanting to attract any undue male attention.

"Just try it on. For me," Carmen pleads.

And so I do to humor her, because she does this to me a lot, and I never buy any of the sexy little numbers, because they're just not for me.

"Oh. My. God," I say, when I come out of the changing room to look in the mirror.

The sweetheart neck enhances my usually adequate cleavage to overabundant proportions, made even more so by the softly molding material. It's cut in such a clever way that it makes my waist smaller and my hips rounder and more feminine, and wisps of the silk petticoat flirt around my knees. It covers me completely yet at the same time totally uncovers me.

I *love* this dress. I've never felt so sexy and sirenesque in my entire life. Which is exactly why I'm not going to get it.

"You have to have this dress," Carmen orders me.

"I don't think—" This is a very dangerous little dress.

"Don't think." She holds up a hand, oddly reminiscent of the way Dr. Love held up a hand and told me not to think two months ago.

What harm can it do? It's only one little dress.

I grin back at Carmen's reflection in the mirror.

Fuck it. I'm having it. I can look sexy and hot just for myself.

The fish gazes malevolently, and I shudder. . . .

My good humor lasts until I reach home and walk into my kitchen. The bathroom, directly above it, was completely gutted and replaced six months ago, because it was old and desperately needed it.

I love my new bathroom. It's all lovely mother-of-pearl tiles, and pale green accessories, and calming. But what I do not love is that the shower has developed a leak, and Brian Hirston & Sons, my plumbers, are ignoring my phone calls.

So earlier in the week I consulted my lawyer, and he sent them a very strong letter, very strong indeed. Unfortunately, the leak is getting worse, and there is water all over the kitchen floor.

I mop it up with kitchen towels, cursing all the time under my breath about shoddy workmanship. The amount I've paid Brian Hirston & Sons is enough to put at least one of the grandkids through college, and the least they can do is provide a decent service.

So when my telephone rings I ignore it, because it's probably Mum with more of Gran and the garden gnome story, and I'll get it all tonight, anyway. Plus, I'm still mopping water. And when I check my messages, ten minutes later, I'm even more pissed off. There's a message from Harry.

"Hi, Rosie." His dulcet tones slide over my skin like silk, and I can't help a little shiver. It's because of my lack of sex, I think, and this irritates me.

Harry's called me a few times since Christmas, but I haven't told Carmen or Jess. I haven't told anyone.

"I'm calling to see what you're," he pauses, "wearing. I'm imagining something black, and tiny, and silky, and that I'm sliding my hand down your body," he adds, and I shiver some more. "Anyway, just wanted to see if you're free for dinner tomorrow night," he says, completely changing the tone of his voice from sexy to amused.

I think he thinks that all this blowing hot and cold is sexy and tempting.

I cannot imagine why he's bothering, because I'm always mean to him, but although I have absolutely no interest in meeting up with him—well, maybe only a very little—it's stress-relieving and refreshing to have someone to be mean to. But I can't be mean to a voice-mail message.

Granny Elsie's theory about being mean to keep them keen certainly seems to be working where Harry's concerned. Not that I want to keep him keen, of course, but despite the fact that I keep saying, "No, go away and never call me again," he keeps coming back for more.

Thinking of Granny Elsie makes me sigh.

Eight more garden gnomes have gone missing since Christmas. And although the police are upset about it and are taking it seriously, the current theory is that they have either been (a) kidnapped by one of Hampstead's snootier, gnome-hating residents, or (b) kidnapped by the French.

I kid you not.

The first theory—that a posh neighbor kidnapped them—is the copycat theory. It's happened before. In Brattleby, Lincolnshire, residents in the posh half of the village woke one morning to find that their gardens had been invaded by fourteen garden gnomes, as some kind of retaliation for their garden-gnome snobbery, or so the locals suspect. The case is still open.

The second theory—that they were kidnapped by the French—is also not a joke. The Liberation Front for Garden Gnomes is actually quite serious in France. Their aim: to de-ridiculize the gnomes by rehousing them in their natural environment.

Apparently, gnomes have been popping up all over French woodland groves, and, on one occasion, seventy-four of them appeared one morning lined up in front of the cathedral in Saint-Die. Imagine popping to church for a quick confession and finding that sight before you?

This is both disturbing and upsetting, especially as I have to keep ordering and replacing them before Granny Elsie notices, but today, the mystery was solved when Mum called me at six this morning. This is what happened.

"Darling, you've *got* to tell *Gran* that she's making the *biggest mistake of her life*," is her opening gambit, and I wonder why she isn't asleep at six in the morning like normal people.

"What's happening?" I mumble, because I'm still not completely awake.

"Rosie, I want you to come over right now and tell her that she's being too rash. She can't do this just because of Sid's romantic flight of fancy."

I'd no idea Gran was seeing a Sid. I thought she was still seeing an Alf. So, of course, I'm thoroughly confused. Especially as I only saw Gran when I popped round before my riding lesson on Thursday, and she didn't mention any forthcoming nuptials.

"Mum, slow down a minute and start over, will you?" I yawn, and rub my eyes with the back of my free hand.

"It was the garden gnomes that caused this mess," she wails. "We should never have bothered replacing them. We should just have left them to their fate."

"We" didn't replace them. "I" did. But before I can say anything, Mum's up and panicking again.

"After all I've done for her since Granddad died. I took her in, I put a roof over her head, put food on the table, and now she repays me by—by—casually marrying Sid and moving out."

"My God. Granny Elsie got married and moved out? When did this happen?"

"No, not yet. But if she thinks I'm going to the service, she's got another think coming, I can tell you."

How strange, yet wonderful, to find true love again at her age. But then again, Broadway actress Carol Channing got married again when she was eighty-two, which was a shock, because everyone thought she was dead.

The childhood sweetheart she married thought she was dead, too, so it must have been a surprise when he picked up the telephone one day and it was Carol on the other end, especially as they hadn't seen each other since high school . . .

"You must come over and *do* something." Mum's building up to an ear-splitting crescendo, and I have to hold the phone slightly away from my ear. "We can't allow this to happen."

"Mum," I try to reason with her. "Gran's old enough to decide for herself, don't you think?" Although I do wonder sometimes if Granny Elsie's reverted to a second childhood. "But at least it's not as if he's marrying her for her money, because she hasn't got much."

"But. But I'll be left *all on my own*."

And that, my friends, is the real crux of the problem.

My head starts to throb as I realize that this will, of course, set Mum off on a whole new Why I Should Move Home crusade.

Mum's been doing quite well since Christmas. Once I went through her finances and got her back on track, and hired some of the cleaners from Odd Jobs to give the house a good once-over, and had a serious chat with her about how she was only in her fifties and had to get out and about more, she took my advice and joined the Women's Institute to get out and about more. I thought she was doing really well.

"Please come now," she says, bursting into tears.

* * *

When I arrive at Mum's shortly after seven this morning, I see, immediately, what she means about the garden gnomes.

They are all, including the old, previously stolen ones, arranged in a huge heart on the front lawn.

In the middle of the huge gnome heart is a huge, padded silk heart, emblazoned with the words *My darling Elsie, will you marry me? Yours, forever, Sid XXX.*

How romantic is that?

"Who's Sid?" I ask Granny Elsie thirty seconds later when she opens the front door to me.

"Howdy, stranger," she greets me. She is wearing a red-and-white-checked shirt, blue jeans, cowboy boots and a Stetson. "My new toy boy. I thought Sandra might have called you." An interesting fashion statement for an eighty-six-year-old with a blue rinse.

Blue, it would seem, is the new pink.

Then, before I can ask about her toy boy or her new image, she cunningly changes the subject. "Is it me imagination, or do I have two Gertrudes, two Munchkins, and two Gladyses?" Granny asks me, peering at her gnome heart with a very satisfied expression on her face.

"Maybe they had babies?" I say, and don't mention the fact that if she looks very closely, she'll find two Pucks, two Freds, two Delilahs, two Frodos, and two Annes, too. Although I've always thought that Anne was an unusual name for a gnome . . .

"Don't you start," she says. "It's bad enough your mother losing her grip on reality without you muscling in on the action."

And this from the woman with the toy boy and the blue rinse.

I follow her through to the kitchen, and she switches on the kettle.

"Where *is* Mum?" I ask, because this is the simplest and

least outrageous question I could ask when faced with a whole host of aging gunslinger and toy boy questions.

"She's gone for a lie down to steady her nerves," Gran says, shaking her blue-rinsed, Stetsoned head.

I need a lie down to steady *my* nerves, I think.

"Honestly, I think she's getting worse, not better. She's not been right since your poor dad passed, has she?"

"No," I say, instantly guilty. I should have been better at spotting the signs.

"And don't go suffering pangs of guilt," Gran tells me. "I know you, Rosie. You're a good girl, but you think you have to look after us all. Well, I'm taking over. She just needs to get out and about more, and I'm going to sort her."

This, from the woman who thinks she's Annie Oakley reincarnated?

"I mean, I haven't even said yes to Sid yet and she's in a right state. Just because Sid wants us to fly to Las Vegas and get married by John Wayne. Not the real John Wayne, obviously, because he's dead."

"Well, I'm glad we got that sorted out," I say, just a bit sarcastically. "So, back to Sid."

"He's loved me from afar since I joined the line dancing circle before Christmas," Gran tells me. "He just didn't have the courage to, you know, ask me out. Especially as Alf got in there first."

"Well, he obviously managed to overcome his difficulties if he's asking you to marry him."

"It was *me* who overcame *his* difficulties," Gran cackles. "I asked him if he fancied a pickled onion at the cheese and wine party last month," she says, grinning. "And then I asked him if he fancied me, along with the pickled onion. But I ain't marrying him. I likes me independence."

I wonder if I should tell her that Sid is a kleptomaniac with a gnome fetish?

"Also, I'm not sure about a man who steals my garden gnomes," she adds, and winks.

I know how she feels about the independence thing, I think later that night at the engagement party. I'm so glad that I've decided to give up on men for good, because they cause nothing but trouble. Take Jess's man trouble, for example . . .

"I'm a bit worried about Aster," Jess, who has had her hair cropped and bleached to a spiky, peroxide blond because Aster prefers blond, confides to me as we sit at our designated table.

I'm a bit worried about Aster, too, because apart from all his other faults, he's barely spent any time with Jess since they arrived, and is currently chatting to an attractive peroxide blond at the drinks station. But I don't say any of this to Jess.

"In what way?" I ask her, careful to keep my voice neutral.

"Oh, it's nothing, it's nothing. I'm probably being a bit silly," she says, giving me a rueful smile. "A bit overreactive and silly, that's all."

"But it might help to, um, get it off your chest," I tell her. "You know that old saying—a problem shared is a problem halved."

"Well, I wouldn't call it an actual problem. Not a problem. More of a . . . a concern."

This is the first time she's ever voiced anything remotely negative about Aster, so I must be careful what I say to her.

"Darling, Jess," I say to her, placing my hand on her arm. "It's perfectly normal, and not at all silly, to have concerns about a relationship. Look at me and Jonathan—I was always voicing my concerns about my relationship with him, and you didn't think I was silly, did you?"

"No, of course not. Okay. Okay," she says, then takes a

deep breath and closes her eyes. "Do you think that Aster is an arrogant jerk who's ruthlessly using me for money?" is not exactly how I expected her to phrase it, and wonder if Carmen has said something to her.

"Well." What the hell do I say? If I say no, that wouldn't be right because I think he *is* using her for money. But if I say yes, then it might cause a rift in our friendship.

"Only, I sometimes think that he's only interested in my trust fund," Jess says, and the words come tumbling out in a rush. "Like that suit he's wearing. It cost a thousand pounds. We bought it today, because the other suit I bought him wasn't quite right for a posh engagement party, and he said he didn't want to let me down in front of my friends."

"Well—" And I'm trying desperately for a bit of Amélie channeling, here . . .

"And whenever we go out, he has to borrow money from me so that he can pay his way, but he never gives it back. Plus he lives with me free of charge, and I pay for all the food, and everything, and sometimes I worry that he's not really interested in me as a person at all. And all he got me for Valentine's Day was a Snickers bar, because he said what can you get for the girl who has a trust fund, therefore has the money to buy anything she fancies, so expensive Valentine's Day gifts were just a waste—especially if you happened to be a penniless musician."

"I think," I say slowly, because I'm groping for words here. What would Amélie say? "I think that it's good to help someone out, but it's also good to—to encourage them to stand on their own two feet—" But before I can find more right words, Jess is off again.

"And he's also gone off sex. And I think he hated that sweater I made him for Christmas, because I found it stuffed under the bed all screwed up in a ball."

I don't think I've ever heard Jess string so many sentences together without doing that little word repetition thing she does, and I want to scrumple up Aster into a little ball and throw him out with the trash.

"There," she says, giving me a huge smile. "You were right. I do feel so much better now. So much better."

"You do?"

"And I'm going to sleep on it. Philip," she calls across the table, "would you like to dance?"

"I'd be delighted, dear girl," he beams back at her, getting to his feet. "Gorgeous new hairstyle. Lovely color."

Charlie and his latest man is another good example of why independence is a good thing.

"I definitely thought he would have called by now," Charlie frets, sliding into the seat next to me.

"Charlie, you only met him last night," I say, exasperated. I absolutely love Charlie. And I'm absolutely delighted that he's finally met someone else whom he feels worthy of more than a few dates, but he's done nothing but obsess about Lewis since the moment he arrived at Ned and Flora's party.

"Maybe I didn't seem keen enough," Charlie frets some more. "Maybe I should have, you know, called him—it *is* Valentine's Day, after all. Do you think I should call him?"

"Well, you don't want to appear too eager," I say carefully. Because I don't want to put Charlie off. But after a year of complete indifference, this all-or-nothing situation is a bit, well, worrying. It's almost like he's a love alcoholic taking his first swig of love gin and tonic after a year, and now he's back in headfirst.

"I'm just going to check for messages," Charlie tells me. "Back in a sec."

As Charlie heads toward the hotel foyer, I worry that he'll get burned again . . .

"Paul's definitely going through a midlife crisis. He's also gone off me," Carmen announces as she inhabits Charlie's empty seat. "He just refused to have sex with me on the fire escape. He said he was too tired."

"Carmen," I tell her reasonably, as I channel Amélie. "Paul loves you. Anyone with even an amoeba-sized brain can see that."

"Really?" She looks at me. "Only—"

"Yes?"

"Well, I think he's having an affair."

"When would he find time for an affair?" I am totally exasperated again. I love Carmen, I really do, but she doesn't seem to grasp that just because she is one of those people who only needs four hours' sleep per night, the rest of the human race needs rather more than that.

"Well, because he's not as keen on sex as he used to be, for one."

"He's working fourteen-hour days to build up his business and your old-age savings," I say to her. "In between working and spending time with you, and having sex five times a week with you, when, exactly, does he sneak off for secret trysts with another woman? In fact, sex five times a week must be exhausting. Would it really kill you to slow down a bit?"

"Yes, but, it's a medical fact that men should have sex at least twenty-one times per month. It's good for prostate cancer avoidance."

Is it? My God, that's astonishing.

"Carmen. He is not. Having. An affair," I tell her firmly and glance across to Paul, who is yawning.

He looks exhausted.

"You know what? You're right," Carmen says, smiling a secretive smile as she twirls her hair. "I know exactly what I need to do. Thanks for that, Rosie. You're a pal."

"What did I say?"

"Part one of the master plan begins now." Carmen slides

back around the table to her seat next to Paul. "Paul, darling," she says, taking his glass of brandy away from him. "That stuff will kill your brain cells and rot your liver—you need to take better care of yourself. Here, drink this water instead."

God, she's gone mad.

Half an hour later, I am still rejoicing in my independent state. I am also exhausted.

This party is just for Ned and Flora to celebrate their impending nuptials with, oh, three hundred of their relatives and close, personal friends, and it's tiring being all flirty, and fun, and making the rounds of all the relatives. Plus, my feet, unsurprisingly, are killing me.

But Mum seems okay. Auntie Lizzy, bless her, is making a point of looking after her. She told Mum earlier, "The young ones need to have fun together," thereby relieving me of the need to sit with Mum all night.

Gran, a vision in a long, blue-and-white-checked dress straight out of a Western, and who needs no excuse to have a great time, is generally mingling and chatting to anyone who will chat back to her.

So just imagine my surprise when I discover that among Ned's close, personal friends is Jonathan. Or rather, Jonathan's new girlfriend is a friend of Ned's. She is a nurse at St. Mary's Hospital and has invited Jonathan as her date.

I discover this startling fact when I set off in search of a diet cola, because I'm hot and thirsty and need a caffeine boost.

"Rosie," Jonathan says, his face turning red as he and his new girlfriend stop in front of me. "What a surprise. You're looking lovely," he also says, and I wonder why he sounds so *surprised* that I am looking lovely. Am I supposed to be doing sackcloth and ashes? I mentally thank Carmen for forcing this little red dress on me.

Actually, *Jonathan* looks lovely. And I can't help it. My throat tightens, and I am ridiculously close to tears as I remember all the good times we had.

"Er, this is Samantha," he tells me, and I force myself to smile at the tall, elegant blond. I can't stop myself from taking a quick peek at her feet. Slim, small, dainty . . .

"Hi," she says pleasantly, offering a hand. "It's nice to meet you."

"Hello." I also try for pleasant. "Lovely, um, shoes," I add.

"Er, Samantha's a colleague of, er, Ned's." Jonathan has the grace to look embarrassed. "She's a nurse at St. Mary's Hospital. Didn't realize it was your Flora he was getting engaged to. I'd never, you know, never have . . ."

"What a small world it is, hahahaha," I say, stunned and a lot betrayed that he has gotten over me so quickly and has moved on with his life. And although I thought I was completely over him and had moved on with *my* life, it hurts that I am so instantly forgettable.

"Well, lovely to see you," I babble, because I have to get away from here *right now*. "Got to dash. Got to, you know . . . well, lovely to see you again," I say in a rush and head for the drinks station in search of a large gin and tonic.

So imagine my dismay when I spot Elaine at the drinks station. With Harry. He didn't mention he'd be here when he left that sexy voice mail for me earlier. The cheating rat.

At twenty weeks' pregnant, Elaine hasn't even got the decency to swell and gain excessive weight. Instead, she is a vision of Madonna-like radiance in a white, flowing gown that gently emphasizes her smallish bump.

And although I do not want Harry as my date, nor, in fact, would I want anything to do with him ever again even if he were the last man on the face of the planet, I am more than a bit pissed that he's attempting to pursue me at the same time as he is obviously dating my cousin.

Yes, it's a very good thing I'm not interested in men, I think as I change course and head to the hotel foyer. I just can't face any of Elaine's bitchiness or Harry's two-faced flirting, because after encountering Jonathan I may weaken and give in.

If I fortify myself in the hotel's main bar, in peace and solitude, I will not have to contend with coupledom and ghosts of boyfriends past, because at this point I'm wondering why Ivan hasn't made an appearance.

"Double gin and tonic," I tell the barman, then change my mind. "Actually, make that a triple," I say, pulling myself onto one of the barstools. My feet feel instantly better.

"One of those days?" he asks, smiling.

"You could say that." *Hmmm*, I think as I take a deep swallow of my drink and the gin immediately hits my nervous system.

Peace and quiet at last.

"You know, drinking alone is the first step along a slippery, shady road to ruin," an attractive baritone voice says in my ear. "I definitely think you need rescuing from that. Mind if I join you?"

And as I turn to face the owner of the attractive baritone voice, "Sweet Mystery of Life, at Last I've Found You," begins to play, rather inexplicably, in my head.

And Dr. Love raises a sardonic eyebrow at me.

10

Some Enchanted Evening . . .

Rosie's Confession:

Women blink nearly twice as much as men . . .
    I mention this because I'm blinking like a madwoman,
because <u>I can't. Believe. My eyes . . .</u>

Of all the bars in all of London, he had to walk into this one,
I think rather hysterically as my whole body jumps to immediate alert.

    So, to add insult to injury, as well as the "Sweet Mystery of
Life, at Last I've Found You," soundtrack running through my
head, I am now also channeling *Casablanca.*

    Play it, Dr. Love, I think.

    "It's you," I say like a dimwit, not resembling Ingrid
Bergman in the slightest, because, of course, I cannot think
of anything droll or charming to say.

    I can't think of anything at all, because the rush of adren-
aline has rendered my brain dizzy, and I have lost the power
of coherent speech.

    "Yes, I think it's safe to say that it's actually me," Dr. Love says, smiling his charming smile as he looks down at his chest and pats himself. And looks back at me, and I'm mesmerized by brown eyes and his crinkling smile. "Again. Luke Benton," he tells me, holding out a hand.

"Sorry?"

"We never did get around to exchanging names, did we? And I always make a point of finding out the names of the women I—" He pauses, and my mouth dries up as I wait for him to say kiss. "Rescue," he finishes, and my heart pounds right into my throat.

"Rosie Mayford," I squeak, flushing. We might not have gotten around to names, but *man* did we ever get around to exchanging saliva. It seems rather surreal to be shaking his hand, given our exciting, if somewhat brief, history. Luke Benton. *Luke Benton*, I think, savoring his name.

"It's lovely to see you again, Rosie," he says, holding my hand in his. "Unexpected, but lovely. Why are you torturing your feet with tight shoes again?"

"Me, too. Um, because they go with the dress?" It's true. Yet again, I sacrificed comfort in the name of "fuck me" shoes, but the spiked heels look so good with the dress. God, but his hand feels so warm and solid, and he's even better, so much better, in real life than in my daydreams. I'd forgotten how compelling, how sexy, how dangerous . . .

Reluctantly, I let go of his hand, because I've been holding it for longer than I should, and he must think I'm an idiot.

"So how's the doctoring business?" God, I could kick myself for the drivel coming out of my mouth. What would Ingrid say in a situation like this? "How's, um, Mrs. Woodbridge?" I ask, groping for something scintillating. God, why can't I be scintillating?

"Mother and baby boy are doing very well, although by the time ten-pound Baby Woodbridge decided to make an appearance, poor Mrs. Woodbridge had graduated from calling Mr. Woodbridge all the names under the sun to quite a lot of words I've never heard before. And swearing that this was the first and last time she'd put herself through such torture."

"Ouch. Ten pounds? I expect it's enough to put you off sex for the rest of your life. Oh, I don't mean you," I babble. "I meant—" Oh, God, I didn't mean to mention sex. Why did I have to go and mention sex? Because, of course, all I can think about now is kissing Dr. Love, I mean Dr. Luke, in Piccadilly Circus.

There is an awkward silence on my part, and sardonic amusement on his part, and in desperation I take another gulp of my gin and tonic and study the bar. It has a lovely finish. . . .

"Yes, well, it's surprising how the memory of the pain fades. My high respect for women and their endurance has certainly gone up inestimably since entering the field," he tells me, and I sigh with relief that my sex gaffe has slipped by. "Even more so, as they mostly go on to have completely normal sex lives again, afterwards. Which is fortunate for the human race," he says. "And for men, in general, of course."

"Well, yes," I babble, because his expression has me on the verge of spontaneous combustion. I think this man is flirting with me. "Especially as men need to have sex twenty-one times a month to help with prostate cancer avoidance—I mean, it's medically proven, isn't it?"

Oh. My. Fuck. *What* is coming out of my *mouth*? I'm going to burst into flames any moment now. Or die of embarrassment.

"And I'm sure that men across the land are rejoicing at that one," he grins at me. "So how are you connected to the happy couple?" he asks, rescuing me again.

"I'm Flora's cousin." I grab the new topic of conversation with relief. "And you?"

"I work with Ned."

"Of course you do, I should have guessed immediately," I babble, again. I must try not to babble. "I mean, he's an obstetrician, you're an obstetrician, it makes perfect sense that you'd, you know, know him—"

"Well, it's a strangely small—the world of delivering babies," he says, as I think what a small place is the world of parties, and how happy I am that it *is* so small, because otherwise I wouldn't have seen him again.

"God, it's a good thing the world is small, otherwise we wouldn't have bumped into each other again," he adds. I think he's psychic. I also think he's *definitely* flirting with me!

God, what do I do?

"Um, would you like a drink?" I ask, trying for coquettish, but I'm sure that I'm grinning like a fool. And when he grins back at me, I wonder if I have lipstick on my teeth. Or food between them.

What am I doing? Why on earth would he want to have a drink with me?

"Well, no—"

"Of course you don't want a drink, hahaha." I leap straight back in to emphasize that I am so not flirting with him. "Sorry—of course you need to get back to your, um, table."

Handsome, dangerous doctors like Luke don't have problems getting dates for these kinds of functions. Hell, they don't find it hard to get a date for any occasion. And although I know I'm looking my best, I'm suddenly stricken by the remembrance of the beautiful blond at the Christmas fundraiser, and my confidence fails.

"I was going to say 'nothing alcoholic, but a cola would be nice, because I'm on call,'" he says. "And I don't think the table will miss me, somehow. It's just like all the other tables. It never writes, it never calls . . ." He raises a sardonic eyebrow, and I can't help but laugh.

"You're doing that thing again," I say, charmed.

"My apologies." He smoothes his eyebrow. "It has a life of its own, I'm afraid. Soooo . . . If you're sure your boyfriend can spare you for a few minutes, I'd love that cola. I'm—glad to see it all worked out for you with him," he adds. And I'm confused, because I'm totally enthralled.

"Which particular boyfriend did you mean?" I ask him.

"I have a choice?"

"Of two, on this particular evening," I say.

"God—you're joking."

"I wish. I'm being tortured with exes. They both have a connection to Flora and Ned. At this point in the day, I wouldn't be surprised if Jack Cooper, whom I snogged behind the bike shed in tenth grade, turned out to be Ned's distant cousin twice removed."

"Lucky Jack," Luke says, and my face gets hotter. In fact, every atom in my body is pretty well boiling.

I hadn't meant to mention snogging, either, because of course now my eyes are totally drawn to Luke's mouth and I want to kiss him again.

"That guy—Jonathan? The one from Christmas. I saw him in the men's room earlier, and I just assumed you were here with him—"

"Oh. Jonathan. No, definitely not my boyfriend anymore," I tell him quickly. "We split up the day after—" *I wantonly threw myself at you in the middle of Piccadilly Circus*, I nearly say, but don't. "The fund-raiser."

"Oh, dear, I'm sorry," he says. But he doesn't look sorry at all.

"Don't worry about it," I say. "Well, it *was* a bit of a shock, at first—"

"On account of him having the bad manners to turn up at your cousin's engagement party," he finishes the sentence for me. "*Very* bad mannered of him. But also, possibly as a means of reminding you of what you're missing, thereby instilling in you a burning desire to get back with him," he says, and I wonder if he's fishing for information about whether I'd like to get back with Jonathan. "Unless, of course, he is a distant relation of Ned's."

"In a way. He didn't mean to. Turn up, I mean. His new girlfriend brought him. You probably know her, she's a colleague of Ned's—Samantha."

"Oh, dear. Yes, I do—nice woman. Excellent midwife. You probably didn't need to know that—sorry to rub it in."

"Well, it wasn't exactly the highlight of my evening, bumping into him."

"But it's the highlight of mine, bumping into you again," he tells me, and I shiver at the expression in his eyes.

And despite the fact that I have sworn off men, I am thinking that Luke, although he will probably break my heart, might be the exception to make me break my no-man rule.

"No cheesy comments allowed, Doc," I say but don't really mean, because I'm secretly pleased, but also secretly terrified, that *he doesn't* mean it.

"None intended," he says, then adds, "I meant it."

Oh, be still my beating heart! A change of subject is definitely in order. Things are just going too fast.

"So, tell me about your latest table," I say, to try to (a) lighten the intensity, because yes, I am a coward, and (b) to ascertain just *if* he has a date, or a girlfriend, or a wife, which would be a tragedy, but he actually hasn't *said*. In fact, he knows rather a lot more about me than I do about him.

So it's a bit of a disappointment when Charlie comes dashing across the bar with his cell phone in his hand before Luke can answer me.

"Darling, he called. He *called*. And after all that worrying." Charlie, all flustered excitement, grabs me, kisses me on the mouth, then steals my drink and knocks back the rest of my gin and tonic in one swallow.

"Charlie—"

"He left me a lovely, long message—he's missing me already and wants to know if I'm free for a date tomorrow night. What do you think? Too soon to call him back? Too available if I say yes to tomorrow night?"

Whilst I'm delighted to see that Charlie has finally glued his heart back together sufficiently to dip his toe in the dating pond to risk getting it smashed again, I am a bit irritated, because I am just about to jump in headfirst and risk my own.

What a horrible friend I am, I think, squashing my frustration. I must remember my earlier conviction about helping friends in order to be happy.

"Well, on the one hand—" I begin.

"Why, hel-lo," Charlie says as he notices Luke for the first time. I know that tone of voice. It's his big-brother, who-are-you, and are-you-good-enough-for-our-Rosie tone of voice. It also has overtones of "God, what a lovely hunky man you are."

"Charlie Blake," he says, holding out a hand. "One of lovely Rosie's dearest friends, and also co-owner of Odd Jobs. And you are? Apart from Mr. Utterly Gorgeous, of course," Charlie adds. "Not that I'm interested; I already have my own Mr. Utterly Gorgeous. Or nearly, at any rate."

"It's not Mr. Utterly Gorgeous," I say before I can stop the words from running out of my mouth. "It's *Dr.* Utterly Gorgeous, I mean, Dr. Luke Benton," I correct myself, trying to regain lost ground.

"It's a delight to meet you," Luke says, his eyebrow going up as he glances across at me. My nerves thrum at the promise of "later" in his eyes.

"Ah, I always did love a man in a white coat with a stethoscope," Charlie grins. "Interesting that you're a doctor, because our Rosie here had a bit of a thing about—"

"Thanks, Charlie," I jump in before Charlie can push his foot any further down my metaphorical, yet embarrassed, throat. "Sorry, Luke, you'll have to forgive my usually calm, self-possessed friend here—he's just had a large dose of love gin and tonic after a long drought."

"Looks like I'm not the only one," Charlie says, and I glare at him.

"Back to your question," I tell him. "I think definitely no games. But also definitely go slowly—you only met him last night," I say wisely. Oh, how I should listen to my own advice, because the way I'm feeling at the moment I could do something very rash with Luke. "If you want to go out with Lewis tomorrow night," I add sagely, "then why invent a previous arrangement? Why play games? Just be straightforward and up front."

"Just thinking about him makes me, you know, very up front," Charlie grins evilly, and then to Luke, "Sorry, Doc, that's probably more information than you wanted about a complete stranger."

"No worries," Luke tells him, grinning back. And just as I am relaxing, as much as it is possible to relax with all the heat and sexual frustration I am currently experiencing, about the fact that Luke is fine about Charlie, because you never know with straight men how they will react to your gay best friend, he ups my anxiety even more.

"I know what you mean about the really up front part," Luke says, and my toes blush. I have to stop myself from letting my eyes wander downward to check out how up front he might actually be. And then, in that totally charming way of his, just as the conversation is getting hotter by the moment, he teases me by *completely changing the subject*.

"So, what is it that you actually do?" he asks us both, and I wonder if he does it on purpose to heighten tension. It's certainly working.

"Odd Jobs," Charlie tells him. "You know, you need an exporn star to take care of your rich kitty, or a drag act, or a bridge painter, we're your people."

"Two large gin and tonics," I say to the bartender, because I feel the need for alcohol to blunt the sexual tension. "And a cola for the sardonic eyebrow."

"Sorry," he says.

"I think it's charming," Charlie tells him earnestly.

"Thank you. But Odd Jobs. That sounds fascinating. Where did you two meet? How did you come up with such an original idea?" Luke asks, sounding genuinely interested and impressed. Which makes a change, because all of my previous boyfriends thought it was a totally mad idea and refused to take it seriously.

Not that Luke is, or is ever going to be, my boyfriend, of course.

"In the students' union bar at college," Charlie takes the lead, also taking a sip of his gin and tonic. "We bonded over a shared love of Donny Osmond, Simon le Bon and drag acts. Love at first sight. Although in a sister-sister kind of way," Charlie continues.

"Of course," Luke says, dead seriously. "Although Donny and Simon never rang my bells, I did develop a deep and passionate love for drag after first seeing Roxanne and the Rockettes."

"My, God, now that's a talented group." Charlie is impressed.

"Aren't they just?" Luke shakes his head. "Tell me, did you ever see Sisters Wedge doing 'It's Raining Men'?"

I'm pretty impressed myself. I mean, not every straight man is comfortable with drag, and I wonder if there's something that he's not sharing with us. He cannot be gay. If I've misread all his flirting, and his kissing, and have got it wrong all along, I will have to kill myself from embarrassment.

"Is there something you're not sharing with us here?" Charlie asks the question. "Do you have a closet you need to come out of?"

"No, not at all," Luke laughs.

"Well, that's a crime for the gay community," Charlie tells him earnestly. And then, "Although not for Rosie," and I scowl at him.

"Well, I hope so," Luke says, smiling at me, and then he does that thing of his. Just as my knees are melting, he totally changes the subject. "One of my interns and his partner decided to make a life-commitment declaration to each other, and they thought that if straight couples could have engagement parties and wedding celebrations, then so could they. Which is how I was introduced to drag. Which leads back to you and Rosie, and how you met," Luke prompts Charlie, and I can see that his interest really *is* genuine.

Unless he's just trying to field personal questions. . . .

"I was in my final year of a media communications degree, I'd already begun to dip my toes into the world of drag. You know—wanted to do something more exciting with my life than working for a huge, faceless conglomerate, and I'd arranged for a new, up-and-coming drag act to perform that night."

"I was the events coordinator," I say.

"Rosie, our very reliable gal, was studying business studies. She needed a bit of a shake-up," Charlie says.

"I did not," I tell him. "That's a bit unfair. I know how to take a risk when the occasion demands it." Luke gives me one of his intense stares, and I wonder if I should take a risk on him.

"So you decided to do it in real life, too?" he asks, and I wonder if he means my taking a chance on him in real life, as well as in my daydreams.

"Not at first—no money," Charlie tells him. "Plus, Rosie thought we should be sensible and get 'proper' jobs for a while. Me in a large PR conglomerate," Charlie shudders. "I hated it. And Rosie worked in human resources for an equally faceless company."

"I hated it, too," I say, because I did.

"Especially your prick of a boss," Charlie says.

"I'm convinced to this day that it was his mission in life to torment me and make my life as miserable as possible. Oddly for a human resources director, he didn't like the idea of women getting above their 'station' in life. He never said as much, but he didn't have to."

"His final method of Rosie torture," Charlie tells Luke, "were the requests for totally useless reports on which Rosie would waste copious amounts of time."

"Yes, and the hair that broke this particular camel's back was when he insisted that I research and produce a report on what the company employees were eating, and how it affected their performance. This was due to his belief that the way forward was to instruct and police our employees to follow company food-consumption requirements."

"Which, of course, would never work," Luke says. "Because you can't dictate what people eat, and the board would throw it out, anyway."

"If, in fact, it ever got as far as the board," I jump in. "Which it wouldn't, because, as I said, it was a time-wasting exercise."

"Which prompted Rosie to throw in her job and I joined her," Charlie says. "Although it helped that Rosie had come into a bit of money from her granddad, and I'd made a couple of killer commissions." Charlie winks at Luke. "As I said, our Rosie likes to play things a bit safe."

"Hey, it doesn't hurt to be sensible. Most of the time," I say, going all hot again as I read that would-I-take-a-risk-on-him? question again in his face. I look back at the mahogany bar.

"So, Odd Jobs was born," Charlie says. "And our fame is spreading like wildfire through the London suburbs. Frankly, I'm shocked you haven't heard of us—we provide some stellar cleaning staff to the good hospitals of this city."

"But only in West London," I interrupt.

"You just have no idea about PR," Charlie sighs and shakes his head at me. "How many times have I told you about spin?"

"But where did you come up with the idea of odd kinds of jobs?" Luke asks. "I mean, I did some vacation and part-time jobs myself to help with medical school," he says, which is a surprise, considering the fact that his family can afford staff.

"But your family has staff," I say before I can stop myself.

"This is just getting better by the minute." Charlie is lapping this up. "Utterly gorgeous, saves lives, rich. Carmen's going to love you."

"Charlie," I warn him.

"Who's Carmen?" Luke asks.

"Never you mind," I say. "Forget Carmen. We're fascinated by why you worked to put yourself through college." At least, I am.

"Nothing fascinating about it. My mother believed in making me earn some of the vast quantities of cash she was investing in my education," Luke explains. "But the oddest thing I ever did was stock shelves at the local supermarket. I had very boring odd jobs. Although I did work at a stable one summer, which mainly involved shoveling horse manure."

Which is why he's such a nice, well-grounded, nonsnobby man, I think. God, he's lovely.

"Not bad, not bad," Charlie says. "But you can't beat Rosie for the odd jobs she did in college. She was our inspiration—she spotted a niche in the market."

"Through absolutely no fault of my own, this included dinosaur dusting at the Museum of Natural History and armpit sniffing for deodorant efficiency studies."

"People really do that?"

"And this from a man who delivers babies?" I ask.

"They do a whole host of odd things," Charlie adds. "Which is exactly the point. Including the time we both worked the help line for the baby formula company."

"All those sleep-deprived, neurotic parents in need of a friendly, reassuring voice in the wee hours of the morning," I tell Luke. "It suddenly struck me, one sleep-deprived night. Who knew there were such strange jobs out there? And how did people find out about them?"

"Well, where did *you* find out about them? I've got to say, the armpit sniffing is peculiar."

"For me, it was usually luck—I'd see an ad in my local grocery store, or a friend would pass on the information. But then, we thought, what if we launched an agency that encompassed all these odd jobs? With Charlie's PR and drag act experience, and mine with placing people in the right jobs, plus my business degree, it would be the perfect solution." I shut up as I realize that I'm getting carried away. "Well, there's nothing wrong with loving one's job, is there?"

"Not at all. It's good to love something you spend a good portion of your daily life doing."

"Tell me," Charlie says. "This is something I've thought about before. Doesn't it put you off sex, looking at vaginas all day?"

"Charlie." Honestly, does he live to embarrass me? Before Luke can answer, Charlie's cell phone saves us.

"Ohmigod," Charlie says as he checks the caller ID. "It's

him. It's Lewis. What shall I say? Oh, never mind, I'll think of something," he says. "See you both later." And then, "Sweetie, I was just about to call you back," as he wanders off.

"I like him." Luke's eyes crinkle.

"Well, I make a point of acquiring only likeable friends."

"That's good. What about me? Am I likeable?"

"I haven't decided yet if you're likeable or certifiable," I say, laughing as I deflect his question, because I like him too much.

"And just for the record. I don't, as it happens," Luke tells me.

"Sorry?"

"Get bored. Looking at vaginas."

"I'm so glad you shared that with me." I can't decide whether to laugh or blush, so I laugh to cover the blush.

"I'm so glad our paths crossed again."

"Yes. You said."

"So I was wondering—" He pauses.

Ohmygod. He's going to ask me out.

"Yes?"

I definitely think he's going to at least ask for my telephone number.

And then he does it again. He teases me, he cranks up the tension (like I need more tension at this point) and switches gears.

"What are your thoughts about marriage?"

Well, that's one I wasn't expecting. Is he asking my intentions? Or am I about to get the let's-just-have-some-fun-with-no-commitment speech, because I've heard it before.

"Um—" I begin, but before I can worry about what, exactly, is going to tumble out of my mouth, Charlie comes dashing across the bar again.

"I know this is going to sound trite and vacuous, but I don't mean it in a trite, vacuous way, but you know that line 'Is there a doctor in the house?' Well, they need a doctor in the ballroom."

"What's happened?" Luke says, all business, as he strides toward the entrance and we follow.

"It's Rosie's cousin Elaine," Charlie says. "She thinks she's going into early labor."

"Oh, God." I don't like Elaine much, but I'd never wish any harm to her. "She's only twenty weeks' pregnant."

"I'll just collect my bag from the concierge desk," Luke says. "Make sure someone's called an ambulance."

11

The Best-Laid Plans

Rosie's Confession:

Apparently, about a hundred people per year choke to death on ballpoint pens. I mean, how do they do it?

I mention this because it's pretty depressing to think that I have more chance of, say, expiring through pen misuse than getting laid . . .

"I'll go back to our table and wait," Charlie tells me as we reach the main ballroom. "I'm not really one for, you know, blood and gore," he shudders dramatically, and I shudder too, because neither am I, but am hoping this won't be a blood or gore situation. Poor, poor Elaine!

"Good plan," I say. "They don't want extra sightseers clogging up the airspace. I'll come and let you know as soon as I have some news." Hopefully good news . . .

As I get closer, I can see that Elaine is lying on the plush carpet at the front of the room, with a jacket under her head for support.

She looks so very small and so very vulnerable. I mean, she is small, generally, but she seems even tinier than usual.

People—fortunately, all three hundred of them—have remained quietly in their seats, and the hum of low, concerned voices obviously means that they all know what is going on.

A worried Auntie Pat and Uncle Bill are also with Elaine, as is Harry, and I can't help but wonder if he is actually the father of the baby. Although Elaine is still being very secretive on that score. I hope fervently that he isn't, because all children deserve a father who is faithful and not trying to pick up the cousin of his child's mother, don't they?

Also in attendance are Ned, in his capacity as a doctor, and Flora. She is a rock of calm stability.

And at least there is another obstetrician in the room. My obstetrician, Luke. Thank goodness he is here, because he can take over from poor Ned.

"Everything's going to be fine," Ned tells Elaine. "The ambulance will be here in a minute, and we'll soon have you safely in the hospital."

"Oh, thank you, Ned," I hear Elaine tell him in a small voice. "It's such a *relief* that you were on *hand*. Flora, you're so *lucky* to be marrying a *doctor*."

"You're in the best hands," Flora tells her. "The main thing is not to panic, for the sake of the baby."

"I hope you don't *mind* me hijacking the *groom*," Elaine says as Ned feels her stomach over the top of her thin dress. "It's just that I *know* Ned. I just feel *better* in the care of someone I *know* and *trust*. Especially in a white, impersonal hospital. I hate hospitals . . ." she trails off.

But that's entirely normal, isn't it? I mean, if I were in need of immediate medical attention, much better to get it from someone I actually know, someone who is really and truly invested in my well-being.

"It's fine," Flora says reassuringly. "Ned's first and foremost responsibility is to his patients."

"How's she doing?" Luke asks as he arrives and kneels down next to Elaine, his medical bag in hand. Oh, but he's so cool, so calm, so collected . . .

"A little worried, a little scared, but she looks in good shape," Ned says jovially. And then, "Thanks for the help, my friend, but Elaine's had a shock and wants me to attend her."

"I understand perfectly," Luke says, giving her a killing, yet reassuring, smile. "It's okay, Elaine. I'm Luke Benton, also an obstetrician. Ned and I work together, but if you're more comfortable with Ned taking care of business, that's fine."

"I can't *tell* you how *grateful* I am," Elaine says, her little-girl face stricken with worry as she fastens her eyes on Luke, and I mentally kick myself for having been such a bitch to her in the past.

I feel awful for every bad thing I've ever said about her.

Not that she hasn't deserved it on occasion, but the reality that she might lose her baby is frightening.

"I can't feel any contractions," Ned tells Luke, keeping his tone cheerful as he removes his stethoscope and unwraps the bandage from her arm. "Blood pressure and temperature are perfectly normal."

"It's probably just a very bad case of indigestion." Poor Elaine is pitiful. "And the dizziness seems to have settled a bit."

"And all the excitement of the party," Luke tells her, smiling his charming smile.

"She's been suffering from terrible heartburn," Auntie Pat says. "And morning sickness."

"Both good signs," Luke says. "But one can never be too careful in these circumstances. I'm sure it's nothing, but it won't hurt to make doubly sure by taking a trip to the hospital."

"Thank you, Luke," Elaine tells him, putting her hand on

his arm and squeezing it. Oh, but Luke really is a hero! "And you, Ned. I'll *never* forget your kindness. I just feel so *bad* about ruining your party, Flora. Will you ever forgive me?"

"Think no more about it," Flora says cheerfully. "Just you concentrate on feeling better, dear girl."

And then the ambulance team arrives with a stretcher, and the paramedics, along with Ned and Luke, carefully help Elaine onto it.

"Right, off we go," Ned says cheerfully.

"Oh, I can't drag you away from your own party," Elaine declares dramatically. "I think Luke can manage," she adds with a winsome smile.

And in that moment I really think that her pregnancy has softened her. How lovely that she, at this worrying time, can think about other people!

"Yes, Ned, you must stay," Luke stresses. "I know Elaine is family—or soon to be family, but no need for both of us to go haring off in the ambulance. What about your partner?" he asks Elaine. "The baby's father?"

"Oh, Harry's not the father." Elaine's voice is all pathos. "Harry's just a—an old friend, *supporting* me in my time of *need*," she says, as tears spring to her eyes. "The—the baby's father didn't want to know. When I told him my news, he *deserted* us both."

God, I know I haven't gotten on well with her in the past, and I know she doesn't have to worry about money and such, but it must be a really daunting prospect—having to go through pregnancy alone. Coping with a baby on your own . . .

"I'm sorry," Luke tells her, his handsome face sympathetic yet professional.

"Don't worry about a thing, darling," Auntie Pat tells her. "Mummy's coming with you, too, and Daddy can follow in the car."

"Do you want me to come?" I ask. I feel I ought to do something to help.

"You're such a *sweetie*," Elaine tells me in her little-girl voice as she wipes away a tear. "But the *best* thing you can do for me is *to stay here* and *enjoy yourself*. Harry will look after you," she adds with a small smile. "Luke will take care of me."

How thoughtful of her! That she could wish me well at this difficult time. The comment about Harry looking after me was a bit thoughtless of her, though, but then she's got other things on her mind right now. Pregnancy really seems to be changing her.

And as they leave, I try to make eye contact with Luke.

"Oh, I feel a bit sick," Elaine says, which means that Luke's eyes are firmly fastened on her. I don't even figure on his radar anymore. Which is just as it should be, I tell myself. His total concentration on his patient is so dedicated and doctorly.

But, and I know it's a bit selfish of me, in light of everything that's going on, I'd hoped for just a last few words with Luke. Or more . . .

I can't help it. I immediately slip into daydream mode . . .

Picture this: I am pregnant, abandoned, alone.

Walking along Camden Lock, a hit-and-snatch thief has just grabbed my handbag, which contains only maxed-out credit cards and will do him no good anyway. But because I don't want to harm my baby I let him take it, but unfortunately, the shock sets in and so does labor, and I fall to the floor in pain.

Dr. Love, who just happens to be passing, has seen the whole thing (obviously, he's been watching me because pregnancy has given me a fragile, delicate bloom, but he doesn't know yet that my partner has deserted me, and Luke is kicking himself for not finding me nine months earlier) and comes running to the rescue, medical bag in hand.

As he takes my blood pressure (off the scale, due to my madly beating heart after the thief episode and Dr. Luke being so damned attractive), he looks straight into my eyes.

"Sweet Mystery of Life, at Last I've Found You," is once again playing in the background.

And as I am transported to the hospital, Dr. Love holds my hand in the ambulance. I tell him my tale of woe, and he is impressed by my backbone, my determination to give my child as normal a life as possible.

Dr. Love—I mean, Dr. Luke—and I fall in love between contractions.

And when I am released, Dr. Luke is awaiting me with his car, a huge bouquet of flowers, a magnum of champagne, and a baby seat. . . .

And as we drive off into the sunset to live happily ever after, Harry says, "Well, that was quite a drama. How about we slip away to a nice, quiet bar and get a drink? Or a bottle of something sexy that slides down the throat? We could—see how things go from there."

It was a crap daydream, anyway.

"Oh, but you're smooth."

"Thank you," he beams, taking it as a compliment.

"I can't believe you've got such a nerve," I say, my eyes on the back of Luke's head as he progresses across the room. How callous is Harry, in view of Elaine's predicament?

"You can't blame a bloke for trying. Faint heart never did win fair maid," he says smoothly. "How am I doing? Don't you think it's time we let bygones be bygones?"

I look up into his handsome face, and he's so appealingly rueful. And just for a moment, I'm tempted to do something rash.

"It's seven years, Rosie, and all I'm asking for is a second chance."

He is very enticing. And cute, and endearing. And it's

Valentine's Day . . . maybe I should take him up on his offer, take him home with me, have wild, casual sex with him and then ruthlessly dump him.

But, and this is just a personal-to-me thing, I've just never been one for casual sex. I tried it. Twice. And it just left me cold. I know it's silly in this day and age, but I need to feel invested in a bloke, to at least trust him, before I'll hop into bed with him. Harry I do not trust as far as I could throw him.

And after the day I've had with the garden gnomes and just missing my chance with another tempting, cute, endearing man, and Elaine's worrying exit from the party, I'm not feeling at my best.

"Harry, I'm sure you mean every word," I say, thinking that he probably doesn't. And besides, I'm not sure I'll ever rid myself of the image of him and Elaine at my twenty-first. "Thanks. But no thanks."

"It's just a drink," he says persuasively. "Go on—you know you want to," he says, grinning his charming grin.

Honestly, since when did *no* mean *maybe*?

"Is everything alright, Rosie?" It's Jonathan.

I cannot turn around without bumping into handsome exes today.

"Everything's fine." Why can't they both just leave me alone?

"Only I just wanted to make sure that you were alright. It must have been a scare for you," he adds, and I so don't want to be here making polite conversation with him.

"Harry, meet Jonathan." I'm just too exasperated to bother. "You have a lot in common. Me," I add over my shoulder as I leave the scene.

Uncle Bill takes the stage, and his voice booms over the loudspeaker system. "Everything's under control," he tells the room. "My daughter, Elaine, isn't feeling quite herself, and because she's pregnant, we thought it best she gets checked at the hospital.

"But I know she wouldn't want that to stop your enjoyment of the evening, and I'd like you all to continue to have a good time. Please raise your glasses to the bride and groom-to-be."

I'd better go check on my mother, I suppose.

A half-hour later, as Auntie Lizzy and I settle Mum and Gran into the limousine Auntie Lizzy insisted on calling for them, I am still worrying about the Elaine situation. I am not the only one, because Mum, as usual, is worrying enough for the whole of London.

"You'll call?" Mum demands. "You'll check with the hospital as soon as there's news?"

"Yes, Mum."

"Elaine's never been one of my favorite relatives, as you know, but a family has to stick together in its time of need," she announces rather dramatically.

"I know, Mum," I say again.

"And you'll call again when you get home? Just so I know you're safe?"

"Give the girl a break, Sandra," Gran tells her. "She might get lucky and find some nice hunk to go home with," Gran adds, which is not helpful.

"Mother, Rosie's not like—"

"Sex is good for the soul. And for bad nerves," Gran cackles as I close the car door. "You should try it sometime. In fact, I might give Sid a call when we get home. Or possibly Alf—I can't make up me mind."

Mum really needn't bother worrying about me getting lucky. She has plenty to worry about with Granny Elsie. And Elaine, of course . . .

As I make my way back to my table, I don't feel much like being cheerful. How can we have a good time, knowing that poor Elaine is in the hospital? But for Ned and Flora's sake Elaine didn't want the party ruined, so it's only right that we at least try to follow her wishes, isn't it?

"Is she okay?" Jess asks me anxiously as I slide into my seat.

So I repeat the sequence of events but omit the part about Luke and me in the bar.

"Oh, it's so awful, awful," Jess says, putting her hand over her mouth.

"She's fine, really," I say. "At least, the doctor thought it was just indigestion. Elaine thinks it's indigestion, too, so that's a good sign, isn't it?" I am trying for upbeat.

"The only thing awful here, I'm thinking, is Elaine's strange desire to be the center of attention at all times," Carmen says, her voice hard and unsympathetic, which jolts us all into silence. "I'm hoping I'm wrong, but if what I'm thinking is true, then I may have to kill her for doing this to Flora."

No. Surely not even Elaine would do something like that? I mean, she's been a pain in the past, but surely she wouldn't deliberately set out to wreck the party?

"Don't you think you're taking this a bit personally?" Paul asks her.

"No." Carmen gives him a glare that would shatter stone. And then does a complete hundred-and-eighty-degree turn as she smiles and switches on the charm. "You just don't know her very well, darling."

"But maybe it's, like, real," Jess says. "And if she did lose her baby, and we didn't believe her, then that would make us heartless. Heartless."

"Um, I know Elaine's pulled some horrible stunts in the past," I say, "but even she wouldn't do something so underhanded and—"

"You two are so nice sometimes, I worry about you," Carmen tells us. "Aster should take you on a nice minibreak," she adds to Jess, and I know that this conversation isn't really about Elaine.

"But she does have a point," Philip points out. "And at this time, we should give Elaine the benefit of the doubt. God would give her the benefit of the doubt. Although I wouldn't put it past her to— No, sorry people. Scrub that."

"You are too nice sometimes, too," Carmen tells him, patting his hand. "But I guess it comes with the territory. Phil, if you could go on a nice, calming minibreak, where would you choose?"

"Don't you think you're jumping to an overreactive conclusion?" Paul asks, totally missing the minibreak hint. "Because you do have a tendency to overreact before you get all the facts." He obviously likes to live dangerously.

"You just don't know Elaine," Carmen tells him with a dangerous glint in her eye. "But darling, how can you base a judgement on three seconds of talking to the woman?" she asks. Her voice is so reasonable and understanding that I'm starting to worry. "You only met her for the first time, tonight, whereas we," she waves an arm around, "have known her for years, and it's not the first time she's rained on someone else's parade."

"Yes, but what happened?" Charlie says impatiently. "I had to put off a highly important telephone call for this, I'll have you know."

"Well, let's see," Carmen says. "Not that I think that your cousin *is* a lying, conniving cow who hates not to be the center of everyone's attention," she says. "Who figures out a way to grab it back when she's not. But as it happens, the minute the room fell silent because Ned was about to make his speech about how lovely and wonderful Flora is, and how lucky he is that she's agreed to be his wife, Elaine's contractions started. Which caused a panic, and thank God Ned didn't have to go to the hospital with her, which is probably what Elaine wanted, but didn't get," she finishes with a flourish.

"You've got to admit it does sound a bit far-fetched," I say. I think Carmen's taking this a bit too personally, too.

"Well, even if it is true—and I'm not saying that it is true—it didn't work," Charlie jumps in. "Thanks to Rosie's utterly gorgeous doctor friend, the groom is firmly back in place having fun with his bride-to-be."

I do wish Charlie hadn't mentioned Luke.

"What gorgeous doctor friend?" is Carmen's immediate, unsurprising response.

"Well, I think you're being a bit harsh on her," Jess starts, then stops as she catches up with us. "Is it the same one as before? The one you snogged at Christmas?"

"He's not *my* gorgeous doctor friend." I avoid giving a straight answer. I can't quite lie to them, so will instead give the impression by careful choice of words. "I'm glad he was able to take over, though. It would have been a damp party without the groom," I add, trying to change the subject.

"You were getting on like a house on fire for two people who've only just met." Charlie rides roughshod over my attempt. "You should have been there," he adds to Carmen, who hates to miss out on anything. "Gorgeous, fascinating, rich—and totally into our Rosie. My fuck, I nearly self-combusted from the heat and smoldering looks flying in that bar."

"Charlie's love gin-and-tonic strikes again," I say to my friends. "It was just a casual chat, that's all. I'll probably never see him again—which is fine," I add, and then change the subject again. "So what's happening with the wonderful Lewis?" I ask Charlie, who immediately takes the bait and launches into a blow-by-blow account of their conversation.

"I know a nice doctor," Jess confides in me just as Charlie is describing Lewis's eyes. "At least, Mummy does. She absolutely swears by Dr. Lockwood, and how nice he is, and what a shame it is that an eligible young man like him doesn't have a nice girlfriend. I think he'd be perfect for you. Perfect."

Great. That's all I need to complicate my life. But it's a sweet thought.

"Thanks—but I don't think—" Actually, I think I'm getting on very well with my nice, organized, man-free life. Apart from the lack of sex . . .

"And he likes feet—he specializes in feet. So on the plus scale, you'd never have to be embarrassed about your shoe size again."

"Well—" Why did Jess think me, doctors and feet, all in the same thought?

"Mummy thinks he's an angel—she won't let anyone else near her bunions."

"Wow, man, was that like dramatic or wot?" Aster has at last decided to grace us, and Jess, with his presence. "I fink I'm going to write a song about your cousin. What do you fink? Move over, will you, Vicar," he says to Philip, who obliges, albeit a bit reluctantly. Aster slides into the seat next to Jess and puts his arms around her.

"I think that's wonderful," she says, gazing into his eyes. At least it's distracted her from the foot doctor.

"Yeah. I'm gonna call it 'Only Wimmin Bleed.' Good title?"

"Actually, old chap," Philip says, rather coldly, "I think you'll find that one's been done before."

An hour later, as soon as is decently possible, after I have spent enough time making the rounds and generally pretending to be happy, bright and unconcerned about anything, after I have fairly successfully avoided Jonathan and Harry and avoided committing to a date with the foot doctor, I make my escape.

My feet hurt from the pinchy shoes.

My head hurts from all the events of the day.

My heart hurts, just a bit, but this is only because it is Valentine's Day, and everyone else seems firmly entrenched in coupledom.

Except for poor Elaine . . .

I want to go home, phone the hospital, put on sweats, watch late-night TV, and eat simple comfort food. Beans on toast comfort food.

And as I wait outside the hotel for the next black cab to pull up, I take off my shoes and feel instantly better.

I feel even more instantly better a few seconds later. Instantly better, but at the same time instantly scared to death, too, when a cab pulls up and out climbs Luke Benton.

12

An Apple a Day . . .

Rosie's Confession:

. . . Keeps the doctor away. Or so they say.
   I may have to give up apples for life . . .

"She's absolutely fine, just a false alarm," is his opening line, and I feel instantly guilty because just for a moment I'd forgotten all about Elaine.

"Um, that's good news."

"Tell me you're not leaving already?" he adds, and my heart jumps into my throat.

Sexily rumpled, he looks almost disappointed, and I want to smooth the tired lines on his face. In fact I want to do more than smooth them, I want to kiss them. Actually, I want to kiss his mouth. More than his mouth. Dangerous thoughts . . .

"Well, I thought I'd have an early night, you know, catch up on some, um, sleep," I trail off, and wish I hadn't thought about bed. Because thinking about bed makes me think about Luke *in* my bed. And I think it's making Luke think about being in my bed, too, judging from the way both of his sardonic eyebrows have just gone up in a very suggestive manner.

"You know, after the, um, busy day I've had . . . and things are quieting down in there . . ." I try to recover the situation. I really want to tell him how glad I am to see him, how grateful I am to him for taking charge of Elaine, and how I've changed my mind about leaving now that he's back.

"Ah, another of those days?" He takes a step closer, and I can barely breathe, because he's just so edible. "I'm desperate to know all about it."

And I'm even more desperate to kiss him.

"Well, um, my feet hurt, and I can't turn around without falling over ex-boyfriends, and garden gnome problems, and I'm hungry—not that I'm a great cook, in fact I'm a terrible cook despite my best efforts, but I can manage beans on toast, and I feel like beans on toast. Plus, I need to check out my bathroom leak," I say, wishing that I had a script. And a non-babbling tongue.

"That's tragic," he says, shaking his head.

"Not for my stomach, it's not. However, it is for my kitchen ceiling," I babble some more, as he takes another step closer.

"You had me on the garden gnomes," he says quietly, and I shudder. I haven't had him at all, but I want him. I'm sure it's written all over my face. "You know, plumbing and delivering babies have strong similarities. I'm pretty handy with a wrench and a U-bend." Oh, but I bet he's handy all around. Such lovely, slim fingers . . .

"So, um, Elaine's really okay?" I squeak inanely as he moves closer still. Yes, I am a coward, changing the subject, because although I want to know what else he's handy at, things are moving too fast, and I can't think straight.

"Absolutely. Total false alarm. She's resting comfortably," he says, then smiles a bit ruefully, which jangles my already jangled nerves. "Although your aunt does seem very—devoted." His eyes crinkle in a smile. "I had to, um, persuade her to leave her daughter in peace for the night."

"That's a very diplomatic way of putting it." I look up at him, because he's standing right in front of me.

We lapse into silence, and I can't think of a thing to say, because all I can think about is the last time we stood by a waiting cab.

"So, here we are again," Luke says quietly.

"Yes. You came back."

"Well, I thought I'd, you know, catch the last of the revelry. Either that or stay at the hospital. And they don't need me for now. Just thought, with it being Valentine's Day—"

"Yes?"

"That I might at least get—"

The word "laid" springs instantly to mind.

"Fed. Going home alone to an empty house and a microwaved dinner for one just wasn't tempting."

Interesting snippet of information.

"You're in luck if you want dessert. The buffet's been cleared away, but I think there's still cheesecake." I want to take him home and feed him. I want to take him home and do more than feed him . . .

"Tell me something."

"What?" I hold my breath.

"Why do you wear shoes that are too small?"

"Because." God. I can't be bothered to lie. "Because I have large feet. And wide feet. I have problems getting shoes to fit."

"They don't look huge to me," he says, looking down at my feet, then back up into my eyes.

"Tell that to my blisters." My voice is breathy, expectant, and I can't help it.

"Well, I think your blisters need medical attention."

"You do?" Instant images of Luke sucking my toes spring to mind. Not that I'm a foot kind of person. Actually, I *am* a foot kind of person. I have very ticklish feet. Sensitive feet . . .

"Yes. I think they need—"

"What?" What do they need? *Spit it out*, I want to scream, but I don't, because screaming requires additional energy, and I can barely move.

"—a meal," he says, so close to me now that every single cell in my body is on red alert. "Everything feels better when you're—sated. Medically proven fact."

"Really?" I ask, mesmerized by him.

"No, I made it up because I thought we could, well, go and get something to eat. Together. Beans on toast," he adds, and I laugh, but it's a nervous laugh. I'm anticipatory, edgy, and incredibly aware of him. Aware of the things that we're saying, yet not saying.

"I haven't got all night," the cab driver says, pushing his head out of the window. "Make up yer minds, will yer?"

And Luke's so close now that I can almost feel his body heat, and I want to touch him.

"There's a great café in Victoria Station. It does bacon, eggs, beans on toast . . . we could meander down there and . . ." He trails off.

And then I realize something. He's just as nervous as I am. At least I think he is. This thought is enormously empowering.

Oh. God.

I really shouldn't do this. I should run, screaming, for the sanctuary of my nice, safe, organized little house. To my nice, safe, organized life.

But oddly, barely knowing him, I trust him.

"Or we could go back to my place," I say. And I can't be-

lieve I just said that. What must he think? Actually, he's probably thinking that I've just invited him to have his way with
me. He'd be right. "Um, I make a mean plate of beans on
toast," I tell him, trying to keep my voice steady and failing
miserably.

"Sounds . . . delicious," he says, lowering his head, pausing,
as if asking permission. "What's for dessert?"

I move my face closer.

"Is he getting in the cab with you, or wot?" the cab driver
pushes, but I barely notice.

"Well—"

"Yes," I say.

And then he kisses me.

Love is a many splendored thing, I sing to the bathroom tiles
the next day, as I scrub between them with an old toothbrush. And then I giggle like a mad fool when I catch sight of
myself in the mirror.

My skin is flushed, my eyes are bright, and my hair is
glossy and full. It must be true what they say about women
in love having that "glow," because I've definitely got a glow.

I'm in love, I'm in love. With a Wonderful Man.

God. Now I'm channeling Mitzi Gaynor and *South Pacific*.
How corny can I get?

More so, it seems . . . as corny as Kansas in April, I want to
run up and down the stairs, I want to spin around in circles, I
want to shout about my Some Enchanted Evening from the
Highest Hills and to the Golden Daffodils . . .

Yes, I know I sound hackneyed and trite, but I can't get all
those old, romantic songs out of my head. I blame my grandmother for making me watch all those musicals with her. She
was right about the sex, though . . .

I squirt more cleaning spray between the tiles as I try to

focus. My bathroom is actually spotless, but it's a week since I did this, so it won't hurt to do it again, and besides . . . I just can't settle.

Not after last night.

Last night . . .

So far this morning I have (a) vacuumed the already spotless carpets, (b) dusted the dust-free surfaces, (c) cleaned the immaculate kitchen floor, and (d) replayed last night a gazillion times in my head.

Last night . . .

God, I blush even thinking about the things we did.

Oh, but he was so lovely, and sexy, and vulnerable, and tender, and passionate and just so . . . *everything*.

And then, when I first woke up this morning, and he was gone, I immediately jumped to the conclusion that it was just for the night. I mean, he didn't make any promises to me, or anything, but when I found myself alone in bed I thought that maybe he regretted it.

Or that maybe I was a disappointment.

Not that I'm exactly inexperienced in the sex department, but I bet that the kinds of women he's usually attracted to are far more—inventive. God, I should have borrowed that sex book Jess was nattering on about.

But then I found his note. I've read it a million times already, but I just can't help reading it again and again. Yes, pathetic of me. This is what it says:

Baby Jackson has decided that 4 A.M. is a very good time to enter the world.

I must have been *very* soundly asleep indeed not to hear his beeper. But then, we did have a very hectic time, and we didn't get any actual sleep until around 2 A.M. My face is hot just thinking about it.

A tragedy, because I had plans for breakfast in bed (although your grill might be too sophisticated for my toast-making skills).

Oh, but that toast comment makes me smile. He remembers our conversation in December. Every little mundane bit, just like me!

Back to the point, because I'm wandering away from it—
I had a good time last night. And no, I don't just mean what you think I mean, lovely though it was.
I want very much to see you again, but my life is pretty complicated. We should have talked last night.
It's your call. But I hope you do call.

Luke

PS I'm free tonight.

He wants to see me again! Tonight!

So, of course, I'm going. I know I like my routine, and that I've got my admin and bills to do, but I don't care. In fact, I wanted to call him as soon as I found his note at six this morning, but didn't, on account of him probably still delivering Baby Jackson.

Have to admit that I'm just a bit worried about his complicated life. . . .

I wonder how long I should leave it before I call him? I mean, it's only eleven in the morning. Is Baby Jackson with us yet? Would I seem too eager, too keen, if I call now?

Wonder what he means about his life being complicated?

God. I was so mean to poor Charlie yesterday when he was obsessing about Lewis, and now I'm doing it myself.

Carmen, I know, has a game plan. At least she used to, in

the old days, before she met Paul. Apparently, one should always leave it for two or three days before calling the object
of one's desire, no matter what the temptation. Rather like
Granny Elsie's advice about keeping them keen, now I come
to think about it.

And then I remember my advice to Charlie—not to play
games. I'm definitely not going to tread that slippery slope
toward misunderstanding and dishonesty.

I pick up the receiver of my telephone and stop, placing it
back on its stand. I'll just wait a bit longer . . .

Complications. What could that mean? Possibly his job? I
mean, he probably works long, odd hours, and I'm sure I read
somewhere that doctors are high up on the list of divorce
rates. Maybe he's divorced? Or what if he has some kind of
life-threatening disease? Or . . .

You know what? I think I worry too much, sometimes. For
once, I'm not going to borrow trouble. This time I'm going to
just think positive thoughts. I mean, what complications
could there be in his life that we can't overcome together?

And I can't help it. I fall instantly into daydream land.

It features me, all gorgeous and demure (but in a sexy kind
of way) in a long, white dress, and Luke, all tall and sexily
rumpled in a morning suit.

No, I am not picturing the wedding. I've bypassed the
whole wedding to the honeymoon. To the hotel room, to be
exact.

My blood is pounding so loudly in my ears that I can't
even hear the background music.

Unable to wait a moment longer, we are tugging at each
other's clothes the minute Luke carries me across the threshold and shoves the door closed with his foot.

Before we can make it to the bed we're all over each other
like a rash. In frustration, because his fingers are shaking so

badly that he can't undo the tiny pearl buttons on the back of my dress, Luke slides his hands under my skirt and pushes it up to my waist, and then he's—Oh. My.

And then the telephone rings.

Oh, what if it's Luke? I think, taking deep breaths to still my beating heart. I pick up, my fingers shaking, my whole body shaking.

"Hello," I say, trying for sexy, but instead my voice comes out as a shaky croak.

"Are you coming down with a cold? Only you sound like you're coming down with a cold," Mum says. "I knew something was wrong when you didn't call."

"No, no, hahaha," I say, convinced that my mother will be able to tell what I've been up to merely from the sound of my voice. "I'm absolutely fine, Mum. Never been better."

"Oh. So you're not ill at all?"

Only a massive dose of desperately in love-itus, I think, but don't tell her this. I cannot believe that I've missed out on this all these years. All I had to do was trust myself, take a risk and leap in with both feet. But then I hadn't met Luke.

All my other encounters were just me practicing for Luke, which is why I always backed out when things got too serious. But I don't tell Mum any of this. I want to keep it to myself for a bit. My Secret Love, just until I get used to the idea of Luke and me being together, and then I'll shout it from the Highest Hills . . .

"Rosie? Are you there?"

"Sorry, Mum, the line went all fuzzy there for a moment," I lie.

"Oh. Only I was wondering why you didn't call me to let me know you'd arrived home safely," she says, building up for a panic. "Especially after you promised. I was going to call you earlier, but you know how I hate to intrude on your life,

I don't want you to think I'm one of those mothers who can't manage on their own, or anything—"

"I was just tired," I jump in again. "I went straight to bed when I got home," I say, which is, actually, the truth. I just didn't go to bed alone.

"Granny Elsie thought you'd got lucky," she sniffs. "But I know you're not the kind of girl who casually picks up a man for the night."

"Nope. Not me," I say, because it's true. Because I'm seeing Luke later, therefore am not a one-night stand. I can't believe this is happening. I wonder what I should wear. Something sexy, yet casual. I wonder where we're going for dinner. Maybe I should just invite him over here and order takeout food?

But then again, if we stay in, one thing will lead to another, and we won't get much talking done. And if we're going to have a proper relationship, then I at least ought to know more about him. His family, his hobbies, his background. What his favorite movie is . . . and his life complications, whatever they may be . . .

"I just thought you might like to know that Elaine's fine. I just called Auntie Pat, and she had a comfortable night—they've just brought her home now."

"I know," I say, instantly guilty, because in my happiness I'd forgotten all about Elaine. How could I be so callous and unfeeling?

"Oh. So I take it you've already called her?"

"No," I say, crossing my fingers. "Um, I spoke to one of the doctors," I tell her, which is the truth, after all.

"Well I've promised that we'll call around to visit her. We *should* visit her, because she's family, and we have to make an effort."

"Right," I say, because Mum has a point. I know that a duty visit is in order, and I can be magnanimous in my happiness.

"So, I thought we should take something. Some flowers, maybe. And some chocolates—some Godiva chocolates, because they're Elaine's favorites."

What Mum actually means is that I should procure them. Although from where is a mystery, since they don't exactly stock Godiva chocolates in my corner shop.

"Right. I'll see what I can do." Pointless telling her that—I'll just pick up whatever is handy.

"So you'll be here in an hour? I thought we could walk up to the house before coming back here for Sunday lunch together."

"Right," I tell her.

An hour will be a bit of a rush, but at least it will while away some of the long hours before tonight.

God, I can't *wait* to see him.

I think I'll call Luke after lunch. That way, he'll have had time to finish delivering Baby Jackson . . .

"How *lovely* of you, you really *shouldn't* have," Elaine gushes at me an hour and a half later as she accepts the bunch of daffodils I picked up from the corner shop. "They're very *nice*," she says. "I'm sure we can find space for them in the *kitchen*. As you see, people are so very *kind*." She sweeps her arm around the living room. It is filled with expensive floral tributes.

The daffodils were all I could find, but it is nearly spring, and daffodils are so cheerful and fecund, with the big, fat trumpets sticking out from the center of the petals.

"They made me think of spring and new birth," I tell her sincerely, so happy am I that even her insults cannot pierce my euphoric glow. If, in fact, she is insulting me. Think it's just (a) my suspicious mind, and (b) previous dealings with Elaine that have made me cynical. In my current euphoric glow I must attempt to let bygones be bygones.

Elaine, pale and elegant in white, is lounging on the chaise longue with a silk blanket draped across her legs. Despite her indisposition, her hair and makeup are immaculate. Everything about her is immaculate. Including her taste.

"Oh, you brought me *Dairy Box*, how *thoughtful* you are," she simpers, placing my chocolates next to the several boxes of Godiva offerings currently inhabiting the coffee table.

"So you're feeling all better?" I ask her. "You gave us all quite a shock yesterday," I add, because in my happiness, I love the world.

"The doctors said that everything's going to be alright," she says rather pitifully. "Although it was touch and go for a while."

Um, that's not what Luke said. He said she was fine, it was just a false alarm. But if Elaine wants to play the part of a heroine in a Victorian melodrama, then let her have it, I think—after all, single motherhood is a scary thing, so a bit of melodrama is only to be expected.

"Well, I expect they told you to take it easy for a few days, then?" I really am trying hard to make polite conversation. I think I'm doing rather well, too. Only another twenty minutes or so and we should be able to escape back to Mum's.

Actually, I might slip upstairs and give Luke a call on my cell phone. I brought his number with me. And his letter. I mean, if I leave it any longer he might think I'm not interested, or playing games or something.

"They want her to take it easy for longer than that," Auntie Pat says. "One just never knows what can go wrong with a pregnancy. Sandra, please don't put your cup down on that table—you'll mark it."

"Oh, sorry. I—" Mum flusters.

"Can you get a coaster for the table, please, Auntie Pat?" I ask sweetly, because although I'm feeling love for the whole human race, it doesn't mean I'm letting Auntie Pat get away with that, and where the hell else is Mum supposed to put her cup down? And then, "Hospitals these days have all the latest electronic equipment, and the best doctors." I smile, thinking of my best doctor. Even Auntie Pat can't ruin my good mood today.

"The Lindo Wing at St. Mary's is very nice," Elaine says.

No National Health Service for Elaine.

"Only the best for our girl," Auntie Pat adds, smiling benevolently. "And Luke is such a lovely man," she says, and my heart pitter-patters. And I can't help it, I'm beaming at the mere mention of his name.

"He seemed, um, very capable," I say, which is a bit naughty, because I'm thinking of his capability in bed rather than on the ward.

"Yes. A dear, *dear* man," Elaine says, watching me thoughtfully. "He made a point of coming to see me this morning before I left."

"I'm sure he is." I know he is. I smile even more widely, hugging my secret close.

And then my world comes crashing down around me at Elaine's next sentence.

"And his wife is charming, utterly charming," Elaine says.

Wife? Wife? Nonononono.

"Yes, Elaine worked with her on the fund-raiser for the homeless last spring," Auntie Pat says, and my stomach lurches wildly, because this is all wrong.

This must be a mistake. Surely she's talking about a different doctor. Definitely a different doctor.

"I didn't realize that Rowan Smythe-Lawrence was actually married to him before he left, or I would have mentioned the connection to him," Elaine says, her words smashing through my euphoric happiness. "I found out from the nurses. The nurses, of course, all drool madly over him, but he's not interested. Apparently he only has eyes for Rowan. A pity, because I quite fancy taking a shot at him myself. But of course I'd *never* betray another *woman* that way by stealing her *husband*," Elaine adds, full of self-righteousness.

It all falls into place.

Rowan Smythe-Lawrence is the sister of Horrible Boss. I remember this, because Jonathan told me that Sidney's sister arranged that fateful fund-raiser we attended last Christmas.

The fund-raiser, which is where I met Luke. Who was sitting with a beautiful, elegant blond. Ohgodohgodohgod.

A wife definitely qualifies as a complication. . . .

"Devastatingly attractive man though, don't you think, Rosie?"

"What?" I say, as her voice registers from a distance. "Oh, I don't remember," I lie, because despite the fact that the floor is dropping out of my world at a dizzying, sickeningly nauseating speed, I cannot let anyone know what has happened.

"Yes, she's stunning, elegant, rich. Comes from a very good family. She couldn't make Ned and Flora's party yesterday, because she's apparently over in The Hague giving a presentation to the European Parliament, or something."

Oh. Ohfuckohmyfuck. Not only have I betrayed, however unknowingly, another woman, but also she's practically a *saint*. This is too horrible to be true.

"I say, are you alright, Rosemary?" Auntie Pat demands.

"Yes, you are looking a bit green," Elaine says, leaning away from me.

"I think I might have caught Elaine's stomach bug," I croak, putting a hand to my mouth.

"I thought you sounded off color this morning when I called you," Mum sniffs.

"Come, come." Auntie Pat practically hustles me out of the cream chair. "You look like you're going to be sick."

And as it finally hits me that I have slept with a married

man, fallen madly and completely in love with a married man, and had the wool pulled ruthlessly over my eyes by a cheating swine of a lying married charmer, I can't help it.

I'm sick all over Auntie Pat's expensive cream carpet.

Another New Year's Resolution

Rosie's Confession:

Yes, I know that it is not New Year, and therefore this resolution is either too early or too late, but as they say: there's no time like the present.

Am going to forget all about Luke Benton and concentrate only on helping friends in their time of need.

"I'm fine," I lie to Mum on Wednesday morning as I force myself to get ready to set off for work.

Yes, I am a coward.

I have been hiding from my friends, and from the world at large, at Mum's house since Sunday. Mum has deflected all calls, told everyone that I had a flu bug because that's what she has decided is wrong with me, passed on all get-better-soon messages, and generally tried to force-feed me chicken soup, but it is time for me to stop wallowing in my well of self-pity and get myself back on track, because wallowing in self-pity is a waste of time and energy.

But so bad was I on Sunday that I barely remember Uncle

Bill driving us the short distance back to Mum's house and Mum hustling me to bed. And all the while, hanging on grimly to my despair, and not being able to cry, because explaining tears would have been impossible.

My head aches, my stomach aches, my heart aches, my limbs feel heavy, and my joints ache, as though they've aged thirty years overnight. Even my skin is painful to the touch. I may never be fine again, but I *cannot* let my disaster with Luke ruin my life.

It was only one night, after all, I remind myself, my head aching even more as I pinch the bridge of my nose to force the tears back into my lachrymal glands. I cannot cry. Not even one tear, because one tear will lead to a lot of tears, and I *refuse* to allow that to happen.

I *will* feel better. And if I'm at work, I'll have less time and less available brain cells to think about him. That's all I need—to get back into my normal routine. It wasn't as if Luke was ever *part* of my normal routine, which is good, which also means that I won't miss him for long, on account of not having all those additional memories. . . .

"Well, I think you should stay home for the rest of the week," Mum frets, wringing her hands, and what she really means is that I should stay home at her house another few days so that she can fuss over me more and make it even harder for me to leave.

"Don't fuss so much, Sandra," Granny Elsie says, patting me on the shoulder.

"At least until your birthday," Mum adds. "It will be lovely to all be together for your birthday."

I had forgotten about my impending twenty-ninth, on Sunday.

"She looks fine to me," Gran says. "And besides, work will be good—keep her mind off of things." Granny Elsie can be very astute sometimes. Although I have not mentioned a word of my disaster with Luke, she keeps giving me these curious, supportive little pats.

I can't even spill the beans and share this with my lovely friends. Much as I love them, the only way to keep a secret, which it must be, is by not telling a soul.

Charlie is a gossip hound. He just can't help himself. He has the best of intentions, but he always manages to let things slip out of his mouth, and before you know it, half of the population of London knows all about it, too.

Jess, dear girl, has a very expressive face and tells Aster everything. And let's face it, if Aster finds out, he'll probably write a song entitled "Achy Breaky Heart" or "Can't Help Loving That Man of Mine," or similar, featuring a woman who has been deceived by a married lover, and then dedicate it to me, so everyone knows who it's about.

And Carmen has very strong feelings about cheating men—she wouldn't mean to, but she wouldn't be able to hide her feelings or her strong views from Rowan Smythe-Lawrence. Or from Luke.

You see, despite my misery, I have thought about this very carefully. I may be a shriveled-up prune inside, but I cannot bear the thought of causing pain to Rowan Smythe-Lawrence.

I have to face the fact that my friends may all, highly probably, meet her. I also have to face the issue that I will probably meet her myself.

It stands to reason that if Luke is one of Ned's best friends, and he came to the engagement party, then the odds are extremely high that Luke and Rowan have also been invited to the wedding. Which means that I can't breathe a word to Flora, either, on account of it upsetting her and casting a black cloud on her special day.

And as for me having to see Luke again, I will face that particular problem when I come to it . . .

But I'm feeling much stronger, I really am. After two days of being coddled and fussed over, I have moved on from hurt and disbelief and bewildered pain to anger. To cold fury. Aimed at Luke, but mainly at myself for doing something so stupid and out of character.

Never again.

"I could call Charlie for you again and tell him you're taking just one more day, if you like," Mum says hopefully. "I'm sure he can manage. You do look peaky. Doesn't she look peaky, Mother?" she asks Granny Elsie.

"Nothing a bit of fresh air won't sort out," Gran says. "What do you think of this?" she asks me kindly, holding up a red Stetson with a large black feather tucked into one side. "Alf thinks red is the true me, on account of me bein' excitin'." She winks at me and places the red concoction atop her blue rinse.

"It's gorgeous," I smile, because the sight is just so—so incongruous.

"That's better," Gran tells me, smiling back. "You have a good day at work—don't go worryin' about things you shouldn't be worryin' about," she adds as she heads to the stairs, the red hat bobbing as she sways in what she considers true cowboy style. "I got to get ready for me line dance practice with Alf—we're doing an exhibition next week and I want to be perfect."

"What happened to Sid?" I ask.

"I don't want to seem too keen," Gran calls as she climbs the stairs. "I haven't decided which one of 'em's the most comfy fit yet. I'm keeping me options open, so I'm seein' both of 'em." Wise woman, my Gran.

"Honestly, your Gran will insist on making an exhibition of herself," Mum says. "That episode with Sid has turned her head. She thinks she's a sex siren."

"Thanks for everything, Mum," I tell her, kissing her cheek.

She's been great, she really has. And despite all her fussing, it was good to be home with her for a few days.

"At least—at least come back here tonight so that I won't worry about you having a relapse," she says, handing me a woolen hat. "And put this on. You lose most of your body heat through your head, you know. It's a medically proven fact."

Medically proven fact inevitably leads me back to Luke, and I take the yellow-and-orange wooly hat, in which I wouldn't usually be seen dead, and pull it on my head. Bad hat sense must run in the family.

But right now I don't care. I look terrible, anyway, and the hat will only distract people from looking at my washed-out face and old, comfy black sneakers. They make my feet look like bargepoles, but I couldn't wear my good sneakers, on account of them being covered in sick. Ruined. I had to throw them away . . .

What a fool I was to take such a risk, I think, as I set off down the road, pulling the collar of my quilted, heavily padded coat around me as the cold chill of the February air joins forces with the freeze that has taken hold of my body. The coat adds about twenty pounds and twenty years to me, but I don't care about that, either, because it's the warmest thing I have at Mum's house. I just need to feel warm again.

What an idiot I was to be taken in by a smooth, charming, lying, deceitful operator. I mean, I was such an easy conquest. I practically threw myself at him. *How he must have laughed at the effortlessness with which he got me into bed,* I think, as I push money into the ticket machine. All that acting endearing and nervous. What a farce.

And as for his bloody note, well, I ripped it to shreds and flushed it down the toilet, where it belongs. Yes, I've washed that man right outta my hair, as the song goes, and I think of another of Gran's favorite old-time music hall songs . . . the one where the cheating, lying man can't get away to marry his sweetheart, because his wife won't let him.

Honestly, the cheek of Luke Benton. Wants to see me again—Indeed! Has a complicated life that he needs to talk to me about. *That's such a good line*, I think, scowling at the poor, innocent London Underground employee as I feed my ticket through the turnstile and march toward the packed elevator.

I wonder, as I get carried along by the flow of people into an even more tightly packed tube, how he would have broached the subject of, you know, that little complication of being married.

"My wife doesn't understand me," is, I believe, the favored line. "We're just staying together for the sake of the children," is always a handy favorite, too.

Oh. My. God. It never even occurred to me until right this moment that he might have kids.

The train lurches, and my stomach lurches along with it, and I fall into nightmare mode, because this episode in my life has cured me of daydreams.

Picture this: Luke and I are sharing an illicit weekend of passion at my house. Illicit because he still hasn't gotten around to telling me about his wedding certificate and off-spring. His cover for his wife: He's attending a medical conference in Geneva, while she is home looking after three golden-haired children. Golden-haired because this is my nightmare and they take after their angelic mother rather than their devilish father.

I have also given them names and ages, because it adds greatly to my misery and anger if I can humanize them. They are Holly, age two, Sam, age four, and Luke Junior, age six.

Rowan, while emptying the pockets of his suits so that she

can take them to the dry cleaner, because she is the kind of woman who takes care of these details, finds a note I wrote to Luke.

My note says, "Darling Luke, I'm hot and willing for our weekend of passion. Don't forget to pick up a giant box of condoms," or something equally obvious, and because I want myself to feel even worse than I already do, it also contains my address.

And just after Luke and I have had wild, rampant sex on the rug in the living room, the doorbell rings. I pull on my bathrobe and open the door, because I'm expecting it to be our food delivery.

But instead of pepperoni pizza, it's Rowan and three sweet little angel faces with despairing, accusing eyes.

From now on, I vow, as I walk up the tube station steps and into Notting Hill Gate, I am going to be the perfect safety zone.

No more risk . . . no more broken hearts.

"Darling, you look terrible," is what Charlie says the moment he sets eyes on me when I push open the door and walk into the main reception area at Odd Jobs, and I'm touched by his sympathy for a few seconds until I realize that he's referring to my apparel rather than my face.

"What on earth are you wearing? Is this some kind of fashion development I know nothing about?"

"I hope you're not still contagious," Shirley, our secretary, says rather dourly as she peers up into my face from her computer screen.

"Nice to see you all, too," I say dryly. I know this is only her way, but am a bit hurt, all the same.

"Only I've just got over a cold and I don't want to catch the flu. You know how long it takes me to recover from these things," she adds. Shirley, who is forty-nine, suffers with her illnesses.

Shirley's colds are always worse than everyone else's. All of her medical problems are worse than everyone else's, because although she is a remarkably organized person, Shirley can be a bit of a hypochondriac at times.

"Yes—we lived through each one with you," Gloria, our receptionist, tells her. "You should eat properly, then you wouldn't get ill so much."

This is one of the dramas that make office life so interesting, I remind myself before I can groan. Shirley, who is always trying to lose twenty pounds, has tried all the diets under the sun, and eating more is not on her agenda.

"God, she's right. I missed the pinched look on your face due to the astonishing headwear," Charlie says. "Good ploy, by the way, for removing attention from the pinched face."

"She just needs a few square meals inside her, that's all," Gloria, unsurprisingly, says again. Good, square meals are something she believes in with conviction.

Gloria is, we guess, at least sixty, based on the fact that she has two children in their forties, but she won't commit herself to actually telling us what her real age is. She's five feet nothing, and one hundred pounds, and her square meals are something she amazes us with on a daily basis.

I've never seen anyone so tiny eat so much. Or someone so remarkably well preserved. If I didn't know better, I would give her fifty-five, max.

"I must introduce you to my mother," I tell her, because Mum has been providing good, square meals along with the chicken soup. Plus, I'm glad to talk about the mundane, rather than get cross-examined about my time off. I'm still nervous that I will spill all if pushed . . .

"Don't you worry, you tell your mum that I'll make sure

you continue the good work," she tells me before picking up the telephone. "Good morning, Odd Jobs, this is Gloria speaking. How may I help you?" she bubbles down the telephone line.

"Are you sure you should even be here? We can manage without you for a couple more days if you need it," Charlie says, peering at me with real concern, and I am almost undone. "You really don't look so hot."

"Thanks for the concern," I say a bit croakily. "But really, I'm fine."

"No, we can't actually manage without her," Colin, the voice of reason, says in his deadpan voice. "Glad to see you back, by the way," he adds to me, and then back to Charlie, "not unless you want to sort out Mrs. Hamilton's Brutus, the condom testers, the doggy breath sniffer and the Bingo caller."

"Oh, good," I say, thinking of condoms, which is not good and makes me think of Luke. I push him determinedly out of my mind. "I'm ready for a challenging challenge—bring them on." I begin to unbutton my coat.

"I've got your friend Jess on the line," Gloria tells me, and I head toward my office. "She says it's urgent."

"Oh, good," I say again but don't mean. Not because I don't want to speak to Jess, but because I'm worried that in our first post-Luke conversation, I'll slip up and tell her all about him.

"It's me, it's only me," Jess says after I close my office door and pick up. "How are you feeling? Are you better? We were worried about you."

"I'm good," I tell her. "Just, you know, a touch of the stomach flu. No other reason for me being incommunicado, ha-haha, just one of those fluke bugs you get from time to time," I babble, and then stop. God, I even *sound* guilty.

"That's what I thought," she chirrups in that cheerful way

of hers. And then she renders me speechless. "Anyway, the thing is. The thing is I've taken your advice and given away my trust fund to charity so that I can properly ascertain whether or not Aster loves me or my money. And I need a job so that I can, you know, pay the bills, and eat and everything. Have you got anything that might suit me?"

"Slow down a minute." I can already feel the headache getting worse. "Just run that by me again. You've given away *all* of your trust fund?"

"No, I'm not that stupid," she says, and I sigh with relief. And then she adds, "Only for this half year. I get the second half at the end of June, but Aster doesn't know that."

"But . . ." *How will you survive?* is the question that immediately springs to my lips as I try to remember exactly *when* I told her to give away vast amounts of cash and pauper herself, but before I can ask her, Jess launches into another speech.

"Don't worry. I've paid all the current bills, and everything, and I've stocked the refrigerator and freezer, and I've kept three hundred pounds until I can start earning."

And I'm panicking. Jess, you see, has never had a real job. When I say real job, I mean one that pays money. Not that she's lazy, because since college and her fine arts degree she's always been remarkably busy. She's always either taking interesting courses or knitting or volunteering for all kinds of charitable things. But she's not exactly qualified for anything.

"Why don't you come in so that we can have a chat about what type of thing you might do," I say carefully. Well, I asked for challenging.

"Excellent. Excellent. I'm free now. How about now?"

"How about this afternoon, after I have a chance to review what we have, and what might suit you?" I don't want to dampen her enthusiasm, but really, this one needs some thought.

Looking on the bright side, though, this might just be the key to getting rid of Aster.

"I like the idea of the supermarket job," Jess tells me after lunch, which surprises me, because I didn't think that stacking shelves and working the checkout would be her kind of thing.

"How about the admin job at the museum?" I ask her, because I thought it would be perfect for her. The job is very junior, and involves filing and making tea and coffee, but would at least involve looking at fine paintings on a daily basis.

"No. No." Jess shakes her spiky peroxide head. "The supermarket's perfect. It's in Portobello Road, which means no traveling, and also means interacting with interesting people."

"I'll set up the appointment," I sigh. And then, "Have you told Aster yet?"

"I wanted to present him with a fait accompli," Jess says, her face pinched and miserable. "Do you think he'll come through for me?"

"I think—" I begin, not knowing what I think. Actually, I do. I think Aster will get fed up with the no-money situation. I think Aster will move on pretty quickly when he realizes that it means no more designer clothes and expensive equipment for his band, but I don't want to hurt Jess's feelings.

"You're right, you're right," Jess interrupts. "He'll not be very pleased about it, will he?" She shakes her head, and I try for positivity.

"Sometimes people surprise us," I say, patting her hand, and then my phone rings.

"Rosie, it's me," Philip says, surprising me. "How are you?"

"All better, thanks, Philip," I say, wondering why he's calling me at work.

"You're probably wondering why I'm calling you at work.

Well, I have something a bit, um, delicate to discuss with you. Are you free sometime this week?"

"Absolutely." My mind is racing. What on earth could Philip want to talk about that is delicate? "When were you thinking of?" I ask carefully, because I'm being delicate in view of the fact that Jess (a) knows who I am talking to, and (b) Philip said it was a delicate situation.

"Say hi to Philip for me," Jess says.

"Jess says hi," I tell him.

"Oh. She's there with you?" He sounds a bit panicked. "Actually, I was hoping you'd come to me. I, um, don't want to be seen at Odd Jobs, because Charlie will ask questions and—well, as I said, it's a bit delicate."

"How about later today?" It's been busy today, but my curiosity has been whetted. Plus, busy is good. No time to think about anything. Or anyone. Also, helping others distracts me from my own woes.

"Perfect. Come for afternoon tea? And Rosie—please don't, er, mention this to—you know, anyone."

"No worries," I tell him as I look at Jess.

And when I hang up the phone, it rings again straight away. "Sorry," I say to Jess.

"That's okay," she says, getting to her feet. "You're busy. I'll go. Just let me know about the interview. Soon?"

"I'll fax your resumé this afternoon," I say. "And Jess?" She pauses at the door of my office, her face unhappy and pale. "Call me if you need me. Take care."

"Thanks, see you Friday night at Knit One Purl Jam?"

"Absolutely," I nod. I don't feel much like knitting, but at least it will get me out of the house and back into routine, and won't allow time for brooding. I pick up my phone.

"What gives? I just called your mother and she said you were back at work?" is Carmen's way of greeting me as soon as I say hello. "You spend two days incommunicado, then slope back to work without a word."

"Thank you, Carmen, I feel much better," I say.

"Well, I was worried. I thought you were close to death's door the way your mum was carrying on."

"It was just a bug. A nasty, virulent one," I say, just a bit bleakly, as I think about Luke.

"It's not like you to stay over at your mother's. Was it seeing Jonathan on Saturday night? I thought it might have brought back sad memories, and then you realized that you'd loved him all along and were suffering from grief or something."

Carmen's a bit too astute for comfort, sometimes, but thank God she doesn't know about Luke.

"No, nothing to do with Jonathan at all," I tell her quickly. "Nothing to do with any man, in fact, hahahaha," I say, digging the hole deeper. "Just a simple bug, hahahaha."

"Well, if you're sure," she says, not sounding sure.

"Absolutely," I tell her cheerfully. "How's Paul?" I ask, thereby cunningly changing the subject before she can dig any deeper.

"The picture of domesticity," she says rather sarcastically. "He's taken up some vigorous housework to relieve his stress levels. And because I'm working longer hours at the store, it's not fair expecting me to do ninety percent of the cleaning."

"You've extended your store opening hours?" Carmen, it has to be said, is not the most domestic of goddesses when it comes to housework. She must have an ulterior motive. "What's the ulterior motive?"

"Oh, ye of little faith. I'm hurt," she says, but I can tell by her laugh that she doesn't mean it. "It's part of my campaign to earn more money and add more to the savings account. See—I took your advice. I'm compromising with Paul."

God, I wish I could remember all of this good advice I've been handing out. I should also remember to take it myself!

"A-ha—if you can't beat 'em, join 'em?" I say.

"Exactly."

"Sneaky." I'm impressed.

"Isn't it?" she laughs. "In fact, he's doing the cooking on Sunday evening because I'm keeping the store open until seven. You are still coming, aren't you? Because we're planning on turning it into a surprise birthday dinner party in your honor, which is why we're doing Sunday instead of Saturday, but I know you hate surprises, which is why I'm telling you now. So just remember to act shocked when you come in through the door and we all yell *Surprise*."

I don't mention that I've had enough surprises for one year.

Oh, to be eleven again, when my little heart was full of Barbie, My Little Pony, and ponies, and didn't include faithless, cheating men . . .

Be Careful What You Wish For . . .

Rosie's Confession:

. . . Because I have absolute proof that it can backfire.

When the phone rings at six on Saturday morning, I know, immediately, that it is my mother, because no one else calls me at six in the morning. So it's a bit of a surprise when it is Granny Elsie.

"Happy birthday, Rosie. You'd better come on over and talk some sense into yer mother," is her opening line. "There's a horse in the back garden."

"Um, it's not my actual birthday until tomorrow, Gran," is my automatic response in my still half-asleep state.

"I know, but I thought if I said happy birthday first it would soften the shock of the horse. The one that's in the back garden."

So, of course, instead of braving the Underground I take a cab to Hampstead, and by six forty-five, I am in my mother's back garden with Mum, Granny Elsie and Candy, the chestnut mare.

Candy is perfect. She is beautiful.

I yearn, with all my soul, for her.

But I cannot keep her because I am no longer eleven years old and now know that (a) horses cost a fortune to stable and feed, and (b) I haven't got the time or the money to adequately look after her. Neither, so I thought, does Mum.

"Happy birthday, darling," my mother tells me, clapping her hands with delight. "Surprise."

You can say that again.

"Yes, yes, but she can't stay here, Sandra," Granny Elsie states the obvious. "What were you thinking?"

"Mum, this is sweet of you," I say, flummoxed.

"I've been planning it for weeks."

"And I truly appreciate the sentiment, she's gorgeous. But Gran's right. Candy will have to go back."

"But I've got it all arranged," Mum says. "I thought this was your heart's desire," she tells me, building up for a panic.

"Yes—when I was ten, or eleven," I say gently. "She needs to be stabled, she can't live in the back garden." I try for reason. Let's face it; if the neighbors aren't too keen on Gran's gnomes in the front garden, then they're hardly going to appreciate a horse in the back garden, are they? "And stabling her would cost a fortune."

"I've got it all worked out," Mum sniffs and heads for the French doors that lead to the basement apartment. With a flourish, she opens them into the small living-room area.

It is covered with straw. There is a bale of hay, plus a feed bin and a water trough.

"Mum—" I'm totally flabbergasted. I'm completely floored.

"Good God," Gran says, her eyes as wide as mine. "This is a surprise."

She can say that again. I mean, I'm sure there are council

regulations about who can, you know, live in an actual house. I don't think horses are on the list.

"I, um, know you've been sad since Dad passed away," I begin. "And that's understandable. Um, he was a big part of your life—" Before I can suggest, for the millionth time, that Mum should have a chat with Dr. Morris about her grief, she jumps straight in.

"Are you suggesting that I'm going mad?" she asks *me* for the millionth time, building up to a crescendo, and I mentally curse myself for not handling this well.

"No, it's just—"

"Because I'm not. I've got all my marbles." She leaps right back into her diatribe, tapping a finger against her temple. "There's absolutely nothing wrong with me, I just wanted to give you a special birthday present, and with me having the space in the basement, and the Heath being so handy for riding, you wouldn't have to pay to ride someone else's horse around Hyde Park twice a week, because you could ride on the Heath instead," she finishes with a flourish.

What she doesn't add is that it would also mean that I'd have to practically move home in order to take care of Candy, even if keeping a horse in the basement were a viable, rational thing to do, which it obviously isn't.

"And I thought I was the impetuous, live-by-the-seat-of-her-pants one in this family," Gran says, shaking her head. "I'll just go and pop the kettle on. A nice cup of sweet tea always helps. A nice drop of brandy in it will help us all see reason, too."

"I love Candy. But I'm very worried about how much she cost you," I say quietly to Mum once Gran has gone. "And if we keep her, I'd keep being worried sick about the money you've forked out for her. I'd not be able to sleep at night for it. And I'd help you all I could, but Mum, it would mean I'd have to sell my sweet little house, and I love my sweet little house more than I want a horse. I'd be heartbroken if I had to sell it," I add. I don't mean to be horrible to her, but she has to understand that moving back home is not what I want.

"But I wanted to give you something lovely," Mum protests, her face crumpling. "I just wanted to make you happy. You're all I've got left in the world," she says, and I put my arm around her and lead her into the warmth of the kitchen, where I gently push her into one of the chairs.

"Here." Gran places a cup of brandy with a drop of tea in it in front of her. "Drink this, love."

For a few seconds we all drink our tea-infused brandy, as I grope for the right way to get her to see reason.

"You're right, it was a stupid thing to do. What was I thinking?" Mum says suddenly, bursting into a fresh bout of tears. "I just wanted to, wanted to—"

"No, not stupid, it was a really nice thing to do. But Mum, where *did* you get the money for her?"

"I took out a loan against the house," Mum says, dabbing her eyes with a tissue.

"Neither a borrower nor a lender be," Gran says, which is not helpful. "That's my motto in life."

"This is what we're going to do," I say, placing down my cup. The brandy has helped, but seven in the morning is not a good time to get sloshed. "I'll arrange for Candy to go back to the dealer. We'll probably have to take a reduction in money, but that's alright, I can help with that."

Thinking quickly, if I drop my riding sessions, I could take over what will be left of the loan. I *should* be able to manage it.

"Oh, I'm such a drain on you in my old age," Mum says, rather dramatically, so I head off the new diatribe at the pass.

"And then first thing Monday, we'll go and have a chat with your bank manager—get this business sorted. And then, if you like, while you're not feeling quite yourself, I could, you know, spend more time with you. Come home for a few weekends. We could do more together. Go out a bit. How would that be?"

"Oh, that would be lovely," she says, her eyes brightening. "But only if you really want to. I don't want to be one of those mothers who never let their children go."

"Of course I want to," I tell her. She *is* my mother, it's the least I can do. Maybe I could get her interested in some hobbies, help her meet some more people. "And maybe we could, you know, pay a visit to Dr. Morris togeth—"

"Whatever for, dear?" she asks, smiling at me. "I'm perfectly fine."

Gran shakes her head and sips more brandy.

And so it goes.

So after several hours of complete chaos organizing Candy's temporary stabling, and her return to her original owner, who was more than pissed at me—plus I had to take a sizeable reduction in the refund amount—it was a relief to return to my own little house.

Until I arrive home and discover that the mailman has left me a parcel.

It is from Luke.

It contains my pinchy Jonathan shoes, the ones I left on the sidewalk at Christmas. It also contains this note:

I wasn't sure if you wanted to see these shoes again, but I thought I'd leave that up to you.

I had hoped to deliver them in person, but then I wasn't sure if you wanted to see me again, either.

Take care,

Luke

And I do take care. I very carefully throw the shoes and the note in the trash. And then I very uncarefully burst into tears.

So, all in all it's been a memorable week for one reason or another. And one that I will happily put behind me as I move on to the future, I think as we all sit around Carmen and Paul's dining table for my Sunday-night birthday dinner.

"Are you sure you're alright?" Carmen asks me for the umpteenth time. "Your eyes are red."

"Must be an aftereffect of the flu," I lie, because as we know, I did, in fact, have a very good cry yesterday. I should never cry, because my eyes always swell to the size of saucers.

"This is delicious." I change the subject by taking another bite of the tuna casserole Paul has made. It's actually awful, but it's better than I could cook up, so I'm not complaining.

"Yes, well done, Paul," Philip joins in. "I'd love a bit more, if you don't mind?"

"Me, too." Lewis, Charlie's new squeeze, is adorable. I mean, he could have been all difficult and loud-mouthed and offensive like Charlie's One True Love, but he's totally slotted into our group. I mean, it must be love if he's willing to endure more tuna casserole agony.

"Thank you both for the lie," Paul laughs. "But please don't torture yourselves on my behalf, old chaps. It's atrocious, and I appreciate you all chomping your way through it."

"You haven't tasted *my* cooking." Philip shakes his head. "Now that really is beyond words."

"You'll be happy to know that the dessert and cheese courses came from the supermarket."

That's a relief.

"Um, and thank you for the book on DIY around the

home," I say to Carmen and Paul. "It will be very useful." For
when I call the plumber or electrician, I don't add, because I
have no intention of learning about plumbing or wiring—I
know my limitations, but at least I'll be able to try and understand what the plumber or electrician is talking about,
thanks to the glossary in the back.

"That's what I thought," Paul says. "See, Carmen, I told you
she'd love it."

"Yes, I can see it was a much better choice than the frivo-
lous voucher for a chemical peel that I had in mind." Carmen
tops up our wineglasses. "Come on, drink up. This is a party."

"And this is gorgeous," I tell Jess, pressing the soft, blue angora cardigan that she has made for me to my cheek.

"It's periwinkle blue. I thought it would go beautifully
with your eyes and your French look," she tells me earnestly.
"It's a birthday and thank you gift, all in one. I love working
at the supermarket." She has, however, only worked there for
two days. "Love it," she adds, just a bit unhappily.

Aster hates it. He stormed out yesterday after she told
him about it. And about the lack of trust fund. Not for
good, but he and Asteroid Attack are playing some gigs in
Sheffield as part of their northern tour. None of us wants to
see Jess hurt, but we all secretly hope that this is the end of
him.

"Here's to Rosie, and many more birthdays," Charlie says,
raising his champagne. He's totally in love. And totally relieved that Lewis has fitted in so well.

"To the beautiful birthday girl." Lewis raises his champagne and smiles his sweet smile. "And thank you all for
making me so welcome."

Flora and Ned couldn't make it, because Ned had some
charity function to attend. It was organized ages ago, so he
couldn't back out, but I told Flora that I truly didn't mind if

she went with him. To be honest, I'm a bit relieved, because the thing with Luke is still so fresh, and seeing his best friend might have made me crack. Especially after yesterday . . .

"Thank you, darling," I tell Philip when I open the thoughtful gift voucher he's bought me. I will not think about yesterday's thoughtful gift. It is behind me . . .

"Well, I never know what to buy, so it seems the safest option," he says. "That way, you can get something you really want." He always says this, because he always buys me a gift voucher. He buys them for everyone.

"Perfect," I say. And then, just for his ears only, "How did it go with Grace?"

"She's, er, really nice. Thanks for putting her in touch with me. I think she'll really work out well."

Philip, you see, wants to make a good impression with the powers that be within the church. He needs a female companion to take to a big church function, and being girlfriend-less, he decided to *hire* the perfect girlfriend. What a stroke of genius.

Grace, with her desire for a job not involving sex, was the perfect match. I mean, porn movies count as acting experience, don't they? I did mention this to Philip, but he didn't have a problem with it, and how would the church bigwigs find out unless someone made a point of telling them?

You know what? It makes perfect sense to hire the perfect partner. This reminds me that I will be attending Flora's wedding by myself, which is not attractive. I have eleven weeks to find someone—someone temporary, so that I am not some sad spinster, and yes, I know this is cowardly, but I just don't want to face Luke on my own.

And as my friends all sing "Happy Birthday to You" to me, and as I blow out my candles, I make a wish.

"Be careful what you wish for," Carmen warns me, rather

dryly. "You might get it." I don't tell her that I already have the Candy T-shirt on that particular issue.

As I blow out the last birthday candle, and as my friends cheer and clap, I wish for Mum to feel better, and for a return to my nice, ordered life. And then another thought occurs to me.

"Jess, tell me more about that foot doctor."

"Oh. Oh, are you interested? That's fabulous. Fabulous. Let's see—he has a practice in Harley Street, and he does the feet of famous or rich people, and he has a lovely apartment in Grosvenor Square," Jess tells me. And I get a nasty feeling that I am about to make a huge mistake.

"So what's wrong with him, then?" Because there must be something wrong with him, mustn't there, if he has such a great resumé and no girlfriend. Or maybe he's just not handsome. But handsome is superficial, as I have discovered, and it's not like I want to bear his firstborn or anything. I just want someone nice and kind I can invite to Flora's wedding.

"His wife left him for another man," Jess says, shaking her head. "For the builder, actually, which was a bit of a blow."

Oh, the poor, heartbroken man . . .

"So shall I set something up?"

But think of the dangers. I don't want him to transfer his affection to me on the rebound, and then I have to break his heart all over again, because that would be totally callous of me, wouldn't it?

"Um, let me think about it a bit."

15

Table for Eight

Rosie's Confession:

You know, mosquito repellants don't actually repel mosqui-
toes. They hide the human.
   I wish I could get a spray that would forever hide me
from the attentions of the male sex, because I am giving up
men forever . . .

Let's just say that this was a mistake . . .

Yes, in my ignorance, I decided, with only three weeks to go until Flora's wedding, that I'd give Dr. Foot Fetish a chance. Obviously his name isn't really Dr. Foot Fetish, it's actually Giles Lockwood, but I shall forever remember him as Dr. Foot Fetish. And he sounded perfectly charming (if a little overwhelming) on the telephone, too.

This is what happened . . .

I'm so *excited* to be having afternoon tea at the *Ritz*. His suggestion. And I'm completely impressed, because they have a waiting list of around *six weeks* at the Ritz.

This is a classy joint. Think opulence, splendor, luxury, five star all the way, baby. Just in case I didn't make myself clear enough, I am utterly charmed by the idea, because I've never had tea at the Ritz before.

As the waiter leads me to the table, as I absorb the magnificence of the Palm Court, I am in awe. It is everything I imagined, and more, complete with a huge chandelier and a harpist harping gently in the background.

As soon as I see Giles Lockwood, I am totally shocked, too.

"Rosie, how lovely to meet you in person—you're every bit as beautiful as Lady Etherington promised," he says as he stands and takes my hand.

What a promising start!

He is tall, blond, and while not exactly handsome, he is nice looking. And I'm thinking that the fat lady just sang . . .

And I'm really glad that I made the effort to dress up. I'm wearing a discreet little black number (it's actually Bill Blass, but I got it secondhand from Carmen's store), and a pair of sexy, yet elegant, high-heeled shoes. Uncomfortable ones, obviously, because we all know about my trouble with finding sexy shoes that actually fit my clodhopping feet.

"Hello," I smile and shake his hand. "I'm—" *pleased to meet you too,* I nearly say but don't, because I don't get the chance.

"What are you waiting for, man?" Giles suddenly barks at the waiter. "Come on, chop, chop. Help the lady to be seated." And before I can even register shock at his Mr. Hyde about-face, he beams Dr. Jekyll at me.

"I think this calls for champagne, don't you think?" he asks jovially. And then to the waiter, "Two glasses of champagne, and a full high tea for two. And be quick about it. Honestly," he smiles at me. "What is the world coming to? You just can't get the waitstaff anymore. I tell you, my dear, I've been coming here for years, and the standards have slipped. Which is reflected in the tip I don't leave these days," he adds, glaring at the waiter again.

"Thank you," I say to the poor waiter as I hand him my menu with an embarrassed smile.

"So, Rosie, I understand you own and run an employment agency. That's completely fascinating, and I want you to tell me everything about it, absolutely everything," Giles tells me. "The Ritz should use you to get some better staff, ha, ha."

"Well—" Before I can utter another word, Giles leaps right back in.

"I'm sure dear Lady Etherington's charming daughter told you, but I'm a member of the medical profession. And you're probably wondering why I specialize in feet."

"Um—"

"Tell me, my dear, because I couldn't help but notice that you're wearing shoes that are a tad too small. Why do you girls insist on wearing shoes that are too small?"

"Um—"

"You simply can't do that to your poor feet. My dear Rosie, don't you realize that you're running the risk of corns and bunions? And corns can lead to a nasty ulcer, you know."

"I—" *didn't know that.*

"And that's only the beginning," he tells me earnestly as the waiter brings our high tea and champagne. "About time, too," Dr. Foot Fetish barks at the poor man. "I tell you, the service here could do with a good shake-up." Dr. Foot Fetish shakes his head.

"Actually, I think—" *that was incredibly quick.* We've barely been here five minutes. But I don't get the chance to say that, either, because, of course, Dr. Foot Fetish's mouth is running full steam ahead.

I don't think this is going so well . . .

"Yes, we had to operate on her bunions," he tells me ten minutes later, as I stuff a smoked salmon sandwich into my mouth.

"But do you realize how common is toenail fungus? Nasty business—all thick yellow or brown toenails. A nightmare. You wouldn't believe it, my dear, even, it has to be said, amongst the titled and famous. And you wouldn't believe how many of them don't have a weekly pedicure—"

I grab a cream cheese and chives sandwich as I try to phase out Dr. Foot Fetish.

"—heel fissures—all cracked and bleeding, you just wouldn't believe the state of her feet," he blathers on.

I drink the rest of my champagne.

"Waiter? Waiter! More champagne for the lady."

I fill my mouth with delicious lemon meringue pie and glance discreetly at my watch.

Yes, I am using that old trick again. If I just keep filling my mouth, I won't be able to talk. Not that Giles is exactly expecting me to talk, because the man hasn't stopped since I arrived.

"—my, that was one of the nastiest cases of an ingrown toenail I've ever seen—"

"Thank you," I smile pleadingly at the waiter as he brings me another glass of champagne. I've given up on the food, because who can eat with all this talk of fungus and cracked, bleeding feet?

"You're welcome, ma'am," he tells me politely, with an understanding smile.

"Where's my glass of champagne?" Giles demands. Which is odd, because he's only drunk half of his first glass.

"Sorry, sir—"

"What are you waiting for, man?"

God, I need to get out of here, I think as I make inroads into my champagne. This was a terrible idea, I should have known from the start that this was a terrible idea.

And then it becomes even more terrible.

Luke Benton is seated at a table at the far side of the room. With him are the beautiful blond woman from the Christmas fund-raiser and an older, elegant woman.

"—best remedy for athlete's foot—"

I have to get out of here.

"—bursitis—"

Right now, before he sees me.

"—people just don't trim their toenails properly—"

"Sorry, Giles, I have to leave," I say, abruptly getting to my feet. "Splendid to meet you, lovely tea, thank you so much," I babble. Because, of course, I always seem to babble in the presence of Luke Benton.

Any second now he'll turn his head and he'll *see* me. And although I haven't done anything wrong, because I didn't know about his wife before I slept with him, I am filled with guilt. I feel sick. It's just that I wasn't expecting to see him . . .

"But we've only just met—"

"I've just remembered, um, an important appointment," I babble, jumping to my feet as I grope for an excuse. "With—with my plumber."

"When can I see you again?"

"Good-bye. Thanks again."

My legs are so shaky that I think I need to sit down.

"Ma'am, is everything alright?" our waiter asks me as I reach the entrance. "May I be of assistance? Do you need a cab?"

"Yes, please," I tell him with relief and hand him a twenty-pound note.

"That's not necessary."

"I insist," I tell him gratefully.

*   *   *

Flora is the perfect May Day bride, I think as she's helped out of the car by her dad, as Carmen, Jess and I all walk down the church steps to greet her.

"Are you sure I look alright?" Flora fusses, as Carmen discreetly slides up the skirt of her own dress and pulls a small silver flask out of a pocketlike, elasticated arrangement that she has strapped around one of her calves.

"You are completely fucking breathtaking," Carmen tells Flora. "'Scuse the bad language, Mr. Mayford," she adds to Uncle Greg, who is looking a bit green himself. "Take a swig of this brandy, Flora. It will settle your nerves. What?" she adds to me as I raise quizzical eyebrows.

"I've never seen you more gorgeous," I say to Flora, because it's true. And then to Carmen, "What a nifty idea."

"Well, I made it specially so I could bring the flask yet not have to bother actually carrying the flask, so to speak. In case of emergencies."

"Can I have some emergency brandy, too?" I ask, because I'm also a bag of nerves. But not for the same reasons as Flora.

"Lovely, you're absolutely lovely," Jess sighs, partly in complete wonder and partly in sadness, and we know that she's thinking of her own dashed hopes for a wedding.

Jess's much more meager earnings as a condom tester (yes, testing condoms, because the supermarket job didn't work out) didn't go down very well . . .

Aster, it seems, got over Jess far more quickly than Jess got over him. We know this because he took his new girlfriend, Maureen, to the supermarket where Jess was working, just to rub Jess's nose in it. Good riddance to bad rubbish, I say.

"Here, have some Dutch courage." Carmen, after taking a swig herself, hands the flask to Jess. And then, "How about you, Mr. Mayford?"

"Call me Greg, dear girl," Uncle Greg tells her, gratefully accepting the flask from Jess. "And I don't mind if I do."

"Paul, please stop snapping pictures of the bride, the bride's father and the bridesmaids knocking back brandy," Carmen commands. "It's hardly the material bridal albums are made of."

"I want some reality shots," he protests, and Carmen glares at him. "Look, don't tell me how to do my job, and I won't tell you how to do yours," he says sweetly, but he's gritting his teeth. "I think it's a cozy moment, you all gathering up your courage and nerve to walk down the aisle with Flora. It's sweet."

Actually, he has a point. It's not as if we're knocking back a bottle each, or anything. Paul snaps a photo of Carmen glaring at him and walks into the vestibule.

"Think of the film you're wasting, darling," Carmen tells him sarcastically. "We don't want to waste money, do we?"

"I'll be inside getting ready for the main shots," he says. And then to Flora, "Good luck, Flora. You're gorgeous. Ned is a very lucky man, so no need to be nervous."

Paul and Carmen, I feel, are in for a plate-smashing session later, and I wonder if Carmen is deliberately goading him. You see, Paul, in his desire for a more settled domestic life, has asked Carmen to marry him.

She's accepted, but she wants a long engagement while she makes up her mind about actually following through with a wedding. Secretly, I think she's delighted, but she's keeping him waiting to set the date. I don't know why, because she's crazy about him.

"Spontaneity," she tells me, reading my thoughts. "I want a bit of our old spontaneity back again."

Sex in odd places, and plate smashing. Well, it takes all sorts, I suppose.

"Right, are we all ready?" Uncle Greg asks. "Shouldn't keep

the poor chap waiting too long, Flora, it's pretty nerve-wracking for him, too, if the bride doesn't appear."

Five minutes later, after we've all had a couple more sips of brandy to warm our stomachs, smoothed Flora's dress and veil, and straightened our bouquets, the very slightly tipsy bridal party sets off down the aisle.

Flora's dress is of ivory silk, beaded with tiny pearls. It is formfitting and shows off her lovely, statuesque figure. Neither a frill nor a flounce to be seen; she is the epitome of elegant good taste and glowing prettiness.

As the organ booms, as all eyes descend on us, as she walks the aisle on Uncle Greg's arm, and as Jess, Carmen and I follow her, I thank God that she's so generous of heart that she didn't force us into horrible, disgusting dresses designed to make us pale into frumpy insignificance beside her.

I don't know why some brides feel the need to do that. I mean, I know it's the bride's day, and everything, and she *should* have the best dress and look the loveliest, but really, a disgusting bridesmaid dress is just one of the most unkind, nastiest things ever to foist on someone you call a friend, isn't it?

Instead, we are wearing lovely, pale blue, elegant dresses that echo but don't overshadow the bride's dress. A color and style that all of us agreed were the best combination to suit our differing hair colors and complexions. Jess, post Aster, has adopted honey blond as her new color and has grown out her punky spikes.

Flora didn't ask Elaine to be a bridesmaid. She explained to Elaine that it didn't seem appropriate for a thirty-one-week pregnant woman to act as bridesmaid, and that she would be happy to have her as matron of honor, instead. But Elaine balked at the word *matron* as being too old and frumpy.

So instead, Elaine is sitting on the front pew, on the bride's side of the church. She is also wearing ivory silk, of a style more elaborate than, yet similar to, Flora's wedding dress, and when I first saw Elaine earlier I was tempted to say something very rude indeed, because, of course, upstaging the bride is such a spiteful thing to do.

But I didn't, because this is Flora's special day, and everything must run as smoothly as possible. Plus, I am trying to give Elaine the benefit of the doubt—that she really didn't mean to overshadow Flora. I mean, Elaine can't help being beautiful, can she?

The style that lends Flora an elegant, glowing prettiness makes Elaine look like a breathtaking, fecund, glorious goddess.

Elaine has also invited Harry as her partner for the day. I don't know why she bothered, unless she's developed a fondness for him, but I am happy to say that Harry really means nothing to me.

Since Flora and Ned's engagement party, he has called me a few more times, but I can't even muster the energy to be angry with him anymore. He's just an irritating irritation, so I usually just tell him to go away and hang up.

Jonathan, of course, is sitting on the groom's side of the church with Samantha, the midwife. Flora asked if I minded him attending, because she worries about that kind of thing, but I said I was completely fine with it. Truth be told, I'm not that thrilled, but this is her special day.

I haven't looked for his blond head, because I am doing my best to completely avoid the groom's side of the church. I have other guests to worry about. Two particular guests.

So, all in all, it's rather unsettling to think that there are probably three men in this church with whom I have had sex. Three men I have known in the biblical sense.

I squash all thoughts of sex and reconcentrate on putting one foot in front of the other, because, of course, apart from several swigs of brandy, yet again I am wearing pinchy shoes.

I really tried to get something that would be elegant, sophisticated and comfortable. But as usual, I could only achieve two out of three. And Flora loves these particular shoes, because they echo her own, and as she's paid such a lot of attention to detail (and paid for the shoes), I didn't like to tell her that they hurt.

But pinchy shoes are worth the look on Ned's face as he turns and sees Flora. He's utterly bewitched, totally enamored of her, and as she turns to hand me her bouquet, the same smile is plastered on her face.

For a moment, just for a moment, I am entranced by this bond of complete love between them, and my throat tightens with emotion. *Emotion in motion*, I think, mentally thanking Iris Murdoch for penning such a lovely, appropriate set of words.

"Dearly beloved," Philip begins, his voice echoing around the lovely, brightly lit church. Of course Philip is holding the service. It just seemed so appropriate that he would perform the honors. "We are gathered here today," he continues solemnly, and I lose myself in the quiet beauty of the familiar words.

Grace is also here, somewhere on the bride's side of the church. Although her companionship to Philip began as a professional one, I think that it's developed into a genuine fondness between them.

Well, he certainly didn't book her through Odd Jobs for this wedding, so that's a good sign. I do hope so—she and Philip seem so well suited. Although an ex-fluffer and a vicar is an incongruous mix . . .

Thinking of hired escorts, my own hired escort, Clarke,

smiles encouragingly as I glance across at him and Mum and Gran. Well, I wasn't going to turn up on my own and suffer silently through all the pitying, poor-Rosie glances, was I? Especially with the ex-boyfriend ratio in attendance.

Clarke is lovely. He's a very nice, considerate man. Plus, he's very good with Mum. Since the birthday horse surprise, she seems to have settled a bit. I still suspect she's suffering from delayed depression, or something, but she has been better since I began staying over on the weekends and taking her out and about. I still can't get her to go and see a doctor because she insists that she's fine.

Although she's only met Clarke twice before, she's really taken to him, which is good, but I do feel a bit mean deceiving her by introducing him as my friend. Not exactly a lie—it's not like I said "boyfriend"—but that is what she's assumed. That's what everyone else has assumed, too.

Fortunately, despite being tall, dark and handsome, he's not my type. So therefore there's no danger of anything unprofessional happening between us.

In reality, he's a lawyer studying to take the bar, but he needs to supplement his earnings by moonlighting as an escort. Which is absolutely admirable and fine, as far as I am concerned.

As Philip pauses to allow anyone with an objection to speak now or forever hold their peace, I hold my breath. And then I breathe again as Philip continues. And after Philip says that those whom God has brought together, let no man put asunder, and after we've gone to the little anteroom to witness the signing of the marriage certificate, we're tripping out into the lovely sunlight.

I've been purposely distracting myself from thinking about Luke. I don't even know if he's actually here, because I couldn't figure out a way of asking Flora without drawing attention to him.

In fact, I don't care, I really don't.

In the weeks since our ill-fated night of passion, I have moved on and pushed him out of my mind and heart. Mostly . . . but at least I'm not having sexy daydreams anymore. Or dark images of revenge and retribution involving him being roasted slowly over hot coals.

And so, obviously, the first person I bump into outside the church as Paul starts putting groups of people together for the album shots is Luke.

He's suddenly there, right in front of me, all handsome in his morning suit, as usual. And my heart leaps in my breast, and my organs all leap to attention, also as usual.

God, but he looks so *good* in formal clothes. His hair is still floppy, and he's just as endearing as ever, and I can't help but remember the last time I saw him. He was naked . . .

"Rosie." He nods his head, not smiling. And just for a moment, as his eyes plead for understanding, I'm tempted to listen to whatever he has to say . . . but only for a moment.

"How's your wife, Luke?" I ask him coldly, but I have a polite smile pinned to my face so that no one can suspect that we are anything but polite acquaintances.

"I'm—sorry you found out about that the way you did," he begins, pushing his hands into his pockets. "I wondered if that's why you didn't call me, twice, but there's—"

"But me no buts." I hold up a hand, my smile cracking. If he tells me that his wife—whom I've just spotted talking to Elaine, and she is just as exquisite as she was the first time I saw her at the Christmas fund-raiser and the second time I saw her in the Ritz—doesn't understand him, then I will scream.

"There is a very complicated, yet actually very simple, logical explanat—"

"There always is." I dive right back in, my voice low in case of eavesdroppers. "And you can't have it both ways. It's either simple or complicated, but at the end of the day, you should have had the decency to tell me about her so that I could choose whether or not to cheat on her with you."

Wow, am I giving him chapter and verse, or what!

"And, anyway," I continue, "it was just one of those meaningless things. A one-night stand after a party. It happens," I shrug, as if it meant nothing to me. "Forget about it. I have." A small white lie in the name of pride . . .

Usually, when it comes to this kind of confrontation, which is not a regular occurrence in my life, I become tongue-tied and forget what I want to say. But this time, I am so proud of myself for being so clear and firm, and for not stumbling once.

"I see. Fine, fine," Luke tells me, looking at the floor. "I understand, sorry to disturb you, won't happen again. I just couldn't think of a way to avoid the wedding without hurting Ned—" And as he turns to go, Charlie chooses this moment to come dashing across.

"Luke, how the hell are you?" Charlie grabs his hand, shaking it vigorously. "You're looking as scrumptious as ever, isn't he, Rosie?" he says, oblivious to the undertones between us. "Lewis, this is Luke Benton. Luke, this is Lewis."

"Ah, yes, I've heard all about you," Luke says. "Glad to meet you."

"Luke here was an absolute angel at Flora and Ned's engagement party," Charlie twitters on. "He's a doctor," he adds as Carmen and Jess arrive next to me.

"A-ha, the mysterious doctor who ministered to Elaine," Carmen says, giving me a sly, sideways glance. "I'm Carmen," she tells him, eyeing him speculatively. "What are your feelings about McDonald's coffee?"

God, I can feel my face flaming. Carmen, who is suspicious about everything, knows, somehow, that there is something I am not telling her.

"You'll have to excuse idiosyncratic questions from Carmen," Charlie tells him. "She tends to the suspicious and whimsical on occasion, but we love her for it—you see, our Rosie here has an inclination toward handsome doctors, and Piccadilly Circus, but that obviously wasn't you. Oh, what am I babbling on about?" he laughs. "Let's just say you had to be there—private joke," Charlie finishes, very unhelpfully, and my face flames even more.

"McDonald's coffee is, in my opinion, completely unforgettable," Luke tells Carmen, and I wonder if I should just slit my wrists now. "I drink it at every opportunity. In fact, I wouldn't drink any other brew," he tells her, and I can see that she's instantly charmed by his easy manner.

"I think I'm going to like you," she tells him bluntly.

But I can't help wonder if he means that *I'm* unforgettable. Also, I'm not sure I want him charming my friends.

"You're the doctor who saved Flora's engagement party," Jess, a couple of beats behind the conversation as usual, tells him, holding out her hand. "I'm Jess. Are we talking about Rosie's doctor? She likes doctors. Except for Dr. Foot Fetish," Jess adds, and I wonder if there's an empty grave in this churchyard that I can bury myself in now.

"But that's all changed since she met her handsome lawyer." Lewis, who is a highly perceptive human being, somehow senses my embarrassment, probably because my face is redder than his bow tie, jumps in, giving my arm an encouraging squeeze. "Where is your man?" he asks me.

"Looking after Mum and Gran," I say. "Well. Better go check on my handsome boyfriend, hahaha. I hope you and your wife enjoy the wedding," I add to Luke, glancing at Carmen as I place emphasis on the word "wife."

I'll speak to her later about putting her foot in it.

* * *

Fuck. I don't believe this. Fuck, fuck and thrice fuck.

I am truly beginning to believe that someone out there has it in for me.

"Darling, I'm so sorry," Flora says over my shoulder as I gaze in dismay at the seating plan from hell. "I should have checked."

"It's okay, Flora," I say quickly, because she doesn't deserve any last-minute anxieties. "It's only for dinner. It will be fine," I lie and briefly close my eyes.

"I shouldn't have let Elaine anywhere near the arrangements, but she was so insistent on helping, and Mummy was so busy, and I was totally up to my neck at work—" she says, building up for a panic, which is not like my lovely, unpanicky Flora at all.

"Here, drink this," I say, grabbing a glass of champagne from the tray of a passing waiter. "Take deep breaths." I grab a glass for myself and swallow it in one gulp. "This is *your* day, and a little, piddly thing like a seating plan is not going to interfere with it," I say, in a much calmer, positive manner than I'm actually feeling.

After the encounter with Luke, and the agony of having wonderful, yet embarrassing, friends, and the stress of worrying about Mum, this is all I need.

It truly is the fucking seating plan from hell.

Clarke and I are sitting with Elaine and Harry, Jonathan and Samantha, and, of course, Luke and Rowan. But at least no one knows that I've slept with Luke, which is a relief. Having to make small talk with his wife, however, is not.

"Are you sure, dear girl? I'm sure we can do some last-minute switching if we need to—"

"What are you doing?" I ask her. "Stop this. Go on, get back in there and find your lovely groom. I'm *commanding* you to have fun."

"Thank you," she says and kisses my cheek. "Thank you."

"Shoo," I add, and she sets off toward the top table, where the bride, groom, best man and parents of the bride and groom are all to sit.

"I hope we're sitting together," Carmen says as she and Jess come over to check out the floor plan.

"You two are," I say. "You're sitting with Paul, obviously, and with Philip, Grace, Charlie and Lewis. Unfortunately, I'm not so lucky." I grab another glass of champagne.

"Grace seems very nice," Jess says, obviously not quite with me. "Are she and Philip, you know, an item?"

"I'm not sure," I tell her.

"Because he deserves to find a nice girlfriend, doesn't he?"

"Absolutely," I say, finishing my second glass. As the bubbles hit my bloodstream, I decide that there's only one way to get through this. Every time anyone says anything to me at dinner, I will simply fill up my mouth with whatever comes to hand, and thereby avoid the need to speak.

"Jesus fucking Christ," Carmen fumes, her eyes blazing fury. "She's done it again. If she weren't pregnant, I'd take a swing for her, I swear I would."

Did Elaine do this on purpose? I mean, I really thought she'd softened . . .

"Oh dear, oh no," Jess sighs, as she finally gets it. "I'm sorry. But at least you have Luke and Rowan to chat to. They seem like really nice people."

"Yes, they do," Carmen says, eyeing me speculatively, and I flush. "Rowan's lovely—apparently she's involved with a lot of charitable events. Christmas fund-raisers, and such."

"Really?" I am all nonchalant.

Because after I left them with Luke, earlier, I did notice that they were all having a very nice, cozy chat with him. And then he introduced them to his wife. I mean, that's just so bloody unfair, isn't it? These are *my* friends. I don't want them hobnobbing with the enemy.

Not that they know that Luke *is* the enemy . . .

"Yes," Carmen tells me. "In fact, she arranged that function you attended last Christmas."

And I know that Carmen knows. She's always been too clever for her own good.

"Well, what a coincidence," I say, brazening it out. "And while we're discussing coincidences, can we please forget all about that McDonald's event in Piccadilly Circus? Honestly, it was just so awkward of you to put me on the spot like that."

"Excuse me for breathing," Carmen says, eyeing me suspiciously. "It was supposed to be a private joke. He wouldn't get it, anyway. I was just teasing you for fuck's sake."

"Well it wasn't funny," I say.

"My God." Carmen puts a hand to her mouth. "Methinks the lady protesteth too much. It was him, wasn't it?"

"Who?" Jess asks.

"The cheating, skanky—"

"No. I was the one who did the actual grabbing—remember what I told you?" I say, backtracking on the story, breaking up her rant before it can get into its stride. "I did the instigating. He did the nice, saving-me-from-Horrible-Boss thing. Then the post-grabbed-and-kissed-by-strange-woman shocked thing. And if you say or do anything, I will never speak to you again," I tell her, meaning it. "Promise me."

"Well, well, well," Carmen says, grinning rather inexplicably. "At least you have good taste. And to be fair, you didn't know he was otherwise taken. And you didn't, you know, exchange telephone numbers or anything . . ."

"Promise."

"Of course. I wouldn't do anything to embarrass you or

ruin Flora's wedding," she says, and I'm immediately guilty for not trusting her. Of course she wouldn't. "Actually, I'm impressed you had the balls. What was it like—remind me again?"

"I'll just go and grab Clarke, shall I?" I say, determined to change the subject. I feel terrible. What would she say if only she knew I'd slept with him?

"But who did you kiss?" Jess asks, and then her eyes widen. "Not Dr. Foot Fetish?"

"No one," I say brightly. "No one. And they didn't kiss me, either. It's not important," I stress and head off to find my rent-a-man.

I really shouldn't call him that, even in my thoughts, because everyone thinks he's my super new boyfriend.

I feel a bit guilty deceiving everyone, but it would be even more embarrassing to admit that in my quest for a date I went to an escort agency. No, I didn't advertise myself, because then Charlie would have known, and his mouth is larger than the Atlantic at times.

Clarke and I will simply become incompatible. In a couple of weeks' time, he'll disappear from my life and they'll forget about him.

"You must get all kinds of cases," Grace is saying to him as I approach.

"Well it's rather like Philip, here," Clarke tells them both. "Philip saves their immortal souls, and I save their mortal bacon."

"I hadn't thought of it quite like that," Philip tells him, as Grace smiles even more brightly at Clarke.

"Darling, there you are," I say breezily as I join them. "They're calling us to dinner."

"Oh, good," Granny Elsie cackles. "The Savoy does lovely food—this is going to be great."

"I hope I'm sitting with you, Rosie," Mum says, frowning.

"Only with all these strange people around, I want to sit with someone I know."

"You're with Gran at table three," I tell her, crossing my fingers, because I don't know any of the people who are actually sitting at her table.

"Lovely," Granny Elsie, resplendent in fuchsia polyester dress and matching hat, jumps in immediately. "We'll be fine together, won't we, love?" she says to Mum. "Just you and me."

"It's only for the meal," I tell her. "As soon as it's over, people will get up and mill about, then I'll be able to come over and sit with you," I soothe her, because this is Flora's day and I don't want any panics from Mum to upset it.

"I bet you'll have a lot of fun, Mrs. M." Clarke flashes her his kind smile. "In fact, we'll escort you there before we take our own places, won't we, Rosie?"

"For goodness' sake, you're all treating me like some kind of invalid. There's nothing wrong with me, I'm not a child, you know," Mum says, rather indignantly.

And after we've settled them, and we head to our own table, I feel like Daniel walking into the lion's den.

16

Cursing Cousins

Rosie's Confession:

Did you know that the milk from young coconuts could be used as a substitute for blood plasma?

I mention this because it would be quite handy to have a few metaphorical young coconuts around just in case of Cousin Elaine stabbing me in my metaphorical back.

Note to self: am never going to hire a date again. Is just too risky . . .

"You must be Clarke," Elaine singsongs in her little-girl voice, smiling coyly at him as we arrive at the table.

I can't imagine why I thought Elaine's pregnancy had changed her malicious streak. Because I know that I have her, specifically, to thank for this seating plan from hell.

"I've heard so much about you from Auntie Sandra, I can't imagine why Rosie's been hiding you away from us," she burbles, and I can't help it. I'm filled with nervous dread.

At this point, it would just be my luck if Elaine discovered that Clarke and I have a financial arrangement rather than a romantic one and publicly announced it.

"I'm Rosie's cousin, Elaine. Do sit here, Clarke." She pats the empty chair next to her. At least there is no danger of Elaine stealing Clarke away from me, I think, smiling cynically at her flirting.

The table is arranged boy/girl, boy/girl, and so my designated place is opposite Luke, whom I am trying very hard not to look at, because I'm going to pretend that he's not there, even though his proximity is having a very undesirable effect on my breathing.

Also, I am to sit next to Jonathan. Which is good, because Jonathan is the least of the three evils, as far as I'm concerned.

"Rosie, you sit next to Jonathan." Elaine states the obvious as she continues to hold court. And then, "Of course, Rosie knows practically everyone here, don't you, darling?" she adds, and I know that she's going to somehow embarrass me.

"Except me, I think," Rowan smiles and holds her hand out to me across the table. "I'm Rowan Smythe-Lawrence," she adds warmly, and I take her hand. "I've heard wonderful things about you," she tells me sincerely, and I'm puzzled.

"Rosie Mayford," I smile a bit hesitantly, not daring to look at Luke. "And this is Clarke Bradley." I search her features for some sign of an ulterior you-bitch-you-slept-with-my-husband motive, but don't find it.

"Hi everyone, glad to have your company today," Clarke says very agreeably as the rest of the table introduces themselves. Harry scowls at me a bit sourly from his position between Rowan and Elaine, and I smile sweetly at him, glad that I have (a) a handsome escort, and (b) taken to ignoring both him and his phone calls at every opportunity.

"Actually, it's rather funny, but Harry and Jonathan are

both Rosie's exes." Elaine—as we know, not one for being out of the limelight—announces to the table at large, and laughs her tinkly laugh. "But it's all water under the bridge, now, isn't it?" she tinkles again, then stops, placing a hand to her throat. "Oh, dear, I didn't mean to embarrass you in front of your new man, Rosie."

"You didn't," I say, smiling sweetly, but seething. Now I could say something really awful, like "Yes, but we both had Harry, didn't we, you mean bitch for stealing him on my birthday?" But I don't. Instead, I grab a bread roll and start stuffing bits into my mouth.

Why on earth this woman feels the need to belittle her family is beyond me. Actually, I do. Elaine, as we all know, is a nasty piece of work who has few friends because they all find out that she is a nasty piece of work at some point in the relationship and then drop her. How could I have believed that she'd changed?

Also, I think she hates it that I have such a great circle of old and new friends who love me. She also hates it that Flora, Philip and I get along so well with each other, and not her, and feels left out. But if only she were nice to people, she'd get on a lot better in this world, I think, feeling sorry for her, because it must be lonely being her, mustn't it? But I don't feel that sorry for her, because of the tortuous seating plan.

"Rosie and I don't worry about each other's past histories," Clarke adds loyally. "I mean this in the nicest way," he nods to Jonathan and Harry. "But I'm very fortunate that you're her exes rather than her currents, or I wouldn't be here with her." Which is not actually a lie but is a very limited version of the truth.

Apart from the fact that I am totally ignoring him, I am acutely aware of the fact that Luke now must think that I have slept with every single man at this table. Not that I care . . .

"Very wise," Rowan tells him. And then, "Rosie, I understand you run an alternative kind of employment agency in Notting Hill."

She does? "Yes," I say, my heart pounding at double speed as I wait for the other shoe to drop. How does she know that? From Luke? Surely I don't deserve another public humiliation? God, I hope he didn't confess all to her. Not that I like deceiving her, but God, I hope he didn't tell her.

"Ned and Flora told me all about how you'd found an untapped niche in the market. And Luke, of course," she adds, flashing him a warm smile, and I feel like dirt. "It's so encouraging to see a woman succeeding in business," she says, and I feel even worse that she's praising me.

"Well, I do have a business partner," I say, squirming a bit from her attention. Oh, how I just want to be left alone to stuff more bread into my mouth. Underneath the table, I slide off my pinchy shoes, because if I'm going to have a rotten time, it might as well be with comfortable feet.

"Charlie, yes. Delightful man. I was chatting to him at the church. He says you're the lynchpin."

"Well, I wouldn't say that—" I trail off. Why is she being so nice to me?

"I've always thought that I'd be good at placing people in the right jobs, myself," Elaine says, ever one for putting herself forward. "I'm a very empathic person."

"Actually, Rosie has a great talent for matching people to the right jobs," Jonathan pipes up rather surprisingly and smiles at me. "I remember that failed juggler from Covent Garden," he says to me, and then to the table, "he lost his patch to a group of fire-eating gymnasts, so Rosie came up with the perfect idea of him becoming the entertainment for children's parties. He was doing fabulously well, the last time I heard . . ." Jonathan trails off, flushing, and I remember quite well the last time we talked about the juggler. We were in bed.

"Well, Charlie, my partner, has a lot of contacts in the entertainment business," I say quickly to cover his discomfort, because it's true. And I'm a bit baffled that Jonathan would be speaking up for me. Although it has to be said, he was always very supportive about my work.

"You know, you're very familiar, Clarke." Elaine changes the subject, and my nerves stand to immediate alert. "I have a feeling we've met before."

Christ. I hope not. This wedding really could not get any worse, could it? I reach for my champagne and guzzle it down. I know it's supposed to be for the toasts, but desperate times call for desperate measures.

And as I place my empty glass down, Luke is watching me, not smiling. His expression is curiously tender as he raises a sardonic eyebrow, as if to ask if I am okay, and I look away. The passing waiter obligingly refills my glass.

"I don't think so. I'm sure I'd remember meeting such a beautiful woman," Clarke smiles gallantly, and my stomach clenches even more tightly with nerves.

"I know this is supposed to be a wedding, and a party," Rowan says to me, "but I'm putting together a fund-raiser for domestic violence awareness, and I wonder if you might be interested? I'm looking for successful businesswomen to take part. You'd be perfect. What do you think?"

"Um, yes," I say, before I can absorb what she's said. Um, yes? I must gain back control of my vocal cords, but I'm stunned by the turn of the tides. Not that I'm going to take her up on the offer. I mean, she's Luke's *wife*.

"Great," she beams and holds out a business card across the table, and I'm struck once more at the contrast between us. Of course Luke would marry someone like her. And I can't help it, my eyes slide over to Luke. How could he cheat on someone so nice?

"Here's my contact information. Please do give me a call, and we can chat about the details. And now I'll shut up about work," she says, smiling around the table.

And I hate myself even more for cheating on her. Even though I didn't know I was cheating on her. And in that moment I hate Luke even more, because she seems really genuine.

"I might be free to help out, too," Elaine jumps in, because she hasn't been the focus of attention for at least thirty seconds and must be suffering from withdrawal. "As you know, I'm heavily involved in charity work, myself," she tells the table at large with such selflessness that I'm struck by a strange desire to write to the Pope and beg him to make an exception to the rule of making someone a saint while they are still alive, and to canonize her immediately. Even though she isn't Catholic . . .

"Less, these days, because of my delicate condition. And, of course, I'm the result of domestic abandonment." She pats her bump. "I can relate to how a lot of these women are feeling."

Heads nod around the table, because she is so convincing. It's only because I now truly know that her sweetness is a façade that I can hear through the sincerity to the false woman behind it. And as Elaine burbles on, I phase her out.

"Everything okay?" Clarke says in my ear.

"Absolutely," I say back in his ear, and we smile into each other's eyes. "Tell me you really haven't met Elaine before?" I whisper, as if I am whispering sweet nothings. "This would be a disaster, believe me," I add, giving him my most coquettish smile.

You see, when I first interviewed Clarke as my possible escort (to be thorough and efficient), I indicated that there might be a faced-with-exes situation, and we've kind of practiced our strategy. He is to treat me as if I am the only woman on the face of the planet.

Simple strategy, but effective, I think as I catch Luke watching us from the corner of my eye.

"I'm pretty sure," he says quietly. "I think you're safe. Now just relax and let me take care of any difficulties. That's what you're paying me for," he grins.

And so I determinedly keep my attention on Clarke, and he on me. And all the while I am pretending to flirt with Clarke, I am aware of Luke's constant glances my way. I am also aware of Jonathan casting sideways glances my way, too. And Harry's occasional scowls.

God, I'm beginning to feel like a scarlet woman. I can't imagine why I'm the recipient of so much unwanted male attention.

And as we listen and cheer through the speeches, I drink more and more champagne for courage. And flirt even more with Clarke.

Also, my guilt increases as Rowan makes an effort to chat to me from time to time, in between being monopolized by Elaine. I am curt to the point of rudeness, which I don't mean, but how can I make nice with her? It's just so hypocritical. God, I'll be glad when this is over . . .

The wonderful food courses for which Auntie Lizzy and Uncle Greg have paid a king's ransom are ashes in my mouth. The top-quality wine that accompanies them is equally lost on me, and I cannot help but remember back to the Christmas fund-raiser.

"So how have you been?" Jonathan asks me as Samantha, Luke and Rowan are engrossed in conversation about a new neonatal unit and as Elaine ignores Harry and tries to charm Clarke away from me. If only she knew the truth. . . .

"Fine, fine," I nod my head, thinking how nice Jonathan is. And how easy he was to be with. "And you?"

"Oh, good. You know. Busy."

"Sidney still as difficult as ever?" I can't help it, I have to ask. "You do know that he's Rowan's brother, don't you?"

"Yes—and she's been a great help sorting out Sidney. Actually, he's been replaced."

"Really?"

"Well, the family decided that he needed a long holiday in rehab after receiving the threat of a lawsuit from a female executive from a company we were doing business with. I'm really sorry I didn't support you as much as I should have done," he says. "Got a bit caught up in the whole thing."

"That's alright," I say, patting his arm. Because I mean it. "Although your breakup line could use some improvement."

"I know," he says, looking down at the table. "What can I say? I'm a bloke. I just thought that leaving you a voice message would be less, you know, messy. Easier on both of us. I'm just not great at all that kind of stuff. I did mean to call," Jonathan adds. "You know, to see how you were feeling. But then, you didn't call me, either."

"Well, it wasn't exactly the high point of my life."

"No, I don't suppose it was. Well, I'm sorry."

"Apology accepted," I say, meaning it. "God, let's forget about it, shall we? Can we talk about something cheerful—this is a wedding. How's your mother?"

"Oh, *Clarke*, I've just *remembered* where we've *met*," Elaine chooses just that moment to shriek with delight. "Actually, we *didn't* meet at *all*, but it was *you* at the Hamiltons' engagement party last month with *poor* Mitzy Stanford, wasn't it?"

"No, sorry, Elaine, it must be a mista—" Clarke jumps in, but before he can valiantly lie to save my pride, Elaine carries on.

"We all felt so *sorry* for *Mitzy*. I mean, having to resort to hiring an *escort* so that she didn't have to attend on her own.

We weren't supposed to *know*, but her sister, Agnes, had a row with her just before the party and made a point of telling everyone." Elaine collapses in a fit of giggles.

I cringe as the whole table, apart from Elaine, obviously, who cannot contain her mirth, falls silent.

I just knew I shouldn't have gotten out of bed this morning. All I need now is for my newly mended bathroom pipes to explode and newly plastered kitchen ceiling to fall in on me.

"Grief, that's so funny," Clarke steps in. "Not for poor Mitzy, of course—how terrible of her sister to do such a horrid thing. But to think—I must have a doppelgänger wandering around London—goodness. But you know what they say. We all have a double, somewhere in the world."

"And we all know that Rosie would never resort to hiring an escort." Jonathan also leaps to my defense. "She's such a lovely girl, she has the men lining up in droves for her." He squeezes my hand under the table, and I'm grateful for the crumb of comfort.

"Actually, I can see why many women choose to do precisely that," Rowan says. "It's hard, sometimes, to find the right partners for all the functions we have to attend. On occasion when I've traveled to functions alone, which is a lot, you'd be surprised at the number of sharks who think I'm fair game."

Oh, if only she knew what her cheating husband gets up to while she's away, I think.

"This is the twenty-first century, after all," the cheating husband says. It's the first time tonight that he's engaged in a conversation in which I am involved, and I'm glad that he's been keeping his distance.

"And even if Rosie did decide to hire an escort," he says, looking across at me, "there shouldn't be a stigma attached. As Rowan says, it's sometimes a smart decision. Almost like hiring a bodyguard. Frankly, I feel very sorry for poor Mitzy having such an awful sister."

Oh, God, and his eyes are so sympathetic. In that moment, I know that he knows . . .

"Oh, well, yes, of course," Elaine does an immediate about-face. "We all did feel very sorry for her. Agnes can be such a bitch, at times. But you know what they say—sometimes you have to laugh, else you'd cry. And," she adds, patting Harry's arm, "Harry and I are just good friends. I, too, am a vulnerable woman who felt the need for a partner at this function," she sighs.

And before I can wonder at her complete two-faced gall, Granny Elsie arrives at the table, a flurry of worry and urgency.

"Rosie, love, I think we'd better get yer mum home," she says a bit out of breath. "She's not well."

"What's the matter?" I'm on my shoeless feet before the words are out of my mouth.

"I think she's having, you know, a bit of a turn," Gran tells me. "She's with Auntie Lizzy in the ladies' room."

"Poor Auntie Sandra's never been the same since Uncle John passed away," Elaine announces to the table. "We're all so *worried* about her. We think she needs to see a psychiatrist, in fact Mummy's always *telling* her she needs to seek medical help," she lies. "But she can be so *stubborn*."

"Grief can be a serious issue," Luke says, getting to his feet. "I'll come, I might be able to help," he tells me earnestly.

"It's okay." I shake my head. "I can manage." At least I think I can. And the last person's help I need is Luke's.

"But you're an obstetrician, not a psychiatrist," Elaine jumps in, her face falling at losing one of her captive audience. "I'm sure she'll be *fine* once Rosie gets her home."

"I insist," Luke says. "Depression can often manifest itself as a physical illness. Let's go."

* * *

"I'm such a drain on you," Mum says sleepily as I tuck her into bed. "I don't mean to be."

"Not one bit," I tell her, leaning over to kiss her forehead. "Now you get a good night's sleep as per doctor's orders. And don't worry about a thing," I add, worrying about her.

"Such a nice young man," she tells me, sleepy from the sedative that Luke has given her.

In many ways he is, I think as I switch off the light and close the bedroom door. He's certainly been kind to Mum.

Mum started crying, you see. Well, more like sobbing and sobbing her heart out, and she couldn't stop. It was the wedding, and seeing Flora and Ned together. It reminded her of her and Dad's wedding. And that Dad was no longer with her. Her grief just caught up with her, and the floodgates opened.

Luke was so calm and assertive. He got her into a cab and insisted on coming home with Mum, Gran and me. He checked her out, then gave her the sedative to help her sleep.

And despite Clarke being a good sport and playing the devoted boyfriend right up to the end, I'm wishing that I'd let him come back with us, because now I have to talk to Luke, and I could do with a buffer.

I take a deep breath and walk into the kitchen, where Granny Elsie is plying him with tea-infused brandy.

"You should be careful," I tell them. "Two mouthfuls of that and you'll be on your back."

"Good," Luke says, drinking deeply. "I could use it after the day I've had."

"Another of those days?" I say before I can stop the words from coming out of my mouth, and he raises a sardonic eyebrow at me as he takes another sip.

"I don't know about you young people, but I'm all done in," Gran says rather pointedly. "I'm taking my brandy to bed.

It was lovely to meet you, Luke," she says. "You've been marvelous with Sandra."

And I panic, because I don't want her to leave me alone with him.

"It was a pleasure to meet you, too." He smiles his lovely, charming smile, and my heartbeat picks up speed.

"I've made one for you, love. Drink it up, then you should do the same," Gran tells me, giving me a meaningful wink before she trundles toward the stairs.

Ever one for seizing an opportunity, I know what that meaningful wink of Gran's means. It means, "Take this one to bed with you." Honestly, the woman has no shame!

"Goodnight, Gran."

"Don't do anything I wouldn't do," she adds, and I scowl at her.

"I'll be following you in a couple of minutes," I say rather pointedly, then flush at the abruptness of my tone.

It sounds like I'm trying to get rid of Luke, and after all he's done for Mum, this is not kind. But then, it's not every Saturday night a girl finds herself in her mother's kitchen with her married one-night stand, is it? What the hell am I going to say to him?

But before I can say a word, a horn honks outside the house.

"I should leave you in peace," Luke says, finishing his tea and getting to his feet. "That's my ride home." He grabs his bag.

"Okay," I say flatly. "I'll walk you to the door."

And as we get to the front door, he pauses, handing me a card.

"Stephen Miller is a good friend. We were at med school together for a while," he says, and I'm confused, which is not an unusual occurrence these days. "He's a top man. Great psychiatrist. Your mum should see him."

Stephen Miller might be a great psychiatrist, but he also has an expensive Harley Street address. Which means expensive Harley Street medical bills.

"Thank you," I say, concentrating on the card, because I don't want to concentrate on Luke.

"He takes National Health Service patients, too, so no worries that he'll be too, um, expensive."

His kindness brings a lump to my throat, and I make the big mistake of looking up into his face. Huge mistake, because what I see there fills me with a longing to throw myself into his arms. Which is ridiculous.

"Rosie?" he says gently.

"Yes?"

"About that—night—"

"No," I say, holding up a hand. Because I don't want to think about that night, because if I think about that night I might do something rash. Like kiss him. "Thanks for everything, but you'd better leave," I say in a rush, taking a step back. "Good-bye."

"Well, then. Good-bye."

I close the door before he's barely over the doorstep.

New Beginnings

Rosie's Confession:

Okay. I admit it. Living alone can be a bit lonely after a while.
But only a bit. And only sometimes . . .

"Miss Mayford, she just won't do," Mrs. Granville-Seymour
booms down the telephone line at me.

I'm a bit cross about this because, as per New Year, I lined
up a selection of perfectly good people with cat experience
from whom Mrs. G-S could choose the perfect companion
for dear Maxie while she and her companion head off to
Paris for a few days.

They're leaving on Monday. This gives me precisely today,
Thursday and Friday to conjure up a replacement out of my
magic hat.

"What, exactly, seems to be the problem?" I ask her, completely hiding my crossness as I wrack my brain for an alternative. Mrs. G-S has, after all, generated a lot of business for
us in the rich-pet-carer business.

But Karen, a very nice English literature major in her final year, was all lined up to move in.

"I made it quite clear that dear Maxie needs twenty-four-hour companionship. I can't have her tripping out whenever she feels like it, leaving him all on his own. I'll be leaving adequate supplies. There will be no need for nipping to the corner shop for tea bags when I have a perfectly good tea caddy full of Earl Grey. And lemons in the refrigerator, naturally."

"Naturally," I say, but don't mention the fact that some of us find the taste of the bergamot oil in Earl Grey too much for our palates.

Frankly, I don't understand why Maxie *needs* twenty-four-hour supervision. He's a *cat*. It's not beyond the realm of possibility that the poor girl might need to go out and buy, oh, I don't know, luxury items such as milk and bread, is it?

I mean, it's not like Maxie's going to throw a secret party while she's out and invite all the neighborhood felines for a mouse fest, is it? God, I can just see it now. The house will be trashed with cigarette butts and empty beer cans on account of all the carousing cats. The police will have to break it up, because the hip-hop music will be too loud. . . .

But Mrs. G-S is paying very well. God, it's only ten in the morning, and already I have a pounding headache.

There aren't many people available with full degrees, or almost full degrees, like Karen, to cat-sit in June, and Grace, the other perfect candidate, the ex-fluffer, is already fixed up. Literally.

She and Clarke, apparently, took a real shine to each other at Ned and Flora's wedding last month. Not that they showed it at the wedding, because they were attending with Philip and me, and therefore it would have been unkind on Grace's part and unprofessional on Clarke's, since I'd paid him.

It happened shortly after the wedding, when they bumped into each other in a supermarket in Islington, because, it seems, they lived just around the corner from each other. And, according to Grace, who told me because she wanted to make sure she wasn't stepping on my toes, whilst swapping special offer information, they also swapped telephone numbers.

Anyway, talk about thunderbolts of lightning—they decided to get married almost immediately. They're currently honeymooning in Brighton. Which is why Grace can't cat-sit dear Maxie.

Philip said not to bother finding him another "girlfriend" for the vicarage garden party he's throwing in July, on account of not wanting to appear too flighty with the church hobnobs. Poor Philip. I think he was quite keen on Grace.

"Let me check through my files and get back to you," I tell Mrs. G-S, envisioning me spending five days in her mansion. "If I can't find anyone else, then, of course, I'll be very happy to step in myself." I make a mental note to pack tea bags.

"Thank you, Miss Mayford," Mrs. G-S says, startling me, because she's prudent with praise. "You did an excellent job with him over New Year. He really took to you."

And then my phone rings again, immediately, and as I pick it up there's a knock at my door, and I'm more than surprised when an unfamiliar brunette wearing glasses sticks her head around it. Actually, she looks familiar. . . .

"Hello, hello, can I come in?" Jess asks, and I nod, smiling, although mentally sighing, because this probably means that the condom factory has let her go. I don't know what else I've got that would suit her. Really, I'm drying up, here. On the bright side, there are only three more weeks to go before she gets the next installment of her trust fund, and therefore only three weeks until her life can go back to normal.

I wonder about the change of image, too, as she breezes across the room in her sensible, loose black pants and sensible, loose black shirt.

"Dr. Miller thinks it would be a good idea for me to get a job," is Mum's opening comment. "Just part time. Just two or three hours in the afternoons, I was thinking. That way I'll have plenty of time to get ready, and such. Somewhere within walking distance, because you know how I hate traveling on the Underground, and taxis there and back every day just wouldn't be cost effective."

"Well—" It's great that she's improving. Luke was right about his doctor friend. And in the month since Mum started seeing him twice a week, she's really come along. The non-addictive prescription has also kicked in, which helps, too.

"And maybe not every afternoon," Mum jumps right back into her soliloquy. Before I can tell her that job beggars cannot be choosers, and that sometimes one has to adapt oneself to whatever the company stipulates, she's off again.

"Three or four afternoons would be good. But not Fridays, because I've joined a widow and widowers support group, and they meet on Friday evenings, and I need to get my hair done before I go. Dr. Miller says it's good to have a schedule, see, so Friday afternoons I've scheduled a regular wash and blow-dry."

"Right," I say. "Got all that."

"So what have you got?"

"I'll check and get back to you later. Is that alright?"

"Well, shouldn't you set up an interview for me?"

"But I haven't checked what we've got yet," I explain patiently.

"No, I meant with *you*. I'm supposed to come for an interview, aren't I? How about now?"

But I *know* her, why on earth would I need to interview her?

"How about tomorrow morning?" I sigh, because it's going to be one of those days. I can just tell.

"How about tomorrow afternoon?"

"Okay."

And after I hang up with Mum, I turn to Jess, who has ensconced herself in the seat opposite me.

"Jess. Lovely to see you," I say brightly. What I don't say is, *Why are you not at work?*

"You're probably wondering why I'm here, and not at work," she says, her smile failing. "I got fired. I'm just no good at anything. I can't even test condoms. I'm unemployable. Completely unemployable," she adds, shaking her newly brunette head.

"That's a different look for you," I say, trying for upbeat.

"I'm trying for pensive and intelligent," she tells me from behind the clear, prescription-free lenses. "What do you think?" she asks, getting to her feet and holding out her arms as she rotates three hundred and sixty degrees.

"Well—" It's a bit frumpy, but she's so serious that I don't have the heart to tell her.

"It's a bit frumpy, but I thought it would make a nice change. Having everyone take me seriously. You know?"

"We do—" *take you seriously*, I begin, but she doesn't give me the chance to finish.

"Grace is very attractive, isn't she?" Jess utterly confounds me by changing the subject.

"Um, yes, yes she is." Grace is a brunette who wears glasses, I think, as I try to follow Jess's line of thought.

"I haven't seen her or Philip since the wedding. I expect they've been too busy to come to the Saturday-night dinners. She seems just like the right kind of woman for Philip. She'll make a great vicar's wife." Jess frowns and sits back in the chair.

And I have A Great Idea.

"She dumped Philip just after the wedding and married Clarke. Remember Clarke?"

"Really?" Jess asks, brightening. And then, "I expect

Philip's suffering from a broken heart, then, which is why he hasn't come to any of the Saturday-night dinners."

This is ve-ry interesting.

"Actually, Philip's not upset—he's just been busy," I tell her, channeling Amélie in my quest to help Philip and Jess. "And he and Grace were, and still are, I think, just good friends." Which is not the full truth, but sometimes it's good to be a bit judicious with it—no need for Jess to find out about the financial arrangement.

"Oh. Really?"

"Actually, I think he's lonely," I say, digging in my point just a bit deeper, because I've always thought he had a soft spot for Jess. "Such a shame," I shake my head. "I think he'd love to find the right woman and settle down."

"That's nice," Jess says brightly. And then, "I'm knitting him a sweater for his birthday. You are coming on Saturday night, aren't you?"

"Absolutely."

I'm definitely not going to miss this Saturday night— partly because it is in honor of Philip's birthday, and partly because if it involves Jess making a move on Philip, I wouldn't miss it for the world.

"Anyway, what have you got for me? It's only for a few more weeks," Jess reminds me.

I sigh, and Jess sighs with me. But defeat is not something we admit to at Odd Jobs. And I have Another Great Idea.

"How do you feel about cat-sitting?"

And after Jess goes off to meet dear Maxie and Mrs. G-S (who is delighted at the thought of Lady Etherington's daughter as a companion for Maxie, plus she is also delighted that Jess has a degree in art), and as I am mentally congratulating myself for my triumph at having (a) rescued myself from five days of only Maxie for company, and (b) fanned the flames of young love, thereby possibly solving Philip's woman issue in more ways than one, I'm not expecting Colin's news.

"Have you got five?" he asks me in his deadpan voice. "Only my mother's moved into a nursing home and the house is in her name. It's got to be sold to pay for the home."

"Of course," I say, because it's a while since he's had one of his depressions, and he sounds depressed.

"I'm not depressed, if that's what you're thinking. Mum really has gone into a home, and the house really does have to be sold. In fact, the contracts are being exchanged next Monday."

"Oh, I'm sorry, Colin," I say, meaning it. How awful.

"It's the bloody government I blame," he tells me but then doesn't say why. "I'm only telling you because I'll need time off to go looking for some disgusting, poky bedsit in some terrible area, because that's all I'll be able to afford."

"Of course, Colin. You must take as much time as you like," I tell him, ignoring my ringing phone. "And if there's anything I can help with, just let me know," I add supportively.

"I shan't be offended or anything if you want to ignore me for a few minutes and take that call," Colin deadpans on.

So I pick up.

"Rosie, it's me." It's Jonathan. "How are you?"

Well, knock me down with a feather. But I'm oddly happy to hear his voice.

"I'm great," I tell him. "How about you?"

"Oh, I'm good, you know. How's your mum?"

"Much better. Improving daily." I'm a bit puzzled that he's called me about Mum, though.

"Look," he adds, without any preamble. "I told you I was no good at this stuff, so I'm just going to spit it out. Samantha and I broke up. Seeing you last month made me realize how much I miss your company, and I'd love to take you out to dinner. What do you say? No strings attached."

"You've got a spare bedroom, haven't you?" Colin pauses at my office door. "How do you feel about a lodger? Only, you did offer to help and I'm a bit stuck," he says, and I'm barely listening to him. It's hard to concentrate on two conversations at the same time.

"Yes, I'd love that," I find myself saying, because, well, I would love that. I can't remember the last time I was taken out to dinner by an attractive man. In fact, the last time was with Jonathan.

"Great," Colin tells me. "I really appreciate it, Rosie. It won't be for long. I hope. When can I move in?"

"Great," Jonathan tells me. "Which night are you free?"

"Um, how about Sunday?"

"I thought that was your admin night?"

"I can be flexible." See, this is the new me. I can bend my schedule a bit.

"Okay, I'll pick you up at, say, seven-thirty?"

"I'll need a spare key," Colin says. "I'll come around about six, if that's alright."

"Perfect," I say.

"See you then," Jonathan says, hanging up.

And then it hits me.

Oh, God. I can't believe that I've just agreed to let Colin move in with me, however inadvertently. But in my good humor, I can afford to help my fellow men.

Today is turning out to be rather a good day, after all.

At least it is until six-thirty in the evening.

As I step out of Paddington Station and into the hustle and bustle of Praed Street, and wonder in which part of the cluster of buildings that constitutes St. Mary's Hospital I might find the Lindo Wing, and also worrying that finding the Lindo Wing might also involve bumping into Luke, I'm more than a bit surprised to see Charlie and Lewis coming out of one of the doors.

"Hey, you two." I dash across to them, bouquet of flowers in hand. "Thank God. I had visions of trekking around forever. Did you find her?"

"Oh, Rosie, hi," Lewis says, a baffled, horrified expression on his face.

"Didn't expect to see you here," Charlie says, equally baffled and horrified.

"Of course I'm here," I say, waving the bouquet. "I might not like her, but she *is* my cousin, and although I'd rather be at cookery class because it's chocolate mousse tonight, I thought I should pop by and pay a duty visit—" I break off.

Because I've just remembered something. Charlie wasn't in the office when I got the call from Mum. He left early this afternoon because, so he said, he had to go to Vauxhall to see a drag queen about a gig.

So, therefore, Charlie doesn't know that Elaine went into labor early this morning . . .

"Elaine had her baby three and a half weeks early. She had a little girl, five pounds two ounces, just before lunchtime. Baby and mother are fine, which is a relief, but they might keep her in hospital for a little while. But as I said, they're both fine," I babble cheerfully.

I'm trying to distract myself.

Vauxhall is nowhere *near* Paddington.

So Charlie and Lewis must be visiting someone else, but why wouldn't Charlie just have told me? Or maybe one of them is sick—I cut off that thought.

"Well, that's lovely. Isn't that lovely, Lewis?"

"Oh, yes. Babies—adorable creatures."

"Um, everything alright?" I ask, not wanting to borrow trouble.

"We were just, hahahaha, you know, visiting a sick friend," Charlie says in a rush, pinning an overly bright smile on his face. "Yes, um, after I got back from Vauxhall, I had a message from, oh, remember our friend June from the Horse and Feathers? Well, we thought we'd better drop by and say hello, and here we are," he says, and the smile falls from his face.

And I know that he's lying. He's a terrible liar.

"You're a terrible liar," Lewis tells him, squeezing his arm, and then he smiles. "Which is one of the reasons I love you, but Rosie's a good friend."

"But I thought you didn't want anyone to—" Charlie begins, and breaks off, which is a shame, because I thought I was about to find out whatever it is that Charlie thinks Lewis doesn't want me to know.

On the other hand, what I don't know can't hurt me, right?

God, I am such a coward. I'll only fret that it's something terrible if they don't tell me anyway.

"Um, whatever it is, if you want to talk about it, then fine. On the other hand, I'll just mind my own business and never mention it again," I say, in as much of a rush as Charlie was just now. I know my expression is full of worry, because full of worry is exactly what I am.

"Rosie, look," Lewis begins, then smiles at me. "I think we could do with somewhere a bit more private for this."

The middle of a busy street isn't a good place to receive bad news, is it? Because I think that's exactly the kind of news they have.

"You'd better visit Elaine first," Charlie tells me. "Why don't you come over to my place afterwards. I'll cook supper. Then we can talk."

"Okay." Oh, I just know this is going to be bad.

"Rosie—stop frowning—and stop worrying." Lewis gives

my arm a friendly squeeze, and impulsively, I lean across and kiss his cheek.

"Thank you," Lewis smiles gently.

"I'll see you both in a bit," I say, also kissing Charlie on the cheek.

"I think you had a point about unexciting sex," Carmen tells me, Flora and Jess on Saturday night as she lowers herself rather gingerly into a deck chair on Flora and Ned's patio.

"I didn't say unexciting sex," I say. "I meant comfort—as in doing it in bed. Don't put words in my mouth." Although I wouldn't mind a bit of any kind of sex, unexciting or not, because it's been a long time.

"What happened?" Flora asks her. "Wasn't the minibreak all you imagined it would be?"

Paul, who is currently in charge of the pork chops, has also been, shall we say, rather gingerly sitting down, too, now that I come to think about it.

In a bid to be more exciting and spontaneous, he conspired with Carmen's assistant so that he could whisk Carmen away on a spontaneously exciting minibreak in Norfolk.

Actually, it's another Amélie coup on my part. Paul and I had a little chat about lack of spontaneity, and how worried he was about not having any, and I suggested a surprise minibreak. But no one else has to know . . .

Anyway, they only got back this afternoon, so we haven't had the chance to catch up yet.

"Oh, it was exciting, alright. He took me on a surprise picnic this lunchtime—champagne, lovely gourmet food followed by open-air sex," Carmen tells us, and I'm a bit envious, because that sounds really romantic. Plus, I miss sex . . .

"That sounds really romantic," I tell her. "What's wrong with that?"

"Nothing—except, in the heat of passion, we rolled over rather vigorously into a patch of nettles."

"Ouch," Flora says and bursts into a long, gusty laugh.

"Oh. My. God," I say, and I can't help it—I'm laughing too, and so is Jess.

"Traitors," Carmen tells us, but she is laughing too.

"What's so funny?" Ned calls across from his place by the burgers.

"Yes, don't feel you have to keep it to yourselves," Charlie tells us. "I hate to miss a good joke."

"Just ask Paul about the picnic," Flora tells them, a warm gleam in her eye as she looks at her one-month husband. "Hmm, I may have to try that myself," she says. "But without the nettles part."

"Are vicars, you know, allowed to have sex out of wedlock?" Jess asks. Then blushes. "Oh, Flora, I didn't mean anything by that. Nothing at all."

"Dear girl, don't you worry about a thing," Flora laughs, then changes the subject because she is very good at making people feel better. "By the way, I love the sweater you made for Philip. It's just the ticket."

"Thank you," Jess beams, glancing across to Philip, who is helping the men with the barbecue.

His sweater is black, with a white neck, and on the front it says God Is Groovy. He hasn't taken it off since he opened the gaily wrapped packet, even though it is, strictly speaking, a bit too warm for a sweater. Especially standing so close to the barbecue.

It's been completely sweet watching them together tonight. I just hope Philip takes the hint from all the doe eyes, and touching, and flirting from Jess, and asks her out. They're two such caring people—they'd be perfect for each other.

Talking about caring makes me glance at Charlie and Lewis, and I have to bite my lip to stop myself from laughing.

To think on Wednesday I jumped to all the most horrible conclusions about why, exactly, they were visiting the hospital. I mean, it's easy to do, isn't it, jumping to all the most horrible conclusions? Especially in this day and age. I think, sometimes, that I worry too much. Oh, I am such an idiot!

You see, I needn't have worried at all . . .

Lewis, apparently, has a large mole in an extremely, um, private place. At least, he used to have a large mole in an extremely private place. Before his trip to the hospital last week. Charlie, because he's so caring (and because he can be a bit of a worrier, a bit of a mother hen at times), swore that the mole was getting larger, and so Lewis, who's had the mole for oh, his entire life, said it really hadn't changed, but because he loves Charlie, and because Charlie was uberly fretful about it, Lewis agreed to have said mole removed.

Result: a benign nonmole in an extremely private place. Which is a lot embarrassing, and which is exactly why Lewis didn't want anyone to find out about it.

I'm sworn to secrecy.

Charlie catches me watching him and gives me a quizzical smile. I beam back at him and cough to hide my laughter.

"Here we go," Lewis tells me, handing me and Carmen plates of food, and I immediately take a bite of sausage. If I concentrate on the food, maybe I won't dissolve in a fit of giggles . . .

"Everything alright, Rosie?" Lewis asks me. "Sausage not too—big?" he teases.

"Mmmm," I mumble, and as Lewis winks at me, I stuff even more sausage into my mouth.

"And two more," Philip says, handing one to Flora, and another to Jess. "Gosh, I just love this sweater, Jess," he tells her for the millionth time tonight.

"Well, I made it especially for you," she tells him, also for the millionth time tonight, as she bats her eyelashes at him.

Go Jess, I think.

"So, dear friends, now that you're all completely familiar with every single detail of our sex lives," Paul says as he raises his glass of Pimm's, and we all laugh with him, "I feel that I should be the one to tell you that Carmen, my lovely girlfriend, has finally consented to commit."

"Hey, buddy, you're raining on my parade," Carmen objects, but we can see she doesn't mean it, because she's laughing, too.

"After my valiant struggle with the nettles, I feel I deserve to have a somewhat more memorable moment of glory," Paul says. "So, raise your glasses and mark your calendars for one month from today at Marylebone Registry Office."

"Congratulations to Paul for finally getting his Carmen," Charlie says midst the cheers, and good wishes, and congratulations and clinking of Pimm's glasses. "But darling, why the hurry? Is there something you're not sharing with us?" is Charlie's immediate reaction as he glances at her midriff.

"Hey, don't give Paul ideas," Carmen tells him. "I'm marrying him, not signing a breeding contract."

"Quick, because I wanted a ring on her finger before she could change her mind," Paul jumps in. "An event that we hope you, our dear friends, will share with us, and then partake of a delicious curry at the Bengal Tiger afterwards."

Only Carmen and Paul would have a quickie wedding followed by a curry.

"I love it, love it," Jess says, clapping her hands.

"It's so *you*," I tell Carmen.

"Excuse me, but while we're sharing good news," Charlie pings the side of his glass with his fork, "Lewis and I would like to invite you all over for a delicious dinner sometime in the very near future to celebrate the purchase of our house."

"Et tu, Charlie?" Carmen throws back her head. "Finally,

another lost soul joining the ranks of the sensible home-owning brigade."

"Well, he had to grow up sooner or later," Lewis shakes his head. "Before you know it we'll be like an old, no-hope married couple," he says, but we can see that he doesn't mean it because he's never looked happier.

He looks across at me and smiles even more widely, and he winks again.

"So, while we're at it with the good news, any more takers?" Ned asks. "Any more weddings, living together or nettle stories?"

"Not me," Philip shakes his head. "I can't even get a date for the garden party next month."

"Well, what about me?" Jess asks. "You haven't asked me, and I'd love to be your date."

"Would you?"

"Absolutely."

Actually, with all this coupledom and happiness around me, I'm feeling like a bit of a spare part. As if I'm that kid standing with her face against the window of the sweet shop but don't have the money to go in.

"How about you, Rosie?" Charlie says, more than a little flushed with the heat and the Pimm's. "Any new doctors on the horizon in Piccadilly Circus, these days?"

I'm just never going to live that down.

"No, not a doctor in sight," I tell them. "But I am having dinner with Jonathan tomorrow night."

18

Ménage à Trois

Rosie's Confession:

Each of an ostrich's eyes is bigger than its brain.

I mention this odd, yet interesting, fact, because I strongly suspect that I have ostrich tendencies. Especially when it comes to sticking my head in the sand . . .

I am nearly late. I am so nearly late, which I hate, I think, as I squeeze my feet into the only shoes I could find to go with my dusky pink dress. They are, naturally, not wide enough, and I foresee yet another day of tortured feet ahead of me.

My alarm failed on today, of all days.

Or rather, I failed to set it correctly, so instead of getting up at eight-thirty and having a good hour and a half to get myself ready and out of the house, I woke up at nine-thirty because I had a late night.

It is now three minutes after ten, and where's the bloody cab? Why is everything conspiring against me? I grab my purse and dash down the stairs.

"You're going to be late." Colin states the obvious in his deadpan voice as he eats toast and reads the Sunday papers at my kitchen table.

"Thank you for that," I tell him a bit sarcastically and dial the cab company's number. I booked a cab for ten sharp, but it's still not here. Okay, so I was not quite ready at ten sharp, but that's hardly the point.

"If you'd had an earlier night, you wouldn't be in such a rush," Colin tells me as the man on the phone assures me that my cab is on its way. God, living with Colin is almost like living with my mother.

"Not that it's any of my business, but maybe you should have stayed over at Jonathan's last night," Colin adds unhelpfully.

I wish I *had* stayed over at Jonathan's place last night, but I just thought it would be easier for me, getting ready in my own home.

I went out on another date with Jonathan last night.

Yes, another date with Jonathan, because we're back together again. Over the past eleven weeks we've slipped right back into our old relationship, minus the Sidney portion, obviously.

I think our time apart really helped me realize how dear he is to me and how well suited we are, because if anything, I'm fonder of him than ever.

"Or you could have asked Jonathan to stay over here," says Colin, whose presence is the *exact reason* I didn't ask Jonathan to stay over, and I take a deep breath to stop myself from screaming.

Call me old fashioned if you like, but having Jonathan to stay while Colin is in the house would be rather like having my boyfriend stay over at my parents' house. Even if sex were a remote possibility, which it's not, on account of my walls being too thin.

"Any luck with the apartment hunting?" I ask, just a bit pointedly. "Anything leap out of the classified section?"

Colin shows no sign of moving out, because all the apartments he's checked out are just not quite right apparently.

"They're just not quite right," Colin sighs. "Just say if I'm in the way," he adds, and I feel guilty. "I know it's a bit difficult, what with you and Jonathan being together, but I'm not a prude."

No, that would be me, I think as a cab horn honks.

Finally.

"Of course you're not in the way," I lie, heading for the door. "Will you be in later?"

"Yes."

I don't know why I asked, because Colin doesn't go out anywhere. He's a homebody, but it's just awkward, because there's never any peace and quiet. Oh, he's not noisy, it's just that he talks all the time. Even if we're watching a movie, he feels the need to either (a) give me a running commentary on what happens, because he's seen it before, or (b) give me a running commentary on what he *thinks* might happen, because he *hasn't* seen it before.

Sometimes, sometimes, I just *wish* I could have a quiet evening home on my own. Or in my home with Jonathan.

Thank God I don't have to collect Mum and Granny Elsie, I think as I jump in the cab and give the driver the address of the church.

"Don't be silly, darling," she said on the phone yesterday when I called her to check. "I'm a grown woman, a working woman, you know, and I'm perfectly capable of organizing a cab," she told me. She emphasizes the working woman part practically every time I speak to her.

Actually, that was rather a coup on my part.

Or rather Mrs. Granville-Seymour's part. Mrs. G-S, you

see, has an elderly aunt living in a mansion on Hampstead Heath, and she just happened to mention, when calling me to sing Jess's praises regarding care of dear Maxie, that the poor old dear had problems with her eyesight, and wouldn't it be nice if I could find someone to sit with her several afternoons a week, just for a couple of hours?

Oddly, although Maxie obviously requires someone of degree standard to converse with him, her aunt does not. So I suggested Mum. Mum loves it because (a) it's close to home, and (b) she has a captive audience to talk to.

Actually, Mum's become quite fond of Colin since he moved in with me. She often calls for a chat with him instead of me.

At last. *Thank fuck,* I think as the cab driver pulls up at the church. I'm only a few minutes late. I am in such a fluster that I just thrust a pile of notes at the cab driver, jump out of the cab, and make a dash for the church steps.

And because I am so worried about being late, I am not being particularly observant, so when I arrive at the church door and find Luke arriving at exactly the same time, it's quite a shock.

Luke, whom I have not seen since the night of Ned and Flora's wedding, when I practically closed the door on him before he was out of Mum's house.

God, he looks gorgeous, is my first thought, as I'm suddenly hotter. But it's August, so hot is okay, I can get away with hot. Oh, but why does he have to look so fabulous in formal clothes?

"Oh, it's you," is again the first thing to come out of my mouth. I should just glue my lips together and save myself the embarrassment.

"Yes," he says, giving me a very faint smile as his sardonic eyebrow does its thing. "I think we can safely say that it is, in fact, me," he adds, and my heart leaps as I'm reminded of the first two times we met, when Luke was an unknown, exciting risk, instead of a lying adulterer.

"Well," I say, speechless. Because (a) I'm puzzled as to why he would even be at Baby Becky's christening, and (b) I'm grateful for the way he helped Mum at Flora and Ned's wedding.

"You're looking as gorgeous as ever," he tells me, and before I can be either (a) thrilled, because this lying charmer still has the power to weaken my knees, or (b) furious, because he has the nerve to say so, he does that thing of his and changes the subject on me. "How's your mother?" he asks.

"Better," I say, a seething mass of nerves as I look down at my pinchy shoes. "Inside the church right now, I hope. Um, Dr. Miller's been great," I babble. "Really great. Thanks for referring Mum."

"My pleasure. Nice shoes," he says, his eyes crinkling a little, and I nearly forget to breathe.

"Thank you."

"Tight shoes?" he asks, smiling faintly.

And I'm about to tell him that yet again I have been lured into wearing shoes that are too tight, because these pink suede pumps are the only ones I could find that match my pale pink linen dress, and then I remember that we're not exactly friends, so I shut my mouth.

"Well, I expect we'd better go inside," he says, and for a moment I'm completely disappointed that he doesn't want to waste any more time speaking to me. Then I remember that we're late.

"God, I hate being late," I say without thinking.

"One of those mornings, was it?"

"The radio alarm."

"A-ha. Now I understand. How's your plumbing?" he asks, reaching for the heavy, old-fashioned handle.

And God, I just can't help it. The mere mention of my plumbing takes me right back to that night, and if it's possible, I get even hotter.

Before he can open the door, and before I can say anything, it's pushed outward, and Jonathan is in front of me.

"There you are, *chérie*," he says, bending to kiss my cheek. "I was getting worried about you."

"I had trouble with the cab," I say, aware of Luke's eyes on us.

"You should have stayed at my place last night," Jonathan smiles. "Never mind, you're here now," he adds, looking at me as if the sun shines out of me. Which is lovely, and warming, and makes me feel wanted. "You look lovely," he tells me.

"Um, thank you." And then Jonathan notices Luke.

"Luke, hello," he says, offering a hand. "Great to see you again. Your lovely lady wife not with you today?"

Yet again I'm reminded of why Luke is a dangerous quantity. Yet again, the familiar old guilt at having betrayed Rowan fills me with shame. Yet again, I feel awful for not calling her about the fund-raiser after Ned and Flora's wedding. I just couldn't do it.

"She couldn't make it," Luke says.

Ah. That old story.

I tuck my arm into Jonathan's arm, and we walk into the church.

"Well, I think that all went off rather well, considering the last-minute arrangements, don't you?" Philip asks me.

Now that Baby Becky has been blessed in church with holy water, we are all blessing her in Auntie Pat and Uncle Bill's drawing room, with Auntie Pat and Uncle Bill's gourmet buffet. And their fine wines.

"You were wonderful." I pat Philip's arm. "Absolutely word perfect."

"Still a bit shocked that she asked me to do the honors," he says, shaking his head. "I've never been one of her favorite people."

"Me neither." I take two glasses of Chardonnay from the passing waiter and hand one to Philip. "But then, today has been another day of surprises."

Apart from the Luke surprise, that is. I'm steering clear of him as much as possible. And since Elaine seems to be monopolizing him, that's been quite easy. Actually, Elaine seems very fond of him . . .

Since the birth of Becky ten weeks ago, she seems to have undergone a personality meltdown for real, this time. Maybe it was having Becky three and a half weeks premature, and Becky's having to stay in the neonatal baby unit until she gained a bit more weight. Elaine probably bumped into Luke quite a lot, come to think of it.

"I, personally, wouldn't be at all surprised if Elaine had been abducted by aliens and they carried out an experimental personality change on her," Jess says, and I reconcentrate on the conversation. No more thoughts about Luke.

"Interesting theory," Philip says, shaking his head.

"Do you know, that's exactly what I was thinking." I swallow the last of my first glass of Chardonnay. The first of several, today, I feel. "It would certainly explain that emotional scene in church where she asked me to be second godmother."

Apparently her friend Pookie was supposed to do the honors, but due to an unforeseen accident involving a pair of skis and a patch of black ice, she couldn't make it. So I could hardly say no, seeing as Elaine sprang it on me in front of the entire family.

"Don't get too emotional about it," Carmen says bluntly as she joins us. "For godmother, read free babysitter. And the fact that Elaine invited us all to the christening is pretty surreal."

"Well, it did cross my mind that she might have some startling announcement to make that would somehow belittle me, or Philip, or Flora in the eyes of our peers, but that would be completely fucking psychotic of me," I say bluntly, and Jonathan gasps and nearly spills his drink.

But on the other hand, I truly wonder if it's because she really doesn't seem to have any friends of her own.

My friends all decided to attend, anyway. I suspect that Auntie Pat and Uncle Bill's munificent hospitality has something to do with their presence. As Carmen quite bluntly pointed out, Sunday afternoons tend to be a bit boring, so they might as well avail themselves of the lovely food and drink.

"I thought you got on well with her," Jonathan says.

"You *are* kidding, right?" Carmen jumps straight in. "Did Rosie not tell you what happened on her twenty-first birthday?"

"Oh, let's not rehash old history." I drink more of the Chardonnay. "At least Harry isn't here today, which is a relief."

"That's the chap from Ned and Flora's wedding, right?" Jonathan frowns.

"Ex-boyfriend of Rosie's," Carmen explains.

"Well, I knew that part."

"Rosie caught him with Elaine," Carmen adds. "More specifically, in a bedroom."

"No." Jonathan's face has gone quite pale. "That's—"

"It's okay, darling, it was years ago." I squeeze his hand. "Thank you for getting upset on my behalf, but I'm over it."

"Your cousin is surreal," Charlie says as he and Lewis also join us. "I nearly fainted when she kissed me and Lewis and wished us all the happiness in the world."

I think that Elaine's world must be pretty lonely.

"What are we talking about?" Flora asks as she and Ned arrive.

"Elaine being surreal."

"You know what? I think she's just lonely," Flora tells us in her matter-of-fact voice. "Think about it—today, of all days, her friends should have been there for her. Especially Justin and Portia Landsdowne. I mean, very bad form not turning up when she'd asked them to be godparents."

Apparently dear Justin and dear Portia had to attend some deadly dull but vital garden party at the French embassy, so they couldn't make it, either.

"Speaking of aliens," Jess, a few beats behind the conversation, says to Philip, "did I ever tell you about my alien abduction experience in college?"

"No, truly?" Philip's eyes widen with amusement.

The vicarage garden party was a huge success. Jess, to get into the role, started attending every single one of Philip's sermons, just to prepare herself. But since the garden party, she's kept it up. She even helps with the church flowers. Philip is a doomed man, I think, but in a very good kind of way.

"Do you want to hear about it? I mean, it wouldn't be, like, some blasphemous thing against God, or anything, would it?" Jess frowns.

"Absolutely not, dear girl," Philip beams at her. "Come on, let's go find somewhere to sit, and you can tell me every single detail."

"You know, it could also have been those strange herbal cigarettes my roommate smoked," Jess says, as they wander out of the French windows and onto the lawn.

"They are just so perfect for each other," Charlie sighs, and we all sigh too, because he's right. "Anyway, while we're talking of perfect," Charlie says, "we've painted, we've sanded, we've fixed. The house is done to perfection."

"Or rather the builders have painted, sanded and fixed," Lewis laughs.

"And we're now in good shape for that dinner party. How about next Saturday?"

"What dinner party?" Elaine asks as she, Luke and Baby Becky join us.

"Our housewarming dinner party." The words are out of Charlie's mouth before he can think up an excuse. I wish, sometimes, that he were a better liar. Because I know what's coming next.

"Oh, how lovely. Congratulations on getting the house," Elaine singsongs to them, with just the right amount of pathos in her tone.

"You must come," Charlie tells her. "And you, too, Luke. Bring that lovely wife of yours with you."

"Darling, do come upstairs with me and help me put little Becky down," Elaine coos at me, rather surprisingly. "I think she's had enough excitement for one day. She's such a sweet baby, isn't she, Luke?"

"As sweet as her mother," Luke says, smiling, and my heart does a flip. I know that he's out of bounds, and I know that I have dear Jonathan in my life again, but I just can't help it.

"Come along, Rosie," Elaine says. "As one of her godmothers, it will be nice for you to get to know her a bit better," she adds, and I have no choice but to follow her up the stairs.

"Um, how is she sleeping?" I ask, because it's one of those things everyone asks new mothers, isn't it? Plus, I am trying to make an effort to be nice. "Letting you get plenty of rest, I hope?" Elaine, as ever, is immaculate. She's even got her perfect figure back.

"Well, I do have Nurse Hodges in residence," Elaine tells me, placing Becky down in her cot.

"It must be nice to have some help with her." Yes, indeed, it must help having a full-time nanny-cum-nurse on hand at all times.

"Becky wakes up several times, but that's to be expected at her age, because she likes her feeds little and often, don't you, dinkums?" she says. "And we're such a fussy baby, aren't we?" Her voice is even more babyish than usual. And then she turns back to me. "I'd be a nervous wreck if it weren't for Mrs. Hodges—she's an absolute godsend. She's under strict instruction to only wake me if there's a problem. Us new mothers need our beauty sleep, you know."

"It certainly suits you," I say, because it does. I think, again, that motherhood really *has* softened Elaine.

"I'm so happy to see you and Jonathan back together again," she tells me, changing the subject as she gazes down over the crib at Becky. "I always thought he was so perfect for you."

Did she? She never said.

"Well, it's early days—"

"He adores you," Elaine interrupts, and I'm searching her expression for an ulterior motive. "It's obvious from the way he looks at you. I can tell these things, because I'm a very empathic person, you know." She clasps her hands together. "He *deserves* a second chance. I just know that if you could find it in your *heart* to open up to him, you'd be *so* happy together."

"Well, thank you." I didn't know she was so invested in my happiness.

"Life's too short," she tells me. "You have to *jump* at your opportunities and make the *most* of them."

I think of Charlie and Lewis, and of Ned and Flora, and of Philip and Jess, and of Carmen and Paul. They certainly seem to have seized their opportunities and made the most of them.

"You know, we haven't been as close as we might, in the past, have we?" she asks in her little-girl voice, her eyes full of sympathetic pleading, and I soften even more.

"No," I say, shaking my head.

"And it bothers me, Rosie, it *bothers* me," she says, shaking her head even more emphatically. "Since giving birth, I've had time to reevaluate what's *important* to me," she adds, walking toward the window. "Because giving birth can be dangerous—why, it's almost like a near-death experience. And then, with little Becky being so small, it was touch and go . . . oh, I don't know *what* I would have done if something had *happened* to my little darling . . ." She trails off, wiping a tear from her eye.

Well, Becky was a bit small, but I hadn't realized she'd been in any danger. In fact, this is the first I've heard of it, and if there had been a problem I'm sure that Auntie Pat would have wasted no time putting the world in the picture. But I don't say this. Instead, I will magnanimously allow Elaine her moment of melodrama.

"It must have been such a worry," I say instead. Because if Elaine can hold out an olive branch, then the least I can do is accept it. "But she's looking lovely and healthy now, isn't she?" I try for upbeat.

"Yes, she is, isn't she? Her lovely little face reminds me sometimes of her father . . ." Elaine trails off, looking tragically down over the garden.

I hold my breath. Elaine never did tell us who it was; I wonder if this new, touchy-feely, friendly Elaine will want to confide in me.

"You just can't imagine how hard it is to be alone, with a poor, fatherless child," Elaine says dramatically, and then she does an about-turn. "But all that has changed since Luke came into our lives."

Luke?

"Um, he seems very nice," I say, all nonchalant.

"Oh, Rosie. I shouldn't tell you, I shouldn't tell anyone, but I'm so *happy*," she says, innocent eyes widening as she puts a hand to her mouth. "I have to confide in someone or I'll *explode*. We just—bonded, in the neonatal unit."

Oh. My. Fuck. I don't believe this. The lying, cheating, adultering . . .

"But he's—he's married."

"That's not the whole truth. Oh, I'm bursting with it, I just can't keep it in," Elaine bursts out. "Of course, you can't tell a soul. Not for now, at least."

"Um, of course." What does she mean, it isn't the whole truth?

"Come, sit with me." Elaine perches on the overstuffed cream sofa and pats the cushion next to her.

And as I walk across and sit down, my heart in my mouth, I can't help but marvel at the choice of a cream couch for a baby's nursery. I mean, I thought babies had, you know, a tendency to be sick and stuff . . .

It's strange, isn't it? My cousin, who until this moment has been Bitch Cousin from Hell, has suddenly had a character-changing experience, wants me to be her new best friend, insists on confiding something to me that I am sure I do not want to know, and all I can think about are cream-covered sofas.

"It's Luke and Rowan," she says. "They're getting divorced."

"Oh." If she'd just told me that an alien craft had landed outside the Houses of Parliament, and that the Prime Minister and, in fact, the entire government had been replaced by a group of three-headed, ten-legged, yellow Urgs from the planet Zoon, I wouldn't be more surprised.

Luke and Rowan are getting divorced? A cold layer of ice forms around my heart as I worry about whether this has something to do with the fact that I slept with him.

"I know. It's unbelievable, isn't it?" Elaine laughs. "I know I shouldn't be happy about it, but you see, it hasn't been a real marriage for years."

"Really?"

"Oh, yes. Luke has confided everything in me. *Everything*," she says, shaking her head. "They're very good friends, and she's a lovely person, and everything. But apparently they got married when Luke was fresh out of medical school because it was expected by both families. They'd been engaged since they were both twenty-one."

"That's young to get engaged," I say absently, thinking, thinking all the time, as the cogs in my brain click and whir.

"Too young to know one's mind," Elaine tells me. "But neither of them could envision marrying anyone else, and they'd been friends forever, and they just kind of fell into it."

Well, that sounds like a good reason to get married to me. I mean, the passion doesn't last forever.

My night of passion with Luke springs instantly to mind. And the friendship that began to form between us at the Christmas fund-raiser, and in the bar at Flora and Ned's engagement . . .

"They just didn't have any passion," Elaine tells me. "Right from the start. Of course, Luke hasn't told me that, but I could tell from the look in his eyes," she adds, and I wonder how much of what she is telling me is a fabrication. Because let's face it, Elaine has been known to give the truth a bit of a helping hand on more than one occasion.

Maybe she's not fabricating. I mean, the note Luke left me that morning said that his life was complicated, and that he needed to explain something to me, and— Oh, fuck, I don't know what to *think* anymore.

Warning bells ring in my head as it all starts to fall into place.

"But. But. But why stay married for so long? I mean, they've been together how many years?" I squeak, trying to get a grip on my vocal cords.

"Five. But you see, staying married suited them. They've

lived very amicably side by side for a while, so why scuttle the boat if there's no reason? Neither of them had met someone else . . . until now." Elaine laughs her little laugh, and the ice around my heart hardens, because I can almost guess what's coming next.

Oh, why didn't I give him a chance to explain himself to me back in February?

But, I remind myself, married or not, he should have told me about Rowan before climbing into my bed. Then again, I didn't exactly give him the chance. I mean, I was all over him the minute we got inside my front door. . . .

"Also, you see, there's all the charitable donations that her family makes. They're a very conservative bunch, they don't really approve of divorce, and Luke and Rowan had to make sure that they didn't destroy the planned agenda of charitable donations her family has made this year. Including a hefty amount for neonatal research."

Oh, it all makes sense.

"As soon as the time is right, Luke and I will be able to *declare* our *love* to the *world*," Elaine finishes, watching me closely.

"Well." I'm bemused, confused. I just can't think straight.

But one huge, unmissable thought shines thorough like a beacon in my fog-infused brain. The one that is telling me that I might have made the biggest mistake of my life not giving Luke the chance to explain things back in February.

"Darling, you're such a good friend," Elaine tells me, taking my hands in her own. "I just hope you can find it in your heart to be happy for us."

"Of course, of course," I say, pulling myself together. "Um, that's completely wonderful news," I add. "And you and Luke can both rest assured that I won't breathe a word of it to, well, anyone," I babble, infusing my voice with false enthusiasm.

"Oh, it's just so exciting," Elaine tinkles at me.

And as Baby Becky begins to cry, I am tempted to join her, without really understanding why.

"You've been very quiet tonight," Jonathan says as he pulls up outside my house.

"Oh, just thinking about, you know, Elaine being a mother, and that kind of thing," I lie, because I can hardly tell him the truth, can I? It all fits. I mean, if I'd really wanted Luke, then I would have listened to him, despite thinking he was a cheating, lying scoundrel. Which means that subconsciously, I was rejecting him.

"So have I. In fact, I've been thinking a lot about the future just recently."

Colin must still be up. All the downstairs lights are on. I just don't know if I can face listening to him tonight.

"Me too," I say, thinking of Colin's future.

"Rosie," Jonathan begins, then stops.

"What?"

"I know this isn't the most romantic setting in the world, and it should usually involve fine food, and violins, and expensive rings. And I know that we've had our difficulties, but I think that we've come full circle. Will you—will you marry me?"

I'm shocked by his question. It's the last thing I was expecting, but as all my jumbled thoughts whirl in my brain, it becomes the most logical, natural question in the world.

We know each other so well; we're that comfortable pair of old shoes.

We're fond of each other and have a lot of the same interests. French, to name one.

And I think of Charlie and Lewis, and how Lewis got his embarrassing mole removed because Charlie was worried. He compromised.

I think of Flora and Ned, and how happy they are in their newly wed state.

I think of Carmen and Paul, and the compromises they made for comfort as well as spontaneity.

I think of Philip and Jess, and how well suited they are.

And then I think of Elaine and Luke.

"You don't need to answer me now," Jonathan adds, an endearingly earnest expression on his face. "Take all the time you want."

"Yes, Jonathan," I tell him. "I will marry you."

Dinner for Nineteen

Rosie's Confession:

They say that too many cooks spoil the broth.
    I just don't think that cooking industrial is my thing . . .

"Are you sure you don't need any help with that?" Colin
deadpans rhetorically at me two weeks later as he pushes
past me to run hot water into the kitchen sink.

"I'm fine, thanks," I lie brightly. "You go back inside and
have fun."

"Let me just clear the decks for you," he says, ignoring me
as he begins to clear the utter chaos that is my small kitchen,
and generally get underfoot as I stir yet another pan of
spaghetti Bolognese.

I know that he is only trying to help, so I bite my lip as I
have to move out of the way for him to collect more dirty
dishes and wipe down the sauce-splattered side.

Although I am a self-confessed neat freak, comparison
with Colin pales me into insignificance on the fanatically-
clean-and-tidy front. Since he moved in "temporarily" oh,

eleven weeks and six days ago, I've taken to leaving dishes unwashed, and squeezing the toothpaste from the top, just to hurry along his search for alternative accommodation. I'm fond of him, but I really hope he finds somewhere soon. He's driving me crazy. Especially tonight, when I need to concentrate on the task at hand.

"We can do that later, Colin," I tell him patiently, because although he truly means to help, he's more of a hindrance. This is a bloody, fearsome war, and I need to plan my campaign.

"Everything alright in here?" Mum asks from the doorway.

"It's all under control," I lie again, because it will be a miracle if I can produce nineteen plates of hot pasta and nineteen servings of hot pasta sauce without having a nervous breakdown.

"Oh, Colin, you're never washing all those dishes on your own?" Mum bustles into the kitchen. "Here, I'll wash and you dry up. We'll have this spick and span in no time." This from the woman to whom the term Domestic Goddess cannot be applied.

I chew even harder on my poor lip as my mobility in the small space is even more severely restricted. I know that they mean well, but in the words of Marlene Dietrich, I just want to be alone. If only they would leave me in peace, I could fight my way through my assault on the spaghetti dinner.

Tonight was *supposed* to be my night of culinary triumph. An intimate dinner party for my nine nearest and dearest friends. A challenging occasion on which I would repay everyone's hospitality for previously eaten dinners prepared by them.

On the two other occasions when it has been my Saturday-night turn to entertain my friends, I took the precaution of ordering (a) Chinese takeout and (b) Indian takeout, thereby ensuring gastronomic delight, because they all knew that I could not cook and forgave me for sidestepping this element.

But that was before I completed my night school cookery course.

Yes, tonight was one of those best-laid plans of mice and women. A chance for me to display my newly acquired knowledge and skill. And also to serve as a low-key engagement celebration, because Jonathan and I have decided on a low-key wedding. We're paying for it ourselves, and why splurge out all that extra money on a huge affair that only lasts one day when we should be investing in our future?

Anyway, I've had several practice cooking runs, just to ensure success. I've calculated ingredients, cooked them, and measured them onto ten plates. The first couple of attempts were a disaster, but I really did a decent job the third time, and the results are currently frozen in individual servings in my freezer.

Oh, yes, I'd planned how to accommodate ten people around a table by opening the partition doors that separate my living room from my dining room and extending the dining-room table by the cunning addition of Carmen's collapsible table, covering both with large tablecloths. I'd even planned to borrow four extra chairs, crockery and cutlery from Jess or Carmen. I had it all worked out perfectly to a T, and in my state of organized euphoria, I should have *known* that something would go wrong.

It began yesterday at lunchtime.

I'd taken an extended lunch break so that I could make a thorough reconnaissance of the supermarket and purchase everything that I needed for the dinner party. With list in hand, I waged a successful campaign that had all the ingredients purloined, taken home, unpacked, and put away, ready for the next stage of the assault.

So when I arrived back at the office just after two and

found that Elaine had arrived minutes earlier, you could have knocked me down with a feather. This is what happened when I pushed open the door and walked into the main reception area . . .

"She shouldn't be much longer," Shirley tells Elaine as she sneezes into a Kleenex.

"Here, love, I've made you a nice cup of tea and cut you a slice of my homemade chocolate cake. That'll keep you going until Rosie gets back. You look like you need feeding up," Gloria says, holding out a cup and plate to Elaine. And then to Shirley, "Are you eating enough greens? Only if you ate more vitamin C you wouldn't get so many colds."

"No, thank you," Elaine tinkles, taking a horrified step back from the germ-infested Shirley and the calorie-infested plate of cake. "I'll just wait in her office, shall I?"

This is the first time Elaine has ever condescended to visit Odd Jobs, and before I can absorb my shock and surprise, Colin unintentionally lands me in A Situation.

"Here she is," Colin monotones as he sees me. "Get everything you need for the engagement party tomorrow night?"

"Darling, *there* you are," Elaine singsongs at me. "I was just passing on my way to Luke's new house. I'm helping him with the interior design—you know what men are like when it comes to that kind of thing," she adds, laughing her tinkly laugh.

Luke's got a house? I suppose it makes sense that Elaine makes sure that she likes the décor. I mean, it will be partly her house too, won't it?

Luke and Rowan are officially separated. They announced it just after the christening, and it even got a mention in the daily newspapers. Not that it has anything to do with me. Not that I'm remotely interested.

"So I thought, why not pop in and say hello to Rosie?" Elaine continues. It's all part of her newly reformed character. Since Charlie and Lewis's housewarming party with Luke, she's taken to calling me to fill me in on what she and Luke are planning next.

"Um, lovely," I say with a bright smile on my face, as I wait for the other shoe to drop. Maybe she missed it? "So, how's Becky?"

"Gorgeous. Nurse Hodges has taken her for a walk in the park. So important for infants, you know." And then, as she absorbs Colin's words, "Oh, are you having an engagement party? I thought you weren't going to bother. I thought the wedding was low key."

"It's *not* an engagement party," I stress, feeling my heart sink. Thank you, Colin. "It's just, you know, a few friends and a plate of spaghetti Bolognese. Nothing elegant, just, um, pasta and supermarket wine."

"Oh, but that sounds so—so spontaneous. And fun." Elaine adds just that perfect bit of pathos to her voice, and I'm immediately guilty for excluding her.

"Well, if you've nothing better to do, you're more than welcome to join us," I say, infusing my voice with false eagerness. "I just didn't think it was your, you know, kind of thing, but—"

"Darling, we're not snobs," Elaine jumps in, and I cringe at her use of "we," because, of course, I know that she's not referring to herself and Baby Becky. "Luke and I would *love* to come to your little spaghetti party. Although I didn't think that you could *cook*, hahaha."

"She's been taking lessons," Shirley tells her. "Oh. Well, I hope you all have a lovely time," she adds dourly, then blows her nose, and I feel like the meanest person.

"I suppose you're going, are you?" Gloria asks Colin. "I

mean, with you being Rosie's lodger. Not that I'm angling for an invite or anything," Gloria adds with a big beam on her face. "But if you need any help with the cooking, you know my number—just give me a call. I'll be happy to stay in the background and just—help."

"I haven't got any fixed plans," Colin monotones back at her. "I thought I'd spend the evening checking and dusting my model train collection."

Fuck, fuck, *fuck*.

I didn't mean to hurt Colin's feelings. I just assumed that he wouldn't *want* to join us. I mean, on the previous two occasions I had my friends around, Colin just disappeared upstairs, even though I told him that he was welcome to join us. I assumed tomorrow would be the same, so I just didn't ask him. How did I suddenly become the most heartless person on the face of the planet? I take a deep breath. There is no way out of this.

"It's like I said, just a few friends having an informal plate of spaghetti," I say. "But if you all want to come, then that would be lovely. The more the merrier," I add, just a bit hysterically.

How the hell am I going to cook dinner for *fifteen* people? Where will they sit?

I can do this. I can cope. I called Carmen and Jess earlier. They're bringing Jess's fold-down arts and crafts table, plus more additional crockery and cutlery. And chairs.

Christ, they'll all be here in a minute, and I haven't even gotten the water boiling for the pasta yet! Better get a move on.

"Can I just get to that drawer, Rosie?" Colin asks, just as I'm teeming spaghetti sauce from four saucepans (two of which are new, because I needed additional pans to cook additional food) into four tureens (two of which are also new, because I needed additional tureens in which to store the additional food) so that I can keep it hot in the oven while I wash the four saucepans, boil water in them, and cook the pasta.

I sigh, put down the ladle and move out of Colin's way.

"Rosie, Colin's just wiped that kitchen surface, and you've dirtied it again," Mum fusses, and I hold my breath and count to ten. "Here," she says, handing me a small plate and a cloth, and I fight the strong urge to scream in frustration. "Put the ladle on the plate and give the side another wipe, there's a love."

Mum wasn't originally on the invitation list for tonight, either, but that all changed when Mum phoned this morning to invite Colin to go to bingo with her. They've become very chummy these days. Colin, of course, told her I was having an engagement party.

What else could I do to preserve world peace but invite her? So, of course, I also had to invite Granny Elsie. And Sid and Alf, because she's still embroiled in her love triangle and didn't want to play favorites.

"Everything under control?" Jonathan asks from the doorway. "We're doing nicely out here. Not to make you panic or anything about dinner being late, but people are starting to arrive. Just thought I'd see if you needed a hand, but you know how useless I am in the kitchen. But I can see you're fully manned—I'll go and sort out the drinks," he says, beaming at Mum and Colin, totally missing the desperate, madwoman expression on my face as he disappears back into the living room.

"You'll have to get that sauce into the tureens and into the oven if you're going to have enough pans to cook the pasta," Colin tells me wisely, and I want to shake him.

"Have you got another ladle?" Mum asks. "I'll give you a hand. Oh, have you got the plates in the oven keeping warm? Why don't you let me—"

"Can I help?" Luke asks brightly from the doorway, and I panic even more. He came, then. *Yet another pair of helping hands*, I think hysterically, as I also remember just what those hands are capable of. And what happened last time he came. . . .

"No, no," I say brightly. "All fine, all okay, lovely to, um, see you, hahahaha."

Luke, always observant, as we know, recognizes the desperate, madwoman expression on my face for what it is and does something rather startling and kind. He raises that sardonic eyebrow at me and gives me a gentle, understanding smile.

And then he rescues me.

"We're in dire need of some help out here," he tells Mum. "Flora and Ned have just arrived with the extra table, and we need you to—organize setting it up."

"Oh, well have you opened the French doors onto the patio? Only we'll need to extend out onto the patio if we're all going to fit," Mum says, heading toward the door. "Honestly, Rosie, it's not like you to be so disorganized and leave things until the last minute."

"Colin, we're still in need of two additional chairs. If you could just get the vanity chair from Rosie's room and the stool from the master bathroom, that would solve the seating situation problem. I'll take over down here," he finishes, just as Carmen, too, arrives in the kitchen to hear every word.

My face flames, because the only way Luke would have this information is if he'd actually been upstairs in my bedroom and bathroom. Which he has . . .

"Yes, I—noticed the extra seats when I used the master bathroom earlier," Luke adds as he realizes what he said.

"Certainly," Colin tells him, his expression not flickering as he wipes his hands on the dishcloth. But then his expression never flickers, so who knows what he's thinking? "If Rosie's sure she doesn't need me in the kitchen any more?"

"No, no, I'm fine. Um, thank you, Colin. Carmen," I squeak. "How lovely to *see* you," I add just a bit desperately, which sounds completely manic because I saw her earlier when she called around to drop off some cutlery and crockery.

"I was going to ask if you needed some help," she tells me, looking back and forth from me to Luke with a very strange, speculative gleam in her eye. "But I can see that you and Luke have everything in hand." She twirls a lock of her red hair—a bad sign that she is thinking and putting together two and two and coming up with, well, four.

She eyes me with an expression that says she didn't believe a word of Luke's excuse and promises "Later you will spill all." She smirks at me as she leaves us to a difficult silence.

"Right—you finish the ladling," Luke tells me, all business. "Hand me each pan as you finish, and I will wash and add water for pasta. How does that sound?"

"Thank you," I tell him in a small voice, concentrating furiously on the sauce.

"You're welcome," he tells me gently. And then, "Sorry about that comment. I didn't think. Do you think she bought that excuse?"

"No," I tell him, getting hotter by the minute. "But I'll work on her."

"Right, right."

For the next few minutes we work in tandem in a vacuum of speech, my brain totally befuddled and confused as I wonder *why* he's helping me, and how I can best explain the situation to Carmen.

"Darling, I wondered where you'd *gotten* to," Elaine, a vision in pale blue silk, says to Luke as she comes into the kitchen. "Oh, you're helping with the *cooking?* I thought you'd been taking *lessons*, Rosie," she says, following it with her tinkly little laugh, somehow managing to make me sound inept. "Luke, you're supposed to be a *guest*. I'm sure Rosie can *manage*. In fact, I'll help, too, if you like?"

"That would be lovely, but we don't want you to spoil that beautiful dress with spaghetti sauce," Luke tells her, and Elaine takes a step backward, her face a picture of horrification at the thought. "However, instead, could you be an angel and tell everyone to take their places? The food is on its way," he smiles at her fondly.

And I remind myself that Luke and Elaine are together, just like Jonathan and I are together. Which is good. Great.

"Right, how about we serve in here?" he asks me as he drains pasta and I retrieve the sauce tureens from the oven. "I'll dish up the pasta, you ladle on the sauce, and I'll be waiter. Does that sound okay?"

"That sounds great. Why *are* you helping me?" I blurt.

"Well, I know how daunting it is to cook for so many, and I have previous experience roommating with a gregarious Australian in med school who regularly invited twenty fellow students for Saturday-night pasta. And besides," he adds quietly, "it's your engagement party, and so far you've spent it slaving away the entire day in the kitchen, I would guess. Plus," he goes on, wielding two plates of pasta for me to cover in sauce, "I, um, owe you one. I'm—sorry about what happened. The lack of communication. I should never have—" He breaks off and takes a deep breath.

"*We* should never have. Consider it forgotten." I'm aiming for cheerful and unconcerned, but instead I sound like a mouse on speed.

"I didn't mean it quite—" He pauses, sighs, and looks down at me. And then closes his mouth as Jonathan comes bustling into the kitchen.

"Do we have any more red wine?" Jonathan asks, and the moment is lost. Which is just as well, because I'm not sure that I want to hear what Luke has to say.

The spaghetti is a success. Well, not exactly perfect, but it is, at least, entirely edible. As is the chocolate mousse that I made this morning and carefully spooned into nineteen small bowls.

And as my friends and family eat, drink and raise their glasses to the chef and to the happy couple, I'm strangely sad at Luke's last words.

That he regrets having gotten involved, however briefly, with me. That he regrets having slept with me.

Of course, I regret it, too. Of course I do.

"If I was thirty or so years younger, I'd give you a run for your money," Granny Elsie cackles, batting her eyelashes and clacking her false teeth as she flirts with Luke. "Or offer to show you my garden gnomes, or something."

"Why let a couple of extra decades come between us?" Luke charms her. "I'd elope with you in an instant, but I fear Sid and Alf would track me down and beat me to within an inch of my life."

Sid and Alf are (a) eighty-four, five feet six maximum, rotund, and (b) a toy boy of seventy-five, five feet six maximum, skinny. They would probably challenge Luke to a game of gin rummy and swindle him out of the contents of his bank account for Gran, but physical they are not. Well, not that kind of physical, obviously. I immediately squash all thoughts about Gran's sex life.

"Ah, well, you can't blame a girl for tryin'," she flutters at him from under her lilac rinse. Lilac, it seems, is the new blue. "I shall just have to content myself with my love triangle. Of course, our Rosie is the exact spitting image of me at her age. And she ain't married. Yet," she adds rather unhelpfully, and my pulse kicks up speed as she wobbles back to the kitchen, and to Alf and Sid, who are taking her line dancing shortly.

She still can't choose between them, and they seem to be content to share her. But I guess at her age she can do pretty well what she likes.

I am trying to distract myself.

Luke and I are alone in the hall, and my face heats up as yet another uncomfortable silence forms between us. I say yet another uncomfortable silence because over the course of the past four weeks since the spaghetti dinner, I can't seem to move without falling over Luke.

Every time I go to a Saturday dinner party, or on the odd occasion I babysit Baby Becky, there he is. With Elaine, who somehow is a regular at our Saturday-night dinners. Not that it bothers me.

Actually, that's a lie, but it's, you know, probably that old saying about the grass always looking greener on the other side of the fence.

Unfortunately, Gran has taken a huge liking to Luke and thinks that I should ditch Jonathan and sleep with him instead.

Luke is watching me with an odd look on his face.

"Just ignore my grandmother, hahaha," I babble, cursing myself for sounding like an idiot. "She has some strange ideas, sometimes, hahaha." God, I should just shut the hell up.

"I love her," Luke tells me, not smiling. "She's unique, just like her granddaughter," he says, and my heart skips a beat. And then he does that thing of his and changes the subject. "How are the wedding plans coming along?"

He always asks me about wedding plans when we have these awkward silences.

"Um, good. Good."

But did he mean good unique or bad unique? Before I can

even think about it, and not that I care, because it's bound to involve more regret for what happened between us, Charlie and Lewis stagger in through the door.

"That's the last of the boxes," Charlie says as he and Lewis carry what I think is Colin's computer screen down the stairs to the basement apartment.

Currently, Luke's helping Charlie, Lewis and I move Colin from my spare room to Mum's basement.

Yes, Colin moving into Mum's basement was a bit of a coup on my part—another Amélie moment. Mum, after the spaghetti fest, started including him for Sunday lunch along with Jonathan and I, because she didn't want him to feel left out, and when I saw how well they got along, it seemed like a good idea to plant the seed. Mum thinks it was her idea, but I don't mind her claiming the glory.

"Thank God that's the end of Colin's stuff." Luke's sardonic eyebrow does its thing as he pushes his hair off his forehead. "Who knew one man could own so many model trains?"

Oh, I wish he wouldn't do that. It's too—too damned sexy.

You know my feelings for Luke in formal clothes, but my fuck, the sight of him in a pair of old jeans and a tight T-shirt is bad for my nerves. Not that I'm interested, of course, because I'm marrying Jonathan in eight weeks' time.

I wish Jonathan were here, instead of in Manhattan on a business trip. It's just lust transference, that's all.

"We're all set," Colin tells us all in his deadpan voice as he, Charlie and Lewis reappear from the basement. "Thanks so much for your help."

"No problem, old man." Charlie slaps him on the back.

"I think this calls for some liquid refreshment," Lewis says, rubbing his hands together.

"What do you say, lads?" Charlie grins. "We can't abandon Colin in his time of need, and if he's going to live here, we should at least help him out by familiarizing him with the local watering holes."

"I'm up for it," Luke nods his head.

"Darling, we've had this conversation before," Charlie teases him and winks at me. "We know you're up for it."

"I'm not a big drinker," Colin, unsurprisingly, protests, as my head begins to ache.

"Come on Col, live a little," Lewis tells him.

"But—"

"No buts." Luke holds up his hand, and my heart thuds in my ears as I remember the time he said the same thing to me. And being lifted into his arms and whisked away to Piccadilly Circus shortly afterwards.

I really must stop doing this.

You see, instead of daydreams where Luke rescues me and we drive off into the sunset, or nightmares involving hot coals and roasting, I have now begun to relive every second that I spent with him. Including the sex. This is not good, but I think it is just a sign of bridal nerves.

See, after I marry Jonathan, he'll be the only man I ever have sex with again. I mean, that's a pretty daunting thought, isn't it?

"I suppose I could manage a pint or two, then," Colin monotones.

"How about you, Rosie?" Luke is so tempting. So tempting . . .

Instantly, my fertile imagination conjures up an image of Luke in his white doctor's coat, with a stethoscope around his neck, which is odd, because I've never seen him in his doctoring environment. He is naked beneath it. Oh my.

"Tempting, but no." I must not weaken. "I have wedding plans to plan."

* * *

"Luke's already here," Elaine tells me as she opens the front door of her Hampstead house.

Oh, good. Another chance for an awkward silence and erotic conjuring, I think sarcastically.

Elaine moved back to her own house with Nurse Hodges and Baby Becky not long after the christening. She said it was because she wanted her life back, because Auntie Pat fusses too much, but I suspect it was because she wanted her privacy back so she could have sex with Luke.

I must stop doing this. I must not think of the words *sex* and *Luke* together.

"You know," Elaine says under her breath as she links arms with me. "I think he's going to pop the question any day, now. Oh, I'm so *happy*. He's *perfect*, don't you think?"

"Um, well—"

"Of course, I'm asking the wrong woman," she trills. "Obviously not for *you*, because you're so in love with *Jonathan*."

"Yes." I nod. Because it's true. I really love Jonathan, whom I am marrying in two weeks' time, because he is comfy, just like a pair of old shoes. With patience and perseverance, he's molded to my metaphorical feet into a perfect fit.

So it's a shame, really, that the shoes he brought me back from his Manhattan trip are too small. Jimmy Choo again. This time, ivory, to go with my wedding dress. An extravagant gesture for our low-key, cut-price wedding, but he wanted me to have something special, which is sweet, isn't it?

Obviously, this has involved me ordering my true size at the website, and I'm just hoping they arrive before my special day does.

"Well, I don't think it will be too long before we follow you down the aisle. Of course, we have to wait for his divorce to come through. Actually, Rowan organized the fundraiser we're attending tonight. It's so civilized to be on speaking terms with one's near ex, don't you think? Of course, I shall have to put a stop to all that after the wedding. I was thinking an autumn wedding next year. That will give Mummy plenty of time to plan it."

"Lovely," I smile, but my facial muscles feel strained.

"Anyway, mum's the word," Elaine tells me under her breath as we enter her living room. "Look who's here, darling," she trills to Luke. "Our lovely bride-to-be."

"Great to see you, Rosie."

"You too," I lie, because it's not, because he's wearing formal clothes again and I'm already hot under my red angora sweater. Instantly, my fertile imagination conjures up an image of Luke, in a dinner jacket and bow tie. Underneath, he's naked . . .

"How are the wedding plans?"

"Oh, darling, Jonathan did the most romantic thing," Elaine trills. "He bought Jimmy Choo wedding shoes for Rosie. Don't you think that was thoughtful?"

"Very," Luke smirks, which I think is a bit unkind.

"I'll just get my coat," Elaine says, "and then we'll be off. Baby Becky should sleep through until eleven. Nurse Hodges fed her about half an hour ago, before she went off duty."

"Do they fit?" Luke asks as soon as Elaine leaves in search of her coat.

"Of course," I lie.

"I'm sorry. That was a bit unkind of me," he surprises me by adding. "Well, then. I wish you all the happiness in the world. Rosie?"

"Yes?" I look up into his face. My throat aches with suppressed tears.

"I—" He takes a deep breath. "I always meant to, you know, clear up that time we—"

My nerves jump to attention. *Danger looming*, that little voice in my brain screams at me.

"Ready, darling?" Elaine singsongs from the door, ruining the moment, which is a relief.

"Absolutely. Goodnight."

And then they're gone.

Bride-to-Be

Rosie's Confession:

You know, I heard somewhere that single women live longer than married women . . .

So it makes perfect sense for a bride to have second thoughts on her wedding day . . . doesn't it?

"Are you sure this is what you want?" Granny Elsie asks me.

Which is an odd thing for her to be asking me as I'm putting on my wedding dress on my wedding day, isn't it? Of course I'm not having second thoughts. I'm just distracted, a bit, about something I discovered yesterday. . . .

"Of course," I tell her, smiling radiantly as I loop great-grandmother Mayford's pearl earrings into my ears.

Something old . . .

At least, I *think* my smile is radiant. It's just bridal nerves. "Why do you keep asking?"

"Oh, Jonathan's a nice bloke and everything. I just worry a bit that he's not excitin' enough for you."

"Gran, he's my perfect pair of comfy, old, worn-in shoes," I say as I slide the lace garter onto my leg.

Something new . . .

I'm confused, you see, and am trying to think it through. Yesterday yielded rather a large surprise. I received a bill from Mum's therapist, Dr. Miller. It was for several hundred pounds, and when I called his office, the clerk told me that yes, it was correct. But when I asked her to check, an older woman came on the line and told me that it was all a huge mistake, and it had been explained to the new clerk that Dr. Benton was taking care of it, and sorry to worry me . . .

Luke, it seems, has been paying for Mum's therapy.

"Yes, but comfy old shoes don't mean boring old shoes," Granny Elsie adds, and this is not helpful. "I mean, my shoes are old shoes," she says, looking down at her green kitten mules with yellow bows.

You need sunglasses to look at them, but she has a point—they're certainly not boring. Oh, I'm already a bag of worry. I know it's supposed to be the happiest day of my life, but do you know how much stress it is?

"Now that Luke, there's an excitin' man," she cackles.

"He's Elaine's boyfriend," I tell her, exasperated. "They're practically engaged."

"But they ain't engaged yet. It's not too late to, you know, change yer mind." This is the same theory she's been expounding ever since Luke became the apple of her eye.

But how kind, yet strange, to pay for Mum's therapy. I shall have to speak to him about it. I'm not sure what to say, but I definitely have to pay back every penny . . .

Oh, what does it all mean?

"I've been on this planet for nearly eighty-seven years and I know what it means when a man looks at a woman in a certain way," Gran says, her lilac head bobbing. "Let's just say that he don't look at Elaine that way."

"How about a nice glass of sherry?" I ask, changing the subject as I fasten Mum's pearls around my neck.

Something borrowed . . .

"You don't look at Jonathan in that certain way, either," she adds, and I try again.

"Please, Gran, let it be," I plead.

"Alrighty then," she nods. "Just remember, when Philip says that bit about if anyone knowing why you and Jonathan shouldn't be joined, it's still not too late to change your mind."

"Gran." My voice is all strangled mouse.

"I'm not sayin' another word on the subject. I'll go and get that sherry, shall I?"

"Who needs sherry when we have champagne?" Carmen puts her head around my bedroom door. "Tada! Your brides-maids have entered the building," she announces rather dra-matically, as she and Jess come into my bedroom. "Thank fuck you didn't make us wear something ugly," she says, twirling in the champagne dresses she and Jess chose. "God, you look amazing. I thought we were supposed to put the dress on you, but I forget, sometimes, just how practical and organized you are," she scolds me, but she's smiling.

"Happy wedding day." Jess brandishes the champagne flutes, and they clink dangerously as she puts them down on my dressing table. "Oh, you're exquisite, exquisite. I can't wait for my turn." She clasps her hands together, and I smile, because she's so infectious.

She popped the question to Philip. He was astonished, but he did say yes. Well, she'd be waiting forever if she left it to him. She even bought him a ring.

"I'll leave you girls to it." Gran wobbles toward the door, resplendent in bright green and yellow polyester. "I'll keep yer mum busy, and give her plenty to fuss about without comin' anywhere near you," she winks.

"Right, here we go." Carmen winces as the cork pops out and the bubbles pour over the neck of the bottle. "Not that I make a point of making emotional, mushy speeches," she laughs as she fills the glasses and hands one to each of us. "But let me just say, as one of your oldest friends, that I hope you'll be as happy with Jonathan as I am with Paul."

And at that moment, the lump in my throat gets even bigger as emotion tears build behind my eyes. I really love these girls. Am I doing the right thing?

"Just remember to smash a few plates, occasionally, to liven things up," Carmen says with a cheeky grin, lightening the mood.

"And as happy as I'm going to be with Philip." Jess, a couple of beats behind, clinks her glass a bit too forcefully against mine, and it shatters. "Oh, sorry, sorry," she says. "I didn't mean to do that quite so hard, I just get a bit too enthusiastic sometimes."

"Here." Carmen whisks the broken glass out of my hand. And then she grabs my hand and holds it away from my dress as a bright red spot bubbles on my finger. If I were a superstitious woman, which I'm not, I would take this as a bad sign.

"Oh, you're bleeding, you're bleeding," Jess panics.

"It's okay, it's only a little cut," Carmen tells her. And then to me, "Here, press this tissue against it. Pressure will stop it in a moment. Jess, you go get us some more glasses, and *don't* tell Mrs. Mayford what's happened. She'll only dial the emergency services if you do," she jokes, and I smile.

"But the glass—"

"I'll do it. Shoo." Carmen waves her off. "Actually, this is rather a fortuitous moment," she says as soon as Jess is out of the room.

"What?" My nerves are already stretching to breaking

point. "Do you think this is a bad omen, and that Jonathan and I are doomed?"

"No." She raises a hand. "Don't you start, that's all we need, you panicking too. Here, hold out your hand," she says as she peels the back off a bandage and sticks it to my finger. "I just wanted to ask if you're sure about this?"

"Et tu, Carmen?" I sigh.

"I shan't mention it ever again. But I just want to make sure that you're marrying Jonathan for the right reasons. That you're not getting caught up in all the coupledom fever that's exploded amongst us in recent months and you think you *ought* to do this rather than you *want* to do this. That you're not secretly harboring something a bit more than basic lust for a particular mysterious doctor who is exciting, and risky."

My God, she's far too perceptive for my good, sometimes.

"My God, that was a long speech." I stall for time.

"Well, I had to get it off my chest. Besides, you *know* I know there's *something* you're not telling me about that certain McDonald's-coffee-drinking doctor." She pauses. Then adds, gently, "Speak now, or forever hold your peace."

Her last line, straight out of the marriage service I will be hearing in about an hour's time, stops my denial on my lips.

"Charlie and Lewis are downstairs." Jess comes bubbling back into the room with some plastic cups. "Oh, your gran gave me these," she says as Carmen and I are still looking into each other's eyes. "Oh, and Luke's here, too. He wants a word with you," Jess adds, and we both turn and look at her instead. "I told him to wait while I checked you were decent."

"Knock, knock," Luke says, from my bedroom door. "Your gran said to just come right up."

"Um, hello. Come in. This—this is a surprise," I say, because it is, because he's the last person I expect to see.

God, but he looks lovely.

As he steps into my bedroom, my heart picks up speed as it usually does, and I want to smooth back his hair.

"Um, I know that this is unusual, but would it be alright if I had a quick, private word with the bride-to-be?" he smiles at Carmen and Jess.

"Absolutely." Carmen, immediately all business, flashes me a meaningful glance, only I'm not sure what it is that she actually means. "Come along, Jess." She hustles Jess out of the room. "We'll be right downstairs."

"But—" Jess begins, but doesn't get the chance to add anything else.

As Carmen closes the door firmly behind them, another awkward silence settles between us.

"I didn't want to leave without saying good-bye," he tells me finally, pushing his hands into the pockets of his chinos. And then I notice that he's wearing chinos, and not a morning suit, and I wonder what's going on.

"You're not—" I break off. He's not coming to my wedding?

"I'm sorry. I felt I should say good-bye in person. Seeing as you'd taken the trouble to invite me to the wedding and everything."

"You're leaving?" My heart leaps into my mouth. Which is ridiculous, because I'm getting married to Jonathan in approximately fifty-five minutes. Why should I care if Luke's there or not?

"Yes. A last-minute opportunity presented itself, and there's nothing holding me back, so I thought, why not? I'm exchanging with an American colleague. I'll be spending the next six months in New York."

"Isn't that a bit sudden?" I panic, which is also odd, because Luke's geography on the face of the planet shouldn't have such an impact on me. But New York. It's so far away . . .

I'm going to be Mrs. Jonathan Leicester, I remind myself.

"Last-minute decision," he says, not smiling as he looks at me in that endearing way of his. "Another colleague was supposed to take part in the exchange, but he had to back out at the last minute. Last night, in fact."

"Isn't it a bit of a risk?" I shouldn't care if Luke comes to my wedding or, in fact, leaves the country at a moment's notice, should I?

"Well, sometimes you have to take a chance. You know, make a snap judgement about something in life. And even if you do it once, and it doesn't work out, you shouldn't let it stop you from, you know, risking everything again—" He breaks off and changes his mind about whatever it is he's going to say. "There's nothing to keep me here anymore," he finishes.

"But what about Elaine?" He's divorcing his wife for Elaine. "You love Elaine," I blurt. "I thought you were getting married. You know, once your divorce comes through," I babble on. He can't just be leaving.

"I'm not in love with Elaine," he tells me, confusion written all over his face. "I'm sorry I gave her, and, apparently, everyone else, the wrong impression, but I have no intention, never did have, of marrying her. I thought we were just friends."

"But you're getting a divorce because of her. Why else would you wreck your marriage? Oh, I know you and Rowan are just friends, and about the family charitable donations and stuff, but why would you bother to upset the apple cart unless—" I babble, then stop, because I sound like an idiot, and I'm making an absolute mess of things, and Luke's divorce is absolutely nothing to do with me.

"Ah, I see. Elaine confided in you about that. I see. I see. Never did get the chance to explain—no. No, it's too late for that," he says and begins to pace the room. "Right. Right," he says, coming to a standstill in front of me.

"What's too late?" I ask, hardly daring to breathe, because I'm not sure I want to know the answer.

"I met someone else," Luke tells me, looking into my eyes.

"What happened?" I ask, every nerve in my body on red alert.

"I was mistaken. She had her own life, and I caught her at a bad time, and, well, I didn't want to, you know. Rock the boat."

"So she didn't know that you loved her?"

"The moment never arose for me to tell her. And now it's far too late. Anyway, I have to go—I have to get myself to Heathrow for my appointment with a Virgin Atlantic plane. I just wanted to drop by and wish you all of the happiness in the world," he says, standing in front of me.

And then, as he leans down and kisses me softly on the forehead, I want to take him into my arms, take that risk that it might be me he loves, but, of course, I don't.

"Be happy, Rosie," he tells me as he heads for the door. And as he pauses, and turns back to me, I want to throw myself at him and beg him to stay. "And," he says, raising a sardonic eyebrow at me, "don't forget to chew well."

As he closes the door behind him, I realize that I'm never going to see that sardonic eyebrow again.

And the bride is the something blue, I think, and I laugh hysterically . . .

"Well?" Carmen asks me thirty seconds later as she, Jess, Charlie and Lewis pour in through my bedroom door.

"He came to say good-bye," I say, and I'm thinking, I'm thinking, as I pace up and down the room. Hysteria has been replaced by sheer, utter terror. And confusion. And the strongest feeling that I am about to do something I never imagined myself doing.

And I'm suddenly reminded of a story I heard in the news about Shrek, the famous New Zealand sheep. Shrek, it seems, had a fear of being shorn. Every year, at shearing time, he would hide in a cave. Each year, his unclipped coat grew longer and heavier, until after six years of unsheardom you couldn't see the sheep for the wool.

And I'm wondering if I haven't been able to see the forest for the trees . . . I'm wondering if I've lost sight of the real Rosie because of having to be organized, safe, dependable . . .

"Yes, darling, but that's why we have the telephone," Charlie says patiently, perching on my bed. "It must have been much, much more than a simple good-bye if he came to tell you in person. I mean, it's not like he's making house calls to all of us, is it?"

"It's not as if you are even that close friends, is it?" Lewis asks, also perching on my bed. "Although the way you two look at each other sometimes has us all on edge. You could bottle it and use it as an antidote to impotence."

"Well, I think that it was very chivalrous of him," says Jess, holding the skirt of her dress as she joins Charlie and Lewis on my bed. And then, "By the way, I know I'm not the quickest of people, but even I haven't missed the sexual tension," Jess tells me.

And I just can't think straight. I mean, how can I jilt poor Jonathan in church, based on a strange flight of fancy? It's just not something that happens in real life, is it?

Shrek's sixty-pound fleece weighs heavily on my conscience, and I feel old, and heavy, as if I'm trying to run underwater.

"Darling," Mum pokes her head around the side of the door. "We're off to the church now. Could I have a private word before we go?"

"Um, yes." I pin a beam on my face and walk onto the landing, closing the door on my bemused friends. Here, in front of me, is one of the majorly, hugely important reasons why I have to go through with this.

It would destroy Mum if I did this to her. For fuck's sake, she's only just coming through Dad's death and moving on with her life. This could spiral her off into another bout of depression and treatment.

The treatment for which Luke has been paying, I suddenly remember, because in the midst of everything I'd forgotten. Another point to add to the dilemma . . .

"Rosie," she says, taking both of my hands in hers, and the tears are stuck in my throat. "You are so beautiful. Dad would be so proud of you today if only he were here. Our little girl, all grown up and heading to her wedding."

"I know," I tell her, smiling weakly.

"You're a good girl," she says, squeezing my hands. "But I just want to make sure that this is what you want. That Jonathan is exactly the person with whom you want to spend the rest of your life. Because marriage is a huge step, and if you felt that it wasn't quite right—well, then, no one would think the worse of you if you changed your mind."

"Oh." I'm so stunned that I can only stand here with my mouth open, guppy fashion.

"The car's here," Colin calls from the bottom of the stairs. "Better get going."

"Coming, Colin. See you in church, Rosie," she tells me, and then kisses me on the cheek. "Whatever you do, be happy, darling." And then she heads off down the stairs.

What the hell am I going to do?

"Look, will you just put us out of our misery and tell us what happened with Luke?" rolls out of Carmen's mouth the minute I go back into my bedroom. "Because I'm not going to buy some weak, half-baked story of saying good-bye, because it's obvious to anyone who looks at him that he's got it bad for you."

My friends collectively nod their heads.

"But why didn't you say anything?"

"We have, darling," Charlie says.

"We keep asking you if you're sure about Jonathan," Lewis jumps in.

"Because we can't butt in too much, because if we were wrong, then you'd not feel comfortable confiding in us, and we had to let you figure it out by yourself," Jess, for once totally on the ball, interrupts. "Just like you let me realize that Aster was bad for me and Philip was under my nose all that time."

"I just *know* there's a lot more to this that Miss Secretive has been bottling up. Spill," Carmen commands me.

And so I do.

And as I do, I feel like Shrek, finally caught and sheared on National New Zealand TV. Little by little, with careful scissors, the shearers chopped off the weight of years.

I begin with the kiss in Piccadilly Circus and feel lighter.

I tell them of our night of passion, and my discovery that Luke was married, and feel lighter still.

I tell them about Elaine confiding in me at the christening.

I re-cover all the ground, every moment I've ever spent with him, and finally, finally, when I tell them what Luke said to me just a few minutes earlier, and that I've only just discovered that he has been paying for Mum's treatment, they are all watching me in wide-eyed silence.

"You dark horse." Carmen, unsurprisingly, is the first one to recover her tongue. "I suspected as much, but I can't believe you've kept this from us for—how many months?"

"Yes, but she thought she'd slept with a married man," Jess points out.

"Well, she did," Charlie adds, grinning widely. "Even if she didn't know he was married. That was a bit naughty of Luke, though. He should have told you before he leaped into bed with you."

"I didn't exactly give him the chance," I say, blushing.

"Yes, yes, but what are we still doing here?" Carmen says. "It's obvious. He fell for you, asked Rowan for a divorce, and then you went and got yourself engaged to Jonathan. I can't believe you took Elaine's comments verbatim. You know how she likes to embroider the truth."

"I know."

"So what are you going to do? Because, sweetie, this is your future you're talking about," Charlie prompts me.

"Sometimes you have to put your faith in someone, despite the fact that it might mean heartache," Lewis adds. "And embarrassing mole moments."

In that moment, as my life flashes before me, as all my thoughts roar around my brain, it condenses down to one thing.

I know exactly what I am going to do.

I'm going to risk everything.

"I want to go to Heathrow airport and find Luke. Whether you're right or wrong. Whether he says yes, or no, and I make a complete and utter fool of myself."

"Yes." Carmen raises a triumphant fist to the ceiling. "Charlie, you and Lewis find out which airlines have flights to New York today in around two or three hours' time."

"He's flying Virgin Atlantic," I say.

"Well, see—that's obviously a sign that he wants you to go after him," Jess tells me.

"I'm going to see if I can catch Flora and Ned on Flora's cell phone before they get to the church," Carmen says. "Ned has a van, therefore we can all fit inside for the journey. Because we're all coming with you."

"But what about Jonathan?" There, I've said it. I still have another layer of wool to shed . . .

"I'll call Philip and tell him what's happening," Jess says. "He'll break the news to Jonathan. He's kind, so lovely and kind, and he's good at this type of thing."

"I appreciate the offer," I tell her, my heart aching for what I am about to do, but do it I must. "But I have to go to that church and tell him myself. If I'm going to wreck his life and break his heart, he deserves to hear it from the horse's mouth."

And as I steel myself for what I have to do, I reach for the too-small Jimmy Choo wedding shoes Jonathan bought for me.

I deserve to feel pain.

21

Leaving on a Jet Plane

Rosie's Confession:

You know, the human heart pumps with enough pressure to squirt blood thirty feet.

I mention this interesting, yet gory, fact because my blood is pounding at least double that with nervous anticipation of what I am about to do . . .

Twenty minutes later, as the hired bridal car pulls up outside the church, and as we scramble out into the cold, November air, I want to be sick.

"My fuck, would you look at your face," Carmen says, pulling up the skirt of her dress and unsheathing the brandy flask from the elastic contraption attached to her calf. "I brought this with me in case of an emergency. I think we can safely say we have a situation. Have some brandy."

I grab the flask, my hands shaking as I gulp down a large swig of the fiery spirit, and it hits my stomach with a whoosh.

"Don't worry, don't worry," Jess tells me. "Worse things happen at sea."

The mention of sea makes me seasick, and I swallow another mouthful of brandy before passing it on to Charlie.

Ned, Flora and Paul are all waiting outside the church, because Carmen called them and filled them in.

Paul, also acting as my photographer today, does not take any cozy snaps of the wedding party glugging back brandy on this occasion, because it's hardly a Kodak moment, is it?

"Dear girl, this is a fine to-do," Flora booms at me, shaking her head, but her eyes are warm and sympathetic.

"I know. I'm an idiot. I'm sorry," I say, meaning it. I feel awful for what I'm about to do.

"No, it's good that you realized before the service," Ned tells me kindly. "Better to sever the ties now. But Luke? I really had no idea. He's not exactly one to confide, although I knew something was bothering him."

"Me, neither." Flora shakes her head.

"We must be the only three," I tell them, shivering with nerves and fear and cold. "Well, I'd better go get this over and done with."

"Good luck, dear girl," Flora says, giving my arm an encouraging squeeze. "Philip's all primed. As soon as he sees Ned open the main door, he's going to send Jonathan to the vestibule so that you can, you know, um—"

"Casually break his heart and ruin his life," I say bitterly.

"Well I wouldn't put it quite like that," Carmen tells me. "You're saving him from certain misery, too."

"But if only I'd done it before the actual, you know, wedding," I wail. "Oh, how hurt and humiliated he's going to be." I put my hands to my face.

"Better to make a clean break," Charlie tells me.

"Rather than leave him in a fool's paradise," Lewis finishes for him, and I smile bleakly at the way they seem to complete each other's sentences these days.

"Are you sure you don't want me to, you know, do the, er, honors?" Ned asks me, pausing at the door.

"No. Jonathan deserves better," I say, frozen to the core, despite the brandy. "Um, you all stay here and, um, I'll see you, you know, afterwards. Okay, Ned, do your thing."

And as I wait for Jonathan in the dark vestibule, each second drags, and my stomach drags, too. The condemned woman waiting for the hangman. And I think of all the lovely times we've had together, and how hurt he's going to be, and how fond of Jonathan I am. But in the end, fond just isn't enough.

"Rosie?" It's Jonathan. "Philip said there was a problem? My, but you look lovely." He looks so nice and handsome, and so kind, that I hate myself even more.

"Jonathan," I say slowly, my voice a death knell. How can I do this to him? I am a horrible, terrible person.

"Is, um, everything alright?" he asks as his face turns a chalky shade of white, and I steel myself to speak.

"Actually, Jonathan, it's not," I say. "Could you please close that door?" I point to the door, which will close off the vestibule from the main church hall. After all, this isn't the Jerry Springer show. And as he complies, I begin to pace as I wonder how to delicately phrase this.

There isn't a nice way to put it.

"I'm so sorry, Jonathan," I begin slowly. "So very sorry. And, um, I know I should have told you sooner, but I didn't know until about, oh, an hour ago, but I've fallen madly in love with someone else, and I can't marry you, because I'd make you miserable and ruin both of our lives." It all comes out in a rush.

And then, before poor Jonathan can take in the awful

thing that I have just told him, the door he has just closed flies open and Elaine is standing in the doorway.

"Oh, this is *all my fault*," Elaine wails, rather dramatically. Which is a shock, because no one invited her along to this breakup party. "I should have *told* you before things got to this stage, but I didn't know *how*," she wails again, loudly.

Loudly enough, actually, for the whole congregation to hear. In fact, the whole congregation is turned toward us and is hanging onto every word.

So much for a private breakup, I think as I also wonder what on earth Elaine's talking about. How can me breaking up with Jonathan be her fault? And how did she know?

"Now, Elaine." Jonathan holds up a hand. "I thought we'd agreed to discuss this later—better to deal with it after the, er, stresses of the day."

"Discuss what later?" I ask, totally confused and bemused. The whole congregation is confused and bemused, too.

"I'll never *forgive* myself for completely *ruining* your *life*," Elaine wails as tears spring to her eyes.

"Um. How, exactly, have you ruined my life?" I thought I was the one doing the life ruining, but it seems that we now have a whole new agenda to which I am not privy.

"I was *so*, so upset after Mungo and I broke up, and then when I bumped into *Jonathan* last August, and he was so *kind* and *sympathetic*, I just couldn't help myself. I fell *prey* to his *advances*."

"What?" Carmen's eyes narrow as she rounds on Elaine, because, of course, my friends heard Elaine from outside the church, so loud was her voice as it reverberated from wall to ceiling, and they have come inside to find out what's going on. I'd rather like to know that, myself.

"Hold on," I say, holding up my hand, my attention focused on Elaine. In fact, the whole congregation's attention is focused on Elaine. Which is bad, because if she's saying what I think she's saying about Jonathan, then it means he cheated on me, and now the whole church knows it. How humiliating!

"Um, could we just, you know, step outside a minute and, um, discuss this in private?" I mumble, my face burning, but Elaine is not to be stopped.

"Oh, I'm so *sorry*," Elaine wails again. Loudly. "I accidentally, because of my emotionally low state at the time, *slept* with Jonathan when you were first *dating* him."

Oh. My. Fuck.

There is a collective gasp from the congregation, followed by a deafening silence as they all try to absorb her rather startling statement. Even Carmen, for once, is stunned into silence and is catching flies with her mouth. Jonathan slept with Elaine? I can't take it all in . . .

"And," Elaine begins again, and pauses dramatically. "There's more."

What more could there be? Oh. My. Fuck. Jonathan is . . .

"Jonathan is Baby Becky's father."

. . . Baby Becky's father.

As the stunned silence deepens into a deeper, horrified calm, I turn to Jonathan. My friends and the entire congregation also turn to Jonathan, because they, like me, are waiting for him to deny this.

I don't need to ask, because the truth is written all over his face.

Despite her tears, I'm sure that smug, triumphant expression on Elaine's face is not my imagination. It really is true, then . . .

"Well, you needn't say it with such a smug, triumphant expression on your face," Jess, surprisingly, breaks the deadlock. Which is also shocking because Jess isn't usually so confrontational. "Especially in the house of God. You're not a very nice woman, not a very nice woman, at all."

And it all falls into place. Elaine was always one for making statements at the time they could be of maximum embarrassment and humiliation to her victim. And I wonder, as I have done frequently through my life, why she feels the need to do this to her nearest and dearest.

"Why—" I begin, and stop to clear my throat. "Why," I begin again, "did you not say something sooner? Why wait for today, of all days?" I know the answer, but I can't quite believe that she has done this to me.

"Well, I just didn't know how," Elaine says. "I was worried you'd be upset."

"You were going to wait until the service, until Philip asked if there was a reason why Jonathan and I shouldn't be married, weren't you?" I ask rhetorically, because I can read the answer in her smug expression. "But when I didn't show up at the altar and called Jonathan to the back of the church, you knew that something was up, so you made the most of the opportunity. You intended to wreak as much havoc and pain for me as you could. But why?"

"Why would I do something so terrible?" Elaine takes a step back as I advance on her, because I'm furious that yet again, I was lulled into a false sense of security. That I really thought she'd changed, and all the time she was saving this little gem of information to share with the world.

"Elaine Mayford, you should be thoroughly ashamed of yourself," Mum tells her as she stalks down the aisle, a lioness protecting her cub. "Ruining poor Rosie's wedding day. You're nothing more than a common trollop. You were always a nasty, spiteful little girl, and now you're a nasty, spiteful woman."

"I say, just who do you think you're talking to?" Auntie Pat, not one for missing out on the action, is a step behind her.

"How dare you speak to Elaine that way, you filthy-mouthed, common piece of work?"

"Oh, do shut up, Patsy," Mum turns on her. "You've deafened us for years with that holier-than-thou mouth of yours, and your aspirations of grandeur. Sorry, Bill," she tells poor Uncle Bill, who has followed Auntie Pat.

"Oh, I agree," is Uncle Bill's surprising comment. "I should have put down my foot years ago."

"William," Auntie Pat turns on him. "Remember your responsibilities."

"Oh, I've been remembering them for thirty years. You never miss an opportunity to remind me, but this is too much. Shame on you, Elaine."

And as Uncle Bill puts down his foot for the first time in thirty years, I turn to Jonathan.

"Why?" I ask him.

"I'm—sorry, darling. It was a slipup. It was just the once—"

"Five times, actually—" Elaine interrupts.

"Dirty little slut," Granny Elsie tells her. "You always were a dirty little slut, though. Always wanted what everyone else had, and you ain't changed."

"This, from a common tart from Bethnal Green," Auntie Pat says, which is not helpful.

"Shut up, Pat," Uncle Bill warns her. "You've always lorded it over Sandra, Elsie and Rosie and, in fact, over dear Edward when he was still alive. Not that you had any reason, either."

"Really, Patsy, you should stop glaring down that snobby nose of yours," Auntie Lizzy wades in to protect Mum and Gran, but they truly don't need it. "And you, Elaine. I just don't know how you could do this to your own flesh and blood."

"Especially coming from the illegitimate daughter of a semi peer of the Realm," Uncle Bill adds, and we all gasp as Auntie Pat turns white.

"But I broke it off with Elaine because it was you I loved," Jonathan insists, taking my hands. "It's you that I love still. You that I want to marry."

"But you conveniently forgot to tell me about your daughter?" I ask. I cannot believe he could be so callous.

"I only found out she was mine earlier this morning when Elaine came to see me," Jonathan says to me and to the congregation at large. "I swear I didn't know. I'd never ignore a baby I'd fathered."

And I feel sorry for him, because I know he's telling the truth. It's just the kind of thing Elaine would do. Especially as she'd just had her romantic hopes in Luke dashed.

I can tell that everyone else believes him, too, because they are all shaking their heads and muttering under their breath.

"But," he continues, squeezing my hands, "we can put this behind us and move on to our future together."

"What about Baby Becky?" Elaine jumps back in. "Are we to be forgotten? You're her father, Jonathan. You have an obligation to her and to me."

It is at this moment that the sheer ridiculousness of our predicament hits me full in the face.

"Oh, dear. I think I've rather upstaged your performance, Elaine," I say slowly. "You saved this prime bit of news to spoil my wedding. But you really needn't have bothered."

"Exactly." Jonathan squeezes my hands again, and I pull them away from him.

"But the only reason I came to the church at all was to call off the wedding."

The congregation gasps collectively. Again.

"I'm, um, sorry Jonathan. Sorry everybody." I feel even more terrible.

"Rosie, dear, are you sure this is what you want?" Mum asks me gently.

"Of course she is," Granny Elsie, not one to be left out, jumps in. "She's in love with someone else."

"But she wanted to do the decent thing," Carmen, unsurprisingly, has found her voice again and is taking her turn to address the congregation. "Rosie, true to her nature, knew that she owed it to Jonathan to tell him herself."

The crowd gasps again—it is a day for gasping, it would seem.

"It's true," I say slowly. "I am in love with Luke Benton." That feels so—liberating. "I'm truly sorry, Jonathan," I say gently, meaning it. "I can't marry you. I really am in love with Luke Benton," I say again, as the sixty-pound fleece of wool falls completely from my shoulders.

What a soap opera, what a drama, I think, as the complete irony of the situation really hits me.

I've never heard of a wedding where (a) the bride wants to call off the ceremony because she's in love with another man, (b) the ex-lover of the groom wants to wreck the ceremony, for some nefarious reason known only to herself, (c) the groom is the father of the bride's cousin's baby, and (d) the bride is wearing pinchy shoes to punish herself for not wanting to marry the groom. I mean, it just sounds so ridiculous, doesn't it?

And I can't help it. I begin to laugh hysterically, because it's better than crying, isn't it?

And then Carmen, Jess, Flora, Ned, Charlie, Lewis and Paul are laughing right along with me, because they, of course, are the only other people who also see the irony of the situation.

The whole congregation—a small congregation, thank goodness, consisting only of family and close friends—soon catches on and is laughing along, too. Not Jonathan's side, obviously . . .

Nor Philip, who is keeping a straight face, because I don't suppose it would be right for a vicar to laugh at such an absurd situation, especially whilst in the actual house of God.

"Well, I don't mean to break up this confession session," Carmen says, trying to stop her laughter. "But time's passing and we have a plane to catch. Don't we, Rosie?"

"Because, Rosie, it's your one chance at true love," Jess tells me insistently.

"Are we going, Rosie?"

This is crunch time. Do I go home and continue with my nice, safe life, or do I take the biggest risk of my life?

"Don't worry about a thing," Mum tells me, smiling widely.

"And don't worry about the reception buffet, either," Granny Elsie winks at me. "It shan't go to waste. Go get your excitin' pair of shoes, my girl."

"Yes," I say, sliding Jonathan's two-hundred-quid engagement ring off of my finger, and hand it to Elaine, who hasn't yet found her tongue since I upstaged her. "Have a good life," I call over my shoulder to her, also meaning it, before we dash down the steps toward Ned's car.

Halfway down the church steps I pause to take off the pinchy shoes. I'm never going to wear pinchy shoes ever again.

"What time is it?" I ask for the millionth time as Ned lurches off the M25 onto the M4, and as the car he ruthlessly carves up honks on his horn.

"Stupid fucking bastard," Ned shouts, giving the driver the finger. Who knew Ned was Mr. Hyde behind the wheel?

"Just after twelve. Stop fussing," Charlie tells me. "Actually, scrub that. Keep fussing," he grins.

"It's nice to see you all flustered for once in your life," Lewis finishes for him.

"Two minutes, in fact, since the last time you asked," Carmen says. "Honestly, I've never seen you so fucking impatient and worked up about anything before. It's fucking fantastic," she grins, and the panic builds in my stomach. What if we're too late?

"What if we're too late?"

"We'll get there on time," Ned assures me. And then, "Fucking bastard, did you see how that shit carved me up?" He solicits agreement.

"Calm down, darling." Flora pats his arm. "Just concentrate on the road." Ned is, it has to be said, not the best driver on the road. As he lane jumps, we all lurch to one side of the van.

"But what if he isn't on the two o'clock flight? What if he was on an earlier one, and right now he's cruising miles above the Atlantic Ocean, and I never see him again?" I fret.

"No chance," Lewis shakes his head. "He needs to be there at least two hours before the flight is due to depart."

"Therefore he must be on the two o'clock. Or a later one."

"But what if—"

"You have to believe," Jess tells me from behind, where she, Philip and Paul are squashed like so many sardines in a can. Yes, Philip, because he didn't want to be left out.

"God will provide," Philip tells me. "Sorry, that sounded a bit pompous, didn't it?" he adds. "Just wanted to make you feel a bit better."

"Are you sure it's terminal three?" Ned booms from the driver's seat as he swerves into the correct lane.

"Oh, God, what if we're going to the wrong terminal?" I fret some more. "Have you got any more of that brandy, Carmen? Only I think I need some more."

"No. You don't need false courage to do this," she tells me firmly. "Besides, we finished it off at the church."

"But are we nearly there yet?" I ask, like some kid in the backseat of a car on a long journey.

"Ned has it all under control," Paul says. "You do, don't you, Ned?"

"Stop." Flora commands from the front seat. "All of you, stop. We *will* get you there on time, Rosie, in the *right* place, in *one* piece, and we *will* find Luke. Now take deep breaths."

I am taking such deep breaths that by the time Ned drops us outside the terminal, I am nearly hyperventilating.

"Go," Flora tells us as we fall out of the van. "We'll park and then come and find you."

As I head to the main door of terminal three ahead of everyone, it suddenly hits me that I don't know where I'm going, and I do an about-turn. My friends all stop in their tracks.

"Virgin Atlantic check-in would be a good place to start," Carmen says before I can ask the question. And off we go again.

And as we dash through the airport, a lot of people pause to stare at us. *A barefoot bride, with bridesmaids, a vicar and three men dressed in full morning attire will have that effect on a busy airport*, I think but don't care as we race toward the Virgin Atlantic desk. Where there is a very long line.

"God, we'll never be on time," I say, taking my place at the end of the line. "It's hopeless."

"Faint heart never won fair doctor," Charlie says, tugging at my arm. "Forget politeness for once, Rosie."

"Our profuse apologies," Carmen tells the line of passengers, taking my other arm, and they pull me to the front.

"Next, please," one Virgin Atlantic representative announces.

"I'm really sorry," I tell the also bemused passengers. "But this is a complete love emergency. Please," I say to the also thoroughly bemused representative. "I know that this is highly unusual, but I find myself in a highly unusual situation and need desperately to find out if a passenger has already checked in—"

"We know that you can't divulge specific information—" Carmen jumps in.

"But it's a case of completely requited love—" Jess adds. "Completely requited."

Oh, I hope she's right.

"His name's Luke Benton—" Paul.

"He's an utterly gorgeous doctor—" Charlie, of course.

"And he thinks his beloved—that would be our Rosie, here—is marrying someone else—" Lewis.

"Because I didn't tell him I loved him this morning when he came to see me before my nonwedding," I wail. "I was an idiot, who didn't know the real thing when it stared her in the face, so he doesn't even know—"

"That she didn't marry the wrong man," Carmen jumps in.

"And he's flying to America and I'll never see him again."

"This is highly irregular," the baffled Virgin Atlantic representative—Amanda, according to her badge—begins.

"Dear lady, I can vouch for them all," Philip, cutting a swathe in full vicar regalia, announces to her. "I am a vicar."

"Well," she says, shaking her head. "This is one I haven't heard before." And then she grins at us. "I shall have to get my manager to check on procedure."

"Everything alright?" Two beefy security guards are by our sides before we can blink.

"These people causing a disturbance?" Two more beefy security guards arrive, and I'm panicking that they'll throw us out of the terminal.

"It's a love problem," Amanda, our new VA friend, tells them, and quickly gives a summary of the problem at hand.

"Basically, this young lady here was supposed to get married. The real love of her life is on a plane bound for New

York, and she's only just realized that it's him she wants, rather than the groom. That about cover it?"

"Yes." We all nod like so many nodding-head puppies or kittens in the back window of a car.

"I'll be right back, if you'd like to wait here?" As if we're going anywhere else! But God, it's already 1 P.M. He's probably boarding the plane already!

"Give the poor girl a break," a woman on line shouts.

"It's true love," another one nods in agreement, followed by a chorus of approval from the other passengers.

"Oh. Well, I like a good love story," one of the guards nods.

"Especially with a happy ending," says another.

"Did you see *Love Actually*? Very tender, very heartwarming."

"Oh, that's one of my keepers."

"I'm sorry," Amanda says as she returns to her desk, and we all hold our collective breath. "I cannot divulge any passenger information."

That's it, then. I'm too late.

"But there must be something we can do—" Carmen insists.

"Show some heart," the same woman on line shouts, to the agreement of the other passengers.

"If you'll let me finish?" Amanda says with a smile. "We're checking with the airport authority, but if you'd like to give us your full name, and that of your loved one, we're going to see if we're allowed to make an announcement over the public address system."

And so I do, and ten minutes later, we are standing by security check-in.

"Will Doctor Luke Benton please make himself known to an airline representative?" booms the address system. "Miss Rosie Mayford urgently needs to tell him that she loves him, and is awaiting him at the security check-in. Repeat. Doctor

Luke Benton. Miss Rosie Mayford is, unlike Elvis, in the building, and she is anxiously awaiting a response to her declaration of love. Please make yourself known to an airport or airline representative."

"My God, it's official," I say, grinning to my friends. "The whole airport knows I love him."

Fuck. The whole airport . . . I'm so nervous that I can barely think of what I'm going to say if he turns up.

"Hey, love, if he doesn't turn up, I'll marry you myself," one of the guards tells me.

"Your Eileen won't like that much," his partner tells him. "He'll be here, love. How could he resist such a romantic gesture? I couldn't resist such a romantic gesture, could you, Bert?"

Five minutes later the same message is announced on the address system, and we have now attracted quite a crowd of spectators and well-wishers.

"Doctor Benton, according to the great Phil Collins, 'You Can't Hurry Love,' but now is not the time to take that advice. Please make yourself known."

Everyone laughs encouragingly as even the public address announcer gets into the spirit. But I'm getting a bit worried, because it is now one-twenty, and the plane must be getting quite crowded.

"It's no good," I say, my heart sinking into my toes. "He probably can't even hear the announcement on the plane."

"Oh, no," a red-coated Virgin Atlantic representative tells me. "I'm not supposed to tell you this, but they've announced you over the plane's address system, too. I can't tell you which plane, or confirm whether or not he's on it, but don't lose hope," she says, winking at me.

"Well, we've come this far, we might as well wait," Philip tells me. "Have some faith."

At one-thirty-five the announcement is made again, and

there's still no sign of him, and the plane must be getting ready for takeoff, and so I have to face it. He's just not coming.

"What's happening?" Flora and Ned finally catch up with us. As everyone fills them in, I sigh and look down at my feet. I did it. I took a risk. I knew that it could go either way, but for a few hours I thought that we might have a chance, that he did love me.

"He's not coming. We might as well accept it. I might as well accept it," I say.

It is now one-forty-five. Far too late. Time to go home. I concentrate harder on my panty-hose-clad toes to avoid all the sympathy stares.

"Well, I expect he had on earphones—you know—was listening to music, or whatnot, and couldn't hear the announcement," Flora tells me, trying for upbeat and failing.

"Rosie," Carmen says in my ear, and nudges me.

"Look," Paul urges me.

"Oh, oh," Jess says.

"God has provided—" Philip. "Oh, sorry, everyone, that sounded a bit odd, didn't it?"

"Rosie, he's coming." Charlie nudges me, too.

"There he is," Lewis adds.

And the crowd roars.

And then I look up.

On the other side of the security check, the crowds have parted to form an informal corridor. In the distance, past the duty-free stores, I can see a man jogging through the corridor.

The crowd cheers as he passes them.

It's Luke.

As he reaches the security check-in, and the security guards pat him encouragingly on the back and let him pass, his eyes are fixed on me. I walk forward to meet him.

He's hot and disheveled and out of breath. And I've never seen him looking so utterly gorgeous, I think, as I reach up and smooth back his floppy hair. I've wanted to do that forever.

The crowd quiets in anticipation as it collectively waits for the outcome of my flight of fancy. And I'm frozen into speechlessness.

"It's you," he teases, breaking the silence, his eyes crinkling as he smiles down at me. And I'm nervous, exhilarated, anticipatory, as my heart pounds so loudly in my breast that the whole airport must be shaking with it.

"I think we can safely say that it is, in fact, me," I smile back, my voice as shaky as my legs. And then, "Just in case there was a slight possibility you missed it, I think you should know that—I—I love you."

"I didn't really believe it until I heard you say it. By the way, I love you right back," he says softly. And then, just before he kisses me, he pauses as he sees my feet. "What happened to your shoes?" he asks, raising a James Bond sardonic eyebrow at me, and I laugh.

"They didn't fit."

"We are definitely going to have to do something about your footwear situation," he says, lowering his head.

And as he kisses me, and as I'm winding my arms around his neck, the crowd lets out a roar of approval as they clap and cheer.

And as he kisses me some more, another announcement booms from the public address system.

"For those very few of you not currently crowding the security check-in area, you'll be delighted to know that Miss Rosie Mayford has located Doctor Luke Benton. We'd like to take this opportunity on behalf of Virgin Atlantic and all staff at Heathrow airport to wish them a happy future. The weather is fair for a happy landing."

*   *   *

Ten months later . . .

Luke and I got married this morning, and he kept his promise about looking into my footwear situation.

His wedding gift to me was a pair of beautiful, custom-made, Italian silk shoes, and they fit like a glove.

"Thank God," Luke murmurs against my mouth as he carries me over the threshold of the honeymoon suite and closes the door with his foot.

I'm all gorgeous and demure (but in a sexy kind of way) in a long, white dress, and Luke is all tall and sexily rumpled in a morning suit.

"Sweet Mystery of Life, at Last I've Found You," is not, thank God, playing in the background, because my blood is pounding so loudly in my ears that I can't hear another thing.

Unable to wait a moment longer, we are tugging at each other's clothes.

Before we can make it to the bed we're all over each other like a rash. In frustration, because his fingers are shaking so badly that he can't undo the tiny pearl buttons on the back of my dress, Luke slides his hands under my skirt and pushes it up to my waist, and then he's—

Oh.

My.

It's a crime what this man can do with his hands . . .

Want More?

Turn the page to enter
Avon's Little Black Book —

the dish, the scoop and the
cherry on top from
MICHELLE CUNNAH

An International Chick's Guide to Life, Love, the World, and ... Shopping!

Introduction

Because I'm a bit of a globe-trotter and have lived abroad for a good deal of my life, it is more usual than not that I find myself in foreign countries (well, countries in which I was not born). And it's a fairly good bet—if I were a gambling kind of gal, which I'm not—that one of the first things a new friend, acquaintance, shop assistant or restaurant assistant will ask is this: Are you from Germany?

It's absolutely true!

This has happened to me on several occasions, but especially when I am shopping at my very favorite shopping place in the world—the Secaucus outlets in New Jersey.

I've no idea why Germany, because I don't (a) look German, on account of not being tall and blond (except in my dreams), (b) I've never lived in Germany (although I have, indeed, visited Germany—lovely, lovely place and lovely, lovely people), and (c) I don't have a German accent.

The other question I am asked a lot (especially at those Secaucus outlets) is this: Are you Australian?

Although I haven't ever been to Australia, I have met a lot of very nice Australians on my travels. I hear that it is a lovely country, too, but the spiders, snakes and creatures with big teeth put me off. But no, I am not Australian.

Maybe a lot of Germans and Australians frequent the Secaucus outlets. . . .

Once established that I am not from either Germany or Australia, when people ask me where, exactly, I come from, I have a hard time answering, because I secretly think of myself as a bit of a nomad, even though I'm originally from the north of England.

In short: I. Am a citizen. Of the world! Yay!

Subsequent questions, when people learn that I am a writer: do I write "real" books? (Um, that would be in comparison to "unreal" books?) Can they purchase my books in, say, German? (Still don't get the German connection, but suspect my true calling is to become blond!) How have my international travels affected my writing? And do I get my ideas from real life?

Admitting yes to this last question brings forth a whole host of other questions. Such as (a) did I really find myself at a function only to realize that I had slept with every man at my table? (b) Did I ever accidentally bare my boob in public? (c) Have I ever ruthlessly stolen someone's garden gnomes in a bid to rehouse them in their natural habitat? And (d) can I tell them how to curse in, um, German?

In a bid to answer some of these questions, and to have a bit of fun, I got the idea of writing this short piece of advice on international etiquette, why the United Kingdom and the United States can sometimes be (in the words of Sir Winston Churchill, one of my personal gods amongst men) two countries divided by a common language, possible hazards in Dutch public parks, and . . . why I prefer French bra sizes . . .

Enjoy!

An International Chick's Advice on . . . A Tricky Social Situation

What to do if you attend a function in Britain and, by some quirk of fate or other nefarious reason (i.e., the person who designed the seating plan has a grudge against you), you find yourself in the awkward situation of having slept with every male (or female) at the table.

There are several courses of action available to you:

1. **For the less faint-hearted:** Introduce possible couples to each other at the table (because, of course, you already know half of them intimately). Add a pinch of personal information. For example, you might say: "Jane #1 (let's call her Jane #1), meet John #1. John #1 is maniacally obsessed with oral hygiene and does not exchange tongues during kissing. His mouth is a vacuous black hole. John #1, this is Jane #1, an oral hygienist, therefore she knows all about the germ-killing properties of mouthwash."

2. **For a less drastic approach:** "Jane #1, John #1 has an amazing collection of dental floss. John #1, Jane #1 is an oral hygienist and has a fascinating collection of tooth-picks." Not only have you diverted attention from your-self, you've introduced two people to their karmic soul mates!

3. **For the more faint-hearted:** Fill your mouth with what-ever food and drink happens to be handy. Every time someone asks you something—for example, Jane #2 is interested in how well you know her boyfriend, John #2 (i.e., is it in the biblical sense?)—simply cram your mouth full of food. After all, it is rude to talk with your mouth full.

4. **For the diplomat:** Wax lyrically about the weather. In Britain this works every time because British people love to chat about the weather. This diversionary tactic will avoid a multitude of embarrassments. And family feuds.

5. **For the coward:** Develop a sudden and debilitating mi-graine, excuse yourself from the table, and slink away to the bar for a medicinal brandy . . . or three.

Although I have never found myself in this particular quandary (but it is true that I did once briefly date a very nice guy who didn't understand that tongues were a good thing during kissing), something similar did happen to an acquaintance of mine several years ago. Let's call her Jane #3.

Jane #3 was invited to a wedding. She was an ex-girlfriend of the groom. She had also dated the groom's cousin, the best man, and various other men on the invitation list (it was a very small town and she was a very emancipated Jane #3).

Although it sounded like a recipe for certain disaster, Jane #3 accepted. When I asked her why, she replied that (a) the invitation had come from the bride, because she was also an old friend of the bride, and (b) why turn down a perfectly good opportunity for free drink, free food, and a rollicking party? Plus, it was a prime opportunity to meet men.

An International Chick's Advice on . . . Unexpected Public Boob Exposure

Well, after the "have slept with every man at the table" situation, this one is merely a trifling inconvenience!

1. **In a social situation or at work.** Tuck errant boob back inside dress/top and continue chatting (chat about anything that takes your fancy—as previously mentioned, the weather is always good). Your co-chatter will be so engrossed in your description of the high-pressure area coming in from the west that they will not notice a thing. Simple, see?

2. **Whilst on stage.** Continue singing (if it is a musical) or acting (if not a musical) and use actorly over-the-top arm movements to discreetly tuck boob back inside costume. Audience will be so entranced by stellar performance that they will not even notice errant boob. Hopefully . . .

3. **At a wedding.** Simple! Refrain from wearing possible boob-revealing attire, thereby totally avoiding the possibility of inadvertent boob exposure. Wear only buttoned-

to-chin tops/dresses. With long sleeves. You won't make quite the fashion statement you'd hoped, but it is very bad manners to upstage the bride, anyway.

4. **On a beach in the south of France.** Quickly whip off your dress/top and reveal the other boob. Beaches in the south of France are topless, so with only one boob on display you would be severely overdressed, anyway. Additionally, it is a good idea to wear a minuscule, bottom-revealing thong, too, or people will think you are a prude . . .

5. **On a beach in the Netherlands or, indeed, in various other parts of mainland Europe.** See 4.

The boob-revealing incident, I confess, really did happen to me. When I was a single gal living in London, I worked by night in a half-gay bar in Notting Hill. Everyone loved this place—it had Old World charm and was unique because of its mixed clientele.

Sadly, the pub was making a loss, but everyone wanted to help keep it going. A fairly famous drag queen came up with the idea of producing an amateur drag act to raise money. Somehow, and I don't quite know how, and even though I am a girl, I managed to get roped in. Our Christmas pièce de résistance: Campalot. A camp version of Camelot, with me as Queen Guinevere.

Picture this: The pub is packed. I am stunning (in my dreams, but this is my anecdote, therefore I am also blond) in a strapless dress. I am emoting away when . . . Merlin (no, not the real Merlin, my friend who was acting Merlin) whispers those immortal words in my shell-like ear: "Your zipper's come down and your boob's hanging out."

Of course, I continue emoting, complete with odd arm movements, and I quickly replace my boob before anyone notices. The soul of discretion, that's me! I mean, I reasoned with myself, in a bar full of predominantly gay men, who was going to pay attention to a female boob here or there?

After our performance, whilst having a drink with Oh Patient One (my then boyfriend, my now husband), Jane #4, a lesbian, and also a dominatrix who whipped men for a living (literally), approached me and told me (a) how much she'd enjoyed the boob incident and (b) offered to show me her, um, whips: Oh Patient One laughed so hard that he nearly fell off his barstool . . . Sorry, Jane #4, but I am just not a lesbian. . . .

An International Chick's Advice on . . .
International Flights

1. When flying, do not, under any circumstances, glance out of window and rather thoughtlessly ask, "What's that big wing-shaped thing out there?" It is a wing. Planes need them to fly. Don't ask me why, they just do. Do not be surprised to discover that the plane has two of them. No, I have never personally said this, but I know someone who has . . .
2. Also when flying—for example, on a package tour vacation to the Caribbean—you should refrain from asking the stranger sitting next to you where he/she is going. They are going to the same place as you. No, I have never asked this of the stranger sitting next to me on an international flight, either, but I know someone else who has . . .
3. Plane toilet doors can be very tricky. It is especially important to doubly check that the door is locked so that either (a) the elderly man who opens the door and finds you in, um, mid-flow, does not have an instant coronary, or (b) the gorgeous, utterly edible man you spotted two rows ahead of you does not walk in unexpectedly and get a really good look at your, um, cellulite. I got the elderly man. Fortunately, he didn't have a coronary. He was just very, very embarrassed and refused to look at me as I came out of the bathroom. But at least the gorgeous, utterly edible guy two rows in front didn't get a good look at my cellulite!

4. "Mile High Club," as we all know, has nothing to do with drinking club soda whilst flying one mile above planet surface. See earlier advice about securely locking plane bathroom doors . . .

5. Never. Ever. Crack a joke. With. An immigration officer. Although very nice people, they have more power than God when it comes to allowing you into their country. For example, when an immigration officer asks you, "Are you carrying any fresh food or meat products?" the correct response is not to batter one's eyelashes and say, "If I answered yes would that involve a strip search?" The correct response is, "No, sir." Never, under any circumstances, do you want to be strip-searched. No, this has not happened to me, but it did to someone I know. She still shudders at the memory. You have been warned . . .

An International Chick's Advice on . . . Visiting the United Kingdom

1. The British Sense of Humor is a mysterious, yet wondrous, thing. When approaching a cab driver, or any other person, to ask for directions, you might say, "Pardon me, sir" (or madam, obviously). When the cab driver (or whoever) responds with a jaunty, "Why, what have you done?" they are joking. They are "pulling your leg." It's a British thing.

2. To male tourists. When a northern British male answers whatever question you might have asked, do not be surprised when he calls you "love" or "duck." Trust me when I tell you that he (a) doesn't think you are a duck, (b) doesn't love you, and (c) he isn't gay (well, okay, he might be). The "love" or "duck" endearment has nothing to do with being gay or nongay. It's just another British thing.

3. When a Brit promises to "give you a ring" they are not proposing marriage or promising to present you with a

Tiffany's engagement ring any time soon. What they mean is that they will "give you a call."

4. When admiring a British person's pants, the correct wording is, "I really love your trousers." If you say "pants" by mistake, they will assume that you have X-ray vision and can see through their trousers to their underpants. A slap on the face could be a possible result.

5. If you are female and refer to a female friend in a nonlesbian kind of way, you should not call her your girlfriend. In Britain, "girlfriend" means lover. A good female friend is your "mate." Yes, although the word "mate" has connotations of, um, mating, it doesn't mean anything sexual here. Men also refer to their best male friends as their "mates." You will just have to trust me on this one.

An International Chick's Advice on . . . Strange British Words

Arse = Ass or bottom. Also referred to as "bum." Yes, a "bum" in Britain is a body part, not a poor, down-on-their-luck, homeless person.

Tramp = Bum. Tramp, just to confuse you, can also mean to traipse around—to tramp around. And on this occasion it has nothing to do with a poor, down-on-their-luck, homeless person.

Mardy = Sulky/whiny. Ergo, don't be a mardy arse = don't be a sulky/whiny person.

Please pass me the rubber = Please pass me the eraser.

Pissed or pissed off = Pissed or pissed off. However, just to confuse you, "pissed" can also mean *drunk* in Britain. Ergo, pissed as a fart = Really, really drunk.

Knickers = Underpants/briefs. However, when someone answers you with a vehement "Knickers," they are not discussing your underwear. They are simply disagreeing with you.

Tart/Slag = A ho. "Slag" is far more horrible than "tart." Should you find yourself in a pastry shop, "tart" also means an edible pastry—a pie without a pastry lid. Also, it is not uncommon for women to greet their close girl buddies with a friendly, "Hello, you old tart." They do not mean it as an insult. In this situation it is a term of endearment.

An International Chick's Advice on . . . Visiting the Netherlands

1. **Dutch public parks.** Picture this: You are taking a walk in the public park when all of a sudden . . . there are a lot of naked people. They are not protesting or making a political statement. They are simply taking full advantage of the lovely sunshine and the park's nudist area.
2. **Sightseeing in Rotterdam.** Picture this: You are heading toward a metro station in central Rotterdam. The sign for the metro station features an advert for plastic surgery. It also features "before" and "after" shots of (bare) boob jobs and (thonged) bottom jobs.
3. **Dutch TV.** Don't be shocked by (a) naked boobs, (b) naked (or thonged) bottoms, (c) curse words, and (d) explicit advertisements for sex chat lines.
4. **Dutch alcohol regulations.** The legal age for purchasing alcohol in a New Jersey bar is twenty-one. In Britain it is eighteen. In the Netherlands it is sixteen. But you will be reassured to know (or not) that at sixteen you can only order either beer or wine.
5. **Dutch saunas.** I have one piece of advice for you here: If you are at all shy about disrobing in multi-gender situa-

tions, check that the sauna is "women only" or "men only" before you decide to pay a visit.

An International Chick's Advice on . . . International Shopping!

Reklame! Opruiming! Korting! My favorite Dutch words! They don't even need literal translations, because I have absorbed meanings via osmosis. Little hint: These words often grace banners in stores, therefore it is easy to surmise that they mean either (a) bargain! (b) sale! or (c) reduced! Oh, but shopping is an international language!

On the odd occasion, as you do, I have wondered why we don't have a universal size chart, because it can be a bit confusing knowing one's size when visiting a foreign country. But I have seen the light! I now have the answer!

1. **Clothes sizes.** American size 6 = British 10 = European 36.
2. **Shoe sizes.** American size 8½ = British 6 = European 39.
3. **Bra sizes.** American and British size 34B = European 75B. Except for France. In France, this is size 90B.

And so, my very final piece of advice to you is this: Always quote American sizes when shopping for clothes. Always quote British sizes when shopping for shoes. And always, always, quote French sizes when shopping for bras! The best of all worlds!

Ciao! Auf wiedersehen! Au revoir! Tot ziens!

Michelle

MICHELLE CUNNAH

Yvette M. Feliciano

MICHELLE CUNNAH Originally from England, Michelle spent six years living just outside Manhattan. She has lived in quite a lot of other places, too. Currently she can be found weebling ineptly along the cycle lanes in Rotterdam, the Netherlands. She aspires to be able to cycle without hands. Maybe one day . . .